Best wishes
Richard + Tracey
from John

THE PROPHET MOTIVE

John J Bimson

MINERVA PRESS
LONDON
MIAMI DELHI SYDNEY

THE PROPHET MOTIVE
Copyright © John J Bimson 2000

All Rights Reserved

No part of this book may be reproduced in any form,
by photocopying or by any electronic or mechanical means,
including information storage or retrieval systems,
without permission in writing from both the copyright
owner and the publisher of this book.

ISBN 0 75411 275 6

First Published 2000 by
MINERVA PRESS
315–317 Regent Street
London W1R 7YB

Printed in Great Britain for Minerva Press

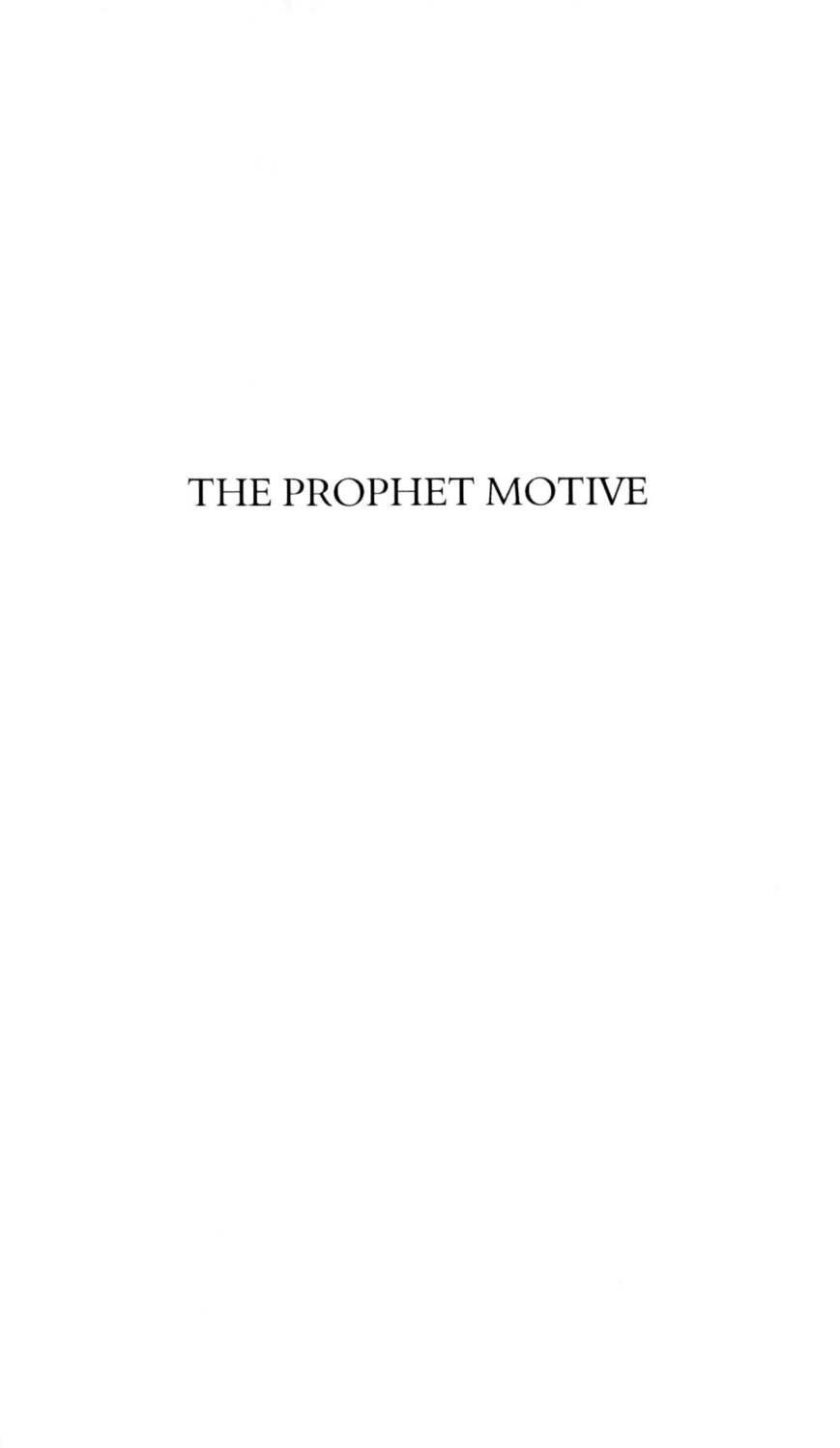

THE PROPHET MOTIVE

All characters and events in this book are fictional,
and any resemblance to actual places, events or persons,
living or dead, is purely coincidental.

*Many thanks
to Marc Catley for background music and a great one-liner;
to Joseph Steinberg, who first allowed the Rev. Oral B Swyver to
express himself in print;
and to Maya, James and Tom
for putting up with me while I lived in another world.*

*Special thanks
to Berj and Susie Topalian
for encouragement throughout;
this novel is dedicated to them.*

Contents

Part One
Swyver

Chapter One	13
Chapter Two	25
Chapter Three	33
Chapter Four	49
Chapter Five	65
Chapter Six	75
Chapter Seven	85

Part Two
The Caves of Nahal Shuhan

Chapter Eight	99
Chapter Nine	109
Chapter Ten	122
Chapter Eleven	131
Chapter Twelve	141
Chapter Thirteen	159
Chapter Fourteen	173

Chapter Fifteen	188
Chapter Sixteen	201
Chapter Seventeen	209
Chapter Eighteen	219
Chapter Nineteen	230
Chapter Twenty	242

Part Three
The Seventh Seal

Chapter Twenty-One	259
Chapter Twenty-Two	269
Chapter Twenty-Three	280
Chapter Twenty-Four	295
Chapter Twenty-Five	307
Postscript	315
Bibliography	317

Then, after this, in the tenth week and the seventh part, there shall be the eternal judgement, and it shall be executed by the watching angels of the eternal heaven...

In those days, when he hurls terrifying fire against you, where shall you flee, and where shall you find safety? ...The whole earth shall be shaken and tremble.

I Enoch 91:15, 102:1–2

The end of the world is one of the oldest products around. It's been sold over and over again, and people are still buying it.

Arlo Guthrie

Part One

Swyver

At the waterfall near the edge of the aqueduct, on the east side of the outflow, dig down seven cubits: nine talents of silver. In the cavern north of the entry to the ravine of Beth Tamar, in the arid land of Gar-pela: all that is in it is devoted to the Temple.

The Copper Scroll 3Q15, 9:11–16

Chapter One

1

Nathan Willard grimaced. The soothing meanders of Bach's *Cello Suite No. 4* had been cut off in mid-flow, and now Barbi-Jo Butterfield was squealing like a stuck pig.

> Lead me to that fabulous man-
> That great big fabulous man-
> That great big fabulous mansion in the sky...

Swyver had arrived in the building.

The lift opened at the thirtieth floor and Willard stepped out. Following a short passage he approached a door inlaid with designs in which the letter 'S' was the dominant motif. He aimed a remote control unit at the door and it slid aside. As it closed behind him, shutting out the shrill country and western chorus, he breathed a sigh of relief.

The room was large and circular, its exterior walls were glass from floor to ceiling, and it glowed faintly throughout with the first light of dawn. Willard pressed the remote control again. With a barely audible hum the room began to rotate. Setting down his briefcase on the nearest table he walked over to the curved wall of glass.

A pale wash was spreading from the east, dimming the last few stars. To the west the clustered lights of Memphis still shimmered through an urban haze. One hundred and fifty metres below, sprawling in every direction, the campus of BIOSES was taking on colour and definition: lecture halls, accommodation blocks, conference centres, libraries and laboratories set in a mosaic of manicured lawns and tree-lined drives. For the first time it struck Willard that, from the perspective of its rotating summit, it was surprisingly easy to imagine the Power Tower as the world's one fixed point around which everything else revolved. Was this an illusion Swyver had deliberately set out to create?

The phone in Willard's briefcase ended his ruminations with a muffled trill. He walked over to the case, opened it and lifted the phone from its holder. Barbi-Jo's lyrics seeped faintly from the earpiece, accompanied by a man's loud, tuneless humming.

'Good morning, sir.'

'"The night is far spent!"' quoted Swyver, '"The day is at hand! Let us therefore cast off the works of darkness, and let us put on the armour of light!"'

'Romans, chapter thirteen, verse twelve?' asked Willard.

'Right!'

'And how are you today, sir?'

'Never felt better! Nathan, have you finished the security checks?'

'There's just the revolving restaurant, sir. I was about to get started when…'

'Good, good. When you're finished up there, I want you to do the fish, Nathan.'

'Sir?'

'Not the ones in the lake,' said Swyver, answering Willard's incredulity. 'Just the fish in the lobby. The CIA could've bugged one before they were delivered.'

'I think we can discount that possibility, sir. The device would have to be…'

'Do the fish, Nathan. Can't be too careful. Today's a big day in world history.'

2

What was arguably the most influential announcement of the end of the world came in 1970 with Hal Lindsey's book *The Late Great Planet Earth*. It spawned a whole genre which is still thriving.

Mike Totley considers the last sentence for a moment, then deletes it. Instead he types:

It was followed by a flood of imitations, some of them by Lindsey himself.

Much better, maintaining a note of derisory wit.

In *Late Great Planet*, Lindsey argued that history 'seems to be headed for its climactic hour'. While never predicting exactly when that hour might come, he suggested a date 'within forty years or so of 1948' – a claim specific enough to excite his readers, but sufficiently vague to avoid a charge of error in the event of Christ failing to return in 1988. Another writer on biblical prophecy, Edgar Whisenant, was less cautious; unlike Lindsey's books, Whisenant's two-million-copy best-seller, *88 Reasons Why the Rapture Will Be in 1988*, stopped being a best-seller in 1989.

3

A bizarre black fish with outsized bulbous eyes stared back at Nathan Willard, its peculiar features magnified by the thick glass, then it joined a mixed shoal surging to the top of the tank in a flurry of excitement. A man brandishing a long pole usually meant food.

Willard frowned with concentration, alert for a tell-tale signal from his earphones. Nothing. His features relaxed. He removed the earphones, letting the headset hang loosely around his neck, and surveyed the lobby to make sure this was the last tank.

The lobby of the Power Tower was a vast, circular space enclosed by glass panels and sliding doors. At its centre, running up the entire cylindrical building, was a gigantic column housing lifts and staircases; at its perimeter was a cloister formed by a ring of free-standing pillars, each about four metres high. Pillars of marble alternated with what appeared at first sight to be pillars of varicoloured glass. The latter were in fact tanks of water in which tropical fish moved among tall fronds of aquatic greenery. As Willard had expected, all twelve had tested negative.

He folded the scanner's telescopic antenna, replaced it in his briefcase and approached the lifts.

Oooooh, Jesus, come,
Come right now and take me!

Oh, Jesus, how I long to see your face…

shrilled Barbi-Jo Butterfield as the doors hissed open. Willard groaned, replacing the earphones as he stepped inside. Muted but audible, the orgasmic ululation continued:

> As the sinners go to fry
> I'll be raptured up on high!
> Jesus, come and take me to a better place.

If a place where Barbi-Jo could not be heard was a better place than one where she could, Nathan Willard was soon there. In his office on the Power Tower's second floor he filled a plastic cup with black coffee and sat down at his desk. He sipped the coffee, took off the headset and looked at his watch. He'd been at work for over five hours and a long, tense day still lay ahead.

Then the significance of the time dawned on him. He swivelled his chair to face a bank of closed-circuit TV screens that filled one wall of his office. Without taking his eyes off the monitors he reached for the phone on his desk and punched out Swyver's personal code.

'"This is the day which the Lord hath made!"' declaimed Swyver, '"We will rejoice and be glad in it!"'

'I believe that's Psalm one hundred and eighteen, sir.'

'Verse twenty-four. How's it going, Nathan?'

'Everything's okay, sir. I screened each place personally, like you said.'

'And the fish?'

'They're clean too, sir.'

'Great!'

'Sir, the first guests are arriving as we speak.'

A camera on top of the main gates showed a limousine parked in the shadow of the gatehouse, while a security guard checked its occupants' passes. Then a barrier lifted and, as it moved off along the drive, morning sunlight gleamed from the limousine's roof.

'Wonderful!' exclaimed Swyver. 'Everything ready?'

'Yes, sir. Students are in place to escort the visitors to Lecture Hall 5. I've briefed them on what to do and say, but they don't know the identity of the guests or the purpose of the meeting.'

'Good, good. I'll see you there, Nathan. It's going to be a great day!'

4

> This is the problem facing every writer on prophecy who wishes to predict Christ's imminent return: while setting a specific date is the surest way to galvanise the fervour of followers, it also runs a very high risk of losing them altogether. The potency of the year 2000 has highlighted this tension. Predictions cluster around it like iron filings around a magnet, but relatively few fix exclusively or decisively on that year. The phrase 'some time around the year 2000' has become greatly overworked. And the tendency is not confined to Christian writers predicting the Second Coming; Drosnin, for example, leaves us wondering whether his 'Bible code' points to 2000 or 2006 as the date of a horrendous global conflict. A degree of vagueness is vital for keeping apocalyptic tension alive – and, it is tempting to add, one's books in the best-seller lists.

Mike Totley sits back from the keyboard and reads through this last paragraph. Then he takes a large book from the top of his computer and reflects on its title, printed in gold on a wine-red cover: *Till the Son of Man be Come: the Modern Age and the Soon Coming of Christ*, by the Rev. Dr Oral B Swyver, PhD. Isn't there some rule against using an adverb with a noun? He turns the book over. From the back cover a man in his fifties, with a broad, smooth, slightly podgy face and abundant silver hair, regards the beholder with persuasive sincerity.

5

The PA system crackled as Willard adjusted the microphone.

'Good morning, gentlemen. My name is Nathan Willard and I'm Dr Swyver's chief security officer.'

His speech was rapid, edged with nervous precision. The importance of the occasion was weighing on him. He cleared his throat and paused, surveying the one hundred and twenty men who lounged on the plush, raked seating. All were middle-aged or older. Some were oil barons, sporting their traditional lace ties, ostentatious belt buckles and Stetsons. The rest wore expensive suits and the faintly surprised expressions which come with multiple facelifts.

'Welcome to the Bible Institute of the South-Eastern States. Before Dr Swyver speaks to you, there are a few preliminaries to be gotten out of the way. First, the important matter of security. This room and the one in which you'll be eating later have both been screened for bugs and are guaranteed clean. We are also protected against long-range listening devices by the same type of shielding system which protects the White House. Like everything else here, this system has its own power supply which cannot be interrupted from outside. Nothing said today will ever get beyond these walls – unless one of you is foolish enough to speak of it. And I'm sure that when you've heard what Dr Swyver is proposing, you'll all appreciate how extremely dangerous that would be. If the world got to hear of this project, there would be misguided opposition and alarm on an unimaginable scale.'

Willard paused again while this took effect. The silence in the room acquired an almost tangible mass. His audience looked suitably overawed and nervously attentive. One oil baron fumbled in his pocket and pulled out a cigar the size of a small Zeppelin.

'Secondly,' said Willard, 'may I remind you that smoking in the lecture hall is forbidden. You may smoke later over lunch.' The oilman grunted, stuffing the Zeppelin back in his pocket. 'And now it's my pleasure to make way for the man behind this most exciting of projects, the Reverend Doctor Oral B Swyver.'

Willard stepped down from the dais, took a seat on the front row and led the applause.

6

Mike stirs his coffee, takes the last of three books from the kitchen scales and returns to his study. Squaring up to the keyboard he types:

> The blurb on the cover describes this as 'the weightiest treatment of end-time prophecy ever published', and a simple experiment seems to bear this out. At exactly 1300 grams, it is 25g heavier than J Barton Payne's *Encyclopedia of Biblical Prophecy* and 75g

heavier than J Dwight Pentecost's *Things to Come*. The blurb also claims that much of the book was directly inspired by the Holy Spirit as Swyver prayerfully pondered the Scriptures, and that this inspiration bypassed the normal limitations of a human brain. Whatever readers may make of the claim to divine inspiration, most will have no difficulty accepting that this book is not the product of a normal human brain.

Swyver's basic premise is that most prophecies in the Bible are long term, and are only now being fulfilled. Ignoring recent work on apocalyptic language as a complex metaphor system, Swyver follows his own approach with single-minded determination. Ambiguity, irony and multivalent readings have no place here; the text has only one meaning and Swyver is the man to tell us what it is. And the upshot of his ingenious interpretations, for those who are convinced, is that Christ's return has to occur within a handful of years. However, in keeping with the trend noted above, Swyver holds back from offering a precise date.

7

Swyver entered from the wings and strode to a lectern at the centre of the dais. A large man with an aura of massive self-confidence, he smiled at his audience then raised a hand to stem the applause. Born in 1948, on the same day as the state of Israel – a fact which his parents, steeped in biblical prophecy, had invested with deep significance – and named after the famous Pentecostal preacher Oral Roberts, Swyver had acquired a sense of destiny along with his first teeth. Now a billionaire, media mogul, televangelist, director of Swycorp Research, founder and honorary principal of BIOSES, he was a man who could have run for president but believed he had more important things to do.

For a long moment he said nothing, savouring the expectant atmosphere. Then he gripped the lectern squarely with both hands and boomed:

'Gentlemen, the long-awaited time is at hand! He is near, even at the doors! It's time to prepare for the great and terrible Day of the Lord! Yes, my friends, I can now reveal the date when Christ will return in glory to wreak vengeance on sinners and reward the righteous!'

8

To give a few examples of Swyver's method at work: the seven-headed beast described in Revelation 13 is 'easily recognised as the so-called G7 nations'; Swyver is unperturbed by the fact that these recently became the 'G8' with the addition of Russia, because Russia – under the leadership of the neo-nationalist faction – will soon go its own way; indeed, it will become leader of the hordes which attack Israel 'out of the north parts' in Ezekiel 38; references to 'Babylon the great' in the book of Revelation mean that the site of that ancient city will be rebuilt as a new capital for modern Iraq; the drying up of the River Euphrates (Revelation 16:12) will allow Iraqi troops to march on Israel for the battle of Armageddon – no planes or missiles, apparently! One has to admit there is something awesome about the single-mindedness with which Swyver applies this approach, undeterred by its improbable results.

9

Swyver's reputation as a preacher was well deserved. He spoke without notes and lavished unnerving levels of eye contact on every member of his audience. His voice had a remarkable dynamic range and he employed it to great effect; sometimes, clutching the lectern with his huge hands, he leaned close to the microphone and almost whispered, his voice tremulous with fervour; at other times, leaving the lectern altogether, he paced the stage with dramatic gestures, his voice rising to a stentorian bellow.

'So you see, brothers,' he declared, employing the latter mode, 'this earth has seen the last millennium before *the* Millennium – the big M, Christ's glorious thousand year reign on earth! The supernatural blessings of that age are about to burst upon us!'

To a chorus of amens and hallelujahs, Swyver produced a Bible from the lectern and proceeded to spell out what those blessings would be. He promised that Old Testament prophecies of miraculous harvests, limitless prosperity and the end of sickness and senility would soon be literally fulfilled.

'But that's not all, brethren. Turning to the book of Revelation, we read in chapter two that he who perseveres to the end will have "power over the nations, and he shall rule them with a rod of iron". And in chapter twenty it says the Lord will give them thrones, and they "shall reign with him a thousand years"!'

Today, he said, he was offering nothing less than the opportunity to join that privileged class. However, the privileges of millennial rule would also bring awesome responsibilities – chief among them the task of replenishing the world's population after the devastations of Armageddon.

'Once again the command to be fruitful and multiply will be paramount. Then we shall see the words of the prophet Jeremiah fulfilled: "Their children shall also be as aforetime." Brothers, what this means is that believers who enter the Millennium in their natural bodies will have the responsibility of begetting children throughout the thousand years!'

Swyver paused. A frisson passed through the gathering as the implication sank in. Not only would the Millennium bring unimagined health, wealth and power; it would also provide those who were there at its inception with a thousand years of unhampered sexual activity.

The atmosphere was broken by the first question from the audience. A plump, sweaty Texan raised a tentative hand.

'Er, may I ask, brother Swyver, I mean, well... What I mean is, will we be doing all this begetting with our present wives?'

Tension hung in the air.

'Sure,' said Swyver, 'provided your wives are born-again Christians who will therefore survive the Great Tribulation. As with Abraham and Sarah, age will be no obstacle; it'll be a time of miracles!'

But enthusiasm began to haemorrhage from the room. Some of these men's marriages had long since staled with neglect; others had married simply for money or to ensure dynastic survival. The thought of extending those relationships by a thousand years cast a pall over an otherwise glorious prospect.

'Of course,' added Swyver, sensing the mood, 'in order to fulfil adequately the command to replenish the earth and subdue it, it'll be necessary to reintroduce the Old Testament practice of concubinage.'

After another pause an elderly, cadaverous man with suspiciously dark hair asked, 'Could you clarify that, Dr Swyver? Do you mean we'll have handmaids, like Abraham and Jacob did, who'll be like, sort of, secondary wives?'

'That's *exactly* what I mean!' said Swyver.

No one actually said 'Hallelujah!' this time, lest he be thought unspiritual, but enthusiasm swept back into the auditorium like a returning tide.

10

In one sense, little of this is new. During the Cold War era Lindsey and others produced apocalyptic scenarios by interweaving biblical prophecies with contemporary political tensions. Most notably they promoted the idea that biblical passages like Ezekiel 38 and Zechariah 14 describe a nuclear holocaust, precipitated by that 'evil empire', the USSR, invading Israel. The remarkable thing about Swyver is that he manages to adapt these interpretations to the post-1989 situation, still maintaining that Ezekiel 38 describes an attack on Israel by a Russian-led alliance. However, unlike his Cold War predecessors, he does not see nuclear war as the outcome; instead, the catastrophes of Ezekiel 38 etc. are devastating earth changes, sent by God to forestall a nuclear holocaust, punish Israel's attackers and purge the world for the return of Christ, which will immediately follow.

Another surprising feature is Swyver's revival of a notion, popular with American writers on prophecy in the nineteenth century, that America will have a special part to play in the 'last days'. Undeterred by the fact that no biblical prophet had ever heard of America, Swyver finds it mentioned in a fleeting reference to 'the merchants of Tarshish, with all the young lions thereof' (Ezekiel 38:13). Apparently the 'young lions' are the youthful states of the New World, founded by 'merchants of Tarshish', understood as settlers from Britain and Western Europe. Swyver is in no doubt that America's wealth and global influence will equip it for its end-time role, though he does not spell out what that role might be.

11

'It's an undeniable fact,' said Swyver, 'that almost all biblical prophecies of events preceding Christ's return have now been fulfilled: the rebirth of Israel in 1948, the recapture of Jerusalem in the Six-Day War of 1967, and so on and so forth. In fact, only two preconditions remain – further proof of how close we are to that wonderful climax of all the prophecies! And here's the amazing thing, friends: it's now within the power of men to fulfil those preconditions! Can that be mere coincidence? Of course not! What's more, I believe we are the particular men to whom the task has been given!'

He rested his arms on the lectern and adopted an intimate tone.

'Like a welcoming committee preparing for the arrival of an honoured guest, it will be our task to make sure everything is ready for the return of this world's heavenly king – to set the stage, if you will, for the final drama of human history. As you all know, I myself have devoted much time and money to that goal in recent years, preparing not only men's hearts but also their digital telecommunications network. Thanks to Swycorp, we can now transmit wide-screen, high-definition pictures from anywhere on earth to everywhere on earth, so that, when he "cometh with clouds" as it says in Scripture, "every eye shall see him"!'

Murmurs of 'Amen!' and 'Hallelujah!' rumbled around the room.

'Completing the task will require a great deal of money, my friends. I make no bones about it: you're all here today because you're not only the wisest, but also the wealthiest men in the CRAP. Without further delay, let me introduce the ultimate project for which your moral and financial support is needed. For reasons which will become obvious, I call it Project Peter.'

Swyver prodded a couple of buttons on the lectern. A backdrop of red curtains parted to expose a white screen.

'This video presentation will introduce our basic aims. I'll explain the practicalities later.'

The screen came alive to a sonorous fanfare. As massive chords set the auditorium vibrating, an impressive building of pale stone came slowly into view through a thinning cloud of smoke. To judge from a group of tiny human figures standing before it, its height was equivalent to about fifteen storeys. It had no windows, only a huge doorway which reached about halfway up the facade. The fanfare faded to a more subdued background of spacious chords, over which a voice said:

'With the aid of computer-simulated images, you are about to witness a ritual which has not taken place for over nineteen centuries...'

12

> Swyver's smorgasbord of pernicious notions is of significance to serious scholars for two reasons. Firstly, it provides important insights into the popular revival of millenarian hopes within Protestant Christianity; secondly, it challenges those of us who teach biblical hermeneutics to do our job better. Failure in that quarter will only encourage the proliferation of such apocalyptic poppycock as this book represents.

On rereading the final paragraph Mike replaces 'smorgasbord' with 'pot-pourri'. Satisfied with the improved alliteration he sits back to finish his coffee.

Chapter Two

1

> Dr Michael J Totley
> Dept of Religious Studies
> Whitfield University
> PO Box 220, Alpha Campus
> Whitfield, WH4 2GL

8 April 1999

Giles Waterman,
Editor, British Journal of Religious Studies,
Rangeford Academic Press,
Unit 5, Fairhome Way,
Rangeford, RF8 4GF

Dear Giles,

The review you've been pestering me for is on the enclosed disk. I'm sorry it's a bit late, but I've had a lot on my plate recently. I've been invited to give a paper on apocalypticism in the Dead Sea Scrolls at the big ASBL/ASTR conference in November, and had to submit a summary and title by the start of this month – which meant drafting the whole thing.

When I finally read Swyver's book I was quite surprised you'd sent it. It's an example of what Moltmann calls psychological terrorism – not the sort of thing to which serious academic journals normally devote space. I've reviewed it as an example of the current dispensational premillennialism, but you'll find I haven't pulled any punches.

I've managed to get a short sabbatical next spring so I'm looking forward to doing some serious archaeology again. I've missed the buzz more than I expected.

Best wishes,
Mike

★

From: m.totley@univ-whit.ac.uk
To: waterman@rangac.co.uk
Date: 30 June 1999
Subject: Swyver review

Dear Giles,

The current issue of BJRS reached me this morning. I naturally turned at once to the book reviews to see how much of my contribution had survived the editorial secateurs, and frankly I was appalled. I know you reserve the right to trim reviews for reasons of space, but mine has been not so much trimmed as hacked to death. The paragraphs placing the book in its socio-religious context have been removed; my quip about Swyver not having a normal human brain has gone; the closing paragraph has completely disappeared; and other biting comments have been rendered toothless by feeble emendations.

This isn't the first time you've taken liberties with my reviews, but in the past I've been prepared to overlook them. This time your bowdlerising tendencies have gone too far. I do not think it is acceptable for an editor to mangle a contribution to this extent without consulting the author. In future I will not write anything for you without an undertaking that all changes will be submitted to me for approval.

Best wishes,
Mike

★

From: waterman@rangac.co.uk
To: m.totley@univ-whit.ac.uk
Date: 1 July 1999
Subject: review moan

Mike,

Sorry if upset you, but only mad changes were essential. Americans very litigious; bets to err on sid of caution. Don't worry – your irony still there in spadfuls, no chance anyone mising your drift!

Gills
PS Glad to hear you're gong to ARSE-BLASTER in Nov. I hop to be there myself so my bum into you among the crows.

★

From: m.totley@univ-whit.ac.uk
To: waterman@rangac.co.uk
Date: 1 July 1999
Subject: review moan

Dear Giles (or Gills if you prefer),

A feeble excuse (so far as I can understand it – your email was practically incomprehensible due to typos). If you do bump into me among the crowds in Washington I intend to pick this bone a lot more thoroughly. And you'd better be right about no one missing my drift – I'd hate readers to think I had any sympathy with this kind of stuff.

Best wishes,
Mike

★

The Rev. Dr Oral B Swyver
Honorary Principal
BIOSES
Memphis, Tennessee
USA

5 August 1999

Professor Michael J Totley
Department of Religious Studies
Whitfield University
PO Box 220, Alpha Campus,
Whitfield WH4 2GL
UK

Dear Professor Totley,

Please excuse me writing you out of the blue like this, but I wanted to thank you most sincerely for your very kind review of my book Till the Son of Man be Come. *One of my research assistants brought me the latest issue of the* British Journal of Religious Studies *with your review marked for my attention, and it warmed my heart to read it. This is the first time any member of the mainstream academic establishment has endorsed my work in such positive terms, so your support is especially welcome.*

Since reading your review I have taken the liberty of discovering a little more about you. I was very interested to learn that you are not only an evangelical scholar but also a professional archaeologist, with special expertise in the Dead Sea Scrolls. I wonder if by any chance you would be free next April–June to take part in an excavation I am organizing in Israel? It will involve exploration of some caves in Nahal Shuhan, a canyon – as you probably know – on the west side of the Dead Sea. Who knows what may be in there? We might even find some new Dead Sea Scrolls!

I aim to finalize details by the end of November, and was wondering if there is any chance we might meet before then to discuss at length the possibility of your involvement. I am prepared to fly to England, or to meet the cost of your fare over here, if that is the only way. I am most anxious to have you on board, and look forward to hearing from you when you've had time to think things over and consider your schedule.

May the Lord bless you!

With sincere Christian greetings,
Rev. Dr Oral B Swyver PhD

★

Michael J Totley,
Dept of Religious Studies
Whitfield University
PO Box 220, Alpha Campus
Whitfield, WH4 2GL
UK

18 August 1999

The Revd. Dr Oral B. Swyver
Honorary Principal
BIOSES
Memphis, Tennessee
USA

Dear Dr Swyver,

Thank you for your letter of 5 August, which I was most surprised to receive.

I am intrigued by your proposed dig in Israel next spring and would like to hear more about it. It just so happens that I will be in Washington DC for 15–19 November, attending a conference at the Sheraton Washington Hotel. If you were able to be in Washington at that time, perhaps we could meet one evening. Would such

an arrangement be convenient for you?
I look forward to hearing from you.

Yours sincerely,
Mike Totley

★

BIBLE INSTITUTE OF THE SOUTH-EASTERN STATES
Memphis, Tennessee
USA

FAX MESSAGE

From:	Rev. Dr O. B. Swyver
To:	Prof. M. J. Totley
Date:	27 August 1999

Pages including this one = 1

Dear Professor Totley,

Thank you for your letter of 18 August 1999. May I suggest we meet on the evening of 18 November? I have arranged to stay at the Omni Shoreham Hotel that night and would be delighted if you would be my guest for dinner.

The Omni Shoreham is just across Calvert Street from the Sheraton Washington, so it will be real handy for you. I will be waiting in the lobby at 7.30 p.m. You should have no problem recognizing me; the photo on the back cover of my book is an excellent likeness, and I will be in the company of two bodyguards.

If I do not hear from you in the meantime, I'll assume this arrangement is okay for you. I look forward very much to our meeting.

May the Lord bless you!

With sincere Christian greetings,
Rev. Dr. Oral B. Swyver PhD

2

'I reckon we've got him on board, Chuck,' said Swyver, sliding Mike's letter across his desk. 'He's practically said yes.'

Charles Sinnet sat down, took the letter and read it thoughtfully. He was a weathered, sinewy man in his fifties with a massive square jaw which made his head much wider at the bottom than the top.

'I'm still not sure about this,' he said, dropping the letter back on the desk. 'Bringing in a guy we don't know…'

'I don't think we have much choice,' said Swyver. 'You may not get an excavation permit without him, not since that explosives fiasco at the Ascent of Ziz.'

Sinnet uncrossed his legs and massaged his left knee. The incident was one he preferred to forget. Renewing eye contact he said, 'And you think having Totley on the team will tip the balance? He isn't exactly a big name.'

'But he trained with Zederbaum, and names don't come any bigger than that among Israeli archaeologists. Anyway I had Willard check him out and I like what I hear: he's single, thirty-one years old, British, solid academic record, full-time archaeologist for three years before he settled at some university in the north of England last year – and he obviously sings from the same hymn sheet.'

Sinnet stroked his jutting chin. 'And if he says no?'

'He won't,' said Swyver with perfect confidence. 'I intend to offer a very attractive incentive.'

Chapter Three

1

'Sorry, but your flight's delayed for three hours,' said the young woman at the check-in desk. 'Fog at Newark International.'

Mike watched morosely as his suitcase wobbled out of sight through a curtain of black plastic strips. 'Did you know,' he said, 'that the word "travel" is derived from the Latin *trepalium*, meaning an instrument of torture?'

'Never mind, sir. You should still be all right for your onward flight to Washington.'

He sighed, took his boarding card and turned away. He'd been up since 4.00 a.m.; it was now 9.30 and he hadn't eaten breakfast yet. He wandered off to find some. Half an hour later, fortified by fried eggs, sausages and toast, he sat in one of Heathrow's cafés reading the *Guardian* and drinking his fourth cup of coffee.

'Hi! Didn't I see you check in for the flight to New York?'

A large man with a red face and full beard sat down at Mike's table, one hand extended in greeting. He was dressed in a plaid lumberjack shirt, check trousers and a tartan body warmer.

'Newark International, actually,' said Mike.

'Same difference. Shame about the fog. That's my flight, too. The name's Woodbridge Belhammer, with only one L. My friends call me Woodbridge. How about yours?'

Mike thought his friends would call this man boorish and badly dressed, but he suppressed the temptation to say so.

'Mike Totley.'

'Hi!' repeated Belhammer. 'So, what takes you to the US of A, Mike?'

'I'm delivering a paper.'

'God, that must be one precious piece of paper! Couldn't you send it by post, or fax it or something?'

Mike gave up trying to read the *Guardian* and folded it sharply.

'When I say I'm delivering a paper, I mean I'm going to *read* a paper at an academic conference.'

'Oh, I get it! What about?' asked Belhammer.

'Apocalypticism,' said Mike, hoping this would kill the conversation stone dead.

'Really?' asked Belhammer. 'The number of the beast, 666 and all that stuff?'

'That's in Revelation; I'm going to talk about—'

'That's gematria, isn't it? The science of relating words to numbers – I know all about that.'

'I'd hardly call it—'

'D'you know it proves that Francis Bacon was the real author of the so-called Shakespeare plays?'

'Pardon?'

'Well, it sure does! If you count the words in roman type in the first column of the first page of *The Histories* – First Folio, of course – the total is exactly 287, which is also the numerical value of the words *Fra Rosicrosse* in the Kay cipher, and of course Bacon was the leader of the Rosicrucian fraternity! Now, on the first page of *The Tragedies*, the first column has 318 words in roman type, but if you subtract the number of letters contained in the words in italics, you get 287 again! Now, is that convincing – or is that convincing?'

Before Mike could object to these limited alternatives, Belhammer was off again.

'I can see you're not totally convinced, so let's take the first page of Bacon's *Essays*; the count for the first line of text is 33, which is the numerological value of "Bacon" in simple cipher, and the total number of roman letters on that page is 259, which is the value of "Shakespeare" in Kay cipher. If you then take away 59, which is the total number of roman words on the short lines, you get 200, which is "Bacon" again in *reversed* cipher! Here, I'll show you how the Kay cipher works. This'll really clinch it.'

The man produced a well-thumbed notebook and a pencil from a pocket of his body warmer and began to write, the tip of his tongue sliding from side to side between his lips. He became so engrossed in his task that Mike was able to slip away from the table unnoticed.

He left the café and made his way to the main seating area. The *Guardian* having proved insufficient protection, he took a Bible from his briefcase and opened it. He assumed anyone seen reading the Bible in an airport would be given a wide berth.

After a few minutes a cultured American voice exclaimed, 'Oh, you're reading prophecy!'

Mike looked up from the book of Daniel and glanced at his new neighbour. She was middle-aged and wore a long blue dress, a matching silk headscarf, vivid red lipstick and wrap-around dark glasses.

'I'm just fascinated by prophecy!' she said. 'Especially Nostradamus. You know his most famous prediction, I suppose? *"L'an mil neuf cens nonante neuf sept mois, du ciel viendra un grand Roy d'effraieur."'* As she delivered the Renaissance French she raised both hands above her head in a theatrical gesture. '"In the year 1999 and seven months, a great king of terror will come from the sky!" What do *you* think he meant?'

'No idea,' said Mike, to whom Nostradamus's quatrains had always seemed incomprehensible doggerel. 'But whatever it was, he seems to have got it wrong – the date having come and gone.'

'Oh, but he was using a different calendar! You have to make adjustments. I've been doing the calculations, and I believe he was predicting an asteroid strike for about this time next year. It'll bring chaos, war and famine, followed by the dawn of a new age of enlightenment, but only the spiritually mature – people like us – will survive to see it. I can tell you're a spiritual person; you have a very interesting aura.'

'Pardon?'

'It's very orange. What sign are you?'

'I've no idea,' said Mike, peevishly.

'Do you know what time of day you were born?'

'I'm afraid I didn't notice. I was very young at the time.'

'My chart shows that in the future, orange is going to be very significant for me.'

'These cellphone promoters will stop at nothing,' said Mike, putting the Bible back in his briefcase. 'Now I'm afraid you'll have to excuse me. I've drunk too much coffee.'

Minutes later, emerging cautiously from the toilets, he decided there would be less chance of getting drawn into weird conversations if he kept moving. Until the call to the departure lounge, he killed time by browsing in shops and observing Heathrow's cosmopolitan bustle.

Mike surveyed the departure lounge carefully before deciding where to sit. Woodbridge Belhammer was already deep in conversation, having found a less nimble traveller on whom to press the Baconian theory. The Nostradamus woman was there too, safely engrossed in a magazine called *X-traordinary Facts*.

When he boarded the plane he was relieved to find his seat was nowhere near either of theirs. On his immediate left was a window, and in the seat to his right sat a small, soberly dressed man with glasses and thinning hair. The man smiled vaguely as Mike sat down, but showed no inclination to talk. As soon as the plane was airborne Mike set his seat in a reclining position and tried to catch up on lost sleep.

2

Unfortunately before Mike could get beyond the outskirts of consciousness a meal was served. At least he supposed it was a meal. The small plastic dish contained a white, rubbery substance, surrounded by a moat of something like sump oil into which a few peas had oozed a bright green slurry. It was while he was hacking impotently at the rubbery stuff with pliable cutlery that the man on his right spoke for the first time.

'That's a tough piece of chicken you've got there, friend.'

'Yes. Should've brought my Swiss Army penknife,' said Mike.

'Oh, you got one of those things, too? Great, aren't they?'

Mike picked up the chicken with his fingers and bit into it with silent determination. He looked out of the window. Below them lay a continuous blanket of grey cloud.

'Just passing over the west of England, I guess,' said his neighbour. 'As a matter of fact I was there until yesterday. Spent a couple of months touring the country, and for the last few days I was in Bath. You know Bath?'

'Slightly.'

'We probably flew over it a few minutes ago,' said the man,

exposing a large wristwatch with an ostentatious gesture. 'Pretty little place.'

They each opened another plastic dish and picked at slices of a dry, tasteless material. Possibly cork, thought Mike. A stewardess brought fresh supplies of coffee and tea.

'My name,' said the man, 'is Effin Clinger. What's yours?'

'Mike Totley.'

'Nice to meet you, Mike. Did I notice you looking curiously at my watch a moment ago?'

'No, I don't think so.'

'It's an intriguing one, isn't it?' said Effin Clinger, unfastening the watch from his wrist and handing it to Mike. 'Go on, take a closer look.'

Mike accepted it reluctantly. He could sense another bizarre conversation coming on. The watch looked well made and expensive. At first glance it appeared to be of the conventional analogue type, but on closer inspection the hands turned out to be luminous lines on the dial, and in place of numbers it had twelve red symbols around the edge. Some were rather too small for Mike to make much of them, but among the clearer ones he could see what looked like a snake, a lion, a donkey, a bunch of grapes and a ship.

'Those emblems,' said Clinger, 'represent the twelve tribes of Israel, and are based on the forty-ninth chapter of Genesis and the thirty-third chapter of Deuteronomy in the Bible. Now, if I press this button…'

He reached across and pressed a small button on the side of the watch. The symbols vanished; in their place, twelve little bearded faces appeared. 'Those are the twelve Apostles of our Lord Jesus Christ. And if I press it again…' The faces disappeared and twelve tiny lights came on – all different colours. 'And those represent the twelve precious stones of the heavenly Jerusalem, as described in chapter twenty-one of the book of Revelation, verses nineteen and twenty. So you see, Mike, this watch not only tells me the time of day; it reminds me that the passing of time sees the fulfilment of God's purposes, and that soon the day will come when our Lord Jesus Christ will return in glory. Are you ready for that day, Mike?'

'Well, yes, I believe I am—'

'I'm glad to hear you say so! But let me make myself absolutely clear. What I'm asking is this: are you a born-again Christian? And I hope you can answer that with all the assurance of President George Bush when it was put to him; he said: "I'm a clear-cut affirmative to that!" Can you say the same, Mike?'

Mike hoped he would never express himself with such flagrant disregard for the rules of grammar. Choosing his words carefully he said, 'Well, if by "born-again" you're asking if there was a decisive moment of conversion in my life, then yes, there was, but the phrase—'

'Hallelujah!' said Effin Clinger, a bit too loudly for Mike's liking. A woman sitting on Clinger's right was jolted out of a postprandial snooze and stared about her, wide-eyed with momentary panic.

Effin Clinger shook Mike's hand and said, 'Praise the Lord!'

'Absolutely,' said Mike, looking at Clinger's watch to cover his growing embarrassment. The display around the perimeter had reverted to the twelve tribes. Mike was now able to decipher some of the more obscure emblems: a water jar for Reuben, a wolf for Benjamin...

'I find that watch a very useful evangelistic conversation opener,' said Clinger.

'I'll bet. Very subtle,' said Mike.

'It's also the most accurate watch money can buy. It receives radio signals from an atomic caesium clock via a network of satellites, automatically adjusts when crossing time zones, and is guaranteed accurate to within one second, even after a million years! Not that I expect the present world to last that long, of course. As a matter of fact, I believe Christ could return any day now. Still, it'll be good to have a dependable watch to see me through the Millennium.'

'Quite,' said Mike non-committally. He turned the watch over and was only half-surprised to find the words: 'Swyver End-Time Enterprises Inc.' engraved on the back. He returned it to Clinger. 'Thanks. Very interesting.' He made no attempt to keep the conversation going. He hoped Clinger would now turn his evangelistic attention to the woman on his right, but she had dozed off again.

'I liked your country,' said Clinger. 'But now I'm looking forward to getting home and seeing how my business is going.'

Good manners compelled Mike to make some response to this, so he asked what line of business Clinger was in. Clinger handed Mike a card. Beneath an address in Bridgeport, Connecticut, were the words:

> Domiciliary Dental Maintenance.
> Express mail order service.
> We make your dental hygiene
> our business!

'I take a back seat these days. My son runs it mostly.'

'What exactly is domiciliary dental maintenance?' asked Mike. 'I'm afraid I've never—'

'Basically, we provide the tools, amalgam and stuff for people to do their dental work at home.'

'You mean, instead of going to a dentist, people buy your equipment and er… do it themselves?'

'Buy or rent. We do kits for extractions, fillings, crowns, plaque-removal – you name it. Everything comes with a how-to video. Our fillings kit is very popular – the extractions kit isn't doing so well though.'

'You surprise me.'

'But I expect sales to pick up now we've launched a false tooth kit to go with it. Would you be interested in buying one? Our kits are so easy to carry, you can take them anywhere. And you never know when a dental emergency might arise.'

'I don't think so, thanks.'

'Our critics say we're making money from people's fear of the dentist, but I disagree. People have the right to maintain their teeth in the comfort of their own homes, just like the right to carry firearms. As a matter of fact I believe our kits encourage regular dental overhauls. Take the scour and polish kit…'

Overcome by tiredness and the monotonous drone of Clinger's voice, Mike found his concentration lapsing. Eventually he drifted into sleep, his mind full of muddled images in which whole small-town communities of do-it-yourself dentists wandered the streets, trying unsuccessfully to communicate through badly repaired teeth.

He was woken by a stewardess handing out immigration cards. After establishing that Mike wasn't a US passport holder and that Clinger was, she gave the appropriate card to each and moved on. Clinger was evidently familiar with this procedure and filled in his card without reading it. Mike examined his carefully, wondering if he was right to detect a vein of humour beneath questions like, 'Is your visit connected with the illegal purchase or shipment of armaments?'

'Now tell me, Mike,' said Clinger, when the task was finished, 'what takes you to the States? Business? Family connections?'

Mike's reply seemed to fire Clinger's interest and more questions followed. When Mike mentioned that he'd done archaeology in Israel, Clinger stared open-mouthed.

'Well, if that isn't the durnedest thing! You're just the man I need to talk to! I want to go on a dig in Israel myself before I get too old for it – you know, as a volunteer – and help confirm the truth of God's Word.'

'It doesn't really work like that,' said Mike. 'The relationship between what you dig up and what you read in the Bible is rather more subtle. Archaeology can rarely prove that particular things happened. It's better at helping us understand the cultural and sociological background—'

'Oh? Well, anyway, how can I get on a dig?'

Mike had no wish to dampen Clinger's enthusiasm. 'Your best bet is to find a library that has this magazine,' he said, writing the title *Biblical Archaeology Review* on the back of Clinger's card and returning it. 'Each January it carries a list of digs in Israel that want volunteers for the summer – gives details of each dig, tells you about accommodation and cost, and gives a contact address.'

'Praise the Lord! That's exactly what I'm looking for, Mike. I must try it while I've still got the strength to lift a pick and spade.'

'Actually, you don't have to do that to be useful on a dig. A lot of work is done with very fine instruments, like tweezers, brushes, dental probes—'

'Dental probes? You don't say! Then archaeology isn't so different from dental maintenance! If I get on a dig I'm gonna take a whole set of our kits along! Did I tell you what's in our plaque-removal kit? It's the works! It would be just dandy for some of that delicate archaeology. Take the double-ended probe...'

3

The election of Patrick Thorn to the presidency in 1996 had brought a raft of right-wing legislation in its wake, including a tightening of immigration controls. Mike was dimly aware of this, but until now he'd failed to appreciate the implications for short-term visitors. At Newark International Airport he had to undergo a lengthy interrogation before an immigration official would stamp his visa.

As soon as the interview was over Mike rushed off to check in for his flight to Washington DC, but at the boarding gate in terminal C, seventeen minutes before departure, he faced another anxiety-provoking delay. Instead of rushing through the usual checks as quickly as possible the woman at the desk spent a long time scrutinising Mike's boarding pass and drumming her fingers. Then she looked up and gave an almost imperceptible nod to two men standing nearby. They approached the desk.

'Dr Totley? Airport security,' said one of them, tapping an identification badge which hung from his lapel. 'I'm afraid we have to ask you to come with us.'

'What? But my plane leaves in about fifteen minutes!'

'I know, sir, but this is a very important matter. If you cooperate you could still catch your flight.'

Mike was led down a succession of branching corridors until he doubted whether he could retrace his steps. Eventually his escorts stopped at an unmarked door. They knocked, opened it, ushered him into the room beyond and then withdrew.

The room had no windows. Its only light came from an anglepoise lamp casting a bright ellipse onto a well-polished desk. On the far side of the desk sat another two men, their faces lit dimly from below by the reflected light.

'Please sit down, Mr Totley.' The words came in a rasping elderly voice.

'*Dr* Totley.' Mike sensed he was in trouble, and hoped his title would provide some protective gravitas.

As he sat down the lamp dazzled him. One of the men leaned forward to adjust it. He was young and fresh-faced with close-cropped hair and a button-down collar.

'We have some questions to put to you, concerning this.' The older man also leaned forward as he spoke. In the lamp's full glare his face looked very white and wrinkled, as though he'd spent a long time at the bottom of a pond. He produced the card Mike had filled in on the plane and placed it very precisely in the centre of the desk. Mike had surrendered the card during his interview with the immigration official, who had seemed to pay it scant attention.

'I hope it won't take long,' said Mike. 'My flight to Washington leaves—'

'That depends on you, Dr Totley. Would you mind explaining the answers you've written here? Are they true?'

'Well, the ones that matter are.'

'All of them matter, Dr Totley, otherwise we wouldn't bother asking the questions.'

'What I mean,' said Mike, 'is – well, take this one for example: "Are you engaged in espionage activities?" Or this: "Is your visit connected with the illegal purchase or shipment of armaments?"'

'To which you have answered "Yes" in both cases,' the younger man pointed out.

'I know. But I was about to say that if you ask someone if they're a spy and they are, they'll say "No", won't they? So these questions aren't worth asking, because you wouldn't get honest answers from real spies or arms dealers.'

'So are your answers true or false?'

'False, of course.'

The older man leaned forward again, his arms on the table.

'And are you in the habit of lying, Dr Totley?' His breath made the card flutter.

'Certainly not!' said Mike with much warmth.

'Yet you admit these answers are untrue?'

'They're not factual, but that doesn't mean they're lies.'

'Oh? Perhaps you could explain that to me?'

'Of course. A lie involves the intention to deceive, and I had no such intention when I filled in that card, because I never expected anyone would be...' (he was about to say 'sufficiently stupid,' but thought better of it) 'would believe those particular answers. They're a kind of irony, saying one thing while expecting people to grasp the opposite. It was meant as a sort of – well, a joke, I suppose. I thought anyone reading this would just...'

'A *joke*?' The man from the bottom of the pond was clearly not amused.

'I don't mean to imply that irony is always humorous, of course,' said Mike, almost forgetting the seriousness of his situation as he warmed to the theme. 'In Shakespeare's *Othello* – assuming for the sake of argument that it was Shakespeare and not Francis Bacon who wrote *Othello* – in Shakespeare's *Othello*, when—'

'Do you mind if we stick to the point?' said the younger man, who knew a hobby horse when he saw one. 'This answer also disturbs us.' He pointed to the question: 'Are you a member of any organisation opposing the values of Western democracy?' Mike had given an affirmative answer to this as well. 'What is it you belong to, Dr Totley?'

'I was thinking of the Church. I should perhaps explain that I don't disagree with democracy as such; it's just that there's very little real democracy about – too much power in the hands of big corporations, public opinion manipulated by an influential elite, private power attacking the public arena. Take genetically modified foods for example, a classic case of...'

'And this group you belong to – what exactly are its aims?' asked the older man, evidently thinking the nub had finally been reached.

'Group? I'm talking about the worldwide Christian Church.'

'So this is a global organisation?'

'Ah... there seems to be some confusion. You think I mean some kind of sect called the Worldwide Christian Church, whereas I simply mean the Church universal, Christianity in all its diversity. Personally I'm an Anglican, but...'

'I see. So this was another flippant answer.'

'I don't consider it flippant at all,' said Mike.

'Well, I do!' yelled the older man, slamming his hand on the desk. 'You may not have done anything wrong, Dr Totley, but you disturb me! You disturb me greatly! Shall I tell you why? Because you are an extremely intelligent, well-educated individual with no respect for authority, and I find that a very disturbing combination! Now, I want you to tell me *exactly* what you'll be doing while you're over here. It says here that you're in Washington for five days, staying at the Sheraton Hotel. Can I assume that's true? Right. I want to know what you'll be doing on each of those days.'

'I've already explained all that to the immigration man, and my flight goes in—'

'Well you're going to explain it again! What will you be doing in Washington?'

'I'm giving a paper at the joint meeting of the Academy for the Study of Biblical Literature and the American Society of Theology and Religion. I'll be there the whole time.'

'Tell me some more about this meeting.'

'Well, it's a big event, held—'

'How big is big?'

'I haven't been to one before, but I gather it usually attracts six or seven thousand scholars from all over the world. Lots of groups meet at the same time – look, I can show you a programme.'

Mike took the thick programme from his briefcase and placed it on the desk. As the older man picked it up and flicked through the pages, a loose sheet fell out. It was Swyver's fax proposing the meeting at the Omni Shoreham Hotel. The two men read it and exchanged knowing looks.

'What's your connection with this man, Dr Totley?'

'Swyver? He contacted me after I reviewed a book of his.'

'I see. You approve of his work?'

'Actually, no. My review was very critical, but I employed irony, and the trouble with irony is that if you don't recognise it, it merely confirms your own prejudice and—'

'I think we've discussed irony enough,' said the younger man, reining in the hobby horse again.

His colleague returned the fax and the programme to Mike and said, 'All right, Dr Totley, you may go.'

Surprised by this sudden end to the interview but too grateful to question it, Mike fastened his briefcase and left the room. To his relief, one of the security men who'd brought him from the boarding gate was waiting outside to escort him back through the labyrinth.

When Mike had gone the older man lit a cigarette and sat back in his chair. 'Well, Jeff, what did you make of that?'

'I think I've just met my first English eccentric, sir.'

'Oh, there's a lot more to Dr Totley than that! As a matter of fact, I think he could be the man our friends in the CIA are looking for.' He opened a drawer in the desk, took out a tape recorder and removed a tiny cassette from it. 'Get this to them right away, would you Jeff? I think they'll be very interested in Dr Totley. Meanwhile…' He unclipped a cellphone from his belt and began punching numbers.

4

As soon as Mike had found his bearings in Terminal C, he ran to the boarding gate as fast as he could. The last few passengers were just disappearing down the covered jetty and entering the plane. Mike rushed to the desk and presented his passport and boarding card. The woman in attendance tapped a keyboard and consulted her computer screen.

'I'm afraid you're too late, sir.'

'What? But I just saw people boarding!'

'Yes, sir, but your seat has gone.'

'What?'

'I'm afraid it's an airline regulation, sir, as printed inside the front page of your ticket: "If a flight is overbooked and a reservation has not been confirmed, and the passenger has not arrived at the departure gate fifteen minutes prior to the scheduled departure time, the seat may be given to another passenger with a valid ticket."' She intoned the regulation in a sing-song manner that fuelled Mike's irritation.

'But my flight was confirmed!'

'Not according to my information, sir.'

'Then your information must be wrong! And anyway, I *was*

here more than fifteen minutes ago. Ask your colleague who was on this desk at the time; she'll confirm it.'

'I'm sorry, but I can't do that.'

'Why not?'

'She's gone off duty, sir.'

'So what am I supposed to do now?' Mike demanded, his sense of helplessness increasing with this woman's unfolding revelations.

'Transfer to another flight, sir.'

'But my luggage is on that plane!'

'That's all right, sir. It'll be kept in a locker at Washington until you catch up with it.'

The muted whine of Mike's plane moving off towards the runway underscored the futility of further argument.

'In that case, could you please transfer me to another flight straight away?'

'I'm sorry, but I can't do that.'

'And why not?'

'They do that at check-in, sir. You have to go back and—'

'Fine. Do you have a room where I can go and scream without disturbing anybody?'

'I don't think so, but I'm new. Would you like me to make enquiries?'

'No, don't bother.'

But Mike was soon regretting his failure to follow this up. At the check-in desk he was told by an efficient young man with brushed-back hair that they could not put him on a flight to Washington until the next morning.

'However,' said the man, perusing his computer monitor, 'I can tell you that your reservation was definitely confirmed.'

'I know,' said Mike, 'I confirmed it myself.'

'So I can't understand why you weren't allowed on the plane, sir. There seems to have been a mistake. I'll look into it momentarily.'

'I hope you'll look into it very *thoroughly*.'

'Of course, sir. You can depend on it.'

'But you just said you would only look into it momentarily.'

'Perhaps we have a language problem, sir? By "momentarily" I mean in a few moments from now.'

'Oh, I see. Sorry. In English it means briefly.'

'We'll also do our best to make up for the inconvenience, sir. I can arrange free overnight accommodation and meals in a nearby hotel, and a guaranteed seat on the 9.15 flight tomorrow morning. Will you accept that offer, sir, along with our apologies? I can arrange transportation to the hotel almost immediately.'

'Momentarily?'

'That's right, sir.'

Mike looked at his watch. It was now 6.35 p.m. local time, 12.35 a.m. by his body clock, and he'd been travelling for over nineteen hours. He accepted the offer.

5

In the leafless Virginia woodlands, about half an hour's drive from downtown Washington, the night staff were taking over at CIA headquarters. But Eugene Hayden stayed on at his desk, papers and infrared photos lying thick in an oval pool of light. He shifted the phone from his right ear to his left and scratched the top of his bald head. His scalp was getting that prickly feeling which it always got when the job of Deputy Director of National Covert Operations began to lose its familiar boundaries.

'But sir, if this guy is from England it's a job for *International* Covert Operations, besides which I have enough on my plate already. As you know, I'm seriously understaffed here, and keeping tabs on those end-time militias in Colorado, Montana and Wyoming has left me really stretched. Those guys are up to something – stockpiling weapons and networking like crazy. I've got no Operations personnel to spare right now. If you'd given me a few days' notice…'

But the voice on the other end of the line was insistent. Yes, the man was British, but he was here in the USA. And it was a matter of seizing the moment; no notice had been possible. If there were no Operations personnel available, what about giving the job to some bright spark in Analysis?

Eugene Hayden flinched. The idea was anathema to him. Having survived the latest staff purges, chiefly because of his meticulous eye for detail and reputation for efficiency, he now sat tight like a hardy fossil while the glacier of change ground its way past him. As far as he was concerned, Operations and Analysis were separate worlds. Analysis was peopled by bearded, tweed-wearing nerds who spent all their time at headquarters; send an analyst on an Operations operation and he would be worse than useless.

Actually, this perception was seriously out of line with the facts. Only a few people in Analysis wore tweed jackets these days, and many did not have beards. In some cases this was because they were women.

Hayden's flinch must somehow have transmitted itself down the phone, because his superior weighed in with fresh arguments, trying to convince him that things had changed; people these days were trained to be flexible, they had transferable skills; and there must be plenty of folks in Analysis who wanted the chance to get out and do something different. Anyway, the bottom line was that he had no choice.

Eugene Hayden put the receiver down with a heavy heart. If he must he must, but someone else could make the selection. He wasn't going to spend his evening interviewing a bunch of hyperintelligent, bearded screwballs who would all peer at him myopically through bottle-bottom spectacles. He buzzed his secretary and asked to see the head of Personnel immediately.

One hour later a fully briefed, tweed-jacketed analyst walked briskly out of the CIA's marble lobby, smiling at the familiar motto on the wall: 'Ye shall know the truth, and the truth shall make you free.'

Chapter Four

1

A polite but persistent knocking brought Mike from the shower. Wrapping a towel around his waist he opened the door a few inches and a hand appeared, delivering freshly laundered socks and underpants. When Mike took the package the hand turned its palm upwards and gave a twitch of entreaty. Leaving a damp trail across the bedroom, Mike fetched his wallet and placed some money in the open palm. The hand closed on the tip and vanished.

Mike dried himself, dressed and went down for breakfast. In the hotel lobby he discovered a vending machine that sold shaving kits, tiny tubes of toothpaste and folding toothbrushes. By the time he set off for the airport, life seemed to be more or less back on track.

Anxious to avoid a repeat of yesterday's encounters he asked the woman at the check-in desk for a seat in a no smoking and no talking section of the plane. She explained that smoking was prohibited on all domestic mainland flights.

'Very sensible,' said Mike, 'but what about talking?'

'Sir?'

'I'd like a seat where no one is allowed to talk to me.'

'I'm afraid we don't do those, sir. But I'll give you a window seat if you like, then only one person will try to talk to you.'

Applying the same logic when he reached the boarding gate, Mike sat at the end of a row. As more passengers arrived he acquired a neighbour, a bearded young man in a tweed jacket whose eyes looked no bigger than newts' eggs behind thick glasses. The man seemed restless and kept looking at Mike as if about to speak. The *Guardian* and the Bible both having failed him, Mike took a fat book entitled *Harlequins and Hermeneuts: the Autonomy of the Biblical Text* by S Goldberg from his briefcase and opened it at random. He hoped anyone looking over his shoulder at chapter headings like 'The Myth of Authorial Intentionality' or 'Metaphors and Anthropopathisms' would think twice before starting a conversation. It seemed to work.

When all passengers were on board the plane a stewardess asked them to fasten their seat belts as the doors would be 'closing momentarily'. Mike's earlier introduction to American usage spared him unnecessary alarm.

With no meals to eat or pointless cards to fill in, he was hoping to feign sleep throughout the flight and run the contents of his paper once more through his mind. He'd just settled back in his seat and closed his eyes when a woman's voice said:

'Hi there! Since we're going to be travelling companions, may I introduce myself? My name's Connie Patterson.'

Mike opened his eyes and turned to face the speaker. Connie Patterson was in her mid-twenties, with an attractive but earnest face, framed by cascades of dark hair.

'Morning. Mike Totley.'

'Would that be Totleigh as in Totleigh Towers?'

'Sorry?'

'Totleigh Towers, stately home of Sir Watkyn Bassett.'

'I'm afraid I couldn't say; I've never met him,' said Mike, though the name sounded vaguely familiar.

'No, you wouldn't have. He doesn't exist.'

This apparent nonsense was too much for Mike. The world seemed to be full of relentlessly garrulous Americans all bent on talking drivel at him. He'd had enough. It was time to go on the offensive.

'Actually it's Totley as in the Totley Tunnel, in Derbyshire, England. The tunnel is three and a half miles, or approximately six thousand two hundred metres, in length. When it was opened on 25 June 1894 it was the second longest rail tunnel in England, being exceeded only by the Severn Tunnel, which measures nearly four and a half miles. It wasn't always known as the Totley Tunnel, because when the line was first opened it only ran from Dore to Chinley, a distance of about twenty miles. The Totley extension was begun in...'

Mike stopped. He'd realised why the name Watkyn Bassett

sounded familiar.

'Oh, I see!' he said, drowning in embarrassment. 'You meant the character in P G Wodehouse's novels! Oh, I'm so sorry!'

Connie Patterson was holding a hand over the lower half of her face, trying to conceal an uncontrollable fit of laughter. Eventually she gave up and released it in a reckless peal. Mike then realised that her face, stripped of its earnestness, was not simply attractive; it was probably the loveliest he'd ever seen.

'You said all that stuff to shut me up?' she asked, when the laughter had spent itself. 'Boy, I must have touched a nerve or something!'

'Not really. It's just that a lot of weird people forced their company on me yesterday, and I thought you were another one. Sorry. It was very rude of me.'

'Don't mention it. It was a very original way to break the ice. But was all that true about the tunnel? Do those places really exist or were you making it all up?'

'Oh yes, they exist all right. In fact Dore was Handel's birthplace.'

Connie Patterson raised a sceptical eyebrow. 'Handel? The famous composer?'

'Certainly,' said Mike. 'I know a lot of people think he was born in Germany, but actually he was one of the Dore Handels.'

She retained a quizzical expression for a moment, then her eyes widened, her face broke into a smile, and she let out another peal of uninhibited laughter. Several adjacent passengers, and some not so adjacent, turned in their seats.

'Door handles! I like it! For a second there I thought you were being serious. You're a wacky guy, Dr Totley!' And she laughed again.

Mike had never known such a gratifying response to this awful joke.

'Please, call me Mike.'

'And you can call me Connie – if you've decided to talk to me.'

'I'd love to. So long as you don't lecture me on the Baconian authorship of Shakespeare's plays, or the interpretation of Nostradamus, or comment on my aura, or try to evangelise me with the aid of an expensive novelty watch, or sell me a kit for taking my own teeth out.'

'Did all that happen yesterday? Poor man! Well, I promise not to talk about anything so boring or bizarre. In fact I'll let you steer the conversation if you like. Oh, we're taking off! If you look out of the window you'll get a good view of New York in a minute.'

It was a morning of bright sunlight and sharp shadows and the views were breathtaking. Mike was able to pick out all the famous Manhattan landmarks before the plane turned its nose towards the south-west. He settled back in his seat.

'Did you fly from England yesterday?' asked Connie.

'Yes. I should've flown to Washington yesterday too, but I was unaccountably bumped – as I think you call it – and had to spend the night in a hotel.'

'Oh, that's a shame! And what will you be doing in Washington?'

'I'm attending a conference. I don't suppose it'll sound very exciting. It's the annual joint meeting of the Academy for the Study of Biblical Literature and the—'

'American Society of Theology and Religion? But that's where I'm going too! Isn't that a coincidence?'

Mike agreed that it was. It was a coincidence that pleased him very much.

'So did you miss a flight yesterday as well?'

'No, but this morning's programme doesn't include anything relevant to my research.'

'Which is?'

'Fundamentalism – from a sociological perspective. I'm just starting my doctoral research. What's your area, Mike?'

'Currently I'm writing a book on apocalypticism – in the broad sense of a belief in the imminent end of the present order. In fact I'm giving a paper tomorrow on apocalypticism in the Dead Sea Scrolls.'

'Really? You're an expert on the Dead Sea Scrolls?' Connie unfastened her seat belt and turned to give Mike her full attention. 'That's something I'd love to know more about! I saw some of the Scrolls when they were on tour over here.'

'Then you probably know quite a bit already.'

'But that was a few years ago. I've forgotten so much, and the rest is probably out of date. Say, why don't I tell you what I remember and you can fill in the gaps and bring me up to speed?'

'If you like,' said Mike. 'Fire away!'

'Well, let me see... they were found in caves on the west side of the Dead Sea and they kept turning up for about ten years beginning, I think, in 1947. They're written in Hebrew and date from between the third century BC and the first century AD. There are hundreds of manuscripts altogether, but some are just itsy-bitsy pieces. And they're important because they throw light on Judaism between the Old and New Testaments. How am I doing, professor?'

'Brilliantly!' said Mike. 'They aren't all in Hebrew; some are in Greek and Aramaic. But that was very impressive.'

'I'm not through yet. Some of the Scrolls are copies of Old Testament books; some give weird interpretations of Old Testament prophecy, and others contain the regulations of a strict Jewish sect called the Essenes, which we already knew a bit about from a bunch of ancient writers whose names I forget.'

'Even more impressive! Actually, some scholars are querying the Essene connection, but I still think it has a lot going for it.'

'One thing I don't recall,' said Connie, 'is why all these documents were hidden in such a remote place.'

'Good question. In the 1950s the remains of a settlement were excavated, close to where most of the Scrolls were found. It's called Khirbet Qumran in Arabic – Qumran for short. It was probably home to the community which produced, or at least owned, the Scrolls – perhaps something between a kibbutz and a monastery. A likely scenario is that when Roman armies invaded the area in AD 68, members of the community hid their precious documents in the caves before they fled, hoping to come back and collect them when the danger was over.'

'But they never did. What do you think happened to those guys?'

'We don't really know. They were basically a bunch of fanatical separatists who expected the present age to end with a war – the Sons of Light, as they called themselves, against the Sons of Darkness, which basically meant everyone who didn't agree with them. They expected to win, in spite of being a tiny minority, because they thought they'd have armies of angels on their side. When the Jews rebelled against Roman rule in AD 66 they may have thought it was the start of the grand finale.'

'Literally the war to end all wars?'

'Exactly. I think they expected to gain control of Jerusalem and the Jewish Temple. In fact the Romans squashed the rebellion and Jerusalem was destroyed; the Temple went up in flames and was never rebuilt.'

'I see,' said Connie. 'So these guys were faced with – what's that phrase for when your cherished beliefs come up against discordant facts?'

'Cognitive dissonance?'

'That's it! They suffered cognitive dissonance, gave up their distinctive beliefs and disappeared?'

'I'd prefer to say we lose sight of them. I don't suppose they died out completely. Sects of that sort usually manage to survive in some form by adapting to a new set of facts. Like the Nostradamus woman.'

'Who?'

'One of the weird characters I met yesterday. She was able to carry on believing in one of Nostradamus's prophecies by adjusting the date. That's a common response to unfulfilled prophecy. The Millerites, the Jehovah's Witnesses – most of those groups have done it.'

'Fascinating! So tell me what your paper's about.'

Mike hesitated.

'I'm afraid I'll bore you if I go into that. It's all to do with the way some of the Scrolls divide time into eras, imposing a pattern on history.'

'Please, Mike, I'm interested.' And she smiled such a winning smile that he yielded, summarising the gist of the paper as simply as he could. 'I think I'll come and hear it,' she said, when Mike had finished explaining the ramifications of a solar calendar.

'What?'

'I'll come and hear you give your paper tomorrow. You don't mind, do you?'

Mike was completely taken aback.

'No, but... are you sure?'

'Sure I'm sure. Even if I don't follow it all, at least I can smile and offer moral support.'

'Well, it would be nice to have a friendly face in the audience. When it comes to question time the knives will be out. To be honest, I'm quite nervous about it. Your reputation can be made or broken by how you're received at these prestigious conferences.'

An announcement from the flight deck informed them that the aircraft was about to begin its descent. Connie stared thoughtfully past Mike and out of the window.

'Well, that's more than enough about *my* subject,' said Mike. 'Tell me more about yours. Fundamentalism, did you say?'

'Mike, I was just thinking; I'm going to feel a bit out of my depth at this conference, and I won't know anyone else there. I'd appreciate it if we could meet up a few times, perhaps have a meal together?'

Mike was flattered that this attractive, intelligent woman wanted so much of his company.

'Well, yes. If you're really sure…'

'Do you know Washington?'

'Not at all. This is my first trip to the States.'

'Then let me take you sightseeing! I know it pretty well. That is, if you don't have anything else planned for your free time?'

Mike had hoped to meet up with several people during the conference, but on reflection he decided he could just as easily discuss things by email when he got home.

'Not really.'

'That's great!'

They talked about when they could meet and what they might visit. Mike said he'd heard there was a good collection of nineteenth-century French paintings in the National Gallery of Art, and Connie said it was one of her favourite places. It was remarkable, thought Mike, how closely their taste coincided. Another announcement from the flight deck told them they were passing over Chesapeake Bay.

'Isn't that just beautiful?' said Connie, pointing to the window. 'Just look at all those little inlets and islands, and the amazing colours!'

Mike looked and was spellbound. The water reflected the sunlight of the clear winter morning like a silver-blue glaze, the wakes of ships forming random brush strokes on its surface. Along the intricate coastline of lagoons and inlets, a drifting dapple of cloud shadows shifted the colour between pale turquoise and deep bottle green. Far to the south the brightness of the water blended in a band of haze with the glowing sky.

Mike felt almost deliriously happy. So what if his critics tore his paper to shreds? He was going to enjoy the next few days enormously.

2

The nineties were an exciting decade for Dead Sea Scrolls research. Not since the fifties, when new Scrolls were still being discovered and the ruins at Qumran were excavated, had there been such a torrent of scholarly endeavour or such a spate of new theories.

The reason lay in the release of Scroll fragments which had previously been in the hands of a small circle of scholars. Most of these fragments came from Cave Four, one of five manuscript-holding caves discovered in 1952. By the 1980s the tardiness of those responsible for their publication had become a source of frustration to the many other scholars around the world who wanted to study their contents. Illicit transcriptions of unpublished fragments started to circulate in the academic community, along with rumours about the contents of others. This merely heightened the sense of frustration; serious academics cannot conduct research on the basis of rumour and second-hand evidence. The thirty-year delay in official publication was denounced as the scholarly scandal of the century. Meanwhile, popular writers produced conspiracy theories, suggesting unpublished Scrolls were being held back deliberately because they contained material which would undermine the Christian faith – a view which overlooked the fact that many fragments were in the hands of Jewish scholars.

Under mounting pressure, steps were taken to accelerate the official publication process, but in September 1991 these moves were overtaken by much more dramatic events. Like a bursting dam the monopoly of the editorial cartel collapsed.

Two separate developments brought this about. The first was the publication – by two scholars at the Hebrew Union College in Cincinnati – of a computer-generated edition of several previously unpublished texts. In a bold and ingenious move they used a computerised catalogue of words contained in these fragments to reconstruct the fragments themselves.

The second development was even more extraordinary. By a remarkable piece of good fortune the Huntington Library in San Marino, California, held an almost complete set of infrared negatives of the Scrolls, including the unpublished fragments from Cave Four. Towards the end of September the library announced that it was making this unique collection available to all *bona fide* researchers, thus bypassing the dilatory procedures of the editorial group.

Members of that cartel were naturally angered by these developments, accusing the perpetrators of theft and the violation of international law. But whatever the rights and wrongs of the matter, general access to the material was now unstoppable.

Early studies of the newly released fragments produced a rash of speculative theories: it was announced that one fragment, known as 4Q285, referred to a slain Messiah, and therefore showed this concept to have been current before the rise of Christianity; alternatively, the Scrolls were actually the work of the first Christians, in which case they discredited the New Testament's account of Christian origins.

But by the end of the 1990s such hypotheses had either been plainly discredited or had died the death of a thousand qualifications, and debate revolved chiefly around competing views of the Scrolls' origins. Were they the product of a small group of separatists, or did they represent the beliefs of wider Judaism? If they were the library of a single group, had that group been Essenes or some other sect? Variations abounded, but the majority of scholars could be divided into two main camps: those who favoured an Essene connection and those who rejected it.

Each new gathering of Scroll experts produced fresh arguments in favour of one position and against the other. Some meetings were carefully orchestrated to promote one point of view; those which weren't were usually heated, sometimes acrimonious.

It was to a gathering of the unorchestrated variety that Mike was to present his paper, and he found the prospect increasingly unnerving as the time drew near.

The first session on Tuesday morning was a swashbuckling, two-hour debate in which famous proponents of rival schools exchanged savage insults and withering sarcasm. It was obvious that anyone daring to challenge the pet theories of either camp would suffer a damaging vitriolic onslaught.

The debate was followed by a break for coffee, after which there was one more item before Mike's paper. This intervening item – an analysis of messianic concepts in a fragment known as 4Q521 – should have interested Mike but he heard none of it, so preoccupied was he with the approaching ordeal. During the question time which followed he imagined the questions his own paper was likely to provoke and realised he could no longer think of the answers.

Just before noon (high noon, thought Mike – oddly appropriate) the woman chairing the session brought questions to an end and thanked the speaker for a fascinating and important contribution. Then she invited Mike to approach the lectern, introduced him briefly and sat down.

There was a ripple of polite applause while Mike placed the text of his paper carefully on the lectern. He looked at the audience of six hundred people and tried to open his mouth. Nothing moved. His mouth was totally dry and its component parts seemed to have fused together. He picked up a glass of water from a table by the lectern and noticed that his hand was shaking. He managed to raise the water to his lips without spilling any and took a sip. He looked at his audience again but was still unable to speak.

He saw a door open at the far end of the lecture hall and hoped someone was coming to announce that the building was on fire. Connie entered and looked around for a seat. There were none vacant so she joined a throng of people standing behind the back row. She waved discreetly to Mike and gave him a dazzling smile.

Mike smiled back.

'This paper,' said Mike, 'offers a fresh analysis of the periodisation of history found in several scrolls from the Qumran caves. I hope to demonstrate the existence of a uniform eschatological scheme in these scrolls, dividing world history into ten periods each lasting 490 years. The authors of these texts believed they were living in the eighth such era – "the Age of Wickedness" – and they expected the ultimate defeat of evil to occur in its final seven years – the years 10–3 BC in the current calendar…'

His delivery was a little halting at first but he soon warmed up and before long was acquitting himself with panache. Forty minutes later he was confidently summarising his conclusions.

'Identifying this eschatological scheme therefore helps us to date the original composition of all texts which adopt it – including the much-disputed 4Q180 – as they could not have been composed after the disappointment of this expectation. Furthermore, we may take it as highly probable that all such texts were the products of a single sect.'

He sat down and the audience applauded. The Chair thanked him for his paper and invited questions and comments. Mike returned to the lectern with renewed trepidation but the response was overwhelmingly enthusiastic. Even scholars who remained unconvinced said his paper contained valuable insights. Without exception, the questions were sympathetic and, to Mike's great relief, answerable. When the Chair finally brought the morning's session to a close several people gathered on the platform to express their appreciation and ask further questions. Connie was among them.

'Sorry I was late,' she said, pushing her way to his side, 'but the elevator insisted on taking me to the top floor before it would bring me down here. You were brilliant, Mike, just brilliant!'

'Really?' said Mike, for whom Connie's opinion had an importance out of all proportion to her knowledge of the subject.

'Yes, really.'

'You managed to follow it?'

'Enough to tell it was brilliant. Mike, I'm in a hurry right now; I'm meeting some people for lunch, but I'll see you tonight – assuming you're still okay for dinner?'

'Wouldn't miss it for anything.'

'Then I'll see you at seven thirty,' said Connie, and she hurried away.

'Well done, Mike,' said Giles Waterman, giving Mike a limp, token handshake. Giles was wearing a hideous tie and an expensive suit with a monogrammed handkerchief protruding conspicuously from the top pocket.

'Ah, Giles!' said Mike, eyeing the tie with visible distaste. 'I was hoping I'd bump into you.'

'Good-looking girl,' said Giles, nodding in the direction of Connie's retreating back. 'Friend of yours?'

'Not exactly. We met yesterday on the plane from New York. Look...'

'Great pair of knockers,' said Giles.

'About that man Swyver...'

'Who?'

'Oral B Swyver. The man whose book I reviewed. You might be interested to know...'

'I wouldn't be treading on your toes, then?'

'What?'

'I'll see if she's free for lunch. Catch you later, Mike!'

Mike would have followed Giles out of the lecture hall but he was prevented by a bearded young man in thick spectacles and a tweed jacket, who seized him by the hand and shook it fervently.

'Professor Totley, I'm really pleased to meet you. My name's Walter Winkelhof.' Mike thought the man looked familiar. 'If you're thinking that I look familiar,' said Winkelhof, 'it's because I sat next to you yesterday at the boarding gate in Newark International. You were reading Goldberg. I wanted to ask what you thought of his views on authorial intentionality but you looked very engrossed. Anyway, I very much enjoyed your paper. You were full of interesting matter.'

'You make me sound like a boil,' said Mike.

'Excuse me?'

'Never mind. What can I do for you?'

'I'm writing a doctoral thesis on the Temple Scroll, and I think you might be able to help me with a few questions.'

'I was actually hoping to get some lunch...'

'Of course. What do you say we have lunch together? You have a favourite restaurant in the hotel?'

'No. There seem to be at least six of them, and I've only had a day to…'

'Then let me take you to mine.'

The lower levels of the Sheraton Washington Hotel were a vast complex of lecture halls and smaller conference rooms connected by a confusing rat run of corridors. With over 7,000 people attending the conference it was not surprising that, during mealtimes and the gaps between sessions, these corridors were awash with name-tagged academics hurrying between venues. As soon as Mike stepped outside the lecture hall he became hopelessly disorientated. But Winkelhof knew his way surprisingly well and led Mike unerringly through the maze to a self-service restaurant overlooking the atrium lobby.

It was a cheerless meal for Mike. He preferred solitude when he needed to unwind, and resented having to make conversation with this complete stranger. To make matters worse, Winkelhof's conversation was not remotely interesting. His questions were prosaic, not at all the sort of thing Mike expected from a doctoral research student. Soon the Temple Scroll was an exhausted topic and Winkelhof turned to other matters. He seemed particularly interested in Mike's career as an archaeologist.

3

In his hotel room six hours later, Mike got ready to spend his next meal in infinitely more pleasant company. He devoted more time than usual to choosing a shirt, combing his unruly hair and examining his appearance in the bathroom mirror, but still arrived early at the hotel's Americus Seafood and Steak Restaurant. He was pleased to find it had a more intimate atmosphere than the one in which Winkelhof had entertained him. He ordered a beer and took it to a table for two which he'd reserved earlier in the day.

Connie arrived as he was draining his glass. She was wearing an open green jacket and matching trousers over a white bodysuit with a low neckline; her long hair, fashionably dishevelled, fell loosely around her shoulders.

'Sorry if I kept you waiting, Mike. It was that stupid elevator again.'

'Do you mean the lift?'

'Really, you English are so lazy when it comes to learning other languages!'

Mike held her chair for her and she sat down. As he took his seat a waiter handed them menus. Connie perused one while Mike simply watched her in a daze of pleasure.

'You really were good this morning, you know,' said Connie, suddenly meeting his gaze. 'Especially the way you handled the questions. You managed to be kind of humble and authoritative at the same time. I admire that; it's an unusual combination in a man.'

'It's kind of you to say so. Actually, I got off lightly. The man who would have been my fiercest critic wasn't there – Elliot Heinzel from Chicago. He's notorious for bitter, personal attacks on scholars he disagrees with – and he would certainly have disagreed with me.'

'And you expected him to be there?'

'Certainly. He's a leading Scrolls expert and normally attends everything, just to push his own point of view. I suspect his absence from my session was the result of a strange incident earlier in the morning.'

'Tell me about it.' Connie folded the menu and leaned forward eagerly, resting her arms on the table. Mike mirrored her.

'Well, the first session was a four-way debate and Heinzel was one of the protagonists. When I arrived at 8.45 the lecture hall was filling up and the four speakers were being fitted with radio mikes. Then Heinzel left the room for a few minutes, evidently to go to the loo. I say evidently, because his mike was already switched on and we all heard a series of loud grunts and plops coming over the PA system, followed by an unmistakable flushing sound. By this point the room was absolutely packed with people.'

'Oh, my gosh!' Connie's large eyes grew even larger. 'Mike, you've got to be making this up!'

'When Heinzel came back there was a mixture of embarrassed silence and suppressed laughter. He obviously sensed he was the focus of it, because he surveyed the audience like a schoolteacher who knows the class has been up to something but can't work out what it is.'

'So what happened next?'

'The debate started and ran on without further ado until the coffee break. That's when I suspect someone with a grudge against Heinzel – and over half the audience probably fell into that category – informed him that six hundred people had heard him relieving himself. I saw him storm out of the room with a face like thunder and he never came back.'

Connie laughed uproariously.

'Mike, that's outrageous! Incredible!'

'It's true, I assure you. Anyway, I reckon that's what saved me from a verbal mauling. Heinzel wouldn't have pulled any punches, and some of them would've been below the belt.'

A waiter reappeared to take their orders. Mike hadn't looked at his menu at all so he simply asked for the same as Connie.

'A funny thing happened to me after your talk,' said Connie. 'A guy wearing an awful tie caught up with me outside the lecture hall and asked if I was free for lunch. He said he was editing a symposium on the Dead Sea Scrolls and was anxious to include female contributors. I know bullshit when I hear it, so I told him I wasn't free for lunch, or dinner, and that everything I knew about the Scrolls would fit on the back of an envelope. He followed me down the corridor and said, "But aren't you a member of the Scrolls Group?" So I told him I wasn't so much a Scrolls Group member as a Scrolls groupie. He followed me again and said he still hoped we might have something to talk about. Then I told him, quietly and demurely of course, where to stick his symposium. He gave up after that.'

Mike smiled at Giles's discomfiture.

'I'm afraid one meets quite a few weird characters at conferences like this.'

'Tell me about it!' said Connie.

'Well, take lunchtime for example. There was this man called Winkelhof – which I believe is Dutch for—'

'No, Mike, I didn't mean that, I meant you don't need to tell me about it.'

'Oh, I see! So earlier, when I mentioned the Elliot Heinzel incident and you said "Tell me about it", you didn't really want to know?'

'Yes, I did.'

'There ought to be some way of distinguishing between "Tell me about it" in the sense of "Tell me about it" and "Tell me about it" in the sense of "Don't tell me about it".'

Connie let out another of her uninhibited laughs. This so startled the waiter, who had just arrived with pumpkin soup and croutons, that he almost dropped them.

There was a lull in the conversation while they both started eating the soup.

Then, looking hard at his spoon instead of at Connie, Mike said, 'I suppose you gave Gi... that man the brush off at lunchtime because you already have a partner?'

'Partner? You mean a boyfriend?'

'Well, yes. I was trying to be politically correct.'

'I approve. It's just that "partner" is ambiguous.' She sipped another spoonful of soup. Mike thought she wasn't going to answer and wondered what to say next. To repeat the question would make his interest rather too conspicuous.

Then Connie said, 'As a matter of fact I don't have a partner right now. I gave that guy the cold shoulder because he was a total jerk.'

Mike stared into his spoon again, wondering at the exhilaration these words had unleashed.

Chapter Five

1

Wednesday morning was bright but cold. Connie and Mike met in the lobby and took the metro to the Mall, where their sightseeing began at the National Museum of American History. After viewing the original 'star-spangled banner', George Washington's uniform, Thomas Edison's printing telegraph and an artificial leg displayed at the first World Fair in 1851, Mike remarked that native American culture seemed somewhat under-represented.

'There's a neat exhibition of Indian cultures in the Museum of Natural History,' said Connie. 'Would you like to see it?'

'Natural History? But we're talking about human beings – as human as George Washington and Thomas Edison. Why isn't it here?'

Connie gave Mike a long steady look and said, 'You really feel strongly about this, don't you?'

'Yes, I do. Do you think that's strange?'

'Not at all. I agree with you. I guess I'm a little ashamed I didn't see it that way myself.'

Mike said he'd rather not visit the Museum of Natural History, so they walked on to the National Gallery of Art. Ignoring the bulk of its collection they headed straight for the nineteenth century European paintings.

They lingered for a long time in front of Van Gogh's *Farmhouse in Provence*, exchanging hushed, enthusiastic comments on the atmosphere of warm stillness that radiated from its rich browns and golds. Then they fell silent before it. Mike wished he could walk through the break in the old stone wall and across the meadow beyond, holding Connie's hand.

He noticed that she'd taken her hands out of her coat pockets and wondered how she would respond if she felt his fingers brush against hers. Was she thinking about him at all, or was she totally

65

preoccupied with this glowing masterpiece? He looked at her face, hoping for some clue. She returned his glance and smiled faintly. He thought he detected a slight tension in her features and wondered what it signified. Suddenly she gave a little shudder, thrust her hands back in her pockets and said, 'Let's go see the Air and Space Museum. It's just across the Mall.'

Aircraft hung in the vast spaces, frozen in mid-flight. Space hardware towered above the knots of wandering visitors. They sauntered along a gallery which traced the development of space suits and other gadgetry.

Connie spoke less and less, and looked increasingly ill at ease. Mike was about to ask if something was the matter when she excused herself, saying she would be back in a couple of minutes. At first Mike assumed she had gone to find what she called a john, but then he caught a glimpse of her talking to a tall, dark-suited man. A moment later she hurried back.

'Mike, let's see the IMAX presentation. You'll love it!'

'The what?'

'It's like a movie – all about space exploration and stuff. I haven't seen it myself yet, but I'm told it's really spectacular.'

'Fine,' Mike agreed, pleased to see the return of Connie's enthusiasm. 'Is there time for a cup of coffee first?'

'I'm afraid it's about to start, but it only lasts about twenty minutes. We'll have coffee afterwards.'

When they reached the auditorium Mike noticed a sign on the door announcing that the next showing would be at 1.30. This was odd, because it was only 11.15. Standing inside was the same man Connie had spoken to a few moments earlier. He nodded respectfully and withdrew, closing the door behind him. Apart from Mike and Connie the auditorium was empty.

'Connie, what's going on?' asked Mike. 'It says on the door…'

'It's kind of a private showing,' said Connie, leading him to the middle of the front row.

No sooner had they sat down than the lights went out. Then the opening bars of Copland's *Fanfare for the Common Man* blasted the auditorium. Mike was still reeling from this acoustic onslaught when Connie leaned close and spoke softly into his left ear.

'Listen carefully, Mike. I work for the Central Intelligence

Agency, and we believe you can help us.'

2

As this revelation sank in, Mike's world went up in flames, and so, apparently, did the world in general. The entire cinema screen, so huge that it filled Mike's visual field, was suddenly a mass of fire. Torrents of flame belched down from giant nozzles. The auditorium trembled with sustained thunder as the Saturn V rocket rose from its launch pad with ponderous power. Even Copland was drowned out by the shattering roar.

'We often use this place to exchange vital information,' Connie explained, her lips brushing Mike's ear. 'It foils listening devices.'

After a few seconds the thunder subsided and Copland gave way to an ambient wash. The flames dissolved into a field of stars and a crater-pocked crescent drifted into view at the bottom of the screen.

'Mike, are you okay?' whispered Connie, as Buzz Aldrin loped across a tract of lunar landscape.

Mike was not okay. He was in emotional turmoil and struggling to disentangle reality from the overwhelming visual images. Buzz Aldrin waved. It was a reassuring kind of wave that seemed to say: 'Hang in there, buddy, it's all gonna turn out fine.' It suddenly seemed natural that this man should have turned to advertising insurance in later life. Mike emerged sufficiently from his disorientation to answer Connie with a slight nod.

'It concerns your meeting with Oral Swyver,' said Connie.

'What?' Mike was sure he'd said nothing to Connie about his forthcoming meal with Swyver. He turned to face her. Connie was poised to whisper in his ear again and their lips touched lightly. She framed his face with her hands and for a split second Mike thought she was going to kiss him; instead she gently turned his face back towards the screen. It was a moment of acute anguish. To make matters worse, the comforting Buzz Aldrin had disappeared and in his place Dave Scott, commander of Apollo 15, was awkwardly saluting the US flag outside the lunar module at Hadley Base. The flag had been especially stiffened so that it would seem to be blowing in a non-existent lunar breeze, and you could tell.

The giant images were now accompanied by a spoken commentary, delivered by a deep, growling voice that sounded like a tea chest being dragged across gravel. The voice was saying something about American achievements in space since the first manned flight to the moon, but Mike was only half aware of it. He was still coming to terms with the fact that Connie knew more than he'd told her.

'Just listen while I explain,' she said. 'We believe Swyver is exerting a potentially dangerous influence on POTUS.'

'And what the hell is POTUS?' Mike demanded, his composure teetering on the brink of disintegration.

'If you have to ask questions, please speak quietly into my ear.'

'I said, what the hell is POTUS?' Mike whispered.

'Sorry, this is Acronym City. President Of The United States.'

An astronaut trundled across the screen in a moon buggy adorned with what looked like an inverted golden parasol. Mike wondered if the parasol had been turned inside out on purpose, to create the impression of another breezy day on the moon.

'The connection goes back a long way,' said Connie. 'Swyver contributed millions of dollars to Thorn's presidential campaign. And there were meetings…'

Mike closed his eyes and tried to give Connie his attention, but it wasn't easy. The gravel-voiced commentator was declaiming facts and figures in an urgent and distracting manner.

'*…missions returned two thousand, one hundred ninety-six samples of moon rock to Earth, weighing a total of eight hundred forty-seven pounds, and took over three thousand photographs for analysis…*'

'…and now Analysis has enough photographs to prove regular contact,' said Connie. 'Sometimes they have prayer breakfasts together.'

Opening his eyes and locating Connie's right ear, Mike said, 'Look, apart from the fact that this doesn't concern me, I can't see why it matters. Prayer breakfasts don't prove influence, for good or ill. Nixon had prayer breakfasts with Billy Graham, and there wasn't much sign of the good doctor's saintliness rubbing off on old Tricky Dicky, was there?'

In spite of his confusion and growing anger, Mike was briefly intoxicated by the warmth of Connie's body and the smell of her perfume. He remained motionless, eyes closed, his nose buried in her hair, until she once again forced him to face the screen.

'Mike, please try to understand; it seems likely that Thorn values Swyver's opinions above those of his official aides and advisers. And because we can't access Swyver's thinking, we don't know which way Thorn is likely to jump if a crisis turns up the temperature…'

'…*and the temperature may reach an astonishing four hundred sixty-five degrees centigrade. Carbon dioxide in Venus's atmosphere allows only half of the planet's infrared radiation to escape…*'

Mike gripped the arms of his seat until his knuckles turned white. He was flying over a buckled, riven landscape at terrifying speed. One moment he was circling a row of towering peaks, the next swerving away to skirt a massive crater; then came a plunging descent into the crater's interior. His stomach, however, remained somewhere outside the rim. He looked for the edges of the vast screen in order to relocate himself in reality, but its curved expanse outreached his vision. He swallowed hard and closed his eyes again, hoping he wouldn't be sick. When he cautiously opened them he was relieved to find that the roller-coaster ride over the Venusian surface had been replaced by a slow, steady approach to the planet Mars.

'…so what we need,' said Connie, oblivious to his battle with nausea, 'is someone who can get alongside Swyver and who has the expertise to understand and anticipate his interpretation of biblical prophecies. He obviously regards them as some kind of blueprint for the future – sort of coded information from God about how events are going to unfold. If POTUS starts basing policy on that, we could find ourselves at war with whoever he decides are the enemies of God.'

'Well, if that's what you're worried about, all you have to do is read Swyver's book. In fact, in the interests of preserving what's left of western democracy, I'm prepared to lend the CIA my review copy.'

'The book doesn't help,' whispered Connie. 'It's got significant gaps. It's as if, on certain issues, Swyver's playing his cards close to his chest.'

Mike had to admit the book was patchy, but he was determined to resist the drift of the conversation. 'Connie, I want nothing to do with this. Whatever you're asking me to do, the answer is *no*.'

'But Mike, do you realise how difficult it is to get anywhere near Swyver? Most of his activities are cloaked in secrecy. The chances of penetrating his inner circle are usually zilch, and you've been offered the opportunity on a plate!'

'No, Connie! *No, no* and *no*!'

They both stared at the screen. Huge boulders came arcing towards them out of pitch darkness.

'...the asteroid belt, occupied by irregular lumps of rock. These range from tiny pebbles to giants hundreds of kilometres across. Thousands have elliptical paths, some of them approaching, even crossing, Earth's orbit. Could one of these erratic wanderers endanger our planet?'

Connie tried again.

'The present danger is similar to that of the Reagan era, but much more serious. Are you familiar with what happened in the eighties?'

'In 1989, a large earth-crossing asteroid passed the exact spot where the earth had been only six hours earlier. Prompted by this close call, a group of scientists lobbied the government's space subcommittee to formulate plans for coping with a potential catastrophe.'

'A group of religious leaders,' continued Connie, 'lobbied Reagan to renounce the idea that the Bible foretells a nuclear holocaust. They were afraid the government would act on that belief, making the prophecies self-fulfilling. It raised enough public concern to force the Reaganite fundamentalists to cool it. This time, with Swyver acting as unofficial chaplain to the White House, it wouldn't be so easy. But you're the ideal person to help us. You've already gained Swyver's confidence; you could get to know what he's thinking quicker than anyone else.'

Mike shook his head, but Connie persisted.

'It's almost impossible for people in the secular, liberal establishment to understand the millenarian mind. That's why the siege at Waco was mishandled – the FBI couldn't get inside the heads of those people. But you combine exactly the right insights, with a healthy detachment from Swyver's belief system. Please say you'll help us, Mike!'

Mike still shook his head.

'At least say you'll think about it!'

But Mike had thought about it a good deal already. He was seeing the last three days in a new and unpleasant light. He felt nauseous again, but this time it had nothing to do with vertiginous images on the giant screen.

'If I don't get some air I think I'm going to be sick,' he said.

Connie sighed deeply and gave in.

'Okay, we'll go outside. But please don't mention anything I've talked about.'

3

They returned to the main concourse of the Air and Space Museum but Mike still needed more air and space. Outside in the Mall he was so relieved to see ordinary people doing ordinary things – walking, jogging, marching in futile protest against government policies – that he wanted to rush among them and embrace as many as possible, but he was too inhibited for that. He stood still, breathing deeply of the cold air, his exhalations forming brief white clouds.

Eventually he said, 'I'd like to walk a bit.' Connie nodded and they set off west along the Mall.

They reached the end of the Mall without speaking. The Washington Monument towered pale and surreal against the pure blue sky; around its base stood a circle of American flags, each one extended vibrantly in a real breeze.

Mike stopped and turned to face Connie.

'Our meeting on the plane was no accident, was it? In fact it was no accident that I lost the seat on my original flight. It was all arranged so that you could sit next to me, gain my confidence and assess my suitability. From the very first words you spoke to me, your friendship has been a sham! You've spent time with me simply to win my co-operation! Putting it bluntly, you're a fraud – a bloody fraud!'

'Mike, that's not true…'

'Don't bother adding more lies to your score. I see it all quite clearly. On the plane, when I told that joke about Handel, you said: "You're a wacky guy, Doctor Totley!" Remember? *Doctor Totley*, you called me! It didn't strike me at the time, but I'd said nothing about having a doctorate! You'd been briefed about me before we met, and I'll bet you knew so much about the Dead Sea Scrolls because you'd done your homework the night before!'

'Mike, listen! I know you might find it hard to believe—'

'It's going to be hard to believe anything you say after this!'

'…but it isn't the way you think! I've genuinely enjoyed your company.'

'Enjoyed…? You don't understand, do you? The last couple of days have meant a lot more to me than that. This may sound stupid after such a short time, but I was actually beginning…'

'Don't say it, Mike! There's no point! This relationship has to remain purely professional.'

'And in your line of work, professional means duplicitous!'

'That doesn't follow!'

'Well, I think it does! Living in a world of subterfuge and deception isn't compatible with normal relationships, because they depend on honesty and trust. Trust is the air they thrive on; deceit poisons them. That may sound like pious claptrap to you, but I happen to think it's profoundly true.'

'Well, now you know the truth, perhaps we can start being really open and honest with each other.'

Mike gave a hollow laugh. 'That's rich! I've been nothing but open and honest with you from the start!'

'Okay, let me try this.' Connie fought to keep her voice low and steady. 'Right now I'm feeling upset, inadequate and scared; upset because you're a decent, caring man and I've abused your trust; inadequate because I'm not on home turf and I'm out of my depth; and I'm scared in case you don't cooperate and this investigation goes nowhere. How's that for openness and honesty? Is that good enough for you?'

Mike didn't answer, just stared at their surroundings: the Lincoln Memorial, the Potomac, the Arlington Bridge, grass and trees in winter sunlight beneath a blue sky and a lattice of vapour trails. Wasted beauty. They should have walked here hand in hand…

Connie broke the silence, her voice still barely under control.

'Okay, I realise you may not be able to forgive me for hurting you, but is there any chance you'll do what I've asked? It really is important, and you're just the person we're looking for. You combine expert knowledge with complete integrity, and…'

Mike let out another hollow laugh.

'Ha! Do you realise what you've just said? If I agreed to do your dirty work, that would mean deceiving Swyver, which would prove that I'm capable of deception; so my integrity would no longer be intact, and you wouldn't know whether to trust me any more. Can't you see what twisted logic you're trapped in?'

'Mike, be careful what you say out here!' For some reason she remembered the motto at CIA headquarters: '…and the truth shall set you free.' Tears welled in her eyes – brought on, she told herself, by the cold breeze. Not wanting Mike to see them she turned away, looking across the tidal lake to the Jefferson Memorial. Reflections of its pillars formed blurred streaks on the water, like lines of fresh paint bleeding into their background.

Still with her back towards him she said, 'We're not asking you to deceive him exactly, merely to find out everything you can and feed us with informed analysis. And think of the greater good.'

'Oh yes? And who decides what that is?'

'Mike, I don't want to get into a theoretical discussion…'

'Of course not! Your convenient relativism might run up against some inconvenient absolutes.'

In an undertone Connie said, 'How the hell did we get here?'

'We're here because your ancestors slaughtered ten million native Americans, took their land and called them Natural History. I suppose at the time it seemed worth it – for the greater good.'

She rounded on him, shaking with emotion and biting her lips. But after a moment of silent confrontation she turned away again and started walking. It wasn't far to where cabs were always coming and going, delivering tourists to the Washington Monument.

Mike called after her: 'I'm sorry, that was out of order. Shall I take you back to the hotel? Connie?'

Connie shook her head and quickened her pace. It was bitterly cold in spite of the sun.

Chapter Six

1

Mike wandered aimlessly. Monumental architecture gave way to brooding dereliction. In the shadow of crumbling tenement blocks, down-and-outs huddled around fires on the pavement. The roads had potholes stuffed with worn-out mattresses. He guessed it was one of those areas tourists are warned to avoid but he didn't care; its atmosphere was the perfect match for his mood.

When he tired of walking he took a cab back to the Sheraton. Having no appetite for food he went straight to his room and tried to read. Then he switched on the TV and sampled a few channels, but nothing held his attention. He browsed through the conference programme and remembered that a paper entitled 'The Messiah of 4Q285 in the Light of 1QM' was scheduled for three o'clock. Hoping it might take his mind off things, he splashed his face with cold water, combed his hair and set off for the lift.

But the enigmas of 4Q285 were a poor distraction. He tried repeatedly to pin his mind to the subject but could only stare at a blank page in his notepad, hearing nothing the speaker was saying. After ten minutes he got up and left.

Without any definite purpose he wandered along a corridor until a handwritten notice attracted his attention. Fastened to the door of one of the smaller conference rooms, it read:

> FUNDAMENTALISM STUDY GROUP
> Dr Melanie Madden's 3 PM lecture on
> fundamentalism and postmodernity is
> cancelled because of illness.
> Instead Ms Connie Patterson will give a
> paper based on her doctoral research,
> surveying movements within
> Islam and Christianity.

Mike looked at his watch. It was almost 3.15. He hesitated for a moment, then quietly opened the door. It led into a small vestibule, the inner door of which was ajar.

'...main characteristics of post-1970 Islamic fundamentalism: a commitment to the *Shar'ia*, the law of God, and a rejection of Western secular culture, viewed as the rebirth of pre-Islamic barbarism or *jahiliyya*. Surprisingly, perhaps, this has gone hand in hand with embracing many advances in science and technology.'

For a second Mike failed to recognise Connie. Her hair was pulled back into a French plait and she was wearing glasses.

'When we examine Christian fundamentalism in America during the same period, we find the two movements have a great deal in common. Beginning with the seventies' fundamentalist revival...'

There were plenty of spare seats on the back row, so while Connie's eyes were on her notes Mike slipped into the room and sat down. He sank low on his chair so that he wouldn't catch her eye, but made sure he could see her between the shoulders of people in front.

After sketching the fundamentalists' move into right-wing politics, the creation of the Moral Majority and the eclipse of moderate evangelicalism, Connie outlined what she saw as an attempt to dominate the intellectual sphere.

'...the rise of fundamentalist universities such as the Oral Roberts University, Liberty University and the Bible University of Memphis – the latter quickly renamed the Bible Institute of the South-Eastern States to avoid an unfortunate acronym.' (Laughter from the audience.) 'BIOSES provides a good example of these institutions: the students have to be "born again" believers, they are encouraged to accept answers rather than ask questions, and French kissing is strictly forbidden.' (More laughter.) 'These institutions also place a strong emphasis on science and communication technology, but with specific objectives: technology is exploited to promote the fundamentalist message and its political agenda, while science is directed to the defence of creationism against Darwinian evolution; Liberty University and BIOSES both have their own Centres for Creation Studies. But alongside all this there's a profound failure to engage with modern culture.

Consider, for example, the Swyver-led organisation called the Crusade to Reconstruct America for the Parousia – whose acronym somehow escaped the scrutiny of its PR people...' (Laughter again.)

Mike realised he'd misjudged her; she was not completely bogus after all. At least she'd told him the truth about her research. There remained a slim possibility that she'd duped her entire study group by delivering a paper written by someone else, but this was eliminated by the way she handled the question time. Her confident responses put her grasp of the subject beyond doubt.

Though still angry at the way she'd treated him, Mike felt a sudden urge to tell her that he withdrew his severest charge. He rose to ask a question.

'I'm very grateful to Ms Patterson for her paper, which has put things in a completely fresh light for me...' He paused, hoping she would catch his meaning. 'I wonder whether she's considered Christian fundamentalism's lack of engagement with modern culture as an aspect of its dispensational premillennialism. It might be a fruitful line of enquiry.'

The sight of Mike in the audience unsettled Connie. She looked nervously at her notes, reshuffled them pointlessly and looked at them again.

'Er, no, I haven't explored that area yet, but I... it sounds like an interesting idea. Perhaps at the end of the session the questioner could suggest some source material? I'd be most grateful.'

But Mike didn't stay until the end of the session. While Connie was answering the next question he quietly slipped away.

2

'Now, Hal and Phoebe, this will decide who gets to keep Kevin, your beautiful Labrador.'

Phoebe leaped to her feet, distraught.

'*He's* always neglected Kevin! *He* never feeds him! *He* even leaves him in the car with the windows closed! Kevin would be dead by now if it wasn't for me! That asshole doesn't deserve Kevin even if he answers every freaking question!'

Mike opened the fridge and took out a beer. Hal won the round. The screen showed the unfortunate Kevin in close-up, giving the canine equivalent of an uncomprehending grin.

'But he's normally so dumb!' protested Phoebe. 'How come he knows so much all of a sudden? I bet he's been reading *books*!'

At this hint of un-American activities the audience was in uproar. A chorus of women yelled 'Cheat!' 'Bastard!' and 'Slimeball!' Some of them even threw things. After several attempts the MC restored silence, apart from the faint sound of Phoebe sniffling miserably into a handkerchief and sighing, 'I'm so sorry, Kevin!'

Mike opened his beer and lay back on the bed. He'd worked out that Hal and Phoebe were getting a divorce. The show was based on the premise that general knowledge questions were an entertaining way to divide the family home.

'Well now, Hal and Phoebe, we move on to the round which will decide who gets your wonderful house, worth over three quarters of a million dollars. The first question is for you, Phoebe, and it's this: Can you tell me, to the nearest ten pounds, the total weight of moon rock brought back by the combined Apollo missions?'

'Eight hundred and forty-seven,' said Mike, and wondered how he'd picked up this useless piece of information.

'Fifty?' hazarded Phoebe feebly.

Mike could bear this woman's suffering no longer. He switched channels and was pleased to find a serious discussion in progress. A slight man with a wispy moustache was advocating gun control.

'...recent years the annual death toll from handgun murders in this country has been fifty times the combined totals for Canada, Britain, Sweden, Switzerland, Australia and Japan. The citizens of most other countries are twenty times less likely to be killed or injured by their fellow citizens. And why?'

'Never mind that shit! Let's get to the bottom line.' The other speaker was an overweight, bull-necked man with the logo of the National Rifle Association stretched across his abdomen on a white tee shirt. 'We all know there's a conspiracy behind this crap. If you disarm the American people there'll be nothing to stand between them and godless tyranny! That's why the right to bear arms is there in the Constitution! God knew there'd come a time when we'd need it, and that time is almost here!'

This drew whoops and applause from an unseen audience, but his opponent came back strongly: when the Constitution was drawn up, 'bearing arms' had meant something quite different, and in context it was clear that the Second Amendment had never intended...

At this point the NRA man launched himself out of his chair and knocked the speaker to the ground. Urged on by a screaming audience and unchecked by a retreating chat show host, the studio dissolved into violence.

Mike felt cheated. He stabbed angrily at the remote control. This time he stumbled into an advertisement slot – a man was brushing his teeth. Why was it, Mike wondered, that people in toothpaste adverts never used toothpaste? Was foam dribbling from people's mouths thought to have connotations of insanity? He was speculating on this when the unexpected happened; the man finished brushing, opened his mouth wide and applied a dentist's drill to one of his molars. Above the whining sound a voice intoned the advantages of Clinger's Domiciliary Dental Maintenance kits.

Mike was about to try one more channel when he heard a knock at the door. He turned down the volume and got off the bed.

3

'Hi,' said Connie, managing a brief smile.

'Hello,' said Mike, who didn't even attempt one. There were several seconds of uncomfortable silence.

'Mike, I was just... I mean, is this a good time to drop by? Only I thought... I'd like to follow up the suggestion you made after my paper, but you left before I could talk to you.'

'Yes,' said Mike, investing the word with no particular meaning.

'Look, I'll go away again if...'

'No, please...' Mike stepped aside and motioned awkwardly to invite her in. He closed the door, crossed the room and sat down at a table strewn with papers and open books. 'There are a couple of articles that might help,' he said, rummaging for a notepad and pen. 'I can't remember all the details, but you should be able to track them down.'

'Thanks.' Connie stood behind Mike's chair, looking at his back while he wrote. The silence was difficult, but she could think of nothing to say.

'D'you like living in Washington?' asked Mike, without looking round.

Connie made no reply. This was dangerous territory.

'I assume you do live here?' said Mike. 'This is where the CIA has its headquarters, isn't it?'

'Not far away.' After a pause she added, 'At Langley, Virginia.'

'So you travelled from here to Newark International on Sunday night in order to be on the plane with me on Monday morning.'

'Yes.'

'You can't have had much sleep that night.'

'No.'

'You did well to stay awake through all my tedious conversation.'

'I didn't find it tedious. Mike, can we stop this, please? I'm sorry, deeply sorry that you got hurt. I never wanted... It wasn't meant to happen that way, that you'd get emotionally involved.'

Mike turned in his chair and gave her a searching look. 'I think I can believe that now, knowing that you weren't being totally dishonest about yourself. That was the point of my comment after your talk; I was trying to apologise for calling you a fraud.'

'Thanks, Mike. That means a lot. Apology accepted.' At Connie's invitation they shook hands.

Mike smiled faintly and the tension eased. He handed her a sheet of paper with references on it.

Connie glanced at it and put it in her pocket. 'And thanks for this, too. As you probably guessed, I've only got a hazy idea of what premillennialism is all about. I'm doing my doctorate part time, so it's slow progress.'

'Putting it simply, premillennialists believe that Christ will return bodily to earth before the Millennium – the thousand-year reign of the saints referred to in Revelation. There are also postmillennialists, who believe Christ will return *after* the Millennium, and amillennialists who take the Millennium to symbolise the present age.'

'It's like my mom always says: look at any question, however complicated, in the right way and it'll turn out to be even *more* complicated.' She turned and noticed the TV was on. 'Oh, I'm sorry if I stopped you watching something!'

'I wasn't really watching, just surfing channels.'

'Find anything interesting?'

Mike got up and began to pace the room. 'To be honest, nothing but drivel – important issues reduced to entertainment, prejudice bolstered by sound bites. Constant immersion in this stream of banality must damage the brain. You know, if you're really concerned about preserving democracy in this country, I think you should be worrying about *that*.' He levelled an accusing finger at the silent TV.

Connie looked at the screen again and said, 'Swyver!'

It was indeed Swyver, tanned and granite-suited, standing before the viewer with a huge, floppy, black Bible open in one hand. Mike sat down on the bed, reached for the remote control and turned up the volume. Swyver became audible in mid-sentence.

'...sure you'll agree, the Post-Tribulation Rapture position is the only one that really satisfies...'

'My God!' exclaimed Connie. 'He's talking sadomasochism!' She sat down next to Mike.

'No, he's talking eschatology. That's the branch of...'

'I know – the branch of theology that deals with the end of the world, from the Greek *eschatos*, meaning the last things.'

'Sorry.'

'So what's all this rapture and tribulation stuff?'

'The Rapture became a popular idea in the nineteenth century, based on an obscure phrase in the New Testament. Saint Paul says that when Christ returns, believers will be "caught up in clouds to meet the Lord in the air". What he meant is a moot point, but literalists like Swyver think Christians will float up bodily to gather around Christ in the sky, forming a kind of escort as he returns to earth.'

'So it's something like parascending,' said Connie. 'And tribulation?'

'The Tribulation refers – actually he's talking about it now.'

'...turn with me to the twenty-fourth chapter of Matthew,' said Swyver, riffling skilfully through his Bible, 'where we hear our Lord say: "For then shall be great tribulation, such as was not since the beginning of the world to this time, no, nor ever shall be."'

'Notice he insists on using the old King James Version, in spite of...'

'Ssshhh! I want to hear this!' Connie leaned forward, her chin in her hands, elbows on knees.

'...the same tribulation foretold by the prophet Daniel. It's also the time when nations will surround Jerusalem and wage war upon it, as we read in the fourteenth chapter of Zechariah: "Then shall the Lord go forth, and fight against those nations, as when he fought in the day of battle. And his feet shall stand in that day upon the Mount of Olives." There we have it plainly, my friends: the great Tribulation will end with the return of Christ to this earth! Then all true believers will be taken from their mundane tasks and lifted up by God to meet the returning Christ in the air! Joined by a mighty angelic host we'll accompany our Lord as he descends upon the Mount of Olives to defeat those heathen armies!'

'There you are!' said Mike. 'He calls it the Post-Tribulation Rapture position because he puts the Rapture immediately after the Tribulation. Some people put it first because—'

'Mike, please! I'm trying to hear what he's saying.'

'Sorry.'

'...and in verse four Zechariah says a mighty earthquake will split the Mount of Olives in two, as also prophesied in chapter thirty-eight of Ezekiel, which tells of "a great shaking in the land" that will bring down mountains. Then he says God will rain down "great hailstones, fire, and brimstone" upon the enemy. And Revelation chapter sixteen agrees, saying that when the invading armies gather at Armageddon there will fall upon them "a great hail out of heaven, every stone about the weight of a talent" – that's about one hundred pounds, my friends! Such will be the Almighty's judgement on a world of sin! He's a God of power and vengeance, not a God of weakness and namby-pamby tolerance!'

Swyver paused for a moment, then slapped his Bible shut and said, in a jovial vein contrasting oddly with his disaster-laden message, 'Well, that's just about it for this week, brothers and sisters. But stay tuned for the infotizements and learn more of how we can serve God's purposes together. And God bless y'all!'

Credits scrolled past while Barbie-Jo Butterfield pleaded to be taken. Mike, who had never heard any of Ms Butterfield's repertoire before, lay back on the bed and groaned in disbelief.

As the music faded Connie tapped him on his right leg and said, 'Mike, take a look at this!' Mike raised himself on one elbow.

The screen now showed a young man in a white lab coat, leaning against a car in a leafy suburban boulevard.

'You know,' he said, 'the events Dr Swyver's been telling us about are probably very close – so close that many of you watching this will certainly get Raptured. But have you considered the implications of that? You see, many of us spend a great deal of time driving our cars these days.' He took one hand from his lab-coat pocket and rested it fondly on the car's roof. 'In fact, some of us spend as much as a quarter of our lives behind the wheel. So it stands to reason that many of us will be driving at that precise moment when Christ returns and we are caught up in the clouds to meet him. Have you thought of the chaos and death that could ensue on our highways and in our cities when believers are snatched away by the hand of God and thousands of cars and trucks suddenly become driverless? Do you think Christ wants to begin the Millennium reigning over a world littered with vehicular wreckage?'

'That,' said Mike, 'is the kind of bizarre scenario you get when you allow crass literalism to...'

'Ssshhh!' said Connie.

'And would you want your unbelieving friends to die in car crashes before they have a chance to respond to the glory of the Lord with repentance and faith? I hope not! Well, we at Swycorp Research have developed a gizmo that can avert those disasters, and you'll be thrilled to know it's now being launched worldwide. It's a computer-aided guidance system that'll control any vehicle and bring it safely to a standstill if its driver suddenly disappears. The Integrated Neural Sensing and Navigation Equipment, as we call it...'

'INSANE,' muttered Mike.

'Not necessarily,' said Connie. 'The University of Pennsylvania has been working on something similar for the military since the eighties – though not for the same reasons, of course.'

'I meant the acronym. It spells INSANE.'

'...fitted to your car at a cost of approximately five thousand dollars, the exact price depending on the type of car. Take a look at this.' The man got into the car, started the engine and pulled away. A camera mounted inside showed the view over his shoulder. He accelerated to 50 mph, then suddenly took his hands off the wheel and his feet off the pedals. The car swerved neatly around a van delivering groceries, avoided a child stepping off the pavement and gradually slowed until it came to a gentle halt. A commanding voice said: 'Reduce Rapture wreckage! Don't delay! Become a Swyver driver today!' The same words appeared across the screen, along with a box number from which the device could be ordered.

'So that's it!' said Connie, her voice shrill with anger. 'All that guff about the return of Christ was to get people to buy his expensive, pointless toy! Swyver's so cynical he'd stoop to anything!' She turned to look at Mike, who was still reclining, propped on one elbow. 'Doesn't it make you sick? Doesn't it make you want to get off your ass and do something about it?'

Mike sat up.

'Hang on! There is another possibility, you know – that Swyver is sincere but misguided. But either way, all he'll do is take money from a few rich people who are stupid enough to believe his wacky ideas. And his gadget isn't completely pointless; it could be very useful if someone was driving to work one day, or perhaps to the shops, and suddenly had a blackout or a coronary...'

Connie stood up, said, 'You're completely unreasonable!' and walked around the bed towards the door.

Mike rolled across the bed and intercepted her.

'Connie, wait! This morning you were concerned that Swyver might use his influence to stage-manage the fulfilment of prophecy – right?'

'Mike, be careful what you say in case we're overheard!'

Mike still had the remote control in his hand. He turned up the volume on the TV and a loud buzzing sound, like the noise of a chainsaw, filled the room. Connie involuntarily glanced at the screen, where a pink-faced man was demonstrating a solar-powered nose-hair trimmer. As the camera moved in for an eye-watering close-up of its depilatory action she winced and turned away again.

'That should foil listening devices,' said Mike. 'Now, my point is this: if he believes the climax of history will involve a massive earthquake, fire and brimstone and hundred-pound hailstones, it puts your fears into perspective, because even Swyver couldn't arrange *that*, could he?'

'No, of course he couldn't! But what if that's a red herring, a sideline, just a way to make a few bucks out of rich idiots? What if the events that really matter to him are political ones, events in which his influence with POTUS could really count for something?'

'There you go again! You're assuming Swyver is a cynical manipulator and a hypocrite.'

'You bet I am!'

'And I'm saying he might be sincere. A tad nutty, but sincere.'

'And on what do you base this charitable assessment?'

'I can see no evidence to the contrary. If I change my mind after I've met him, I'll let you know.'

'Well, thanks, Mike! Thanks a lot!' said Connie, and left. She tried to slam the door behind her but it was fitted with one of those annoying devices that close doors very slowly.

Outside in the corridor she wiped the tears from her eyes, hoping Mike hadn't seen them. They were caused, she told herself, by that close-up of a man doing strange things to his nasal hair.

Chapter Seven

1

There was no sign of Swyver in the Omni Shoreham's opulent lobby. Checking his watch, Mike approached the reception desk and explained why he was there.

'Of course, Dr Totley, we were told to expect you,' said the immaculately groomed receptionist. She nodded to a young man sitting near the centre of the lobby who got up and strolled over. He was impressively well built.

'Dr Totley, my name's Rip Warholler. I'm to take you to Dr Swyver. He's waiting in one of the hotel restaurants. Please follow me.'

At the door of the restaurant another young man of similar physique was standing guard. Warholler joined his colleague on sentry duty and Mike entered alone. Every table in the vast room was empty except for one in the centre. There Swyver sat by himself at a table for two, his head bowed as if in prayer. Mike paused just inside the door and took in the implications of this strange scene. To ensure privacy or personal security Swyver had reserved the whole restaurant for their use. It was a powerful reminder to Mike that he was about to meet one of the ten richest men on the planet.

He hesitantly wove his way between the empty tables. A deep-piled carpet muffled his approach and Swyver remained unaware of his presence. Mike was wondering whether to speak when a waiter approached the table with menus under his arm and gave a discreet cough.

Swyver lifted his head.

'Dr Totley! Good to meet you at last!' He stood up, beaming and proffering a large hand. Mike shook it.

'I hope I didn't keep you waiting, Dr Swyver.'

'Not at all! Excellent! I like a man who looks me straight in the eye and gives a good, firm handshake! Please sit down.' They sat and took the menus from the waiter, who drifted silently away. 'I hope the change of plan didn't confuse you, but I couldn't wait around in the lobby. Strangers who recognise me from my TV shows keep pestering me. Can't stand them. Let's choose our meals and get down to business.'

Swyver donned a pair of gold-rimmed glasses and studied the menu, mumbling softly to himself and drumming his fingertips on his forehead. Mike's first impression was that Swyver in the flesh was quite unlike his pedagogic TV persona; he seemed more affable, almost avuncular. But when the waiter returned and Mike ordered a Caesar salad, Swyver regarded him sternly over his spectacles.

'You're not a vegetarian, I hope, Dr Totley?'

'No.' said Mike. 'But I like salads and I thought I'd try a traditional American...'

'Good. Because I don't hold with these left-wing, New Age ideas. They're inspired by the Devil.'

With some trepidation Mike ordered a main course of pan-fried fillet of skate with mushroom, tomato and garlic sauce. But fish was beyond Swyver's suspicion; according to the Bible, Jesus had eaten it for breakfast on at least one occasion. The waiter waited, pen poised, for Swyver's order.

'Well now,' he said, removing his glasses and tapping them on the menu. 'I'm really not sure about the first course. Can't decide whether to have the warm salad of quail and fennel with cherry vinegar, or the rillettes of duck with apricot chutney.'

'Would you like more time to consider your choice, sir?' offered the waiter.

'Tell you what – I'll have both. And for the second course' – he replaced the spectacles – 'I'll have the pan-fried fillet of venison, garnished with swede quenelles, served in a game and chocolate sauce.'

'Yes, sir.'

'Or should I have the grilled sirloin of veal with sweet potato purée and roast shallots?'

'Well, sir, they're both highly regarded...'

'In that case I'll have both of those as well,' said Swyver. 'And bring two jugs of fresh orange juice.'

'Would that be one each, sir?'

'Of course. Do you think I'd want them both for myself?'

The waiter took the menus with poker-faced tact and withdrew.

Swyver pocketed his spectacles.

'Now, Dr Totley, I suppose you're expecting me to ask you a whole lot of questions. Well, I'm not going to! No, sir! Because I've already found out everything I need to know. Like I said in my letter, I took the trouble of discovering a few things about you after I read your wonderful review – by the way, I loved the part where you said, "The text has only one meaning and Swyver is the man to tell us what it is." Great! Where was I? Oh yes – and recently I've learned a great deal more. You see, I took the liberty – I hope you won't mind, but it will save us valuable time – of sending one of my research assistants, a brilliant young man named Walter Winkelhof...'

'Ah!' said Mike. He began to wonder if any of the conference's seven thousand delegates, apart from himself, were really what they seemed.

'So I'm already satisfied that you're just the man we're looking for.'

Mike cringed inwardly from the ironic echo.

'I see. It's kind of you to say so. But I'm at something of a disadvantage, knowing very little about your project. Perhaps you could...'

'Of course, of course. You know the canyon called Nahal Shuhan?'

'I know approximately where it is – on the western side of the Dead Sea, between Masada and En-Gedi.'

'That's right. The best way to explain it...' Swyver surveyed the table as though looking for something, then gazed around the room. 'Let's go over here.' He moved to an adjacent table with place settings for four people and swept all the cutlery and condiments onto the floor. Then he shook out the napkins, tweaked them into peaks and ridges and formed two converging mountain ranges.

'It's something like this, but instead of a valley between ridges, you've got to imagine a canyon cutting through a plateau.' They sat down on opposite sides of the model landscape. 'Now, let's suppose my edge of the table is near the Dead Sea, where the plateau ends in steep cliffs. You're sitting some place inland, where the canyon narrows and kind of fizzles out. Near my end we've got four caves on the south side, round about here. They were explored in the sixties but the archaeologists were frustrated by debris from roof falls – big rocks everywhere. They tried to chop up the rocks with pneumatic drills so they could move them but it didn't work. Too much dust and not enough oxygen in the caves; the drills kept failing and the men couldn't breathe. But with modern technology we can do a whole heap better. We've got machines – originally developed for rescue work in earthquake situations and adapted by my research people – that'll slice those rocks lickety-split. Then we can do a really thorough job.'

'How accessible are these caves? It's a very rugged area.'

'An old Jeep trail branches off the main road and goes to the foot of the cliffs, about here. There'll be a base there with tents and so forth. Three of the caves can be reached from the bottom of the canyon. The fourth is a lot higher, but there's another jeep trail, goes up on the north side and all around the head of the canyon.' With his finger he traced a route along the napkins to Mike's side of the table and back again. 'Using ropes, you can get down to that one from the top.'

At that point two waiters entered with the first course and the orange juice, stepping carefully over the items scattered on the floor. Mike and Swyver returned to their own table. As Swyver attacked his quail and fennel salad, Mike asked who would be in charge of the dig.

'Oh, we have an excellent team,' said Swyver, chewing while he talked. 'I won't be there myself – too busy and anyway it's not my field – but we have an excellent team. You've heard of Dr Chuck Sinnet?'

'Er...' began Mike, who hadn't.

'How stupid of me – you must have, of course. He heads up my Bible Institute's Centre for Creation Studies. As excavations director he'll be in overall charge. He's a brilliant man, brilliant. Right now he's leading an expedition in eastern Turkey. Its objective is to locate the remains of Noah's Ark once and for all, proving the reality of the biblical flood. That'll confound the sceptics! Bring them to their knees!'

'And who else is involved?' asked Mike, hoping Swyver would name someone of international repute.

'The dig's deputy director and conservator will be Dr Leo Parbunkel. You've heard of him, too, I expect. He runs my Jerusalem Centre for Biblical Archaeology, from where the whole dig will be co-ordinated. That's where you'll all stay whenever you're not camping out at the canyon. The Centre is superbly equipped with every modern facility.'

Mike had never heard of Parbunkel either, and would have said so if given the opportunity, but Swyver paused only long enough to refill his mouth with duck.

'Leo's another fine archaeologist. His long-term project is an archaeological survey of the whole Dead Sea area, its objective being to locate the remains of Sodom and Gomorrah and provide proof of their violent destruction.'

'To confound the sceptics?' asked Mike, who thought these projects sounded strong on objectives but weak on objectivity.

'You said it!' said Swyver, taking another mouthful. 'Bring them to their knees! Then there's a brilliant young woman called Talia Schluter, who's just started working with Leo. She's doing a great job out there. She's going to be the dig's registrar and pottery specialist.'

'You haven't mentioned an epigraphist, Dr Swyver. Since previous digs in that area have produced a lot of written material, it would seem...'

'An excellent point! And that's *exactly* the role I'm hoping you'll fill, Dr Totley! We need a bright, well-qualified epigraphist, and you seem admirably suited to the job. You'd also be a supervisor, of course, in view of your experience. There'll be one supervisor for each cave: Chuck Sinnet, Leo Parbunkel, Miss Schluter and yourself – if you decide to join us. We'll have three or four volunteers working with each supervisor, and we'll give priority to applicants with a solid Christian commitment; that keeps the dig bums away and makes for a better team spirit. Within your own cave you'd have total control; all decisions about strategy and methods would be yours. How does that sound?'

Mike finished his salad and poured himself some orange juice. Remarkably, Swyver finished his double starter at the same time.

'It sounds very attractive. But I still have a few more questions…'

'Of course. Only natural. Ask away!'

'How sure are you of getting an excavation licence from the Israel Antiquities Authority?'

The waiters returned with the main course. Swyver's two choices were delivered on separate plates, but he immediately heaped them together and began to spear the resulting meat mountain with his fork.

'Oh, that's practically settled. Just a few little details to sort out. I'm very confident. We've never had a single one of our applications turned down.' He emphasised this point by wagging his loaded fork, sprinkling liberal amounts of gravy onto Mike's shirt, tie and jacket. Then he crammed the forkful of food into his mouth as though nothing had happened.

'Do you know the exact dates yet?' asked Mike, dabbing at the spattered gravy with his napkin.

'The dig will begin about 1 May and last for six weeks. Leo and Miss Schluter are out there all the time, of course, and Chuck Sinnet will join them in March. They'll be getting things ready for the Nahal Shuhan expedition from around mid-April. If you could arrive soon after that, you could help set things up and establish a good working relationship. Would that suit your schedule?'

Mike consulted his diary.

'I could fly out just after Easter – say, 25 April?'

'No problem. You know, it looks to me like God may be calling you to this job, Dr Totley.'

'Well, perhaps… Could you clarify the aim of the dig? The caves don't have any direct biblical connection, so I assume it isn't to, er… confound the sceptics and—'

'…bring them to their knees? No, but like I said in my letter, there's the possibility of finding new Dead Sea Scrolls. Wouldn't that be something?'

'Certainly. But Nahal Shuhan is a long way from Qumran. I'm

not ruling out the possibility, but…'

'We shouldn't hold our breath? I agree. But there is the Copper Scroll connection.'

Mike was intrigued. Discovered in one of the Qumran caves in 1952, the Copper Scroll was literally a scroll of thin copper, engraved in Hebrew. It listed more than sixty caches of buried treasure, including scrolls and fantastic amounts of gold and silver, but the descriptions of the hiding places were so obscure that not a single one had ever been convincingly identified.

'Have you ever heard of the Reverend Zelophehad Smith?' asked Swyver.

'The name Smith rings a bell from somewhere,' said Mike, trying out Swyver's sense of humour.

'That'll be him!' said Swyver, who didn't have one. 'Do you know his theory about the Copper Scroll?'

'I'm afraid not.'

'He published it privately in a little book called *The Copper Scroll Deciphered*. Distribution…' Swyver paused, raised himself off his chair and broke wind loudly. 'That's better. Where was I?'

'Distribution,' said Mike, fanning the air discreetly with his napkin.

'Oh, yes. Distribution was very limited. Anyway, he shows that the Scroll contains a kind of code, and he seems to have cracked it. If he's right, then one of the hiding places listed in the Scroll is right there in Nahal Shuhan, and is probably one of our caves! I'll send you a copy of the book so you can read it before the dig. That's if you decide to join us.' Swyver put the last morsels of his double main course in his mouth and sat back. 'Do you think you will?'

'How soon do I have to decide?'

'I have to know within a week. Forgive me asking, but is money an issue here? Because I'm willing to pay you the same as Chuck and Leo for the whole time you're out there, and they're among the highest paid men in my entire organisation. They get—'

'No, really, I wouldn't want paying; I'll still be paid by my university while I'm on sabbatical.' This was true enough, but a more important reason for Mike's refusal lay in his disagreement with most of Swyver's opinions. The way he saw it, refusing Swyver's money was a way of retaining his independence and avoiding compromise. He was also determined that his involvement – if he decided to get involved – would be motivated solely by the pursuit of knowledge, not by a fat cheque.

'As you will,' said Swyver. 'By the way, you seem to have got some gravy on your shirt.'

Mike ate his last mushroom and set his fork down on the plate. A waiter brought the menus again. Mike chose Key lime pie for dessert.

'Well now,' said Swyver, settling his glasses on his nose, 'shall I have the huckleberry pie or the tiramisu and raspberry brûlée? Tell you what…'

2

After the conference's concluding papers on Friday morning, Mike had a light lunch and went to his room to pack. He had almost finished when there was a knock at his door.

'Oh! Connie!'

'Hi, Mike!'

'I'm afraid I'm just getting ready to leave.'

'I guessed you would be. I couldn't let you go without saying goodbye.'

Mike stepped aside to let her in.

'You never give up, do you?'

'Sorry?'

'What you really mean is, you couldn't let me go without asking how I got on with Swyver.'

Connie looked at the carpet to avoid Mike's accusing stare. Why did he have to be so confrontational, for God's sake? She took a deep breath and tried again.

'Okay, I'll admit I'm curious. But I also wanted say a proper goodbye. We didn't end on a very good note yesterday.' Her gaze dropped to the carpet again.

'No, we didn't,' Mike agreed, also looking at the carpet. The carpet, of hard-wearing, synthetic fibre in monochrome beige, did not really warrant this amount of scrutiny.

'So, I'll try to stay calm if you will.'

'Agreed,' said Mike, adopting a determinedly positive tone. 'How about a beer?' Connie accepted. He opened two bottles from the fridge and poured the contents into glasses. 'But I'm afraid I haven't changed my mind about Swyver. After meeting him, I'm even more convinced he's sincere.'

Connie took her glass and sat down on the bed. 'Really? So what's he like?'

'Potty, but almost certainly harmless. He has no time for vegetarians, no sense of humour and is blissfully unencumbered by any critical faculties. He puts food away like there's no tomorrow and he's a messy eater; if you ever have dinner with him you should dress to match the colour of his meal. A shade of brown would be a safe bet.'

'Is that all you can tell me?'

Mike sat on the edge of the desk and thought for a moment. 'Oh, yes – he likes a good fart.'

'Thanks. I'll remember to put that in my report.'

'Seriously, he's just a typical enthusiast – except, of course, that he has the money to indulge his enthusiasms on a grand scale. He's interested in a limited number of subjects, about which he knows a good deal and can talk endlessly. In some ways he could be quite a likeable old buffer. It's a shame his religious and political views are so obnoxious.'

'Does that mean you won't be joining his dig?'

'Not necessarily. Swyver himself won't be there. Actually, I find it very tempting. I've never excavated a cave before, and there's a good chance of making significant finds. Forty years ago in a neighbouring ravine, an Israeli archaeologist called Yadin found some amazing...'

'So you haven't decided yet?'

'No. I've got a few days to think about it. Swyver's given me an email address.'

'I see.' Connie drained her glass and stared into it. 'But either way, you won't be having any more meetings with Swyver?'

'No.'

'So there won't be any point my contacting you again.' Her inflection left this wavering somewhere between a statement and a question.

'Definitely not.'

'Well, thanks for the beer.' Connie placed her glass on a bedside table and got up, holding out a hand to Mike. 'I'll say goodbye and let you finish packing.'

Mike stood and shook her hand very formally. 'Goodbye, Connie.'

'Bye, Mike. And I really am sorry…'

'I know. And I'm sorry I didn't turn out to be the right man.'

Connie suddenly leaned forward and kissed him on the cheek. Then she released his hand and hurried from the room. Mike watched her go with a mixture of longing and relief.

This time Connie reached the end of the corridor before the tears began to well. Life, she decided, was basically a bowl of shit.

Part Two
The Caves of Nahal Shuhan

When Solomon built the Temple, he knew it would one day be destroyed. He therefore constructed beneath it, in deep and twisting tunnels, a place in which the Ark could be hidden.

Maimonides, *The Book of Temple Service*, 17

Chapter Eight

1

'Welcome to the Centre for Biblical Archaeology, Dr Totley. May I call you Mike? I'm Leo – Leo Parbunkel.' Parbunkel was a rotund, moon-faced man in his late thirties with receding hair, a dense beard and overgrown eyebrows. He seized Mike's hand and shook it fervently. 'It's good to have you on board. Like some coffee?'

'Thanks, yes,' said Mike. As it was late afternoon he would have preferred tea, but he knew from experience that an American enclave in Israel was unlikely to provide a decent cup.

'I'll get Mrs Spittler to bring some. She's our domestic bursar – looks after everything that's not to do with archaeology or the library. After coffee I'll show you around the Centre.'

Parbunkel never quite managed full eye contact and throughout this exchange his gaze was focused on Mike's chin. Until he got used to this, Mike wondered if his chin was displaying an unsightly smudge or an embryonic boil.

'I look forward to it. But…'

'You'll just love it! It's got everything.'

'Actually,' said Mike, 'I'd quite like a shower and a rest first, if that's all right. I'm a bit travel-stained.'

'Oh, really?' Parbunkel seemed disappointed. 'Well, in that case I'll take you straight to Mrs Spittler. She'll take care of all that.'

Merle Spittler, a grey-haired woman with ornate spectacles, served coffee in her office then showed Mike to his room and pointed out the nearest showers.

'You'll be sharing the room with your assistant supervisor,' she said, 'but he won't be arriving for another two days.'

Mike was grateful for the temporary solitude. He unpacked, showered and lay down for a nap. He'd been dozing for about two minutes when there was a knock on the door.

'Ready to see the Centre?' called Parbunkel from the corridor.

Tastefully clad in Jerusalem's honey-coloured stone, the Centre consisted of four long, flat-roofed buildings, joined to form a rectangle around a shady, well-tended garden. Mike's guided tour began with the accommodation block, his room being located on its second floor. This block formed the north side of the rectangle and also contained the main entrance to the whole complex, with a reception desk fronting Merle Spittler's office. The western side of the quadrangle consisted of kitchens, a refectory, a lecture room and a chapel; the southern building contained a row of offices – one of which was assigned to Mike for the duration of the dig – and various rooms for the treatment and storage of finds.

These rooms comprised the heart of Parbunkel's little empire and he ushered Mike from one to another with childlike excitement, talking in staccato sentences.

'This is the computer room where we keep the er... computers, and this one... where we clean, draw and restore the pottery and... as you can see, light and spacious, like an artist's studio, um... and this is... well, my laboratory, with all the chemicals for cleaning metals, preserving organic matter, that kind of thing, really exciting... and upstairs there's a storage room...'

The eastern side of the rectangle housed the library. While Parbunkel chattered about budgets and purchasing policies, Mike browsed along the shelves. The collection of books, journals and excavation reports was impressively broad and up to date. Above the library was the coffee lounge and from there a spiral staircase continued up to a roof terrace. The views from the terrace were spectacular – to the north, Jerusalem, to the south, Bethlehem and to the east the eroded hills of the Judaean wilderness.

Parbunkel noticed Mike gazing eastwards, where the contours of the hills were sharpened by lengthening shadows. He said, 'You'll be driving out that way tomorrow. Chuck's going to take you to the caves. Now let's go and have dinner.'

2

The road from Jerusalem to Jericho descends from over seven

hundred metres above sea level to about three hundred metres *below* sea level in little more than twelve miles – as the eagle flies. Much of it is steep, winding and potentially hazardous. Chuck Sinnet powered his Land Rover down it at reckless speed.

'Isn't she great?'

'Who?' asked Mike, gripping the sides of his seat. He assumed Sinnet was referring to either Merle Spittler or Talia Schluter, the only women he'd encountered since arriving at the Centre.

'We always go for the best,' said Sinnet, stroking the wheel, 'and the Defender is the best field vehicle around. Got another one back at the Centre. Can carry ten people each, twelve if they have to. Got an old two-seater as well – lots of room in the back for equipment – but I wouldn't like to try its gearbox on this particular route. Fortunately, with just the two of us, there's plenty of room for the climbing equipment in this one. Have you done much climbing, Mike?'

'No, not much. Actually, none at all.' Mike was sure Swyver had said nothing about climbing skills being a prerequisite for the dig.

'Then I'll give you a lesson. Some simple rappelling, that's all.'

'Is that the same as abseiling?'

'That's right. You'll soon get the hang of it. Say, that was pretty good! The *hang* of it! Get it?'

Mike laughed politely. They continued their descent between weathered hills. Reaching the floor of the Jordan Valley they left the Jericho road and turned south.

Here the road follows the western shore of the Dead Sea, passing the tourist spots of Qumran, En-Gedi and Masada, and then carries on to Elat. Lying four hundred metres lower than the surface of the Mediterranean, the Dead Sea coast is the lowest dry land on the planet. Despite the inroads of the tourist and chemical industries, it remains a desolate wilderness in which humanity seems peculiarly out of place. Perhaps for this very reason it has always been a magnet for outlaws, anchorites and fanatics.

In the nineteenth century – when it was far less accessible than it is today – the region evoked powerful reactions from Western explorers. Sir George Adam Smith called it 'this awful hollow, this bit of the infernal regions come to the surface, this hell with the sun shining into it'. Colonel Conder on the other hand waxed lyrical:

> Sitting on the edge of the great cliffs, which drop down a sheer height of some two thousand feet to the rockstrewn shore, gazing on the shining waters of that salt blue lake, I have felt the sense of true solitude such as is rarely known elsewhere.

Away from the noise of the modern road and the occasional monstrous hotel, the solitude can still overwhelm. Here is silence on a massive scale, confronting, probing, stripping the intruder down to essentials. Little wonder that Jesus came here to outstare temptation, or that men like Chariton and Sabas chose it as a setting for the monastic life.

For most of its length the western shore of the Dead Sea consists of a salt-encrusted gravel beach, sloping gently to meet terraces of white marl. Beyond these rise the mountains, stark and haggard, a wall of layered cliffs with crumbling shelves and slopes of scree. In places the cliffs and terraces are riven by deep gorges. These are wadis, seasonal watercourses that bring winter torrents down from the central hills. In summer their channels are parched, barren except for gnarled acacias and tamarisks which somehow survive the long annual drought. Nahal Shuhan is one such ravine.

Opposite the mouth of Nahal Shuhan the main road hugs the shoreline, which lies almost two miles from the cliffs at that point. A good dirt track leads from the road to the gorge, winding its way between strange formations produced by erosion of the soft marl. After about one and a half miles the track divides; one trail zigzags steeply up into the mountains on the north side of the gorge while the other turns south, crosses the watercourse and then runs parallel with it. Though impassable when the torrents are in full spate, by late April the watercourse is dry, with tufts of greenery marking its bed.

Sinnet took the southern route. This never rises higher than a rocky plateau beyond the marl formations, perhaps ninety metres above the wadi floor. About a mile into the gorge the track peters out; the gorge itself curves to the north-west for another half a mile before its bed rises sharply and it becomes a narrow gully, snaking up towards the Hebron Hills.

Sinnet stopped the Land Rover on the plateau in the shade of the cliffs and switched off the ignition. 'This is it,' he announced. 'The end of the road.' He produced a bright yellow baseball cap, stuck it casually on his head and clambered out. Mike stepped down to join him and noticed that a faint whirring noise seemed to be coming from Sinnet's head. He sneaked a sideways glance and saw that the baseball cap had a tiny fan set in the peak to blow air onto the wearer's face.

'Admiring this?' asked Sinnet, patting his cap. 'Neat, isn't it? It's got a small solar-voltaic panel on top that provides the power.'

'I must get one,' said Mike. 'I was wondering – the track we just followed; why does it exist at all if it stops here in the middle of nowhere?'

'It was created specially by the army, for the Israeli archaeologists who explored this area in the early sixties. From here on we follow *that*.' Sinnet pointed to what looked like a mere goat track weaving precipitously up the cliffs. Going to the rear of the Land Rover he took out two water canisters in canvas pouches which they fastened to their belts.

'Drink three sips every fifteen minutes,' he said. 'That's the army way. It could get hot before we're through.' Then he picked up two caving helmets. Handing one to Mike, he exchanged his baseball cap for the other and led the way. 'Oh, and if you notice me limping slightly,' he added over his shoulder, 'don't worry. I was wounded in 'Nam. Bullet through the left knee. Nothing serious. Doesn't bother me at all.'

When they reached the mouth of the lowest cave Mike was surprised to see that a strong metal grille had been fixed across it.

'It's a pity about this,' he said, tapping the bars. 'Spoils the timeless atmosphere.'

'Vital precaution,' said Sinnet, on whom timeless atmospheres were completely wasted. 'The Antiquities Authority fitted them to all four caves at our request. The Bedouin in this area are notorious for clandestine excavations. As soon as they'd gotten wind of our expedition they would've been up here trying to beat us to the best finds, hoping for something they could sell on the illegal antiquities market. As I'm sure you know, Mike, something like a Dead Sea Scroll would fetch millions of dollars.'

In the centre of the grille was a metal door secured by a large padlock. Sinnet produced a key and opened it. The door swung inwards with a metallic squeal, the noise echoing back at them as they stepped inside. Three bats came hurtling out of the darkness, swerved around them and shot through the doorway. Following Sinnet's lead, Mike switched on his helmet lamp and advanced into the cave. It was littered throughout with heavy roof fall; huge angular slabs of rock cast confusing shadows as their lamps swept the darkness. The atmosphere was stuffy and fetid.

'Welcome to Cave A,' said Sinnet. 'I'm afraid we can't do anything about the stink – bat dung. Most of the bats left when the men from the IAA were fixing the gratings, but the smell is here to stay.' This cave, he explained, would have to be Parbunkel's, on account of Leo not being very athletic and this being the easiest cave to reach. 'But I'm afraid you won't escape the smell,' he added, 'because all the caves are the same. We'll have to wear face masks when we're shifting rocks and stuff. The dust is terrible.'

Cave A was basically a single, large, low-roofed chamber with a few small bays and recesses, so it didn't take them long to look around. Caves B and C were higher up the cliffs and farther west, about ten minutes' difficult walk from Cave A. Their entrances were only about thirty metres apart, a single ledge giving access to both.

When they were inside Cave C Sinnet said, 'We thought you could take this one, Mike. Tally Schluter can have B. Is that okay with you?'

Cave C had three chambers opening off a gallery, and relatively light amounts of roof fall.

'That's fine by me, but it leaves you with Cave D, which I gather is pretty hard to reach.' Mike had doubts about Sinnet's agility, in spite of his dismissal of his war wound.

'At present,' said Sinnet, 'but we plan to change all that. I'll explain when we get there.'

3

They drove out of the gorge, joined the northbound trail and were soon crawling steadily up the steep zigzag into the mountains. It was a long drive around the head of the ravine. Sinnet whiled it away with an account of his expedition to eastern Turkey.

'Yessir, it was the remains of Noah's Ark all right,' he concluded. 'Plain as anything. Could've got the samples to prove it, too, if we'd had more time, but the Turkish authorities moved us out. Something to do with a military operation against Kurdish separatists, or so they said. But there's always opposition to proving the truth of God's Word, as I'm sure you've discovered, Mike.'

Mike foolishly admitted that he hadn't encountered this problem in his own line of work.

'Oh?' said Sinnet, his tone suggesting that Mike had been wasting his time on trivia. 'I guess it's different in the front line. That's where I've chosen to serve the Lord – in the front line!'

The mountain road turned out to be much rougher and more difficult than Swyver's demonstration with table napkins had suggested. Even after crossing the head of the ravine and turning eastwards again, the route was by no means straightforward. The south side of Nahal Shuhan is broken by another wadi called Nahal Jamin, and the detour around that added another five, slow miles to the journey. In all, the drive from the bottom of the gorge to the top of the cliffs above Cave D took one and three-quarter hours.

The cliffs there rise to over four hundred metres above the bed of the wadi. From where Mike stood, the ravine stretched away like a great gash in the tortured landscape. The face of the southern cliffs was still in deep, monochrome shadow. Almost a quarter of a mile distant, the sunlit northern side provided a stark contrast. Its brown and ochre tones were changing constantly as cloud-shadows crept over its massive stratified walls, towering crags and chaotic, fractured slopes.

Mike was deep in the grip of this awesome, eroded grandeur when the rattle of a climbing harness broke the spell.

'Put this on,' said Sinnet, 'and I'll teach you some simple rappelling techniques.'

Mike looked around for a nice little rock face, ideally no more than three or four metres high, on which to practise, but the ground here was almost flat to the edge of the cliffs. His stomach tensed as the truth dawned; his first abseiling lesson and his descent to the cave were to be one and the same thing.

While Mike carefully fastened the harness around his waist, Sinnet deftly slipped into his own.

'This is a descender,' he said, clipping a small, metal figure-of-eight to Mike's harness. 'The rope goes through it like so, and you control it like so.' His hands moved with a casual swiftness that was hard to follow. 'In a moment I'll demonstrate properly. Now put your helmet on.' Mike wondered what use a helmet would be if he fell four hundred metres.

Sinnet had parked the Land Rover facing the precipice. He tied the ropes to its bull bars and gave them a final tug to check that everything was secure. 'All set?' he asked.

Mike supposed he must be, since no amount of delay could have removed his trepidation. He nodded grimly, his face deathly pale.

'Then stay close and do exactly as I do,' said Sinnet. 'We'll just walk down slowly – no fancy moves. The important thing is to keep your legs pretty straight. Bend them too much and you could turn upside down.'

With these encouraging words ringing in his helmet Mike carefully copied Sinnet, walking backwards to the edge of the cliff. His first step over the edge, leaning back and trusting his weight to the rope, was a moment of pure terror. After that things became easier. He had to concentrate on where he was putting his feet, so there was no opportunity to look down and be reminded of the huge drop below. The cliff was not perpendicular at that point, so the exercise was more like a steep backwards walk than true abseiling. Even so, when Mike's feet finally touched the ledge they were aiming for – about ninety metres below the top of the cliff – his legs were shaking so much he could barely stand.

Sinnet slapped him on the back, almost knocking him off the ledge, and said, 'Well done, Mike! Better sip some water. The cave's over there, round that corner.' He was pointing to a place where the rock face jutted out and the ledge had given way. 'There's practically no ledge for a few feet, so we have to put most of our weight on the ropes. When you're ready, follow me.'

Mike found this manoeuvre even worse than the descent, because to find the best footholds he had to look straight down. But eventually the ledge widened again and they stood facing the cave entrance. This was so narrow it didn't need a metal grille; the frame of the small door had been fixed directly to the sides of the hole. Mike noticed that a large metal hook protruded from each end of the concrete threshold.

'Those are for a rope ladder,' said Sinnet, guessing his thoughts. 'The Ben-Gurion University of the Negev is supplying one. Has to be three hundred feet long to reach the nearest ledge we can get to from the bottom. Should arrive tomorrow. Then we'll be able to climb to all four caves from our base in the canyon. No more long drives, and no need for a separate camp at the top. Let's look inside.'

Mike soon understood why Sinnet wanted this cave. It wasn't simply that its location appealed to his gung-ho mentality; it also had enormous potential. It must have always been difficult to reach, even when the adjacent ledges were in better shape, and therefore would have made the ideal hideout for rebels against the power of Rome. It was also complex and extensive; a maze of low galleries and small chambers.

'Come see this,' said Sinnet, picking his way among the usual slabs fallen from the roof. At the rear of this particular chamber lay a pile of huge boulders. 'I doubt we can do much about those, not even with the rock slicers. That isn't your average roof fall. Those rocks fill a massive pit that drops way below the cave's normal floor level. Here, take a look.' He detached the lamp from the front of his helmet and angled its beam down into the spaces between jumbled boulders. 'See what I mean? There's no knowing how far it is to the bottom. And if you look up...' He redirected the beam of light to a roof which soared above them like the interior of a gloomy cathedral. 'That's almost a hundred feet above where we're standing. If all that rock came down and filled an existing pit – well, that's a mighty big pit!'

'I see what you mean,' said Mike. 'So even the new equipment can't help?'

'Afraid not. No way can we clear that hole. But never mind, there's plenty to do here. This is a big cave and I can't wait to get started.'

They set off back along the crumbling ledge. Mike found the final climb to the Land Rover every bit as harrowing as his descent; it involved bracing his feet against the sloping rock and pulling himself up, hand over hand, to the top.

It was now the hottest part of the day; the temperature was over thirty degrees and all shade had vanished from the southern cliffs. Sweat ran from every pore of Mike's body, soaking his clothes. When he finally reached the top he threw himself down by the Land Rover and lay in its meagre strip of shade. As he lay gasping for breath, the muscles in his arms aching and stiffening, the words of Indiana Jones came spontaneously from his parched lips: 'This is *not* archaeology!'

Late that afternoon, over coffee with Leo Parbunkel, Mike related his experiences at the ravine.

Parbunkel nodded sympathetically, and when Mike had finished his narrative he asked, 'When the two of you rappelled down to Cave D did Chuck put a safety rope on you?'

Mike said he wasn't sure – he'd been too preoccupied with controlling his fear to take everything in – but he didn't think so.

Parbunkel shook his head. 'That's Chuck Sinnet for you,' he said. 'Caution just isn't in his vocabulary. I guess it's only by the grace of God you're still alive.'

Chapter Nine

1

After breakfast next morning Mike had a briefing session with Talia Schluter. Tally was about thirty, small and wiry, with blond hair pulled back into a loose ponytail at the nape of her neck. As the dig's registrar of finds, her task was to oversee the detailed recording of everything the teams discovered. The four supervisors would each be responsible for recording finds in their own caves, but Tally's job also involved collating the information, checking that all descriptions and measurements of find-spots were complete, and entering the data on a computerised master-register. She explained the procedures she'd devised for all supervisors to follow.

'Of course, you don't have to do all the recording yourself,' she said, noting Mike's frown. 'That's what the assistant supervisors are for – to take some of the load off of you. They're all volunteers with previous experience who can be trusted with that kind of job.'

'And they're all arriving later today?'

'They should be here by this evening so you'll meet them over dinner. I've already assigned each one to a particular supervisor. Yours is called Dave Hirschfeld; he's a really keen amateur archaeologist – spends his vacation on a different dig each year. Leo's is called Wade Brattle, and he's done three seasons at Tell Jawa. Mine's Drew Gessinger, who's worked at Hazor and Jezreel. I don't know anything about Chuck's, except that he's called Rip Warholler; Chuck chose him personally.'

Mike thought this last name sounded familiar, but he couldn't recall the connection.

'Well, I must say I'm very impressed, Tally. You've got everything beautifully organised. Where did you dig before you joined Leo?'

'Jezreel, and the new Hazor excavations. That's how I know Drew Gessinger; we've worked together before.' Mike thought he noticed a slight blush on Tally's cheek. 'Time for coffee,' she added quickly.

2

Parbunkel was in his element.

'Then there's EDM – electronic distance measurement – which records measurements at amazing speed and uses them to generate maps and plans.'

'I think I'm *au fait* with that,' said Mike.

'What about AutoCAD? It can show reconstructed buildings in three dimensions, from any height and any angle, and rotate the model through three hundred and sixty degrees.'

'I've used that too, but things may have moved on a bit…'

'Right. We'll bring you up to speed later. How about photogrammetry?'

Mike had never used photogrammetry.

'It's the cat's miaow,' said Parbunkel. 'Haven't tried it in caves yet, but I'll find something that'll give you the idea.' His podgy hand, fingers fluttering with indecision, hovered over a neat row of boxes like an overweight hummingbird. Then he selected a disk and fed it into the computer. A few seconds later the monitor was showing the interior of a long, stone-lined chamber with a barrel-vaulted roof.

'Computer graphics,' Parbunkel explained, 'based on photogrammetry. You take overlapping colour slides and put them into a stereo plotter, and the computer combines them with basic measurements; then it can produce exact dimensions for any features in the slides, and from those it can generate new images. Fantastic, isn't it?'

Mike was intrigued. He shifted his chair closer to the screen.

'So what are we looking at, Leo? Where is this?'

Parbunkel hesitated, gave Mike – or at least his chin – a long, searching look, then turned back to the desk.

'It's a project Chuck and I carried out in Jerusalem recently.

Only lasted two weeks, but boy... watch this – it'll blow your mind.'

He shifted the computer mouse and tapped the keyboard as he spoke. An aerial photograph of the Old City appeared on the screen, in colour and with impressively sharp definition.

'You're familiar with this, I expect?' He pointed to a large rectangular feature to the right of the picture.

'Of course. The Haram esh-Sharif,' said Mike, using its Arabic name.

'Right. Otherwise known as the Temple Mount – and I assume you know its history?'

Mike nodded. On its present scale this structure was the work of Herod the Great in the first century BC, but its history as a sacred site went back nine hundred years before that, to the time when Solomon built his temple on the same spot. In the sixth century BC the Babylonians had overrun Jerusalem, leaving Solomon's temple a charred ruin. Later that century, Judaean exiles returning from Babylon had built a second temple, which had survived for the next five hundred years.

Then came Herod, with a master plan not only for a new temple but for an enhanced setting – spacious courts requiring a raised platform the size of twenty-four football pitches. Herod's temple was in turn destroyed by Roman armies in AD 70. His monumental platform lay more or less derelict until the seventh century, when it was adopted by the new religion of Islam. Jerusalem's Muslim rulers repaired it and built the Dome of the Rock over the site of the Jewish temple.

Leo moved the mouse again and tapped more keys. The Temple Mount moved to the centre of the screen, was enlarged and then overlaid with red contour lines.

'Then you'll know that the south-eastern corner of Herod's platform was raised high above bedrock by a series of supporting vaults and a massive retaining wall.' He touched another key and the vaults were delineated in green.

'Yes. They're misleadingly known as Solomon's Stables.'

'Right. Well, the western side of the platform is also much higher than bedrock, but here the method of construction has always been a mystery. The western wall includes some fantastically huge stones, the biggest weighing between four and six hundred tons – bigger than any stone in the pyramids or Stonehenge! It can't have been easy to shift stones that size, so there must have been a special reason for using them. It's always been assumed they were put there to withstand enormous pressure, but pressure of what? Just a mass of rubble, or the arches of enormous vaults? Well, now we know. And it's vaults! There's a whole maze of vaults behind there!'

'How did you find out? Ground-penetrating radar?'

Leo waved a hand dismissively.

'We went one better. *We* got inside!'

Mike was astonished. Apart from the practical difficulties, it didn't seem possible to penetrate the Temple Mount without causing a political crisis. It was one of Islam's holiest sites, and threats to its sanctity and security always provoked violent reactions.

'That's incredible! How did you manage to get permission?'

'Oh, the Jewish Ministry of Religious Affairs and the IAA were very cooperative…'

'But the *Muslim* authorities, Leo! The interior of the Temple Mount is under their jurisdiction…'

'And we knew they'd never give permission for what we wanted to do, so we didn't ask.'

'What? But didn't they protest? Why weren't there demonstrations and riots all over the West Bank, like there were when the Western Wall tunnel was opened to tourists?'

'Because the dig was carried out in secret.'

'But… how on earth…?'

'You just mentioned the Western Wall tunnel; have you ever been inside it?'

'No.'

'You should pay a visit. Very interesting, archaeologically. Anyway, the Ministry closed the tunnel for us for two weeks. The official reason was that the roof needed reinforcing. In fact some small-scale repairs were done, but really it was just a cover for the dig. The Muslim authorities had no idea what was really going on.'

The total frankness with which Parbunkel admitted this mind-boggling duplicity left Mike speechless. He simply stared back, open-mouthed.

'The way we see it,' said Parbunkel, responding to Mike's expression, 'religious and political sensitivities can't be allowed to hold up research. Anyway, I'll show you how we did it.' He turned back to the keyboard. A green stripe appeared on the screen, superimposed on the aerial photograph. 'That's the tunnel, running all along the Western Wall of the Temple Mount, and here' – more key-taps, and a small green rectangle also appeared on the western side of the platform, at right angles to the tunnel – 'is one of the original entrances to Herod's structure, discovered by Wilson and Warren over a hundred years ago.'

'Known as Warren's Gate,' said Mike, becoming intrigued again.

'Right. It entered the Temple Mount at street level, but the street was about forty feet lower than the pavement of the Temple courts, so the entrance was like a modern pedestrian subway, extending beneath the outer court for almost one hundred feet. At the far end, steps led up to the surface of the platform. You with me so far?'

Mike nodded.

'Now, this underground passage survived the Temple's destruction in AD 70 and later became a Jewish synagogue. When the crusaders took Jerusalem in 1099 and drove the Jewish community out, they blocked both ends of the passage with concrete and used it as a reservoir for storing water. It stayed sealed for over nine hundred years – until just a few weeks ago in fact. Working inside the tunnel, we broke through the concrete at the western end of the passage and got inside. That's what I showed you to illustrate photogrammetry. You're one of the few people alive who know what the inside of that chamber looks like!'

Leo's fingers rattled over the keyboard and the original view of the chamber returned to the screen.

'As a matter of fact the stonework is now coated with medieval plaster; this shows how it would have looked originally. But we can do better than this.' From behind the computer he picked up a headset with dark goggles on the front. 'Virtual reality. Try it.'

With the goggles in place Mike saw the same view as on the screen, but the sense of being inside the underground chamber was breathtaking. Then it struck him that all this skulduggery in the tunnel still hadn't revealed Herod's vaults.

'But Leo, I don't see how this helped. This chamber doesn't communicate with the interior of the Temple Mount, does it?'

'Not originally, but we knew it had been damaged by a big earthquake in 1033, because a manuscript mentions repairs to the synagogue. We wanted to locate those repairs behind the medieval plaster, hoping they might provide an easy route through the masonry. To cut a long story short... watch this!'

He performed a quick arpeggio on the keyboard and the scene changed again. Mike was standing in a forest of massive pillars which rose amid heaps of rubble. The pillars supported rows of arches, the crowns of which were about eight metres above the floor.

'This is what lies beyond the chamber,' said Parbunkel. 'The vaults supporting the western side of Herod's platform. Impressive or what? But this isn't all. We're going east a bit. This could feel a little strange if you're not used to it.'

Mike seemed to be walking, or rather floating, between two rows of pillars. Ahead of him was a wall of masonry and, as he got closer, he saw that in one place the wall had collapsed, exposing natural rock. In the rock was a roughly hewn hole, large enough for a person to walk through.

'That masonry had already fallen away when we found it. What you see behind is bedrock, part of the hill that Herod built his platform on. The interesting thing is that hole; it was blocked with stones when we found it. We cleared it out, and...'

A second later Mike was travelling down a sloping tunnel hewn through bedrock, the rough limestone pressing close on both sides. The slope was gentle at first, then became a series of badly worn steps. Eventually the passage levelled out, the walls opened up and he was standing in a gloomy, bell-shaped cavern. In its centre was a circular shaft with steps around the interior, spiralling down into darkness.

'An ancient cistern,' Leo announced. 'There's water at the bottom of that hole.'

There was nothing intrinsically surprising about this. Parts of the Temple Mount were known to be honeycombed with tunnels and water cisterns gouged out of the bedrock. In the nineteenth century a few archaeologists had been allowed to explore them and take measurements. As a result of their efforts over forty subterranean chambers had been thoroughly documented. But Mike was baffled by this particular cistern. He was familiar with the plans published in the nineteenth century and was sure that no cistern as large as this had been recorded in the central part of the Temple Mount.

'If I remember rightly,' he said, 'this isn't documented.'

'Right, Mike. It's a new discovery – never entered before in modern times! But the really amazing thing is not the cistern itself but what we found at the bottom. There was only about a foot of water and beneath that was a thick, semi-solid layer of goo – sediment deposited over thousands of years. And almost submerged in the sediment was a box.'

'What kind of a box?'

'A wooden box. I'll show you. But not like this. I'll show you the real thing.'

Mike removed the VR goggles and blinked.

'You mean you've got it here?'

'Right! Follow me.'

3

They left the computer room and entered Parbunkel's laboratory. Opening a door at the far end, he led Mike down a flight of steps and into a long corridor. Two days earlier, when giving Mike his guided tour of the Centre, Parbunkel had said nothing about this basement level. The corridor led to a heavy door which he opened by punching the buttons of a nine-figure combination lock. They entered the room beyond and the door clicked solidly behind them.

The room was quite small, no more than four metres square, and it hummed with the pervasive throb of hidden machinery. Illumination came from a row of translucent ceiling panels. There was nothing in the room except a long table spread with open files, books and papers. The opposite wall seemed to be lined with unpainted sheets of metal riveted together, and in its centre was a large window, completely dark. On the wall to the left of this window was a control panel with push-buttons and a row of winking lights; to the right of the window was another heavy door.

Leo Parbunkel walked over to the panel and pressed a button. The window lit up. Mike moved closer. The glass was very thick and surrounded by a rubber seal. Both the window and the metal wall seemed to be giving off heat.

'What do you make of that, Mike?' asked Parbunkel, rubbing his hands with excitement.

Mike was looking into a small cubicle in the centre of which stood a square, metal table. The table had a wire grille in place of a solid top, and on it sat a large rectangular box of blackened wood. The box was badly warped, but had no visible openings. Mike could see neither the box nor the table very clearly because the cubicle contained a dense cloud of vapour.

'Well?' said Parbunkel. 'Isn't that the cat's miaow?' He was still rubbing his hands together, and shifting from one foot to the other as though he needed a pee. His face was covered with little beads of perspiration.

'Is that what you found in the silt?'

'Right. A wooden box, three feet nine inches long, two feet three inches wide and two feet three inches high. Do those dimensions mean anything to you, Mike?'

'I'm afraid not. I don't think easily in feet. Could you translate them into centimetres?'

'How about cubits? Two cubits and a half was the length of it, and a cubit and a half the breadth of it...'

The penny dropped. '...and a cubit and a half the height of it!' said Mike, completing the biblical quotation.

'Right!'

Leo's habit of saying 'Right' was making Mike feel like a quiz show contestant, but this was no time to vent his irritation.

'Leo, you can't be serious! Are you actually suggesting... do you mean... you actually think this box is the lost Ark of the Covenant?'

'Right! And why not?' Parbunkel brought his excitement under control and dropped his voice to a suitably hushed and reverent level. 'As I'm sure you know, there are lots of legends about what happened to the Ark when the Babylonians destroyed Jerusalem – that Jeremiah hid it in a cave, or it got taken to Egypt, or... and so forth – but there's always been a rumour that it was hidden beneath the Temple Mount. And the dimensions are roughly right, allowing for some small differences of opinion over the length of a cubit. And it's made of wood, and it looks pretty ancient. It's also very heavy – as it should be if it contains the stone tablets of the Ten Commandments!'

'But, Leo...' Mike began, remembering the next verse of the biblical description: 'And he overlaid it with pure gold within and without...'

'No gold covering? I'll admit that's a difficulty at first sight. But suppose a nosy Babylonian soldier had found his way into that tunnel and gone prowling around down there; a plain wooden box under the water would hardly have been noticed, but a box overlaid with *gold*... So if you want to make it inconspicuous, you strip the gold off. Right?'

Mike remained sceptical.

'And you think a wooden box could have survived in water for more than two and a half thousand years?'

'Given the right conditions... anyway, it's not exactly in a pristine state. In fact it's so decayed it's ready to fall apart, and if we'd let the wood dry out, it would've crumbled to dust. We kept it moist until this partition could be installed to create a special environment for it. You see that mist in there? That's part of a preservation process which will eventually allow us to open it without risk of damage.'

'It also makes it hard to see,' Mike pointed out. 'Is there any way of getting a better look?'

Leo shook his head.

'Not at present. The mist is a fine spray of polyethylene glycol coming from nozzles on the ceiling. Mustn't be turned off until the process is complete. It steadily penetrates the cellular cavities of the deteriorated wood and hardens them. The normal method of using this stuff is to submerge wooden objects in a liquid for about two years, but the boys at Swycorp have developed this accelerated process. By converting the liquid into tiny droplets, and heating the atmosphere in there to 70 degrees centigrade, we can reduce the time to less than three months. Unfortunately the temperature, the humidity and the chemicals in the air make the inside of that cubicle absolutely lethal. Without protective clothing and breathing apparatus you couldn't survive. I don't know which would come first – getting cooked or getting poisoned – but either way, you'd soon be dead.'

'But beautifully preserved. And you don't have this protective clothing and breathing apparatus?'

'Not yet. This whole thing took us by surprise, so... But Swycorp's getting a special suit ready and it should arrive pretty soon. When it does, you can go in there and examine that thing up close and personal.'

'Thanks,' said Mike, trying to sound enthusiastic.

'You know, this'll shake the world, Mike. It's not just finding the Ark, though that's amazing enough. Imagine being able to produce the Ten Commandments!'

'You mean like Cecil B DeMille?'

'I mean being able to show the world the original stone tablets, brought down from Mount Sinai by Moses! Proof of the authority of Scripture, a decisive blow to liberal immorality! Think of the revival that would follow!' Parbunkel switched off the cubicle light and adopted a conspiratorial air. 'I'm sure I don't need to stress this, but until we have absolute proof of what we've got in there, and we're ready to issue a press release, this must remain a matter of the strictest confidence. Even the Antiquities people don't know we found it.'

'Of course,' said Mike. 'You have my word.'

'Thanks.' As Leo opened the door to the corridor he placed a hand on Mike's shoulder. 'And, uh... I'd appreciate it if you didn't mention to Chuck that I've told you all this. He can be... well, kind of touchy about who knows.'

4

Mike spent all afternoon in the library, checking facts about the chamber behind Warren's Gate. Everything he could discover was consistent with Leo's story. He came across references to it by the Christian pilgrim Theoderich in the twelfth century, and by Rabbi Samuel ben Samson in the thirteenth. Parbunkel had been right about its use as a synagogue, and about the documentary evidence for earthquake damage in 1033. Charles Wilson had entered it in April 1866, having gained access through a shaft at the top, long since sealed; in Wilson's catalogue of caverns within the Temple Mount it appeared as No. 30. But by the end of his research Mike still didn't know what to make of it all. Although the basic facts checked out, Leo's conviction that he'd discovered the Ark of the Covenant had no more credibility than several similar claims.

In recent decades a whole spate of amateur archaeologists and explorers had announced the discovery of that missing relic of the First Temple – or at least the discovery of its final resting place: Tom Crotser claimed to have photographed the Ark in a cave beneath Mount Pisgah in Jordan; Ron Wyatt had produced video footage in support of his claim that it lay in a cavern near Jerusalem's Damascus Gate; Vendyl Jones believed he'd traced it to a cave not far from Qumran; Graham Hancock claimed it resided in a secluded chapel in Ethiopia. And now there was Parbunkel's discovery to add to the list, seemingly made by chance and with only rumour to back it up.

On his way to his room, Mike considered the worst case scenario: that the box, the cubicle and the preservation process were all parts of an elaborate hoax, perhaps intended to turn an unbelieving world from its sinful ways. After all, the only evidence he'd seen for the western vaults and the newly discovered cistern was a series of computer graphics, and Leo could have concocted those himself. Their authenticity would be hard to disprove without further access to the chamber behind Warren's Gate. But had Sinnet and Parbunkel really penetrated that chamber at all? Had there ever been a secret dig within the Western Wall tunnel? Or was the whole story a fabrication from beginning to end?

In the absence of clearer evidence he could only suspend judgement. If the protective suit for entering the cubicle failed to arrive, or if Leo found some other pretext for denying him access to the box, his worst suspicions would be confirmed. But if the box was a genuine discovery, and he was eventually allowed to inspect it, then it would be only a matter of time before he knew if it really was the Ark.

5

When he got to his room Mike was surprised to find a man of about his own age, with dark curly hair and wire-framed glasses, peering into the wardrobe.

'Who the hell...?'

'Hi! You must be Dr Totley. Can I call you Mike? I'm Dave Hirschfeld, your assistant.'

'Of course! Sorry, I'd almost forgotten...'

'The others have arrived too – Rip, Drew and Wade. I should tell you right away that I'm different.'

'Oh?'

'For one thing I've got a real biblical first name, while those other guys seem to get by with monosyllabic verbs. And I'm a Messianic Jew. I prefer that term to "converted Jew" because that suggests I've stopped being a Jew, which I haven't – not in my view. Also, I live here in Israel and the others are all from the States. I'm from San Francisco originally, but I made *aliyah* – sorry, that means came over to Israel – in 1994. I live in Beer Sheva and work on education programmes for the sedentarised Bedouin. And you needn't worry about my archaeological experience; I've dug so many holes in this country I'm surprised it hasn't fallen apart. Please tell me if I'm talking too much. It's a bad habit of mine.'

'Dave, you're talking too much. But welcome anyway,' said Mike, smiling and offering his hand.

Mike met the other assistant supervisors when they went down for dinner. He immediately recognised Rip Warholler as Swyver's bodyguard whom he'd met in the Omni Shoreham Hotel. During the meal he asked Rip what digs he'd been on. Apparently uncertain how to reply, Rip glanced across the table in silent appeal to Chuck Sinnet who promptly changed the subject.

Taking a folded sheet of paper from his shirt pocket, Sinnet handed it to Mike and said, 'Have you seen this, Mike? It's the latest revision of the team lists. One of the people from your team, a Miss Harrison, had to drop out, so I emailed a guy on the waiting list and he's coming instead. That reduces the women, including Tally, to four, so I've moved Alice Wesson into your team to keep them evenly distributed. The whole gang should be here by the end of tomorrow.'

Mike looked at the new name on the list and thought, 'A man reaps what he sows.'

Chapter Ten

1

[Extract from the journal of Effin L Clinger]

Decided to keep a daily journal to record the six weeks of the dig in detail, for they are sure to be a unique and momentous experience. What a privilege to be here! After three months on the waiting list I'd begun to think it wasn't God's will, but at the last minute someone got sick or died and couldn't come – praise the Lord!

I got to the Center for Biblical Archaeology around noon, one of the first volunteers to arrive. It's on the south-eastern edge of Talpiot, a suburb of Jerusalem about two miles south of the Old City, so should be real handy for sightseeing when we get time off. I've already met the staff and just know it's going to be a pleasure working with them. The director is Dr Chuck Sinnet, well-known author of *Our Youthful Earth* and a big man in every way. Dr Mike Totley from England, known to me personally since last November, is also on the staff and I'm thrilled to find that I'm in his team!

The last volunteers arrived in time for dinner this evening. As we were gathering outside the dining room, something strange happened – so strange it seems worth recording. I was about to approach Mike and ask him about some practicalities when a tall, dark-haired girl walked up to him and said, 'Dr Totley, I presume. It's great to meet you.'

Mike looked like he'd seen a ghost, and said, 'Connie! What... I mean... What...'

She lowered her voice (but I got close enough to hear) and said, 'I'm here to keep an eye on you – and to learn some more about archaeology and Dead Sea Scrolls and things at the same time.'

Mike looked agitated. He took a piece of paper from his pocket and stared at it, then he said, 'But I wasn't expecting...

your name isn't even on the list!'

She said, 'Yes it is. There! Sydney C Patterson.'

He said, 'You used a false name?'

Then she said, 'Don't assume I do everything by stealth and subterfuge. Sydney really is my first name. I don't generally use it, but the application form asked for my name in full. On this list someone's changed Constance to an initial.'

Mike ran his fingers through his hair and I could see sweat on his forehead. He looked at the paper again and said, 'But there are only three women volunteers, and they're all listed: Cecilia Hope-Parsons, Alice Wesson and Shirley Fisher!'

The girl said, 'Shirley Fisher is a man; over there in the green shirt. I see I'm in Dr Sinnet's team. Which one's he?' Mike pointed him out and she said, 'The big guy who looks like a retired baseball coach? I'd better go say hello.'

When she'd moved away Mike stared at his piece of paper and pushed his fingers through his hair again, looking real worried. People started drifting into the dining room and sitting down at the table so I asked Mike if he'd like to join me. He said he'd lost his appetite and was going back to his room. He missed a nice meal.

Bowel movements regular.

2

Leo Parbunkel surveyed his audience. A bloom of sweat spread over his face in spite of the expensive air conditioning. He hated upfront roles.

'Welcome to our orientation session,' he said, speaking too loudly into the microphone. He took a step backwards as his amplified voice rebounded from the walls. The assembled volunteers and staff, arrayed before him in the lecture hall, fell silent before the assault. 'And may I also welcome you all formally to the er... Jerusalem Centre for Biblical Archaeology. I hope our latest arrivals all had a good sleep last night. This session has three aims: one is to er... introduce the Centre and its work; the second is to explain the background to our dig; and the third...'

There was a long silence. Parbunkel had temporarily forgotten the third aim.

'Oh, yes, the third is to tell you how we'll be going about it. I'd like to begin the session by telling you all about the Centre and its work.'

Parbunkel was not a gifted public speaker. He rambled, lost the thread of his sentences and went off at tangents about things that were neither relevant nor remotely interesting. The audience's flagging attention revived briefly when he fiddled with some controls on the hi-tech lectern; blinds glided down the windows, the lights dimmed and a map appeared behind him, back-projected on a large screen. It showed an area from Jerusalem southwards to Beer Sheva, including the western shore of the Dead Sea. Parbunkel tried to indicate the places he was talking about with the aid of an electronic pointer which shone a bright green spot onto the map. Unfortunately his hands shook and the spot gyrated around the screen like a deranged firefly. When he finally relinquished the podium there was scattered and bemused applause.

Mike took his place. He considered the microphone unnecessary when addressing such a small gathering, so he ignored it and strolled around the platform as he spoke.

'Before this expedition gets off the ground – or perhaps I should say *into* the ground' – laughter from the audience – 'you should have a good grasp of some basic facts about the caves of Nahal Shuhan. By the way, *nahal* is the Hebrew word for a seasonal watercourse, one that gets filled up by the winter rains but is dry all summer; in Arabic it's called a wadi.'

Mike walked to the lectern and pressed a button; Parbunkel's map disappeared from the screen and a panoramic view of Nahal Shuhan's southern cliffs took its place. Mike indicated the cave entrances with the pointer.

'All our caves were explored by archaeologists in the early sixties and from the few odds and ends which they found – oil lamps, potsherds and so forth – we already have some idea of the different periods in which they were occupied. A few slides will explain what I mean.'

The cliffs vanished, to be replaced by a close-up of some pottery fragments.

'These are the oldest items found in the caves so far; potsherds from Cave A. For those who are new to archaeology, let me explain the value of pottery for dating purposes. The shapes and decoration of pottery vessels have been changing constantly, ever since the first pottery was produced around seven or eight thousand years BC.'

A loud throat-clearing noise, with strong connotations of disapproval, issued from Chuck Sinnet.

'A pottery expert can tell which period a vessel dates from by recognising what we call diagnostic features; for example, these sherds on the screen are pieces of what we call a hole-mouth jar. Here' – Mike singled out one piece with the pointer – 'just below the rim is a double herringbone design. Shape and decoration are typical of what we call the Chalcolithic period, which lasted from roughly 4000 BC to just before 3000 BC.' (More significant throat-clearing from Sinnet.)

A hand went up in the audience. A volunteer called Travis Roston wanted to know whether radiocarbon dating wasn't better than dating by pottery. Mike explained that in the majority of cases it wasn't.

'For one thing, you can only use it to date organic remains – wood, leather and so forth – which aren't always present. However, we may be lucky and find some because of the very dry conditions. The main reason for not bothering with radiocarbon is that, for the periods we're interested in, its results are often less precise than the dates we can get from pottery. Of course, radiocarbon is vital for dating things in the pre-pottery period – say, earlier than ten thousand years ago.' (Yet more troubled noises from Sinnet's throat.)

The next slide showed an oil lamp. It had a squat, circular body, small enough to sit on the palm of an open hand, and a spout-like neck to hold the wick.

'Now we move forward in time to the first century AD. This oil lamp is from Cave D. Like other ceramics, oil lamps underwent changes in shape and decoration, and these provide clues to their date. This one's typical of the first century and probably belonged to members of the Jewish rebel army during the revolt of AD 66–70. We know they used caves like ours as hideouts.'

Another hand went up. The questioner was Wilbur Wesson, a

tall, lugubrious Southern Baptist in his late forties.

'What I'm wondering, Dr Totley, is how anyone ever got to that cave. It looked pretty much inaccessible in your first picture. Did they have rope ladders like we do?'

'Good question, Wilbur – and please call me Mike. We believe there was a way down from the top of the cliffs in those days. Some ledges have since been eroded away. Even back then, access must have been difficult, but if you're hiding from the Romans you don't want a place with a front drive and a welcome mat.' (Laughter.) Wilbur Wesson nodded and raised a hand in acknowledgement.

The next slide appeared, showing a fragment of parchment bearing some faint lines of Hebrew script.

'No, I'm afraid this isn't a Dead Sea Scroll. Our caves haven't produced any of those – yet.' (Laughter.) 'This is part of a letter discovered in Cave B, and it dates from the time of the Bar-Kokhba rebellion, second century AD. Let me put it in context.

'As you probably know, the First Jewish Revolt broke out in AD 66 and resulted in the destruction of Jerusalem in AD 70. The last outpost to fall was Masada, captured in AD 73 – we'll be visiting Masada on our first field trip. Two generations later, in AD 132, the Second Jewish Revolt broke out. Some thought its leader, Simon Ben Kosiba, was the Messiah so they called him Bar-Kokhba – "son of the star" – believing that he fulfilled the prediction of "a star out of Jacob" in the biblical book of Numbers. One aim of the rebels was to rebuild the Temple, so when Bar-Kokhba gained control of Jerusalem he appointed a High Priest in waiting. But that was as far as they got. Within a year the city was back in Roman hands. Bar-Kokhba died in AD 135 and the revolt collapsed. To get back to our letter: it's very fragmentary but we can read enough to know that it was a message from one rebel commander to another during the revolt. Cave B contained coins from the revolt as well.'

Bar-Kokhba's coins appeared on the screen.

'To sum up, then, we already know that the caves were used at three different periods: Cave A was a Chalcolithic dwelling; in the first century Cave D was probably a rebel hideout; and in the second century Cave B provided refuge for some of Bar-Kokhba's men. So we can expect finds from all those periods, and possibly others besides. And to encourage you, let me show you what the famous archaeologist Yigael Yadin found in the Nahal Hever caves in the sixties – caves which lie only a few kilometres from ours. Everything you're about to see is from the time of the Bar-Kokhba revolt.'

Appreciative exclamations punctuated the slide sequence, which showed bronze vessels, a beautiful glass bowl, baskets, fragments of clothing, human skeletons, knives, a painted jewellery box and a whole archive of letters.

'Finally,' said Mike, as the screen went blank and the lights came on, 'you'll know from the films – sorry, *movies* – you've seen that archaeology is a glamorous and exciting business; we may be attacked by ruthless bandits trying to get their hands on our priceless finds; the dig may be hijacked by crazed extremists; our lives may be in constant danger. But probably not.' (Laughter.) 'The truth is, we've got a lot of hard work to do if we're to find anything at all. We're going to get hot, dirty and tired, there'll be plenty of frustrations and sometimes we'll get fed up with each other. And there's something else you should know: although the caves haven't had any human occupants for nearly nineteen centuries, they've been very popular with bats. The bats have now found alternative accommodation, but they left without cleaning up. The smell can be pretty bad. So if you really thought archaeology was all glamour and excitement, this dig should change your mind.' (Laughter again, mingled with expressions of disgust.)

As Mike vacated the podium to warm applause, Chuck Sinnet stepped up to make the third and final presentation.

'My task is to explain the strategy and tactics of the dig. But before I do that, I feel constrained to correct something my colleague Mike Totley said during his talk. He said pottery was first made about ten thousand years ago, also that the Chalcolithic period began around 4000 BC. These are the conventional dates, but they're grossly in error and we shouldn't believe them. Those of us who accept the Bible as God's literal truth know that the world was not created until about 4000 BC. Therefore the long timescales used by most archaeologists must be wrong. As you may know, I've written a book called *Our Youthful Earth* which argues this case in detail so you'll find my evidence in there.

'But to give just one example: when we drive down to the caves first thing tomorrow, we'll be passing the Dead Sea. Now the Dead Sea is proof that the earth is only a few thousand years old. It's fed by the Jordan but it has no outlet, and the only reason it doesn't keep filling up with water is that it lies in a valley where the high temperature causes rapid evaporation. Now here's an interesting fact: the Jordan brings in eight hundred fifty thousand tons of salt every year, which has no place to go. But scientists tell us the total amount of salt in the Dead Sea is currently eleven thousand, six hundred million tons! Divide this by the annual deposition and you'll find the Dead Sea has been receiving salt for no more than thirteen thousand years! And when you allow for various springs that contribute to its waters, you have to cut that time in half! So the Dead Sea turns out to be only six thousand years old – which is exactly what we'd expect if God created the world in six days around 4000 BC like the Bible says!'

With this he shot Mike a glance which said: 'And don't you dare cross me again, young man!'

3

Leo Parbunkel's fingers danced skilfully over the computer keyboard. On the screen a ground plan rotated, careened and became an elevation. He grunted with satisfaction and tried another manoeuvre, putting the latest AutoCAD programme through its paces. He was so engrossed that when Chuck Sinnet entered the room without knocking, he almost jumped out of his seat.

'Leo, we have to talk,' said Sinnet brusquely.

'Right now?'

'Yes, now. Two days ago you showed Totley the Ark, didn't you?'

'Well, um...'

'I know you did, because I was in Merle Spittler's office at the time and the security cameras were on. I saw you on the monitor, taking him down to the basement.'

'Sure. Well, why not? I mean, he's a member of the team, and a brilliant scholar who knows the field.'

'Because we can't be sure of him is why not.'

'But Chuck...'

'He may be a member of the team, Leo, but he doesn't sing from the same hymn sheet. You heard what he said this morning?'

Parbunkel glanced wistfully at his computer and wished he'd locked the door. He didn't want this conversation.

'Leo?'

'Well, I agree he seems to have a few different emphases, but as an evangelical Christian... Anyway, as director of the Centre don't I have the right to decide who sees what in my own lab?'

'Not in this case, Leo. I'm director of the dig, and in terms of Project Peter I'm also the boss's executive officer here in Israel. That makes me your superior. Decisions of that kind should not be taken without consulting me, and when we disagree you must defer to my judgement. Is that clear?'

Parbunkel then played what he thought was the trump card.

'Chuck, it was Oral himself who okayed Mike Totley. In fact he selected him personally to join the team!'

'Yes, and chiefly because of Totley's review of Brush's book.' The use of Swyver's nickname was a masterstroke of one-upmanship. Parbunkel kicked himself for not thinking of it first. 'Have you read that review, Leo?'

'Um...' Parbunkel hesitated. Nobody can read everything, but academics don't find it easy to admit their limitations.

'Well, I just have,' said Sinnet. 'The journal's in the library. And you know what?'

'What?'

'I think Brush seriously misunderstood Totley's intention. I don't like the tone of that review one little bit, Leo. It's left a bad taste in my mouth and a stench in my nostrils.'

'Like bat dung?'

'Much worse.'

'Really?'

'As a member of the supervisory team, Totley could be a serious problem. Do you understand what I'm saying, Leo? I'm not just talking about the dig. He could be a threat to Project Peter itself. We can't allow that. We'll have to watch Totley very closely from now on, and if he looks like stepping out of line... well, we may have to take steps.'

Parbunkel didn't like the sound of this. He buried his fingers in his beard and scratched his chin.

'You really think it's... it's...?'

'That serious? Yessir, I do. Can't take any risks, Leo. The countdown has started, remember?'

Parbunkel stole another escapist glance at the monitor. In that same instant it reverted automatically to the screen saver, a field of stars through which the observer seemed to be plunging at phenomenal speed. It was an unfortunate coincidence and it made Parbunkel shudder.

Chapter Eleven

1

[Second extract from the journal of Effin L Clinger]

Felt very inspired by our orientation session, especially when Dr Sinnet concluded by saying that he thought an even greater prize than a Dead Sea Scroll might await us in the caves! But it left me with some worries about Mike Totley, who gave us conventional dates for things like the invention of pottery even though they conflict with the Bible, and had to be put right by Dr Sinnet. I sat next to him at lunch and raised the issue again, expecting to find that he'd changed his mind in light of Dr Sinnet's evidence, but he said: 'I'm afraid Chuck Sinnet misrepresented the facts. During the Pleistocene period the Jordan Valley was a huge lake. It dried up around 10000 BC and only then did the river start cutting through its sediments. So 13,000 years of salt deposits isn't out of line with present theory, and his attempt to reduce that by half was arbitrary.'

Totally fixed in his ideas! Must try to win him over. There should be plenty of opportunity when we're working together in the cave.

It's now 9.30 PM and time to turn in, as tomorrow we drive out to the caves very early.

Bowel movements remain regular.

The Dig: Day 1 (Wed. 3 May)

We set off in three Land Rovers while it was still dark. Sunup while we were on the way. Got to the canyon soon after 6.30, the tall cliffs very impressive in the early light.

The plan was to get the preliminaries over before it got hot. First we unpacked the tents and put them up. They're nice bright colours – mine's yellow. There are two people to each tent, and I share mine with a young man called Travis Roston III.

Then Dr Parbunkel explained the tools of the trade and how

to use them. There are big picks for shifting compacted stones and dirt, a little bitty pick called a patishe – which is Hebrew for a hammer, he says, but it isn't a hammer, which is confusing – for loosening dirt in more delicate situations, and for even finer work there's a whole variety of pointy trowels, brushes and dental picks. He said only the supervisors and their assistants would be doing the delicate stuff, which is a pity because I've brought along a whole set of dental things that would be a great help.

Then we all gathered in Cave A so that Rip Warholler, a big guy in Dr Sinnet's team, could demonstrate a rock slicer. We've got two of these machines but only Rip and Dr Sinnet are allowed to use them because they're so dangerous. A rock slicer is for cutting big rocks into moveable pieces. It looks like a cross between a large disc cutter and an industrial vacuum cleaner and it's powered by a battery pack on the operator's belt. So that people in the cave don't choke on powdered rock, the dust gets sucked down a flexible tube into a metal drum and from there it goes through another tube and out of the cave in compressed balls. Some dust still escapes into the cave so we all had to wear face masks. We also wore ear protectors because of the noise. Rip Warholler is so strong he can lift huge pieces of rock single-handed, so Rip and a rock slicer make an impressive team.

After the demonstration Dr Sinnet explained our normal daily routine, Tuesdays through Thursdays. (Things are different Mondays and Fridays, because we go back to the Center for weekends. Today, though Wednesday, is like Monday.) It goes like this:

5.30 AM   Wake up, get dressed, spend some time in private devotions.
6.00 AM   Communal devotions led by Dr. Sinnet or Dr. Parbunkel.
6.15 AM   Light breakfast, coffee, etc.
6.30 AM   To the caves.
9 AM   Return to camp for full breakfast.
10 AM   Back to the caves.
11.30 AM 15-minute break at the caves.
1.30 PM   Return to camp for lunch, followed by rest period.
3 PM   Cleaning and sorting finds, with explanations of what everything is, its date, etc., by the supervisors. This keeps us all in the picture, and we get to learn about dating pottery and so forth.

5 PM   Showers. Our shower – a large tank on a metal frame with a plastic curtain around it – was delivered during the morning. A truck will come out most days to refill the tank, bring food, drinking water, batteries for the lamps, etc.

6 PM   Dinner.

7 PM   Clean up and turn in. Sundown is around 7.30 and it gets dark pretty fast.

This schedule means we don't spend too much time in the unhealthy atmosphere of the caves, and do nothing strenuous during the hottest part of the day. Must say, I was glad to get out of the cave at lunchtime. It's a lot more pleasant in camp where we work in the shade of tarps slung between tent poles.

Once we got started in the cave I tried talking to Mike Totley about his liberal views on the Bible. Choosing an appropriate moment – instead of moving around the cave a lot, he was lying flat on his stomach poking at some incredibly small object with a brush – I asked if he was a Creationist.

He said, 'Probably not in the sense you mean,' and talked a lot about metaphors and 'the literalist fallacy'.

When I challenged him further he asked if we could postpone the discussion because he had to concentrate on an important task. Later it turned out that all he'd extracted from the dirt were some itty-bitty pieces of broken pottery. I'd obviously rattled him.

Praise God, my bowel movements continue regular.

Day 2 (Thurs. 4 May)

Am getting to know the other two members of our team. Alice Wesson is a limber, middle-aged woman whose husband Wilbur is in Miss Schluter's team. Salt of the earth both of them. Dave Hirschfeld is Mike's assistant – a pleasant young man but sometimes he talks so much I can't get a word in edgewise.

During breakfast this morning I overheard another strange conversation between Mike Totley and Connie Patterson. They were sitting on a rock in the shade of an overhang, and they didn't know it but I was close by on the opposite side of a big boulder.

Mike said in a low voice, 'You might have warned me you were coming,' and she said she'd tried to contact him by email. He said something about travelling around too much to catch up with it and she said, 'That's a pity. When we met the other day you gaped like a dead fish. People will have guessed we know each other. We'd better agree on a story.'

At that point some kind of insect got into my shirt. I was afraid it might be a scorpion and tried to remove it. They must have heard me shuffling around because their conversation suddenly stopped. I intend to keep my eyes and ears open for any further light on this mystery. Mike always seems uneasy when Miss Patterson is around. Perhaps they've had some kind of unwholesome relationship. How can we expect to experience God's blessing on our endeavours if there's guilt within the group? This probably accounts for the poor results so far – only a few more bits of broken pottery today. I'm reminded of the failure which the sin of Achan brought upon the Israelites.

Bowel movements still dandy.

Day 3 (Fri. 5 May)

I suspect Miss (or, as she prefers, Ms.) Patterson is even further from the kingdom of heaven than Mike Totley. She joined our cave team for breakfast again and when we were discussing the morning's communal devotions (led by Dr. Sinnet with a reading from Proverbs 7) she said she thought the Bible was 'hopelessly sexist'.

Mike Totley said, 'You should try the Song of Solomon. Even feminist critics agree that's a non-sexist text, celebrating gender equality through its portrayal of lovemaking.'

Ms. Patterson lapped up this nonsense and said she would read the Song of Solomon as soon as she could get hold of a Bible. I saw a chance to steer her away from error and offered her my own – *The Disciple's Amplified and Annotated Life-Guidance Study Bible*, with helpful comments by that great expositor Dr. Kermit Bender on every page. I just had time to get it from my tent before we set off back to our different caves. This group is turning out to be quite a mission field. Fortunately I have with me Thurber Prewett's fine book, *Lost Sheep and How to Catch Them in the Fishing Net of Truth*, which is full of advice for this kind of situation.

During the second half of the morning we at last made a significant discovery in our cave...

2

In the farthest chamber of Cave C, Mike calls for more lights. While the volunteers position them he removes his helmet and wipes his brow with a bandanna which he wears for this purpose. He is squatting in a pit that he and Dave Hirschfeld have spent two hours clearing of stones and earth. Now their efforts are rewarded by a tuft of rope protruding from the infill.

'What the heck is that?' asks Dave, rejoining Mike in the hole.

Mike carefully removes a little more earth with a trowel. Something bulky, woven from rushes or palm-leaves, becomes visible.

'A basket,' says Mike.

Effin Clinger is instantly on hand with a basket.

'No, Effin, I don't *need* a basket. I meant *this* is a basket. Tied up with a rope.'

Alice Wesson voices the obvious question. 'Any idea what might be inside it?'

'Documents, if we're lucky,' says Mike, carefully brushing away more of the dark, dusty earth. 'Or perhaps a collection of bronze vessels. We'll soon know.'

But it takes another painstaking hour to expose the basket completely. Disregarding the practice of his colleagues Mike allows each volunteer to take a turn at removing the earth with small trowels and brushes. In his view, people learn best from hands-on experience. He draws the line, however, at Clinger's request to try out a variety of inappropriate dental implements.

Excitement grows among the little group until finally the basket sits exposed at the bottom of the recess. The silence is profound as Mike slides his hands around the bulging shape and carefully raises it. The basket's weight confirms his suspicions. He looks down at the bottom of the hole to see whether anything remains and notices two small, drab discs. Handing the basket to Dave he stoops to examine them. When he straightens up he is holding the discs in the palm of his hand. For a moment, attention is diverted from the mysterious basket.

'Coins,' he announces. 'They need cleaning before we can read them, but I'm pretty sure they'll turn out to be from Bar-Kokhba's revolt.'

That afternoon the basket, a piece of palm-frond rope and several bronze objects are the source of intense excitement and speculation in the camp. There are a dozen metal items in all: six jugs, five bowls and a shovel.

'What I don't understand,' says Alice Wesson, 'is how Mike guessed what was in the basket before we'd even uncovered it. He said it might contain a collection of bronze vessels, and it did!'

Everyone looks at Mike.

'It was a simple deduction, really. In 1960 Yadin found baskets like this in the Nahal Hever caves. One of them, with a rope attached to it, contained a cache of bronze vessels. They were all items used in pagan worship, probably looted from a Roman temple by Bar-Kokhba's men. Because our find was concealed in the same way as Yadin's I realised it might be more of the same booty. I suspect the rope was originally much longer and was used to haul the basket up the cliffs. When they'd got it to the cave someone cut the rope because they couldn't be bothered to untie the knots.'

'Very clever,' says Sinnet. 'But totally wrong, I'm afraid, because these vessels aren't from a pagan temple. They're from the Jewish Temple in Jerusalem, hidden in the first century on the eve of its destruction. My friends, we could be on the brink of one of the greatest discoveries of all time!'

3

When everyone had returned to the Centre on Friday, Chuck Sinnet called a special meeting of supervisors for Saturday evening. Although Sinnet left the purpose of the meeting vague, Mike had no doubt what it would be about. Their disagreement over the bronze objects from Cave C had spawned a lively debate and Sinnet wanted the matter cleared up.

In preparation for the meeting Mike subjected all the associated finds – the coins and a large collection of potsherds – to a careful examination, missing Saturday's field trip to Masada in order to complete the job. After many hours in the pottery room he was in possession of almost all the evidence he needed. By the start of dinner he had just one loose end to tie up, and hoped a quick visit to the library between the meal and Sinnet's meeting would supply the last link in the chain of his argument. Unfortunately the book he wanted had been wrongly shelved and it took him longer than expected to find it. He arrived at Sinnet's study five minutes late. He gave a token knock on the door and rushed in.

Sinnet, Parbunkel and Talia Schluter were seated around a table on which the disputed bronze objects were neatly arranged on a blue cloth.

'At last!' said Sinnet. 'You've just wasted fifteen minutes of valuable time, Mike.'

Mike checked his watch.

'With respect, I'm exactly five minutes late, Chuck. For which I sincerely apologise. I was looking for this book...'

'But those five minutes have to be multiplied by the number of people you've kept waiting. Now, without wasting any more time may we open the meeting in prayer?'

Silenced by piety, Mike took the seat provided for him and bowed his head. Sinnet clenched his eyes and prayed with solemn fervour.

'Lord, you have promised to lead your people into all truth. So lead us now, and teach us to be of one mind, united in your Spirit. Amen.'

'In my opinion,' Sinnet continued, snapping out of prayer mode as suddenly as he'd snapped into it, 'it's vital that we have a full discussion on the nature of this discovery from Cave C in order to come to a consensus and end the rabid speculation among the volunteers.'

Mike sighed audibly. In his view, the only person guilty of rabid speculation was Sinnet.

'You have something to say, Mike?'

'I hope you'll give me time to restate my case in detail. I do have some additional evidence to bring. That's why I was late. I was finding...'

'Of course, you'll get your chance. But let me begin with my own case, then you can reply. Just take a close look at this.'

Sinnet picked up the bronze shovel and held it reverently. It had a rectangular pan measuring about fifteen centimetres wide and twenty centimetres long, and an ornate handle of the same length. The corners of the pan nearest the handle had two round cups attached, each about six centimetres in diameter.

'An incense shovel,' said Sinnet. 'The incense was placed in the cups, like so; and hot coals in the pan, like so. It's exactly what a priest would have used to make the daily offerings at the Altar of Incense in the Jewish Temple. After transferring hot coals from the Altar of Burnt Offerings to the Altar of Incense, pinches of incense could be taken from the cups and sprinkled over the coals, like so.' He mimed the action. 'To that I add another piece of evidence: according to Zelophehad Smith's decipherment of the Copper Scroll we should find objects from the Temple concealed in one or more of the Nahal Shuhan caves. So I conclude that this shovel, and the other items buried with it, came from the Temple in Jerusalem and were hidden just before its destruction.' Sinnet carefully placed the shovel back on the table. 'Now, what's your counter-argument, Mike?'

Mike closed his eyes for a few seconds to calm himself and to gather his thoughts.

'I have four points in favour of my interpretation. The first concerns the close parallel with Yadin's hoard from Nahal Hever, which I mentioned yesterday at the wadi. As I'm sure you know, the bronze items discovered by Yadin included a shovel almost identical to this one. The whole cache belonged to the time of Bar-Kokhba and everyone agrees they were pagan cultic implements looted from a Roman temple. I see no reason to draw a different conclusion in this case. Secondly, the pottery from Cave C. I've spent today going through every sherd discovered so far and I'm confident it's all second century. There's nothing to suggest that Cave C was entered at the time of the First Jewish Revolt. The same applies, incidentally, to the pottery from Cave B.'

Mike looked to Tally Schluter for support but she kept her eyes fixed on the table and said nothing.

'Thirdly, the coins. Now that Leo has given them the formic acid treatment, it's clear they're silver dinars inscribed with the date "Year Two of the Freedom of Israel". In other words, they date from Bar-Kokhba's revolt. Since they were under the basket, the basket and its contents can't have been placed in the pit earlier than the coins.'

At this point Leo Parbunkel said sheepishly, 'If I might make a... um... have you considered the possibility, Mike, that the coins might have dropped to the bottom of the hole from above the basket while the basket was being excavated?'

'And let's remember,' added Sinnet, impatient with Parbunkel's half-hearted attack, 'that you unwisely allowed your volunteers to excavate that basket; in those circumstances anything could have happened. I'm surprised you didn't find the ring-pulls from a few Coke cans down that hole!'

Parbunkel laughed loudly at this, hoping a spot of jollity might defuse the growing tension, but it didn't and his laughter died an embarrassing death.

'That remark was unjustified,' said Mike. 'I supervised every second of that operation and I personally removed the basket from the hole. The coins were underneath it, pressed into the earth by its weight.'

There was an uncomfortable silence before Sinnet asked, 'You have a fourth point?'

'Yes. I've consulted the *Mishnah*.' Mike lifted the large book from his knees and placed it open on the table. 'As I expect you all know, the *Mishnah* is a compilation of Jewish regulations produced in the second century, but it contains older material, some of it dating back to when the Temple was standing. One section describes in detail how offerings were made at the Altar of Incense. It's quite long, so I won't bore you by reading it out, but I recommend that you all look at it carefully. I'm afraid it doesn't support Chuck's idea of how the incense was offered. It mentions hot cinders being carried in a shovel from the main altar, but it says the incense was brought in a separate golden ladle. You see my point? The shovel used in the Temple can't have had incense cups attached to it.'

An even longer silence followed this disclosure, during which all eyes turned to Sinnet.

'Well,' he said, with discernible discomfort, 'that sounds convincing on the face of it, but I'm sure I don't need to remind a fine scholar like you, Mike, that the interpretation of the *Mishnah* is a complex matter. It may contain an idealised picture of the past rather than a record of how things were actually done in the time of the Temple. As for the pottery and the coins, there are so many uncertainties... circumstantial evidence at best.'

Mike closed the *Mishnah* with a slam that combined anger with resignation.

Chapter Twelve

1

On the north side of the Old City of Jerusalem, not far beyond the medieval walls, stands a prominent scarp of rock. Today it is partially concealed by buildings and a bus depot but in the nineteenth century it was a bare and striking feature. In 1883 General Charles Gordon – later of Khartoum – championed the view, first proposed at least thirty years earlier, that this hillock was none other than Golgotha or Calvary, the site of Christ's crucifixion.

While in Jerusalem, Gordon was befriended by a group of Christians known as the American Colony, effectively an end-time sect whose members devoted themselves to missionary work and acts of charity while awaiting Christ's return. They were led by a family called the Spaffords who owned a house near the Damascus Gate. The flat roof of the Spafford residence gave a fine view of the rocky scarp and there Gordon liked to sit, weaving mystical speculations around his favoured hillock.

At the foot of the scarp and hewn out of the rock stood an ancient tomb, discovered in the 1860s. General Gordon seems to have been the first to suggest that this was the tomb from which Christ had risen from the dead. Although Gordon himself never insisted on the identification, interest in the ancient sepulchre grew and in 1894 a group of English Protestants bought the land which fronted it, turning it into a place for meditation and prayer. Now known as the Garden Tomb, but sometimes mistakenly called Gordon's Tomb, this peaceful spot provides the perfect visual aid for Christians wanting to contemplate the events of the first Easter. In fact this is the only value of the place, for its archaeological credentials are non-existent. Those seeking the authentic tomb of Christ must visit the Church of the Holy

Sepulchre; it may be an unappealing pile, but its pedigree is impeccable.

Each Sunday morning a service of worship is held at the Garden Tomb, often with a visiting preacher from the USA, and Sinnet and Parbunkel decided the Nahal Shuhan expedition would benefit spiritually from regular attendance. Mike was happy to overlook the fact that the place was an archaeological non-starter, and did his best to enter into the spirit of the service. But his attention wandered, preoccupied with Sinnet's clumsy intellectual bullying and abuse of evidence. There had to be a hidden agenda behind it but he couldn't imagine what it was.

After the service Mike offered to take interested members of the team on a walk around the ramparts of the Old City walls. Some had already arranged to go to Bethlehem with Chuck Sinnet, and others preferred to visit the Rockefeller Museum, but four people said they would love to come: Effin Clinger, Dave Hirschfeld, Connie Patterson and Cecilia Hope-Parsons. Mrs Hope-Parsons, a middle-aged Englishwoman from Parbunkel's team, shared both a room and tent with Connie and they were fast becoming friends.

It was a beautiful, blue-golden morning and the air hadn't yet lost its freshness. Swifts wheeled and careered overhead, their shrill cries piercing the sound of traffic and the shouts of street vendors. Mike led the way through the bustling shade of the Damascus Gate to where a small booth sold tickets for the rampart walk. At that point Mrs Hope-Parsons looked up at the walls and said she wasn't sure this was a good idea after all; she felt slightly weary and thought it might be better to save her energy for the dig. Effin Clinger immediately offered to escort her to the bazaars to find a nice place that served coffee. Then Dave said he'd just remembered he was expecting a phone call from Beer Sheva and had to get back to the Centre. So all three made their apologies and melted away into the melange of tourists and souvenir sellers. Mike had been dreading a moment like this. Until now he'd managed to avoid being alone with Connie for more than a few minutes.

He was about to suggest they postponed the walk until next Sunday, in the hope that more people might be able to come, when Connie produced some shekels and bought two tickets.

'This is on me,' she said brightly. 'You can buy me some falafel later. Lead the way, professor, and tell me all about this place.'

So they climbed the narrow steps and set off along the ramparts heading south. Fortunately for Mike there was no shortage of things he could talk about. The remains of more than four thousand years of history lay all around, arranged in a confusing bricolage. And whenever he walked the ramparts of the Old City Mike had a powerful awareness, peculiar to an archaeologist who deals in stratified remains, of history accumulating vertically, centuries embodied in centimetres, extending down beneath those ancient walls through even more ancient stones and earth. The present is never without roots but there they twist through portentous times and awesome depths.

He began with Suliman the Magnificent, Ottoman builder of the walls, who restored a dilapidated Jerusalem in the sixteenth century. He explained how the occupied area had shifted over time so that Suliman's walls didn't enclose the same Jerusalem which Jesus knew, and the site of King David's capital lay outside them altogether. The citadel by the Jaffa Gate, known as the Tower of David, therefore had nothing to do with David; it was one of those misattributions in which Jerusalem seems to specialise.

At the Jaffa Gate they descended to street level to find a café that sold freshly squeezed orange juice. Mike's flow of chatter temporarily dried up; he could no longer escape into history and small talk deserted him. Connie was also unusually quiet; she seemed content to stroll at his side, looking cool and relaxed, taking in the sights and sounds of the busy bazaars.

When they ordered drinks at a stall in David Street the owner offered to buy Connie from Mike for thirty camels. He refused and the price rose to forty, eventually to fifty. Mike still shook his head.

The man laughed loudly and said, 'Good choice! Very lucky man!' If only, thought Mike.

They finished their drinks and returned to the wall.

As they climbed the steps Connie asked, 'Was that guy trying to buy me for a packet of cigarettes?'

'Good grief, no!' said Mike. 'Not Camel *cigarettes*; the real thing – those big animals with humps, bad teeth and a permanent smell of old socks.'

'No kidding? And is fifty camels a good price for a woman?'

'I think so. One has to allow for inflation, of course, but it's certainly the most I've ever been offered.'

'So what happened to your other women?'

'Sold them. I own the biggest herd of camels in Whitfield.'

'You don't say! So why didn't you sell me?'

Mike paused. In different circumstances this line of banter would have had excellent potential. As it was, he saw no point in pursuing it.

'No room for any more camels. Now, on our left is the Armenian Quarter, once the site of Herod the Great's palace. It had gardens, fountains and luxurious apartments, and it stretched from here all the way back to the citadel...'

Travelling east with the Mount of Olives directly ahead they soon reached the Jewish Quarter, into which they descended near the Dung Gate. By now Mike was concerned that Connie might be suffering from a surfeit of sightseeing. He offered to stop but her appetite was insatiable. So they entered the enclosure of the Temple Mount and savoured its spacious tranquillity.

'It's beautiful,' said Connie, after some moments in silent contemplation. 'So very beautiful. Almost surreal.'

'Yes, isn't it? Its name in Arabic is the Haram esh-Sharif, the Noble Sanctuary, which suits it perfectly.'

Through a row of soaring arches they admired the view of the Mount of Olives, its rocky slopes cloaked by olive groves and dark spires of cypress. Mike pointed out the two contenders for the Garden of Gethsemane, and the impressive monuments known as Absalom's Pillar – nothing to do with Absalom – and the Tomb of Zachariah – nothing to do with Zachariah. Then Connie turned to face the graceful, golden-crowned octagon of the Dome of the Rock.

'I especially like the mosque,' she said. 'You don't appreciate how perfect its proportions are until you get up here.'

'One of my favourite buildings,' said Mike, 'a gem of Islamic architecture. But strictly speaking it's not so much a mosque as a shrine – in fact the oldest major shrine in the Islamic world. I thought you might've known all about it, in view of your research into Islam.'

'But I've been concentrating on modern fundamentalism, remember. Tell me more.'

'A caliph called Abd al-Malik built it in the seventh century. The traditional reason is that he wanted to commemorate Mohammed's ascent into heaven, but it's actually a monumental piece of propaganda proclaiming the superiority of Islam over Christianity and Judaism. Inside the dome there's an inscription urging people to reject the divinity of Christ.'

'So that puts the Christians in their place. What about the Jews?'

'Well, for over a thousand years this was the site of the Jewish Temple. In fact this huge platform we're standing on was built by Herod the Great to give the Temple a more impressive setting.'

'So building the shrine here was like saying Islam had superseded Judaism?'

'Exactly!'

They circled the Dome of the Rock to admire its exquisite mosaics. As they walked around its western side, Mike fell silent. For the last two days his thoughts had been so dominated by Sinnet's extraordinary claims that he'd almost forgotten Parbunkel's equally bizarre story of the wooden box. Now it came back to him with a jolt; if the story were true, the underground passage he'd seen in virtual reality must lie directly beneath his feet.

'Mike, can you hear me? I asked how old that is.'

'The colonnade? Fourteenth or fifteenth century, I think. Definitely Mameluke.'

'Are you okay, Mike? You seem…'

'Yes, fine, thanks. Shall we go down to the Western Wall?'

They descended the ramp from the Moor's Gate to the spacious esplanade by the wall, where Jewish men and women were praying in their respective enclosures.

'It's sometimes called the Wailing Wall,' Mike explained, 'because Jews used to come here to lament the destruction of the Temple. But now they're trying to shake off its dismal associations by calling it simply the Western Wall. It's the holiest site in Jewish tradition.'

'Why don't they pray on the Temple Mount itself?'

'There's a rabbinical ruling that no one should set foot there, lest they defile the Holy of Holies. That was the innermost part of the Temple, so sacred it could only be entered once a year on the Day of Atonement, and then only by the High Priest. Originally it housed the Ark of the Covenant, but that was lost when the Babylonians destroyed the First Temple. In the Second Temple, the Holy of Holies was just an empty chamber.'

'I still don't see why the whole of the Temple Mount should be a no-go area.'

'Because nobody knows for sure where the Holy of Holies stood. There's a good chance the site is now covered by the Dome of the Rock, but we can't be certain. So to be on the safe side the whole area was declared out of bounds. In practice, of course, the rule is academic. Gentiles and liberal Jews both ignore it.'

Mike watched the black-coated Hasidic men at their prayers, rocking back and forth from the waist, the fronts of their broad-brimmed hats lightly kissing the wall with each rapid bow.

'Just look at the fervour of those people! Such spiritual intensity, and so natural! I wish I could pray with energy like theirs.'

'I just wish I was sure there was someone to pray to,' said Connie. 'Don't you ever have doubts, Mike?'

'Of course. Doubts are the growing pains of faith.'

'Who said that?'

'I did.'

'I meant isn't it a quote from somebody?'

'Not so far as I know. I do have an original thought every now and then.'

'Oh, sure. It just sounded... well, uncharacteristically pithy.'

Mike was wondering whether he should expand on the subject in the hope of saying something helpful, when he noticed a trickle of people entering a gate on the north side of the esplanade.

'That must be the entrance!' he exclaimed. 'Let's go!'

'The entrance to what?'

'The Western Wall tunnel! Come on!' Mike headed for the gate at a rapid clip, with Connie running to catch up.

Beyond the entrance they took a right turn and passed through various subterranean rooms in which Mike showed no interest, though other visitors seemed totally engrossed. Eventually Mike stopped in a high, narrow passage.

'This is it! We're in the tunnel. It runs from here northwards along the western side of the Temple Mount. These big stones were part of the retaining wall for Herod's platform. I've never been down here before, but we should be able to see... yes, here it is! See this stone? It's almost thirteen metres long and weighs over four hundred tons. No one's sure how Herod's engineers moved it into place.'

Connie let out a low whistle as she walked the length of the gigantic stone. Meanwhile Mike moved further into the tunnel. He stopped opposite an arched recess in the face of the wall and stared at it. This was what he'd been hoping to find.

'Seen something interesting?' asked Connie.

'Er... no. No, not really.' His answer sounded evasive, not like Mike at all.

'Oh, come on, Mike! You're staring like you've just made some amazing discovery.'

'Well, I meant... it's not interesting to most people.' Mike reached out to touch the surface of the wall within the recess. Unlike the rest of the wall, this was not masonry but concrete. 'Two thousand years ago there was a gate into the Temple courts here. People could walk in from the street, along an underground passage and up a staircase to the top of the platform. It's been blocked since the Crusader period.'

But part of the concrete looked fresh. So at least that part of Parbunkel's story was true; Warren's Gate had recently been opened and resealed. But what about the vaults, the cistern and the box? Here in the tunnel he felt tantalisingly close to an answer, and in a sense he was: not far beyond that wall lay tangible evidence which would either prove or disprove Parbunkel's claims.

Mike stepped over a metal barrier, spread both hands on the concrete and placed his forehead against its rough surface. A vague idea that Parbunkel's story and Sinnet's theory about the bronze vessels might be parts of a single web of deceit – twin products of a bizarre Templemania – arose dimly in the back of his mind. But try as he might, he could not drag it out of the shadows to examine it clearly.

Connie watched Mike with growing apprehension. Other visitors to the tunnel looked at him strangely as they walked past, but said nothing. Perhaps they assumed he was a Jew, praying fervently towards the former Holy of Holies. Connie took a step closer and put an arm around him.

'What's the matter, Mike? What are you doing?'

Mike stepped back over the barrier. He put one hand to his forehead and felt the imprint of the uneven surface.

'Sorry. I think I need to get out of here.'

Connie put her arm through his and they walked quickly to the exit. Outside in the sunlight she held his hand and looked at him with tender concern. As their eyes met, Mike slipped further into confusion.

'What's wrong, Mike?'

Too many things: his unrequited feelings for Connie; his doubts about Parbunkel; his loss of confidence in Sinnet…

'Do you want to talk about it?' asked Connie.

But it wasn't that simple. There was no point in confessing he loved her; he'd given his word not to divulge Parbunkel's story about the box; and he could hardly expect Connie to understand the ramifications of last night's confrontation with Sinnet.

'If you think it's something I wouldn't understand,' Connie persisted, 'I guess you might be right; but I wish you'd let me try.'

Mike was still looking into her eyes.

With a strange sense of distance he heard himself say, 'Okay, if you're sure.'

'Sure I'm sure, if it'll help.'

Mike felt an unexpected wave of relief break over him.

'Then how about eating while we talk? I could do with some food.'

2

At Mike's suggestion they headed for the bazaars of the Muslim Quarter. The narrow streets were cool and dim, so overhung with awnings and protruding upper storeys that only a slender stripe of sunlight reached the pavement. They found an empty table in a small café and ordered iced beers, falafel and coffee. Mike rapidly downed half his beer and then began.

'Well, as you must have gathered on Friday, Chuck Sinnet and I don't see eye to eye over the bronze objects I discovered. I expect you heard him say they all came from the Jewish Temple?'

'Loud and clear. He thinks they were brought from Jerusalem and hidden in the cave for protection shortly before the Temple was destroyed by the Romans.'

'Yes. But if he's right the associated finds should all be first century – and they're not; they're second century.'

'From the time of Bar-Kokhba's revolt?'

'Exactly. The coins alone are conclusive, because we know the exact year they were minted.'

'AD 133,' said Connie.

'That's right, and... How on earth did you know that?'

Connie put down her glass and leaned forward.

'I talked to Dr Parbunkel during yesterday's trip to Masada. He said he'd cleaned them on Friday night.'

'I see. Well, the coins were under the basket so the hoard can't have been squirreled away before AD 133.'

They were served with falafel nestling in pockets of warm Arab bread, along with chopped tomato and cucumber and a tahini cream salad.

'Sounds like a knock down argument,' said Connie. 'So what does Sinnet say?'

While Connie ate, Mike outlined the previous evening's exchanges.

'The outcome was a stalemate. I refused to recant my alleged heresy, but in effect the truth has been sidelined in favour of a wacky theory without a shred of evidence to support it.'

'But this is incredible! Didn't Parbunkel and Tally Schluter support you?'

'They'd already been whipped into line by Sinnet. It wasn't exactly a free vote.'

The strong black coffee arrived. Connie took an appreciative sip and set her cup down again.

'And what about this Smith guy and the Copper Scroll?'

Mike was taken aback. He'd deliberately omitted that detail from his account lest it confuse the issue. 'Good grief! You know about that, too?'

'Sure. Sinnet talks about it when we're digging. Seems to put a lot of faith in it. I assume you don't agree?'

'No.'

'Okay, you'd better fill me in on it. But finish your falafel before it goes cold.'

Mike did so and then continued.

'The Copper Scroll is a very strange document, probably the most mystifying of the Dead Sea Scrolls. It has sixty-four entries arranged in twelve columns of Hebrew script, describing locations where huge amounts of gold, silver and other precious things are supposed to be hidden. Unfortunately its directions are so useless no one has ever found a single cache. It says things like, "In the cave of the column with two entrances…," and "In the tomb in the stream at the approach from Jericho…," and so on. Most of the places can't be identified and the few that can have produced nothing. Some people think the whole thing is the work of a deranged mind, especially as the silver and gold would total over two hundred tons.'

'Gosh! That's an incredible amount!'

'Not in the literal sense of the word. One place which might have owned that much is the treasury of the Jerusalem Temple, which functioned a bit like a bank. If the Scroll is factual it could be an inventory of things removed from the Temple in the years leading up to its destruction.'

'Which is what Sinnet believes.'

'Yes, and it's a plausible theory. The Scroll itself hints at some connection with the Temple because it mentions things like sacred vessels, offerings and vestments. But Sinnet departs from mainstream scholarship when he combines this theory with Smith's.'

'So Smith isn't a mainstream academic?'

'Goodness, no! Nor an archaeologist. Just a dilettante who knows Hebrew. As you might have gathered, he thinks the Scroll is deliberately obscure and conceals the truth by means of a cipher.'

'And is that unreasonable?'

'Not in itself. It would explain why the text is so difficult to understand, and it might account for some Greek letters scattered mysteriously through the first four columns.'

'So, where's the problem?'

Mike finished his beer and started on the coffee. Looking at Connie over his raised cup he said, 'Are you sure you want to hear all this?'

'Of course! You can't stop now. I sense we're just getting to the crux.'

'Okay. Did I mention last November that I'd met a convinced Baconian on my way to Washington?'

'A guy who thought Francis Bacon wrote Shakespeare? I vaguely remember it. You're not going to tell me Bacon wrote the Copper Scroll as well?'

'Sillier things have been suggested, but no. This chap believed there were all kinds of ciphers scattered through the plays, containing cryptic allusions to Bacon. When I got back home I mentioned the theory to a colleague in our English department and she lent me a book on the Bacon–Shakespeare controversy by a couple of cryptologists – experts in codes and ciphers. They blow the whole theory out of the water.'

'That's nice,' said Connie. 'So I don't need to amend the title page of my *Complete Works of Shakespeare*. Now can we please get back to the Copper Scroll? I'm still waiting to hear what you've got against Smith.'

'But this is all relevant! You see, I read Smith's theory just after reading this book about the Baconian ciphers. It didn't take much lateral thinking to see that Smith's approach to the Copper Scroll has a lot in common with the Baconian's approach to Shakespeare. Both leap on any strange spellings as indications of ciphers and both indulge in numerology. Most importantly, both have an appearance of reason and logic, but their methods are fatally flawed.'

'You'll have to more explicit, Mike.'

'Well, in deciding whether or not a decipherment is valid, a cryptologist looks for two things. Firstly, the solution should be in language which is acceptable and coherent; mere gibberish won't do. Smith's results survive that test inasmuch as they refer, in passable Hebrew, to places we know existed. The crunch comes with the second criterion: that the keys should never be ambiguous. Basically that means…'

'…that the decipherment must be free from arbitrary decisions, so that several cryptologists, working independently with the same key on the same text, will all reach the same answer.'

Mike was amazed. Connie appeared to have read his mind.

'How the hell…?'

'Cryptanalysis was part of my CIA training.'

Mike continued to stare.

'Carry on, Mike, I'm truly fascinated.'

'Well, er… where was I?'

'I think you were about to say that Smith's decipherment won't wash, because it involves too much latitude on the part of the decipherer.'

'Exactly. I couldn't have put it better.'

'So how does it work?'

'It's all to do with gematria – a system for assigning numerical values to Hebrew words. The letters of the Hebrew alphabet also serve as numerals, so any Hebrew word or phrase can be given a numerical value by adding up the value of its letters. Smith takes a phrase describing the location of a cache, works out the total value of its letters, then looks for a substitute phrase with the same value. In most cases we're talking pretty big numbers, so the scope for finding alternative instructions is quite wide. But in case that isn't latitude enough he creates a bit more. Remember I mentioned some Greek letters in the first four columns? Smith thinks we're supposed to assume more Greek letters in similar places in the other eight columns as well. He says they indicate that the numerical value of the equivalent Hebrew letters should be added or subtracted – whichever suits his purpose at that point – from the lines where they occur.'

'I get it: that gives him the liberty to modify any numerical values he can't make use of in their raw state.'

'Precisely! Or in Smith's case, *imprecisely*. The procedure looks exact because it involves number-crunching, but in fact his solutions are completely arbitrary.'

'So, do you think he's a fraud?'

'No, just deluded, carried away by his own ingenuity – numerologically inebriate.'

They finished their coffee in silence. Then Connie said, 'Have you confronted Sinnet with all this?'

'No point. His critical faculties have taken a holiday.'

'How about using a computer to show that Smith's approach can generate lots of alternatives? That would conclusively invalidate it. Sinnet would *have* to admit it was worthless.'

'I'm afraid I wouldn't know where to begin.'

'But I would! You'd have to provide me with the crucial piece of text and the numerical values of the Hebrew letters. And for a database I'd need a catalogue of permissible Hebrew words and constructions.'

'There are complete concordances of the Old Testament and the Dead Sea Scrolls…'

'Great! Did you bring your copy of Smith's book to Israel?'

'No, but there's sure to be one at the Centre.'

Mike stared thoughtfully at the sweet sludge in the bottom of his cup. He was impressed by Connie's idea but he still wasn't sure if the effect on Sinnet would be worth all the effort.

'Look, Connie, I don't want to sound ungrateful, and I'm sure your results would convince any reasonable person, but Sinnet isn't reasonable. It might all be a waste of time.'

'But it's worth a try,' said Connie. Suddenly smiling, she added, 'You know, I'd almost forgotten how conversations with you could make my mind reel.'

'I'm sorry.'

'Don't apologise. It's exhilarating. Who else could get from a Dead Sea Scroll to Shakespeare and back in a few sentences?'

'You're sure you don't wish you'd gone to Bethlehem with Sinnet, or to the Rockefeller Museum with the others?'

'No way! Perhaps we could do Bethlehem another day. If you recommend it, that is.'

'Oh, yes. The Church of the Nativity has mosaics dating back to the fourth century. In the seventh century it escaped destruction by the Persians because one mosaic depicted the wise men in Persian dress. But there I go again! I'll try to shut up for a while.'

'Wise men from the East,' mused Connie. 'And this morning it's been visited by fools from the West.'

Mike laughed and realised he'd passed a watershed. He was learning to relax in Connie's company.

'Thanks for getting me to talk. And for understanding.'

'My pleasure.' After a pause Connie added, 'But there's something else bothering you, isn't there?'

Mike hadn't realised he was so transparent. 'Yes. But I'm afraid I can't... I gave someone my word, you see.'

This wasn't the answer Connie had expected or hoped for. With her fingertips she silently rearranged a few breadcrumbs on her plate.

'Penny for your thoughts?' said Mike, afraid he might have offended her.

Connie reached across the table and placed her hands on his.

'Listen, Mike, when...' Then she hesitated.

'Yes?'

'No. This isn't a good time. It'll keep.' She sat back, smiled, and in an altogether different tone of voice said, 'Hey, shall we finish the ramparts?'

'If you like. We could get back on at St Stephen's Gate.'

'Then let's do it!'

3

At sunset that evening Sinnet parked his Land Rover in a cul-de-sac near the King David Hotel. After a few minutes a bulky, middle-aged man approached. He wore a shabby white suit and had a half-smoked cigarette dangling from the corner of his mouth. Stopping by the Land Rover he looked around, discarded the cigarette and buttoned his jacket over his spreading waistline. Then he opened the passenger door and climbed in. His left eye was bloodshot.

'Your eye is bloodshot,' said Sinnet.

'I know. Had a small accident. It's okay.'

'So, did you see anything?'

'He went with four others to the Damascus Gate. Then three of them went off.'

'Who stayed? Was it Hirschfeld?'

'No. A girl. Height about five eight. Long hair in a French plait. Brunette. She was wearing a cream cotton top and a pleated skirt in pale brown. Her sandals were brown leather with…'

'Okay, okay. I didn't hire you to be a fashion correspondent. I know the girl you're describing. What did they do?'

'They walked the ramparts as far as Jaffa Gate, came down, bought drinks in David Street. I took a picture.' The fat man passed Sinnet a photograph of Mike and Connie by the drinks stall.

'You're sure they didn't see you take this?'

'Of course they didn't. The Old City is full of tourists pointing cameras in every direction. By the way, notice how I've got the light coming down between those awnings. Really captures the atmosphere of the bazaars, don't you think?'

'I didn't hire you to produce postcards of the Old City either.' Sinnet handed back the photograph. 'What did they do next?'

'Went back to Jaffa Gate, walked the ramparts some more, came down again and did the Temple Mount, the Western Wall and the tunnel. Then to a café in the Muslim Quarter for lunch. I managed to get a table next to theirs. The girl was wearing a nice perfume, either L'Air du Temps or…'

'Yes, yes. Could we keep to the important stuff? I haven't got all night.'

'Okay. They had falafel and salad. I did too, as a matter of fact, and it was very good, a nice, distinctive flavour, made with…'

'Could we skip the Food and Drink section as well? Just tell me what they talked about.'

The man flicked through a small, dog-eared notebook.

'It wasn't easy to overhear. Totley did most of the talking and he was further away from me. Something about buried treasure – silver and gold. After that he talked about bacon.'

'Bacon? Are you sure?' Quite apart from its lack of connection with hidden treasure, bacon seemed an ill-chosen topic for a lunchtime conversation in the Muslim Quarter.

'That's right. I could hear the girl better but she said a lot less. Said she worked for the CIA.'

'What?'

The man turned a grubby page.

'She said something – I didn't catch the word – had been part of her CIA training.'

Sinnet stroked his chin.

'Interesting. Anything else?'

'She said some people who'd gone to Bethlehem were fools.'

'I see.'

'Soon after that they got up and left. I wasn't able to follow because that was when I had the accident. Stuck a Camel in my eye.'

'A camel?' said Sinnet, his imagination struggling with this unexpected scenario.

'Yeah. I'd just got a pack of Camels out of my pocket when the girl's voice went very soft, so I moved my chair back to get closer. Just as I took a cigarette out of the pack and started to put it in my mouth she moved *her* chair back to stand up. It jogged me and I poked myself in the eye with the cigarette. Very painful.'

'One of the dangers of smoking,' said Sinnet. 'You should give it up.'

'Would you like to see any more pictures? I got a really nice shot when they were by the Western Wall plaza. Look, you can just see the Dome of the Rock over the top of the wall. Looks especially nice against the blue sky. Then there's this one…'

'No, thanks.'

'You want me to watch Totley again?'

'I'll let you know.'

As soon as the man had gone Sinnet drove back to the Centre and went straight to bed. But he had much on his mind and real sleep eluded him. Instead he lay stranded on the shoreline between waking and sleeping, where strange but half-familiar phrases drifted in and out of his thoughts: 'It is easier for a camel to go through the eye…' What came next? Whose eye? 'First cast the camel out of thine own eye, and then thou shalt see clearly…' That didn't sound right. But he certainly needed to see clearly. At the moment everything was far from clear, and that troubled him intensely.

4

Mike was also too restless to sleep. He sat alone reading a book in the coffee lounge, waiting for tiredness to creep over him. Just as sleep was beginning to seem viable Tally Schluter put her head round the door. She withdrew as soon as she saw Mike was alone but he called her back.

'Tally, I've been hoping for a quick word. Would you mind? It won't take a minute.'

'Okay. Fire away.' But she sat down with obvious reluctance.

'It's about last night's meeting. I'd like to hear your honest opinion on the pottery. Do you really think it's all first century?'

'Well, you know the problem with pottery, Mike.' Her ponytail was hanging in front of her left shoulder and to avoid looking at Mike she examined it for split ends while she talked. 'Forms don't change overnight to mark the beginning of a new historical era; they evolve slowly, each merging into its successor. It's often hard to assign sherds with confidence.'

'True, but there are plenty of clear diagnostic pieces in our corpus. Surely you can see where the evidence points? Why didn't you back me up against Sinnet?'

'Mike, I know Chuck Sinnet better than you do. His insights are often intuitive. It isn't always easy for onlookers to understand how he reaches his conclusions. But he's a brilliant man. Leo and I have both learnt to respect his opinions.'

Mike noted the import of this last sentence: that it was no use trying to get Parbunkel to support him either. But he persevered.

'I'd be the last person to deny the importance of intuition, Tally, but however a conclusion is reached, if it's valid it must be possible to support it with sound reasoning and hard facts. Scholars can't go around propounding theories like Moses delivering the tablets of the Law. They should submit their views to scrutiny and debate by their peers, and that wasn't happening last night.'

'I'm sorry, but I just can't agree with you on the pottery,' said Tally, finally meeting his gaze but avoiding his argument.

'Can't, or *won't?*'

She got up from her chair.

'I really must get to bed. And I think you should do the same. We're making a very early start tomorrow. Please excuse me.'

Tally left the room and Mike went back to his book. The hope of sleep had receded again.

Chapter Thirteen

1

[Third extract from the journal of Effin L Clinger]

Day 4 (Sat. 6 May)

The first of our educational field trips – Masada. On the way I sat next to Harry Hah, the third member of Dr. Sinnet's cave team. Harry is from South Korea. His English isn't that great, but I learned that he belongs to the Yoido Full Gospel Church in Seoul – the biggest church in the world! Having Harry around is a real inspiration.

We had a great day, with only one small disaster. When we arrived at the top of Masada by cable car a few of us at the back of the group failed to hear clearly an announcement from Dr. Sinnet. He apparently told us to follow Ari, our Israeli guide, at all times, but at that stage the guide's name hadn't really registered with me and I thought he said we should follow Harry. Harry didn't understand the announcement either, and pretty soon wandered off to take video shots of the Roman siege ramp. Wilbur Wesson, Wade Brattle and myself all followed him over a wall, past a sign that said, 'DANGER! DO NOT PASS BEYOND THIS POINT!' in several languages – but apparently not Korean – and down a long, steep slope, and so got separated from the rest for at least two hours!

When we finally found them again Ari and Dr. Sinnet were very angry about our unscheduled detour. Ari said we'd been extremely irresponsible and Doc Sinnet said, 'Don't you realise you could have fallen to your deaths if you'd lost your footing?'

Harry just smiled, patted his camera and said, 'Yes, lots of footage.'

Anyway, we were all together for the emotional climax of the visit. This was when Ari told us the story from Josephus, an ancient Jewish historian, of how brave Jewish freedom fighters defending Masada against the Romans had heroically committed suicide rather than be defeated and enslaved.

Bowels fine again.

Day 5 (Sun. 7 May)

At breakfast I told Mike Totley all about the trip to Masada because he'd had to stay behind for some reason. He was real grumpy. When I told him what Ari had said about the Jewish freedom fighters' mass suicide he said, 'You've been told a load of tosh, Effin. If you read Josephus for yourself you'll find they weren't freedom fighters at all, they were Sicarii – a bunch of extremists who'd been kicked out of Jerusalem by their fellow Jews for murdering people.' When some folks are in a bad mood they don't have a good word for anyone!

All went to the Garden Tomb for morning worship. What an inspiring experience to hear the gospel preached at the very place where Christ arose from the dead!

Spent the rest of the morning with Mrs. Cecilia Hope-Parsons, the only member of the team from England apart from Mike. She is a fine lady, a widow about my age. I'm not sure about her spiritual condition; she says she's an Anglican but so is Mike Totley so this could mean just about anything.

To avoid monotony will not mention bowel movements again unless some irregularity occurs.

Day 6 (Mon. 8 May)

This morning, when we'd all assembled in camp, Dr. Sinnet explained that during the weekend the dispute over Mike Totley's big find had been resolved in favour of a first-century date, and there was no doubt at all that the objects came from the Temple in Jerusalem. He sent us off to the caves with expectations running high that we might find more of these sacred vessels.

As our team started up the track to Cave C I heard Mike Totley say to Dave Hirschfeld, 'Let's hope we find more of those old shovels; we're going to need lots of them if this carries on.'

Dave looked puzzled for a second and then said, 'Oh, I get it – to shift all the bullshit!'

Then Mike said, 'Quite!'

Of course it's possible that Dave said 'batshit', but I don't think so. Mike's lack of respect for the director's opinions is worrying.

It was doubtless because of his bad attitude that we found so little today. Dave turned up some more coins from the Bar-

Kokhba revolt but apart from that it was just the regular pottery. Mike said it was all good dating material but I reckon he was just trying to make us all feel good about a disappointing day.

At lunchtime I asked Connie Patterson whether she'd read the Song of Solomon yet. She said, 'Yes, and I can see how it breaks the stereotypes with its autonomous female protagonist. But I found some of the imagery obscure. For example, what does she mean by asking the man to "be a like a hart on the mountain of Bether"? The notes in your Bible don't explain that kind of stuff at all.'

Unfortunately Mike Totley overheard this and said, 'It would be better to translate that phrase: "…be like a young stag, my beloved, on the cleft mountain." She's referring to her mons Veneris, the cleft being her vulva; she's inviting him to arouse her by clitoral stimulation.'

At this everyone in earshot went quiet. We were all too shocked and embarrassed to speak, except Ms. Patterson who said, 'Oh, I see! And what about the part where the man tells the woman her breasts are "like two young roes that are twins"? That's a strange image for a pair of boobs.'

Mike said, 'Only if you assume the imagery is visual. The two fawns are a *tactile* image, with the emphasis on softness. Viewed the right way it's overwhelmingly sensuous.'

I'm sure his gaze wandered fleetingly to Ms. Patterson's own breasts at that point. I also think she noticed because a shy kind of smile flickered around her lips for a second. There was another silence after this, broken by Travis Roston III choking on a piece of melon. We all gathered round to slap him on the back and check he was okay and then the meal continued and the conversation went on to other topics. I decided not to raise the Song of Solomon again in public. In fact I found the whole conversation deeply distasteful. I can't imagine what the late Mrs. Clinger would have made of it. To think that we used to read the Song of Solomon aloud together, taking it in turns to read the different parts!

Day 7 (Tue. 9 May)

In Miss Schluter's cave, next door to ours, they found a little jug wrapped in palm fibres. There was lively discussion about it in the afternoon session. Dr. Sinnet said it dated from the first century and must have come from the Temple, while Mike Totley insisted the jug was a second-century type and had probably belonged to Bar-Kokhba's followers. He reminded us that a letter and some coins from that time had turned up in the same cave forty years ago. But Doc Sinnet remained firm and I expect he's right.

Only the usual bits of pottery from our cave. Another pleasant conversation with Mrs. Hope-Parsons at lunchtime.

Day 8 (Wed. 10 May)

Dr. Parbunkel dug up some pieces of fabric in Cave A, some of them quite big. He thinks they're bits of a rug which some rebel hiding from the Romans used to wrap himself in at night. He was quite excited because until now his cave has only produced bits of Chalcolithic pottery like the ones Mike Totley misdated in the orientation session. To me it all looked pretty boring but none of the other caves produced anything better.

I'm getting worried about Mike's influence on the younger members of the group. It's not just that he dresses like a hippy with a bandanna tied around his head; his behaviour is often irresponsible. Today at lunch he taught Travis Roston III, Drew Gessinger and Dave Hirschfeld a stupid game which he called Digger's Roulette. This consists of getting one can of Coke for each person in the game, shaking one of them violently (the can, not the person), and then mixing them up so nobody knows which is the shook-up can. Then everybody takes a chance on opening one and the person with the shook-up can gets a soaking when the contents come bursting out. This childish nonsense attracted quite an audience. Ms. Patterson came along with Miss Schluter and said, 'Is this a male bonding thing or can anyone join in?' Mike said, 'Please do,' and they did. Harry Hah even videoed it. I fear this stupidity will now be a regular lunchtime feature.

Day 9 (Thur. 11 May)

More pieces of old rug from Dr. Parbunkel's cave. In ours Dave Hirschfeld found a wooden bowl, very well preserved, and Alice Wesson turned up the pieces of some broken oil lamps. In the afternoon we had the usual arguments about whether they were from the second or first century.

Spent lunchtime talking to Mrs. Hope-Parsons again. She really is a very nice lady. I suspect she's a born-again believer though she doesn't talk about it.

Day 10 (Fri. 12 May)

A day of real excitement at last! A truly amazing find from Dr. Sinnet's cave! It was discovered by Dr. Sinnet himself while no one else was present. Such is his commitment that he continued to work in the cave while the rest of us were having breakfast and that was when he found it. He was so engrossed in the task of excavating it that he was very startled when Harry Hah went back to the cave slightly early. We first knew something unusual was happening when we heard Dr. Sinnet shouting at Harry by the mouth of the cave – but we couldn't hear what he was saying from so far away. Then he radioed down to Rip Warholler to fetch a box and some rope.

We all went back to work in our own caves without knowing what he'd found but by lunchtime it had been brought down to the camp and we all saw it. It was a beautiful stone jar, complete with stopper, wrapped in the same kind of cloth Dr. Parbunkel's been finding. The jar had been buried under stones and dirt in a recess covered by heavy roof fall, so the rock slicers have finally proved their worth.

Dr. Sinnet said the jar and its stopper had clearly been turned on a lathe by a master craftsman. He explained that stone jars were often used in Temple times because they were believed to preserve their contents from ritual impurity. But the most amazing thing was a Hebrew inscription around the shoulder! He translated it as 'Holy to the priests belonging to the Temple of the Lord'. This proved, he said, that the jar, like the other objects we'd found, had been specially made for use in the Temple. Thanks to the cloth protecting it, it was without a scratch. You could almost imagine it had been made yesterday!

As he started to wrap it up again Mike Totley asked if he could have a closer look. But Doc Sinnet said there would be plenty of time for that when we were all back at the Center, and he packed it away in a box. We naturally spent the rest of the day in a state of extreme excitement.

But for me a dark shadow was soon cast over these events. In the lunchbreak I noticed Totley retreat into his tent alone, with his clipboard and a pencil. There was something furtive about him which made me suspicious. Apparently Ms. Patterson also noticed him go because after a couple of minutes she took his water bottle over to the tent to offer him a drink. I felt prompted to listen to their conversation, so I moved quietly toward the tent and bent down, pretending to retie my bootlaces.

I heard Ms. Patterson say, 'Hey, that's really neat, Mike! You're some artist!' Totley said, 'Every archaeologist has to be able to draw.'

She replied, 'But that's exceptional. I recognised it straight away. It's Sinnet's jar. Why are you sketching it?'

There was a pause, then Totley said, 'I wasn't going to tell anyone this, so please don't mention it to anybody else.'

She said, 'Cross my heart and hope to die.'

Then he said, 'I plan to show this sketch to all the antiquities dealers in Jerusalem and…'

Just then Travis Roston III saw me and said, 'Hi, old pal! You okay down there?'

So they knew someone was close by and the conversation stopped. But I'd already heard enough. In the orientation session Dr. Sinnet had told us about the danger of finds being lost to the illegal antiquities market, so it was clear to me what Totley had in mind. He could probably get millions of dollars for a jar that had once belonged to the Temple!

So I hurried over to Dr. Sinnet, who was just packing stuff in his Land Rover, and told him that Totley was planning to steal the jar and sell it. He was naturally shocked and asked how I knew. I quoted the words I'd overheard and Dr. Sinnet looked strangely thoughtful, almost doubtful. I assured him I'd heard every word clearly. Then he put his hand on my shoulder and thanked me for my alertness. He said we should continue to act naturally and not let Totley or Ms. Patterson know that we knew anything. He also assured me that the jar itself was perfectly safe.

'I won't let it out of my sight until we get back,' he said, 'and then it goes straight into a strongbox.'

Day 11 (Sat. 13 May)

Today's field trip was to Qumran where the Dead Sea Scrolls were discovered. However, I wasn't always able to concentrate on the guide's explanations because Mike Totley had decided not to join us and I kept wondering what he was doing instead. He'd told me he was skipping Qumran because he'd been lots of times already, but I suspected he was up to no good while we were all out of the way. In spite of Dr. Sinnet's assurances I can't help worrying about the stone jar.

Day 12 (Sun 14 May)

Went to the service at the Garden Tomb again. Mike Totley came along – hypocrite that he is – but left the group as soon as the service was over without saying where he was going. All very mysterious and disturbing. I'm sure he won't rest until that precious jar is in his hands.

2

In order to pursue his enquiries with greater freedom Mike rented a Fiat Punto for the weekend. After the service at the Garden Tomb he collected it from the underground car park outside the Jaffa Gate and left Jerusalem on the road to Ramallah.

Between Ram and el-Bireh he turned east and followed a twisting, minor road into the central hills. After about four miles he turned off onto an unmetalled track. It ended on a barren hilltop where a cluster of field vehicles stood on a bulldozed patch of ground. From this vantage point he could see down into a broad wadi that meandered south and east towards the Jordan Valley. The wadis in this part of the country were not like the deep ravines further south; they had gently sloping sides, many of them terraced since biblical times for growing olives. This one displayed the characteristic banded pattern – red earth glimpsed between silvery-green foliage.

Leaving the Fiat in the makeshift parking lot, Mike followed a steep track down into the wadi. On a low mound rising from the shoulder of the hill, a dig was in progress. Forty or fifty men and women were busy with picks, trowels, baskets and wheelbarrows. Every work area was covered by a brightly coloured tarp suspended between upright poles, and the workers only emerged from their shade to wheel away barrowloads of earth, or to consult with colleagues in a neighbouring sector.

Mike walked carefully between excavated squares and trenches, admiring their neat dividing baulks and meticulously labelled sections. Clearly, Baruch Zederbaum had not lowered his high standards one jot during the last seven years.

Zederbaum was easy to find in this hive of disciplined activity. He was sitting at a table in his most characteristic posture, bent over some enigmatic find like a living question mark.

'*Shalom*, Baruch!' said Mike, approaching with outstretched arms.

Zederbaum carefully put down his magnifying glass and raised his head. His hair was now more white than grey and his weather-beaten face was as wrinkled as a walnut, but his eyes sparkled like an excited child's and his handshake was as strong as ever.

'Michael! *Shalom*, my dear boy!' He got up from his campstool and the two men embraced with genuine warmth. 'I'd heard you were in Israel-Palestine again. Why didn't you get in touch sooner? Here, unfold one of those stools and sit with me in the shade. The air temperature isn't high but the sun can still burn. Let me pour you some mango juice. This calls for a celebration!'

Baruch Zederbaum pronounced his immaculate English with a heavy German accent. Always a fierce individualist, he'd been unusual among post-war immigrants to Israel in refusing to replace his Teutonic surname with a Hebrew one. Now his adoption of the clumsy term 'Israel-Palestine' expressed his commitment to the ideal of peaceful coexistence between Jew and Arab.

'Thanks, Baruch. I've been meaning to get in touch, but the Nahal Shuhan project has kept me very busy. I'm sorry.'

'Ah, yes, you're with the Americans. All that crawling about in dark holes doesn't appeal to me, I'm afraid. The stale air, the smell…'

'Like working in a giant's armpit.'

'Exactly so! I had enough of that as a student – I was in Nahal Hever with Aharoni.'

'I know. I've been rereading the reports.'

'And what's it like, working with fundamentalists? Not quite your cup of tea, so to say?'

'Not bad. Some of the younger men are good company. You'll be pleased to know I've introduced them to Digger's Roulette; remember teaching me that?'

'I hope you've also retained some of the more *useful* things I tried to teach you?'

'How could I forget? You were an excellent teacher, Baruch. And how are you?'

'I keep well, thank you, Michael. But getting too old for this.' With an extravagant sweep of his arm, he indicated the scene before them. 'I've been digging this site since 1995 but I've scaled the project down quite a lot in the last two years. One more season and my work will be finished – then I plan to retire.'

'I'll believe that when I see it,' said Mike. He glanced at the potsherds arrayed on Zederbaum's table. 'Anything interesting turned up?'

'The site is mainly Hellenistic and Roman, also with some Byzantine and Early Arab occupation. These pieces are late Hellenistic – but of course, you can see that, Michael. One of my area supervisors thinks the bowl had an inscription on it but the marks are so faint it is hard to be sure. What do you think? Is that a *daleth* and a *beth*, or is my imagination getting the better of me in my old age?'

Mike examined the sherd with the magnifying glass.

'Could well be Hebrew letters in badly faded ink. What about the other pieces?'

'Even fainter, I'm sorry to say. But if all my frustrations were like this I'd be happy. You see that over there?' Zederbaum nodded in the direction of a nearby hilltop where a clutch of new buildings reflected the sunlight from rooftop water tanks and solar panels. 'One of those militant West Bank settlements which that idiot Netanyahu allowed to flourish. And within sight of a Palestinian town! So provocative! Every day it pains me to see it. And some days the men come over here and harangue me with their bigoted views and their misuse of the Bible. You see, I've built up a mixed team here – Palestinian students and volunteers as well as Israelis; after all, we're digging up Arab as well as Jewish culture, their ancestors as well as ours. But those settlers hate me for it. Do you know what they tried last week?'

Mike shook his head and leaned forward sympathetically.

'They claimed the whole site was an ancient Jewish cemetery, and demanded – on religious grounds – that we stop digging. They threw stones at us every time we tried to work. I tried to reason with them but got nowhere. So eventually I had to radio the police. It was almost a riot. Do you know what's gone wrong with this country, Michael?'

'I expect you're going to tell me.'

'It started in 1967 with the Six-Day War. When we captured the West Bank and reunified Jerusalem it changed our self-understanding; it made us look and feel like a great power on the world stage. Arrogance crept in, the seeds of moral decay were sown. A new breed of visionary activist appeared, spreading a potent mixture of religion and nationalism. They seized the initiative from the old moderates and started doing evil in the name of holiness. Today their spiritual descendants are plentiful. They think they can use God as an excuse for driving the Palestinians from every square centimetre of this land!'

Zederbaum turned one of the small pottery fragments between his fingers, sighing as though he saw in it a symbol of shattered hope.

'But that's enough from me,' he said, setting the potsherd down again. 'What about you, Michael? How's your expedition going?'

'To be frank, Baruch, I'm having a few problems of my own. And I'm hoping you can help me with one of them. Tell me if you've ever seen anything like this.' Mike pulled the folded sketch of Sinnet's jar from the pocket of his denim shirt and spread it out on the table. 'It's made of stone, very high quality workmanship, about twenty-four centimetres high and about eighteen centimetres across at the widest point. The stopper is also stone. And it has an inscription incised around the shoulder in palaeo-Hebrew script: *Kodesh kohanim l'beth Yahweh.*'

'Remarkable!' Zederbaum examined the drawing with intense interest. 'You found this?'

'One of my colleagues. I prefer not to name him for reasons which will become obvious. He claims to have found it in a recess at the back of his cave, wrapped in a piece of striped textile.'

'Claims to? What are you suggesting, Michael?'

Mike lowered his voice. A few metres away two volunteers were busy sieving earth for small finds and he didn't want to be overheard.

'I've reasons to be suspicious. For one thing he found it during a breakfast break when he was alone in the cave. No one else saw it until it was out of the ground. Normal practice is to let the volunteers watch the removal of the finds. I even let them help, like you used to do. Secondly, the first volunteer to go back in the cave after breakfast was a Korean known for his liberal use of a camcorder. As soon as my colleague realised he wasn't alone in the cave he started yelling at this volunteer, demanding to know how long he'd been there and whether his camcorder was switched on. Poor Harry came to talk to me about it because he didn't understand why he'd been shouted at. That's how I know what happened. It seems my colleague was anxious not to have his discovery of the jar captured on video.'

'And was it? I mean did this man Harry…'

'No, unfortunately. He'd only been in the cave a few seconds when my colleague started bawling him out.'

'I see.' Zederbaum pondered Mike's sketch, grunting inscrutably.

'Well, what do you think?'

'I think this is a very good sketch, Michael. You always were very clever with a pencil. You could have been an artist.'

'You know perfectly well what I mean, Baruch. Could it be a genuine find?'

'Well, they were certainly able to produce very fine lathe-turned stone vessels in the Hellenistic and Roman periods. As you know, we have examples from Jerusalem which are much larger than this. The shape would not be out of place in the Herodian period, though the best parallels are in pottery. As to the inscription, palaeo-Hebrew script was enjoying a revival at that time. The wording, of course, points to a connection with the Temple; it is exactly the same as on the ivory sceptre-head that Lemaire found in 1979.'

'Which adds to my suspicions. That inscription is famous; a forger could easily have copied it.'

'Mmm, perhaps. But if you think the jar was planted you must explain how your colleague obtained it in the first place.'

'I've thought of that. There are two possibilities: either he had it specially made, or he got a genuinely ancient jar from an antiquities dealer and added the inscription himself. The latter would be relatively easy with equipment we've got at the Centre. He could even make the incisions look ancient, given enough time. If he had it made from scratch there's no way I could prove anything; he would have covered his tracks too well. But the dealer theory appeals to me slightly more. Or at least it *did*. I spent most of yesterday going around all the big antiquities dealers in Jerusalem and Bethlehem, showing them this sketch and watching for a glimmer of recognition to cross their faces.'

'With no result?'

'None at all.'

'Which proves nothing. They're an extremely wily breed.'

'But I thought it was worth a try.'

Baruch Zederbaum slowly shook his head, implying that Mike should have known better.

'And now you come to me in the equally vain hope that I can throw some light on this little mystery!'

'Well, you *are* the leading expert on Hellenistic and Herodian culture. You're telling me you can't help?'

'Not with the data you've given me so far. What about the associated finds?'

'That's a bit complex. In that particular cave the evidence is ambiguous. I'd say everything we've found so far is second century – Bar-Kokhba's time – but back in 1960 they found an oil lamp that was probably first century: made on a potter's wheel, with a spatulate nozzle and a knife-pared base.'

Zederbaum spread his hands, inviting Mike to see the obvious.

'So the cave was probably used as a hideout during the First Revolt. Your colleague's jar would not be out of place in such a context.'

'I know. But there's more. Before this jar turned up, two other caves produced some interesting finds – several bronze vessels, and a nice pottery jug which may have contained balsam oil from En-Gedi. In my view both those caves are pure Bar-Kokhba, but my colleague who found the jar insists that all these items came from the Temple just before its destruction. Which suggests a possible motive for faking the jar.'

'Ah, yes! Its inscription establishes a connection with the Temple, not just for the jar but also, by implication, for the other finds as well!'

'Exactly! It tips the balance against my interpretation and in favour of his.'

Zederbaum pondered the matter silently for a few moments and then said, 'But what about the textile you say the jar was wrapped in? Where do you think he got that from if the jar is a fake?'

'That's easy. Another supervisor has been finding similar pieces in a different cave. He could have supplied it. If he didn't enter it on his register no one would know.'

'Ah! Now you're suggesting a conspiracy!'

'What I'm suggesting fits a well-known pattern of scientific fraud. Some scholars and scientists stoop to manufacturing evidence to prove what they already believe by intuition. They rationalise the deception as a way of hastening the advancement of knowledge, bypassing the long search for real but elusive evidence.'

'It's still a very serious charge, Michael. And in my experience forgery is extremely rare. Most of us manage to support our pet theories merely by ignoring some facts and exaggerating others.'

'So you think I'm on a wild goose chase?'

Zederbaum shrugged.

'How can I say? I would very much like to see this jar for myself. Do you think it could be arranged?'

'That's exactly what I hoped you'd say, Baruch! I'll try to get permission for you to inspect it. It shouldn't be difficult – they could hardly refuse someone with your reputation. It would mean a visit to the Centre, of course.'

'In Talpiot? No problem. My wife and I have an apartment in Jerusalem, not far from the National Museum.'

'Your wife?' Seven years ago Zederbaum had been a widower and Mike had heard nothing of this new development.

'Yes, that's right. You must come and eat with us before you leave Israel-Palestine. Rivka would love to see you again.'

Mike stared at Zederbaum in astonishment.

'Rivka? You mean you married Rivka Danin?' He had vivid memories of a statuesque beauty, Zederbaum's junior by about thirty years.

'Three years ago. Don't look so surprised, Michael. Remember Rivka is a museum curator; it's natural for her to be fascinated by an ancient relic.'

Both men laughed heartily, then Mike said, 'Well, my belated congratulations to you both! You lucky old devil!'

'I know. My wife is beautiful, talented, interested in my work, and she cooks the most amazing meals – which is another incentive for you to come and see us. Please give me a telephone number where I can contact you.'

Mike wrote the Centre's number at the bottom of his sketch and tore the piece off. Then Zederbaum wrote his own number on the sketch and Mike returned it to his shirt pocket.

As he got up to go, Mike said, 'There's another favour I'd like to ask of you, Baruch.'

'Then ask it, Michael.'

'Watching your dig going on around us, it makes me realise the Nahal Shuhan volunteers are missing something. Working in the caves gives them a very narrow range of experience. They're not learning anything about stratigraphy, squares, trenches, baulks, sections and so on. I'd like to bring them here one day so they can see a typical, well-run dig in progress. Would you mind? I'd phone you first, of course.'

'It would be a pleasure. I look forward to hearing from you.'

So Mike said goodbye to his old mentor, stepped out from the shade of the tarp and set off back to his car. But as he reached the top of the track there was a deafening explosion. He briefly saw the Fiat, and other vehicles near it, dissolve in an expanding ball of flame before the force of the blast threw him backwards down the steep slope.

Chapter Fourteen

1

The casualty department kept Mike in hospital overnight, suspecting concussion. But at nine o'clock on Monday morning they decided he was suffering from nothing worse than bad bruising and a few cuts.

Dave Hirschfeld had stayed behind at the Centre that morning, waiting for news. When Mike phoned to say he was being discharged Dave drove to the hospital in his own Jeep Wrangler to collect him. He delivered a clean set of Mike's clothes to the reception desk and sat down to wait. A few minutes later Mike appeared, looking slightly haggard but otherwise none the worse for his ordeal.

'Good to see you, buddy!' said Dave, springing from his chair. 'You had us all worried!' He put an arm around Mike's shoulder. 'Thank God you're okay! And I mean that, Mike; your survival was pure *hashgacha* – divine providence.'

'Could you go easy on that shoulder, Dave? It's a bit bruised. Yes, I expect you're right; if I hadn't fallen backwards down that hill I would've been caught in the fireball. It doesn't bear thinking about.'

They walked to Hirschfeld's Jeep in sombre silence.

'Thanks for fetching my clothes,' said Mike, climbing stiffly into the passenger seat, 'but I can't wear these for five days. Do you mind if we stop off at the Centre and collect some more?'

'You're incredible! You want to go back to the canyon today?'

'Why not?'

'Because about twenty hours ago you almost got killed is why not! Look, nobody expects you back at the dig for at least a couple of days, so why not give yourself a break? I can take care of things in the cave.'

'I know you can, but there's no need. I'm fine, Dave, honestly.

And I've had an idea I want to follow up. You know that big rock by the wall in the second chamber? The coins and lamps we found last week seemed to cluster in that area. I'd like to have that rock moved today.'

'I could organise that.'

'I know, but I want to be there. Now, stop arguing and let's get going!' Mike knew that if he stayed alone at the Centre, trying to read or sort pottery, he would brood endlessly on yesterday's close call. Far better to be active and among company.

Dave started the Wrangler and drove off in silence, shaking his head at Mike's stubbornness. They were almost at the Centre before he spoke again.

'So what d'you think might be underneath that rock, Mike?'

'Not necessarily underneath it. Perhaps... well, it doesn't do to speculate too much. Let's wait and see.'

The Centre had a walled compound for vehicles, located outside the labs on the south side of the complex. Dave slowed as he approached and pointed a remote control unit at the gates. They swung open and he drove through. He stopped the Wrangler by the Centre's rear entrance.

'Need any help?'

'No, thanks,' said Mike. 'Shouldn't be more than five minutes.'

2

Mike pulled a few clothes from his wardrobe, thrust them into a rucksack and set off back towards the rear of the building. To reach the exit he had to pass the computer room and he decided to pay it a brief visit. There was something he wanted to try while none of the team were around.

He sat down at the nearest terminal. On the screen, coloured rotating disks performed a hypnotic pavane. Mike tried the keystrokes Tally had shown him for accessing the main register and the disks were replaced by rising columns of data. Mike let them march up the screen until last Friday's date appeared at the top, then he froze their advance. That day's record of finds from Cave D was set out in a familiar format; for each entry it listed a find-spot in three dimensions, a locus number, the nature of the surrounding soil, the material from which the artefact was made, its state of preservation, measurements, period of origin and a record of all photographs taken.

He was hoping to obtain details of the stone jar without quizzing a hostile Sinnet, but at first he could see no entry for it. Then he found the material description 'limestone' against a set of suitable measurements. He was disappointed, but hardly surprised, to see that no photographs were on record. What did surprise him was the heading under which the find had been entered. Instead of the word 'jar' or the more generic 'vessel' it was designated by three Hebrew letters: *qoph, lamed, lamed*.

Conscious of Dave waiting outside, Mike quickly scribbled down a few details, closed the register and left. He was going to ask Dave if he knew the significance of those three letters but as he reached the rear exit he remembered something which drove the question from his mind.

'You okay?' asked Dave as Mike climbed back in the Jeep.

'Fine, thanks, but I've just remembered a message they gave me at the hospital. Would you mind if we made a slight detour between here and the wadi? I have to report to a man called Levit at the Joint Security Base, just outside Jericho.'

3

'Thank you for coming, Dr Totley,' said Commander Yitzhak Levit of the West Bank Joint Security Base. 'I won't keep you long. Please sit down and have some coffee.' He poured two cups and slid one across the desk to Mike.

'Thank you.' Mike sat down carefully. His buttocks were the most bruised part of his anatomy and the chair was hard. In fact the office as a whole was rather utilitarian, furnished with only a desk, two chairs, a filing cabinet and a computer terminal. The wall behind the desk was covered by a large map of Israel and the administration zone of the Palestinian National Authority. The opposite wall bore the only decorative item in the room: a signed photograph of porn star Tabatha Cash, fully clothed for once, standing on the Mount of Olives with an Israeli flag in one hand

and a white dove in the other.

'Now Dr Totley, yesterday afternoon at Tell el-Mikhta, you were almost blown to pieces,' said Commander Levit, who believed in getting straight to the point.

'I know,' said Mike, 'I was there.'

Levit raised one eyebrow. He was a middle-aged, balding Israeli with a thick moustache and an underdeveloped sense of humour. He looked from Mike to the report on his desk and then back to Mike. 'You had a very narrow escape. I have no doubt the bomb was meant to explode when you started your car.'

'May I ask why you think that?'

'My men found bits of the bomber. When you returned to your car he was apparently underneath it attaching the bomb. He probably heard your approach and in his haste to finish the job, a careless slip and – *boom!*'

Although lacking in terms of realism, Levit's impression of the explosion brought a tingle to the back of Mike's neck.

'Er... quite. Any idea who he was?'

'I'm afraid not, Dr Totley. There was not much left – just a few pieces here, a few pieces there. Did you know that a violent explosion at close quarters can completely destroy human tissue? Which is what was meant to happen to you, no doubt. It is because we have so little to go on that I am hoping you can help us. Do you know of anyone who might be wishing to blow you to tiny pieces?'

Mike winced at Levit's bluntness. 'I'm sure I don't have any enemies, if that's what you mean. The bomb must have been intended for someone else. Perhaps they chose the wrong car.'

'It is possible. That excavation is controversial. There are Israeli extremists who oppose Professor Zederbaum's politics and there are Palestinian extremists who object to an Israeli – even a sympathetic one like Zederbaum – heading an excavation in the West Bank. So perhaps the bomb was meant for him. Or perhaps – and this is more likely, I think – it was planted randomly, an act of terrorism against the dig, not against any individual.'

'I hope you're right. I'd hate to think someone was trying to kill Baruch.'

'Don't worry, Dr Totley. We will be particularly vigilant on his behalf whenever he is within our jurisdiction. You have been most helpful. I think we can eliminate the possibility that you were the target of this most regrettable explosion.' Commander Levit rose and extended his right hand. 'But please let me know at once if anyone else tries to blow you up or murder you in any way at all.'

'Thanks, I will,' said Mike, 'unless, of course, they succeed.'

4

A rock slicer whines and coughs, expelling the last glob of compacted dust from its excretory appendage. Sitting on the broad ledge outside Cave C, Mike watches the dark sphere drop into the ravine. Almost the size of a football, it develops a comet-like tail as it falls; then it breaks and becomes an amorphous, spreading cloud which drifts eastwards on the slight breeze.

'All finished,' says Rip Warholler, emerging from the mouth of the cave. 'But if I were you I'd wait a while before you go back in there, let the dust settle.'

But Mike can't wait a while. He has a feeling about this, an expectation he can't articulate. He puts his face mask on. His team are sitting with him on the ledge and when he stands up they follow his example, but Mike turns and raises a hand.

'No, please, not all of you. I'll need Dave's help, but Alice and Effin can stay out here and enjoy the fresh air a bit longer. We'll call you in if we find anything.'

In a far corner of the second chamber they drag away the fragments of the dissected rock. There is nothing whatsoever beneath the rubble. But there is something behind it. A small hole, barely big enough to crawl through.

'I'll take a look,' says Mike, and begins to squirm his way in on his stomach. His bruises hurt and his muscles ache in protest, but he forces his way forwards. After less than a metre the hole funnels out and his helmet lamp reveals a long, narrow, low-ceilinged chamber. Inside there is enough room for him to make progress on his hands and knees.

Two minutes later Mike wriggles back into the main chamber and Dave helps him out of the hole. Without speaking, Mike gets unsteadily to his feet and walks to the mouth of the cave. Outside he leans back against the metal grille, takes off his face mask and breathes deeply. His face is terribly white.

5

[Fourth extract from the journal of Effin L Clinger]

Day 13 (Mon. 15 May)

Incredible news when I woke up this morning. Seems that after I'd gone to my room to write my journal last night, Mike Totley phoned from a hospital to say he'd narrowly escaped death in a terrorist bomb attack! Amazing!

We drove out to the canyon and set up camp again. As Dr. Sinnet was beginning our morning devotions Mrs. Hope-Parsons said we should all give special thanks to God that Dr. Totley had been spared. The sentiment was shared by everyone, of course, but I recalled the text of Dr. Barclay Wright-Winger's sermon at the Garden Tomb yesterday: 'For, behold, the Lord will come with fire, and with his chariots like a whirlwind, to render his anger with fury, and his rebuke with flames of fire' (Isaiah 66:15). Obviously, Totley has experienced God's rebuke, rendered with flames of fire, to turn him from the path of wickedness. If he doesn't heed this warning something worse will surely befall him!

Dave H. brought Totley back to the canyon around noon. I was hoping to alert him to the spiritual meaning of his ordeal but never got the chance because of a remarkable development in our cave. It happened like this:

In the absence of Totley and Dave H., Alice Wesson and I had been continuing our respective tasks from last Friday, with Miss Schluter dropping in from time to time to see how we were doing. When Totley came back he said we must leave the cave for a while because he'd asked Rip Warholler to do some work with a rock slicer. After Rip had finished, Totley and Dave went back inside on their own and when they came out again Totley looked like death. At first I thought he'd just realised how close he'd come to meeting the Almighty with sin nestling in his heart. In fact he'd seen something that had churned his stomach.

In a side chamber, which none of us knew was there, he'd discovered the bones of at least a dozen people – men, women and children – with clothing, jewellery, sandals, coins – all kinds of things, which will take ages to get out and record properly. Sticking to his theory that everything in our cave comes from Bar-Kokhba's time, Totley says these are the bodies of rebels and their families who slowly starved to death while the Romans besieged the caves. Those who survived longest, he says, must've had the awful task of burying their families and comrades as they died. It was terrible to think of it and lunch today was a very sombre occasion. Almost nobody spoke.

After lunch there was a long discussion about how to deal with this discovery and the staff decided to rearrange our schedule for the next few days. Some other volunteers will be transferred to our cave and will work all day today and tomorrow to get the finds photographed, recorded and removed. Wednesday afternoon will be free time to give us a well-deserved break. We will return to the Center at noon that day, taking with us all the stuff we've managed to remove from the burial chamber. On Thursday morning some of the group will stay at the Center to do more work on the finds while the rest come back to the canyon.

Day 14 (Tues. 16 May)

Clearance of the burials is progressing according to plan it seems. I wasn't given a hands-on role myself. There sure is an awful lot of stuff in there! Totley now says there are fifteen burials altogether.

At lunchtime Ms. Patterson returned my Bible and said she was having problems with 'the opaque, antiquated language of the King James Version', and that she preferred a modern translation Totley had since given her. She also said the Rev. Kermit Bender's comments were way off beam, as he failed to mention any of the things Mike said about the Song of Solomon. I told her Kermit Bender was undoubtedly one of the great Bible expositors of our time.

She said, 'That's absurd! Most of what he says is just his own narrow-minded bigotry expressed in pious jargon. Kermit the Frog would probably be more illuminating.'

It was distressing to hear a great man of God compared unfavourably to a Muppet, and it shows the extent of this young woman's spiritual blindness.

Day 15 (Wed. 17 May)

A day overshadowed by terrible news! We all drove back to the Center for lunch, in line with our new schedule, and found Mrs. Spittler (the administrator or something) in a very distressed state and the place full of Israeli police. It turned out that the Center had been broken into last night. Surprisingly, of all the valuable finds and equipment stored there, only one thing seemed to be missing – the stone jar from the Temple! So my worst fears have been confirmed!

After lunch I managed to get Dr. Sinnet alone for a few moments and asked if he'd informed the police of Totley's involvement in the theft. He said no, he hadn't, and didn't intend to, which astonished me. He said that since we knew Totley had been in the camp all night when the jar disappeared we had no proof that he was involved. I said the conversation I'd overheard was strong enough evidence and that Totley must have gotten an accomplice to steal the jar. But Dr. Sinnet said I might've misunderstood what I'd heard and that it was best to leave everything to the police. His attitude amazes me. Armed with my information the authorities could arrest Totley and torture the truth out of him in no time.

For our free afternoon Totley had organised an optional trip to a dig run by one of the country's greatest archaeologists, Prof. Baruch Zederbaum. Apparently this is the place where Totley almost got killed three days ago. Quite a few of us went along and it was all very interesting, especially the burned-out parking lot. If ever I get the chance to go on another dig I'd like to join one like this, where you work in the open air, go back to Jerusalem each evening and get to sleep in a proper bed every night.

Near the end of our visit I was disturbed to notice that Totley took Prof. Zederbaum aside for a secretive conversation. I wasn't able to hear any of it because there was no way of getting close. I sure hope Totley isn't trying to draw this great man into his evil scheme.

6

'I can't tell you how sorry I am,' said Baruch Zederbaum. 'To think that you might have lost your life because some crazy people don't like what *I'm* doing – that's terrible! I was so worried when I saw you carried to the ambulance; you looked so white, Michael.

It was a great relief to hear you on the phone on Sunday night.'

'Have they any idea who did it yet?' asked Mike.

Zederbaum shook his head.

'They can't even decide between Arabs and Jews. But at least we now have good security here. You saw the guards at the parking lot?'

'Yes. Baruch, about your visit to the Centre to see the stone jar; I'm afraid there's a problem.'

'You want to postpone it? I'm not surprised. That multiple burial you told me about must be a lot of extra work.'

'Worse than that, I'm afraid. The Centre was broken into last night. The jar's been stolen. Nothing else, incidentally, just the jar.'

Zederbaum looked around to see how likely they were to be overheard. They had already withdrawn some distance from the Nahal Shuhan volunteers, who were being lectured on stratigraphy by an area supervisor, but Zederbaum took Mike's arm and led him to the crest of Tell el-Mikhta where no one could approach them without being seen.

'This is very suspicious, Michael, in view of what you told me. I assume the police are looking for the thieves?'

'Yes, but they don't have much to go on. The people who did it were obviously professionals. They knew how to disable the alarms and security cameras and they left no fingerprints or other clues.'

'I see. Apart from me, did anyone outside your group know about this jar? Had there been a press release?'

'Definitely not.'

'Were you able to find out any more about the jar than you told me on Sunday?'

'Not really. A staff discussion about it was planned for Sunday evening and that would've been my first chance to examine it closely. By then, of course, I was in hospital. I did manage to get some more accurate measurements from the computerised register of finds, but my guesswork wasn't significantly out. There is one thing, though: on the computer the jar was registered under an unusual name – Kelal.'

'Kelal?' The wrinkles deepened on Zederbaum's forehead and

he involuntarily tightened his grip on Mike's arm. 'You know what this word means, Michael?'

'It seems it's just a rare Hebrew word for a jar. What I don't understand is why it's been used in the register. All other vessels are entered under their usual English names. Baruch, what's the matter?'

Zederbaum was visibly agitated. He looked around again, as though he feared eavesdroppers even in this exposed location.

'We have to talk about this, but not now.' He released Mike's arm, took a diary from his pocket and leafed through the following week's pages. 'Come to dinner next Thursday evening, Michael. Then we can give this puzzle the time it deserves. I wish it could be sooner, but it is not possible.'

'Thanks. I'll check my schedule and confirm it by phone. But what—'

'I told you, I cannot explain it now. I'm sorry to leave you in suspense, so to say, but I can say no more until I've made enquiries and done some thinking. Rivka will be able to help too. In the meantime, you must not discuss this any further with any of your colleagues or volunteers. Don't even mention the word Kelal. Do you understand? That is very, very important!'

7

In the centre of the room a very old man lay on a narrow bed, his arms outside the covers, his head and shoulders supported by a heap of pillows. His hair was sparse and white, stroked back from the wizened features. His eyes were closed, his breathing shallow and noisy. The room was dim, for the blinds were down and the only light came from two candles. Near the head of the bed a young man sat on a chair and kept watch, his body rocking slightly to the rhythm of his murmured prayers. Occasionally he paused and reached forward to wipe a dribble of saliva from the old man's chin and beard with a handkerchief.

There was a light knock on the door and six more young men filed in, their forms crowding the small room with shadows. They arranged themselves silently, reverently around the bed. One of them held something wrapped in a prayer shawl. The man on the chair stood up, leaned towards the bed and whispered a few words close to the desiccated face. At this, the old man's eyes opened and his arms lifted from the bed. His outstretched hands began to shake violently.

The man holding the object in the prayer shawl unwrapped it, placing it gently between the quivering hands. He continued to support its weight while the old man caressed it, feeling its shape, tracing the incisions in its hard, smooth surface. His sight was so poor that the jar was only visible to him as a pale blur, but his gnarled fingers searched out the missing detail.

He tried to speak but only a few faint rasping sounds came from the toothless mouth. His attendant, however, seemed to know what he wanted and carefully removed the stopper from the jar. The old man drew the jar closer until he was almost embracing it. Slowly he placed one trembling hand inside the mouth of the jar, withdrew it again and sniffed at his fingertips. He tried once more to speak. For a few seconds his eyes were large with wild excitement, then they closed again and he sagged back into his pillows, exhausted. His lips were still open and the last dregs of his strength drained from him in a wheezy, disyllabic sigh which might – or might not – have been a word. His attendant turned and looked at the expectant faces around the bed. Then he nodded and gave the hoped-for interpretation.

'Kelal,' he said.

8

After Wednesday the quantity and variety of finds from the burial chamber continued to demand a flexible working pattern. Early on Thursday morning Chuck Sinnet and Tally Schluter took half of the group back to the caves while Leo Parbunkel and the remaining volunteers stayed at the Centre to work on cleaning and preservation. Mike Totley and Dave Hirschfeld remained behind until noon that day, updating the computerised register. This would normally have been Tally's job but, as Sinnet pointed out, Mike was the best person to interpret his own field notes and these were unusually complex in the case of the multiple burial. Burial records had to include detailed information on the position of each skeleton, observations on age (as deduced from the teeth), sex (as deduced from the pelvis), and any evidence of disabilities or wounds; information was also required on the surrounding soil or stones, the latter being classified according to size by a system known as the Wentworth Scale. After entering all this data Mike and Dave set off for the wadi in Dave's Jeep.

'This burial's got Leo worried,' said Dave. 'Have you noticed how jumpy he's getting?'

'I think he's just excited,' said Mike. 'With so much organic material to process, he's like a child with a box of new toys.'

'Not just that. Take it from me, he's a worried man, Mike. And I can see why. Strictly speaking he's breaking the law by keeping human remains at the Centre.'

'Really? Since when has that been illegal?'

'The law changed under pressure from the religious parties after the 1996 election. Before that it was okay for human bones to be kept until a physical anthropologist could examine them, but not any more. Now they have to be handed over immediately, on site, to the Ministry of Religious Affairs for reburial. So we broke the law already when we took the bones to the Centre. And remember, these bones are extra-special; they belong to Jewish freedom fighters who wanted to cleanse the land and rebuild the Temple. I guess Leo's afraid the Centre could face the wrath of the Ultra-Orthodox. You know they're opposed to archaeology because in their view it desecrates burials?'

'Yes, but I didn't realise they'd made life quite so difficult.'

'Difficult is putting it mildly. This is a strange country, Mike, and it gets stranger by the day.'

They joined the Jericho road. After chatting a while about their aims for the afternoon Dave became unusually quiet. Then he said, 'Mike, would you mind if I gave you some advice, as a Christian brother?'

'Not at all. Go ahead,' said Mike.

'"It's better to marry than to burn with desire." Saint Paul's first letter to the Corinthians, chapter seven, verse nine.'

'I'm sorry, Dave, but I haven't a clue what you're talking about.'

'I'm talking about you and that babe Connie Patterson.'

Mike was stunned.

After a long pause he said, 'I don't think Connie would like to be called a babe.'

'Okay, but don't try to change the subject. Your feelings for each other are obvious, and I think it's time you did something about it. I tried to give you a chance in the Old City last week, when that idiot Clinger and Mrs Hope-Parsons decided not to walk the ramparts; I deliberately left you guys alone together. But unless I'm mistaken, you didn't take advantage of the situation.'

Mike smiled at Dave's naivety.

'Dave, I'm sorry to disillusion you, but Connie doesn't see me in that light at all. I can't go into details, but let's just say her interest in me is purely professional.'

'Oh yeah? Haven't you noticed the way she looks at you?'

The question couldn't be brushed aside lightly. On several occasions, something in Connie's gaze had disturbed Mike's carefully guarded equilibrium. The problem was that she'd looked at him that way in Washington too; if it hadn't meant anything then, why should it mean something now?

'And how come,' Dave continued, 'she was so upset on Sunday night when I told her about the bomb at Tell el-Mikhta?'

'She was?'

'You bet she was! After you'd called from the hospital I went up to the coffee lounge and told all the guys who were there what had happened. Connie practically went to pieces. She had to go to her room.'

'She did?'

'Yeah. Didn't look like purely professional interest to me.'

Mike was unable to speak. A glimmer of hope was beginning to challenge his gloomy preconceptions.

'Like I said,' Dave persisted, 'it's time you did something about it.'

'But even if you're right – and I'm still not sure you are, but let's just assume it for a moment – there are complications you know nothing about, a history of misunderstanding that goes back to last November. It wouldn't be as easy as you seem to think.'

'Sure it would! Just take her somewhere nice, like the nature reserve at En-Gedi. You could take her there in the two-seater tomorrow afternoon on the way back to the Centre. Find a quiet spot, get her alone, away from the tourists, and…'

Mike never heard the rest of Dave's extremely interesting recommendations. Suddenly the windscreen was pocked with bullet holes and spattered with blood.

Dave crumpled in pain and his right arm dropped to his side. A second later his left hand flew from the steering wheel to clutch at his right shoulder. The Jeep slewed across to the wrong side of the road and bounced against a crash barrier. The impact threw Dave heavily against the driver's door. He struck his head and passed out.

They had just begun the steepest part of the descent into the Jordan Valley and Dave had been in the act of changing gear when the first bullet hit. The Wrangler was now in neutral, freewheeling down the steep hill and gathering speed. And it was still on the wrong side of the road.

Mike was disorientated but unhurt. He peered through the crazed windscreen and saw a large truck labouring up the hill towards them. As he reached for the steering wheel another hail of bullets ripped through the windows and bodywork. He ducked down and the remains of the windscreen collapsed on top of him in a shower of crystals. He pulled Dave down too, trying to protect him from further harm. Then he heard a horn blaring and remembered the truck. It sounded terribly close, almost on top of them.

Reaching across Dave's limp form he made another grab for the wheel. Again he was thwarted, this time by the Jeep swerving so violently that it threw him sideways. When he carefully pulled himself up and peered over the dashboard he saw that they had somehow missed the truck but were no longer on the road.

Crash barriers are intermittent on the Jericho road, allowing vehicles to turn off onto obscure wilderness trails. The Jeep had apparently swung off the road through a convenient gap and was now careering across a rock-strewn wasteland. Mike at last managed to get hold of the wheel but the steering seemed to be damaged; the wheel refused to turn. Next he tried to reach the brake pedal but Dave's legs were in the way. To add to his problems the Jeep was bouncing crazily over the rough ground. At this speed it was only a matter of time before it overturned or dropped into a gully.

Suddenly their attacker, or attackers – Mike was not sure that the streams of bullets always came from the same direction – opened fire again. Upholstery exploded all around him and he huddled in a foetal ball, expecting death at any moment. But after a few more seconds of violent lurching and bouncing, their progress became smoother and the firing stopped. Mike risked another glance over the dashboard.

They were on a single track road with alarming bends and a sharp gradient. After a few confused seconds Mike recognised it. It was the old Jericho road which follows the south side of the Wadi Kelt, a long, deep ravine twisting through the wilderness from the Jerusalem hills to the Jordan Valley. Nowadays the old road is used only by tourist coaches visiting the beauty spot at Ein Kelt or taking their passengers to view the picturesque monastery of St George on the far side of the wadi.

A busload of tourists was in fact on its way up the hill towards Ein Kelt at the same moment that Dave's Jeep was gathering speed in the opposite direction. For several seconds a bend hid the bus from Mike's view; then suddenly there it was, a monster of painted metal and tinted glass filling the road. There was nowhere to go. To the right was solid rock, to the left a sheer drop into the wadi. Mike closed his eyes.

Chapter Fifteen

1

With meticulous care Tally Schluter removed the concealing layers of bat dung and earth from Cave B's latest find. When it was completely exposed, she brushed away the last traces of fetid dust and took off her face mask. Tossing her ponytail back over her shoulder she leaned forward and gently raised the object from its resting place. Its lower half was blackened with soot but otherwise it was in perfect condition. She stroked her hands around it, feeling the texture of its faintly ribbed surface. Then she handed it carefully to Drew Gessinger.

'Second-century cooking pot,' said Drew.

'Yes. No doubt about this one.'

'But why hide a cooking pot? It's not exactly valuable. And there's nothing inside it.'

'Well, this is just a guess,' said Tally, 'but perhaps they didn't want this chamber to show any signs of activity. They were in a hurry, so they shoved all their everyday things down holes and covered them with dirt. That would account for the oil lamps we've found in strange places.'

'But why?'

'Because – and this is an even bigger guess – there's something really valuable hidden in here, something we haven't found yet. They didn't want the Romans to go poking around so they made this chamber look like they'd never used it.'

'Sounds plausible. So what do you think we should be looking for?'

'I've no idea. And don't get too excited, Drew; remember this is all speculation. But at least we've found a fine example of a cooking pot from the Bar-Kokhba revolt. Now we'd better go down for lunch.'

Outside the cave they saw Chuck Sinnet returning to camp

from Cave D. Tally hung back to wait for him. Walking behind him down the steep track, she told him about the cooking pot. His reaction was predictable.

'Are you sure about the date? Couldn't you be misreading an item from the time of the First Revolt?'

'I'm sorry Chuck, but no. This is a complete pot, not a few nondescript sherds.'

'Then I guess your cave was occupied twice – during the Second Revolt as well as the First. Looks like we've got the same situation in Cave C; the bronze vessels Totley found are from the First Revolt, but the multiple burial dates from the Second, as the coins clearly show.'

Sinnet quickened his pace but Tally was sure-footed and kept up with him.

'Chuck, I hate to raise this again because I know how strongly you feel about it, but the more things we find from the Second Revolt, the harder it is to argue that any of our stuff dates from the First, since we've no unambiguous evidence…'

Sinnet stopped and turned to face her.

'Look, Tally, I may not have what you call evidence for my conclusions, but I do have certain reasons. Strong ones.'

'I know there's Smith's reading of the Copper Scroll…'

'And other reasons which I can't go into right now. You'll just have to go on trusting me, Tally. It'll all become clear soon – very soon, in fact. Trust me, okay?'

Then Sinnet turned around, adjusted his solar-powered baseball cap and continued his descent.

2

The mind can develop strange preoccupations in times of crisis. In the seconds following Mike's realisation that he was about to collide with a large bus, he found himself reflecting on the behaviour of the Jeep's steering wheel. It seemed to be trying to shift anticlockwise in his hands, and it occurred to him that since Dave had lost consciousness the Jeep had done some rather odd things, almost as if…

His next thought was so wild it seemed ridiculous: their lives would be saved if he did absolutely nothing. With a sudden leap of hope he let the wheel run free. He didn't see what happened next because his eyes were still tightly closed. The Jeep made another sudden swerve to the left, leaving the road just in time to avoid impact. But instead of falling through empty space and smashing itself to pieces at the bottom of the wadi, it bounced onto a rough track that dropped so steeply from the road that Mike, even with his eyes open, would never have seen it in time.

The track soon became narrow and dangerous, turning sharply to the right in parallel with the road above. Before reaching the bend the Jeep slewed to a halt in a cloud of dust. Then the engine cut out and there was silence.

Mike opened his eyes. As the dust cleared he saw the Jeep had stopped near the brink of a precipice. He engaged the handbrake and turned to Dave, who was losing a lot of blood from his right side. Mike gently eased him into a sitting position to examine the wounds. There appeared to be two, one in Dave's shoulder, the other near his hip. The latter injury could only have been caused by shots fired from a high vantage point, such as a hilltop overlooking the road.

He opened his window and listened. All he could hear was the distant drone of the bus continuing on its way up the hill. Its driver, he assumed, had glimpsed the liberal sprinkling of bullet holes in the Jeep's bodywork and decided not to get involved. It wouldn't be the first time someone had turned a blind eye to trouble on the road from Jerusalem to Jericho.

Mike searched for a first aid kit and found one under his seat, but its contents were woefully inadequate for dressing Dave's wounds. Whilst Mike was doing his best to apply the single bandage to Dave's shoulder, Dave gave a faint moan.

'Dave? Can you hear me?'

'Where...?' Dave began, then winced, fighting back waves of pain.

'Don't try to talk, Dave, just listen. We've been attacked by some lunatics with assault weapons, but I think we're safe now. They probably think we've gone over the cliff. We're on the edge of the Wadi Kelt and I'm going to St George's monastery to get help. I don't like to leave you but if we both stay here it could be hours before anyone finds us.'

'*Al tidag... Lo ason,*' whispered Dave. Then he passed out again.

Mike cautiously opened his door and clambered out. He had decided to head for the monastery because that seemed the less risky of his two options. The alternative was to walk back to the main road and try to hail a passing car, but if a gunman was still perched on a nearby hilltop Mike would present an easy target.

He peered over the precipice immediately in front of the Jeep. It was much too dangerous for an inexperienced climber, but a few metres back along the trail a goat track angled its way down a slightly gentler slope into the depths of the wadi. As Mike set off towards it he stopped at the rear of the Jeep, bent down and rubbed a layer of grime from the fender. The bumper sticker read: I'M A SWYVER DRIVER. ARE YOU?

3

The first part of Mike's journey to the monastery was painful, hot and terrifying. There was no well-worn route from his starting point. When not following goat tracks, which were invariably narrow and often bordered precipitous cliffs, he had to negotiate treacherous slopes of scree. The loose material made walking arduous and he frequently fell onto sharp rocks or into thorn bushes. As he pushed on he was acutely aware that his next fall could be disabling – or even fatal. It was not without reason that the lower reaches of the Wadi Kelt were traditionally held to be the Bible's 'valley of the shadow of death'.

He intended to walk east along the bed of the wadi but on reaching it he found his progress impeded by a jumble of huge boulders. It seemed the journey was going to take much longer than he'd expected. His concern for Dave was turning to panic, when he remembered that an ancient aqueduct ran along the wadi's northern cliffs. If he could reach it, it might provide an easier route to the monastery.

The climb taxed his remaining strength to the limit. His legs began to stiffen whenever he rested for a moment to catch his breath. The roar of pumped blood pounded in his ears. Sweat poured down his forehead, trickled over his eyebrows and stung his eyes.

Thanks to renovations over the centuries, the aqueduct still carried water from springs farther up the wadi, past the monastery and on to the ruins of Herod's Jericho. At the point where Mike reached it, the aqueduct was a concrete trough, a little over half a metre wide, in which clear, cool water flowed gently towards the Jordan Valley. By walking in this trough he hoped to make progress more quickly than he could over rough terrain; and the aqueduct followed a relatively straight course, sometimes bridging gullies which would otherwise have required difficult detours.

He stepped into the channel and the water came almost to his knees. As soon as he felt its coolness he longed for it to touch every part of his body. He knelt down and the water reached his crotch. Then he lay full length in the narrow channel, submerging himself completely, burying his face in the flow. The water swept through his clothes and hair, caressing his skin, soothing his burning muscles. He held his breath for as long as he could, savouring the exquisite sensation. Then he got to his feet and began the final stage of his trek to the monastery. The water evaporating from his clothes continued to cool and refresh him. Almost weeping with relief he recited aloud some words from the Twenty-third Psalm, words once dulled by familiarity but now so sharply bright they seemed freshly minted: 'He leads me beside the waters of rest, he restores my life... Even though I walk through the valley of the shadow of death, I fear no evil...'

The buildings comprising the monastery of St George clung to the layered cliffs like a colony of barnacles. Named after George of Koziba who had led its community to greatness in the sixth century, it had once been famous for its hospitality to travellers passing between Jerusalem and Jericho. As Mike reached for the bell rope that hung by the door, he hoped the present-day occupants would live up to its ancient reputation.

Several pulls on the rope produced no response. A notice by the door gave the times when the monastery was open to tourists: 8 a.m.–12 noon and 3 p.m.–5 p.m. Mike looked at his watch; it was one thirty. He tried shouting that he was not a tourist and that a friend's life was in danger. He shouted it in English and he shouted it, as best he could, in Arabic, punctuating his cries with more pulls on the bell and thumps on the door, but still there was no response. Then he remembered that St George's was a Greek Orthodox monastery, so he tried shouting in Greek, but that produced no result either.

In the monastery courtyard stood an alcove where a tap dripped water onto the stone flags. A small sign above the tap said, 'You may drink' and a metal cup hung from it by a chain. Mike helped himself to several draughts while he considered the situation. Above him, stone buildings rose up the cliffs in tiers, some well built, some rather ramshackle, but all with doors closed and windows shuttered. In growing despair he looked beyond the courtyard walls in the direction of Jericho, at least another forty minutes' walk away.

Along the track from Jericho a small, hunched figure was approaching on foot with a heavily laden donkey. Mike turned off the water and went out to meet the traveller, hoping to discover a monk who would take a message to his brethren inside. Instead he encountered a wizened, shabby, poorly shaven little man in a Bedouin headdress.

'*Salaam*,' said Mike.

'*Salaam*. Not time,' wheezed the Arab, pointing to the sign by the door.

'I know, but I need help.'

The man shook his head.

'Open only three o'clock. I know it. Bring supplies from Jericho every day.'

'But my friend's been...' Mike began, then thought better of giving too much detail. 'My friend needs help urgently.'

'Friend? Where friend?' said the Arab, looking over Mike's shoulder.

'A long way from here,' said Mike, pointing back up the wadi. 'Near the road.'

'Car out of gas?' The Arab wagged a finger disapprovingly. 'Always should get full of gas before drive into desert. You American?'

'No, English.'

'Ah, English!' said the Arab, as though this explained everything. 'Fish and chips! Anthea Turner!' he added, eager to show that he was *en rapport* with quintessential Englishness.

Mike pointed towards the door at the far end of the courtyard.

'I have to talk to a monk. Can you please get one of them to see me?'

'*No, no, no, no* sir,' said the Arab, shaking his head vigorously to rule out any misunderstanding.

'But you said you were delivering supplies. They must open the door for you.'

'*No, no, no* sir. Three o'clock only.'

Mike couldn't see any logic in this.

'So why come at half past one?'

'Sleep,' he said, pointing to the shade beneath a group of cypress trees. 'At home wife, children, grandchildren, all shouting very noisy. You have children?'

'No. Look, I have to speak to a monk. It's an emergency.'

'You have wife?'

'No. I must speak to a monk.'

'You want be a monk?'

'No. I just want to talk to one. I told you, my friend needs help. He's injured. Bleeding.'

'Ah! He bleed!' The Arab nodded with comprehension. 'Maybe I help,' he said, rasping nicotine-stained fingers over the stubble on his chin. Raising one eyebrow he gave Mike a questioning, sideways glance.

In response Mike delved in his pockets and pulled out all the shekel notes and loose change he could find. 'Okay? *Shahih?*'

The little man fingered the damp notes dubiously, then shrugged and pocketed the money.

'*Shahih, shahih*, I help.' Reaching inside his patched jacket he pulled out a mobile phone. He tapped the buttons with practised nonchalance and was soon conversing with someone in rapid Arabic. Then he put the phone away and said, 'Monk coming now.'

Mike stared.

'But... if you've got a phone, you could have called for an ambulance!'

'You wanted monk,' said the Arab.

In frustration Mike smote the palm of his hand against his brow. Then the sound of grinding keys and sliding bolts came from the monastery door and a second later it swung open. A stately, bearded monk with deep-set eyes stepped into the courtyard.

Mike hurried to meet him and, using his reasonably fluent Greek, began to explain his predicament. But the monk raised both hands in protest and shook his head.

'You don't speak Greek?' said Mike, his despair returning.

'Not much, but my English is pretty good.' The monk's accent owed almost as much to the eastern seaboard of the USA as it did to the eastern Mediterranean. 'No need to look surprised. I'm Palestinian by birth, I speak American English by education and I'm a monk by calling. I'm Father Joseph, the Archigrammateus – which is Greek for Chief Scribe, as I expect you know. In my case it means administrator and PR man. C'mon in.'

Mike followed him over the stone threshold and found himself in a cool entrance hall with benches around the walls. Father Joseph paused to give the Arab a wave of acknowledgement before closing the door. Then he produced a packet of Camels from one of his capacious sleeves and turned to Mike.

'Cigarette? Sure? Mind if I do? Okay, siddown and tell me your problem. We've got total privacy.'

They sat down and Mike told his story as succinctly as he could. As soon as the monk had grasped the details of Dave's location he reached inside his other sleeve and produced his mobile phone. During the next two minutes he spoke to a succession of people at the Joint Security Base, switching with ease between English, Arabic and Hebrew.

'It's all taken care of,' he said, sliding the phone back into his habit. 'The local security people are on to it. They're sending a helicopter with army medics to collect your friend. Should be there in minutes.'

Mike expelled his breath in a long sigh and sagged back against the wall. Father Joseph left him for a moment and returned with a tall glass of water and a bowl of fruit. As he sat down again he studied Mike's face carefully.

'You know, I think I recognise you. Aren't you Dr Mike Totley?'

'Yes. How on earth...?'

'I was at a conference in Washington DC last November. Heard you give a paper on the Dead Sea Scrolls.'

'Really? That's amazing!'

'I was actually attending the Fundamentalism Study Group, but a young woman called Peterson or something said you'd be worth hearing, so I went along.'

'She did?'

'Sure. Seemed a big fan of yours. You know, I'm intrigued by those guys who wrote the Scrolls. They were a lot like some of our monks, the way they took their separatism to extremes. I mean, I've got brother monks here who think we're the only ones who'll be okay at the Last Judgement. They think everybody else – Jews, Muslims, unbelievers, Catholics, Anglicans, Baptists and all the rest – will get condemned to Hell up there by Jerusalem and then... I'm sorry – you're worried about your friend. Perhaps we can talk again in better circumstances. When you've had enough to eat and drink you'd better go to the Security Base.'

Mike said he wasn't sure he could walk that far in his present state.

'Don't worry,' said Father Joseph, 'I think I can arrange some transportation.'

4

An hour later Mike was once again sipping strong black coffee in the main office of the Joint Security Base. Commander Levit was not on duty today. Instead, the chair behind the desk was occupied by his Palestinian counterpart, Commander Rawan Yassine, a slim woman of no more than thirty-five with a pleasant oval face and short, raven hair. Looking around the room Mike noticed that the signed photograph of Tabatha Cash on the Mount of Olives had been turned to the wall.

'I know this must be very tiring for you, Dr Totley,' said Commander Yassine, 'but I will have to ask a few more questions to get things clear.'

'I made them as clear as I could to your colleague at reception,' said Mike. Emotional and physical exhaustion were taking their toll on his patience.

'Yes, we are grateful. But I do need a few more details.' Commander Yassine looked down at the notes she'd received from the reception desk. There were some odd features in the account. 'The car you were in – it seems to have done very strange things. Can you please explain?'

'It was INSANE.'

Commander Yassine looked up.

'I'm sorry, you have had a bad shock. Perhaps I should see you tomorrow, when you…'

'That's the acronym for its automatic guidance system: Integrated Neural Sensing And Navigation Equipment. It's marketed by an organisation in the States.'

Apart from permitting one eyebrow to flicker slightly as she amended the notes, Rawan Yassine showed no surprise.

'I see. Then you crossed the wadi to find help at the monastery. That was a big risk; the cliffs are dangerous. Last summer there was a lost tourist, walking; he…' To spare Mike the details she walked her fingers along the edge of the desk then mimicked a sudden fall with her hand. 'But you were fortunate.' She got up and turned to the map on the wall. 'From the monastery you came here on a donkey, and by the time you reached us your friend was already in hospital. We have a team of experts examining the car, and helicopters looking for the gunman.'

'Or gunmen,' said Mike. 'I did say I thought there might be more than one.'

'In any case there is little hope of finding them; with so many caves and narrow ravines, people disappear easily in that area. And they had plenty of time to get away.'

The phone rang, bringing her back to the desk. She listened for a few seconds without speaking then thanked the caller and replaced the handset.

'That was news of your shot friend. He had lost a lot of blood but is out of serious danger. He will undergo surgery very soon.' She said this as she said everything, with brisk efficiency and no trace of emotion, but when Mike breathed an audible sigh of relief she allowed herself a brief, sympathetic smile.

'Now, Dr Totley, to continue: I do not have many details about your friend. He will, of course, be interviewed when he is well enough, but it would help to have the basic facts. His name is Hirschfeld?'

'That's right.'

'He's an Israeli citizen?'

'Yes, but he's an American immigrant.'

'And he is Jewish?'

'A Jewish Christian.'

'I'm sorry, Dr Totley, can you explain that?'

'He's a Jew who's become a Christian.'

'In that case he's not a Jew any more.'

'Dave would strongly disagree. He's a Messianic Jew – a Jew who believes the Messiah has come.'

'So he's a Jew and a Christian at the same time?'

'Sort of.'

'I see.' The words slipped out as a formality. Commander Yassine was completely out of her theological depth. She wrote in her notes that Dave was an American Israeli Jewish Christian and hoped someone else would make sense of it.

'And why would anyone want to kill him? Does he have enemies?'

'I've only known him a couple of weeks, but I doubt it. He seems too easygoing.'

'If this was not a personal attack it is the second act of terrorism in five days. On Sunday a car was blown up a few kilometres south of Ramallah.'

'That would be mine,' said Mike.

For once there was unsuppressed astonishment in the Commander's face.

'*Your* car was blown up?'

'Well, strictly speaking I'd hired it, but it certainly blew up. Commander Levit took the details.'

Rawan Yassine went to the filing cabinet and pulled out a folder. She sat down again and flicked through the contents.

'I have not yet had time to read his report or I would have recognised your name. So, you have suffered terrorist attacks twice in a few days, Dr Totley?'

'Coincidence, I'm sure. I mean, I don't have enemies either.'

'I'm sorry. This is a troubled time. Not only are there people who wish to destroy the peace process, many religious fanatics have entered the country and some would like to provoke a crisis before the year 2000 is over. They think it will help the coming of the Messiah. One more question: was Mr Hirschfeld able to say anything after he was shot?'

'Yes,' said Mike, remembering Dave's brief return to consciousness. 'He said, "*Al tidag, lo ason.*"'

'Hebrew. You understand it?'

'Yes. Roughly translated it means, "Don't worry, it's not the end of the world." Dave's an irrepressible optimist.'

'And we must all hope he is right,' said Commander Yassine.

5

Mike had left the Arab's donkey tethered to a telegraph pole outside the Joint Security Base. Passing the checkpoint by the gate, he was surprised to see that the Arab had walked back from the monastery and was sitting on the ground next to the animal. As soon as the little man saw Mike he sprang up and came to meet him.

'*Salaam*, sir,' he said, clutching at Mike's arm. 'Very sorry. Here, please.' He pulled an assortment of notes and coins from his pocket and held them out. It was the money Mike had given him in exchange for help. 'You Christian?'

'Yes,' said Mike.

'I Christian also,' said the Arab. 'Please forgive Nabil, your brother. That is my name – Nabil. Father Joseph – the monk – he talk to me and I see I have done a bad sin. Please forgive me, sir.' There were tears in his eyes.

Greatly moved, Mike put an arm around the Arab's shoulder.

'I forgive you, Nabil. Thanks for coming to find me.'

'We can be friends?'

'Of course, Nabil. Please call me Mike.'

They embraced and shook hands. Then Nabil pointed at the top of Mike's head.

'You have no hat, Mr Mike.'

'No. I left it in my friend's Jeep. Don't suppose I'll get it back.'

'Here, please.' Nabil removed his *keffiyeh* and offered it to Mike. 'Sun very hot. Should wear something.'

'But…'

'Please, please. You English, need it more. And I have another.'

Mike sensed it would be rude to refuse. He took the *keffiyeh* and put it on.

'Very good!' exclaimed Nabil. 'Like Lawrence of Arabia!'

Mike laughed.

'Nabil, do you know a good place to eat in Jericho? I haven't had a decent meal since breakfast.'

'Oh, yes. My cousin has restaurant. Very good food. Very clean, nice place. I take you?'

'Thanks. Why don't you join me?'

So Nabil untied the donkey and the three of them set off towards the town.

Chapter Sixteen

1

[Fifth extract from the journal of Effin L Clinger]

Day 16 (Thur. 18 May)

Another dramatic day! Some of us came back to the canyon first thing, like it was Monday, while the rest stayed at the Center to deal with all the stuff we took back yesterday. Totley and Dave were meant to join us at lunchtime but they didn't show up. We guessed their work was taking longer than expected. Then, late in the afternoon, Totley arrived at the camp alone and on foot. He'd gotten a taxi from Jericho to the end of the dirt track and walked the rest of the way.

We were all appalled to hear that Dave had been shot! And for the second time this week Totley himself had come close to death. On reflection this was not surprising, for judgement on the covetous 'lingereth not, and their damnation slumbereth not' (2 Peter 2:3).

Totley was wearing an Arab kerchief which he says an Arab friend gave him. This doesn't surprise me either. It's well known that the illegal antiquities market is run by Arabs. It all fits together.

During our meal this evening Mrs. Hope-Parsons let out a yell. It turned out that an olive stone had loosened a filling in her upper right bicuspid. Fortunately I had a Domestic Dental Repair Kit in my pack and it took only a few minutes to fit a new one. She has a fine set of teeth, enhanced by dental work of high quality. Seems she's a three-times-a-day brusher, no matter what – a real lady!

The same cannot be said of Ms. Patterson, who has recently been wearing a pair of very short cut-offs and a top that shows naked flesh above her waist and even exposes some cleavage. Noticing that her immodesty was distracting our young men (who all glance in her direction when she bends down to pick up a basket of potsherds) I decided to do something about it. I expected only barbed comments if I talked to her myself so I raised the matter with Dr. Sinnet. To my surprise he seemed reluctant to take action. Eventually he muttered something about having to accommodate the weaker brethren and went over to speak to her. I guess he's progressed so far in holiness that he's hardly aware of the sinful thoughts that afflict his fellow-men.

Day 17 (Fri. 19 May)

This morning Ms. Patterson was wearing a shirt and proper shorts. Dr. Sinnet seemed unusually irritable, especially toward me. Perhaps he woke up too late to spend much time with the Lord in prayer.

The burial chamber in our cave is now completely cleared, so today we began work on a new area. Soon after breakfast I made my first discovery – the sole of an ancient leather sandal, which I extracted from the dirt myself! When I showed it to Totley he said, 'It's survived the centuries amazingly well, Effin. A pity it couldn't also withstand your assaults with a dental probe' – an unjustified comment as only a few pieces had broken off. He said I should look for another, because a one-legged man would never have made it up the cliffs. He has a twisted sense of humour.

When we finished work, instead of driving back to the Center with the rest of us, Totley and Ms. Patterson headed off on their own in the two-seater Land Rover. It's obvious they're in this jar thing together.

2

A flock of dark, thrush-sized birds performed communal aerobatics, calling to each other with wild and melancholy whistles. Their wings flashed like burnished bronze as they wheeled and tumbled over the crags.

'They're Tristram's Grackles,' said Mike.

'Oh, they're beautiful!' exclaimed Connie, hugging herself.

She and Mike were sitting on a broad ledge, two hundred metres above the shore of the Dead Sea. A perennial spring splashed from the rocks, creating a streak of verdure down the barren cliffs. Far below, the oasis of En-Gedi lay like a bright emerald in a landscape of ochres and greys.

'Had enough to eat?'

'Plenty,' said Connie. 'It was a great idea to bring a picnic.'

'I'm sorry the food was a bit dull. I didn't think of coming here until yesterday, so all I could get hold of were some things left over from this morning's break.'

'Don't apologise. I like people who do things on impulse. Now, where's this temple you promised to show me?'

They left the shade of pendulous lianas and Mike led the way to En-Gedi's high plateau, where a network of stone foundations lay exposed near the edge of the cliffs. After the exertion of the climb Connie took off her wide-brimmed hat and fanned her face.

'Neat!' she said, walking around the remains.

'The associated pottery dates it to around 3000 BC. At least that's the conventional date, but I'm sure Chuck Sinnet would revise it to fit his compressed history of the world.'

'You don't believe a word of that stuff, do you?'

Mike shook his head.

'Sinnet treats the Bible like a scientific textbook. Doesn't let it speak on its own terms.'

They sat down on a rock and admired the view. Across the Dead Sea, beyond a haze of heat and vapour, the Jordanian mountains rose in massive solidity, scarred by the shadows of deep canyons. There was no shade on the plateau, so Mike pulled his *keffiyeh* from the back pocket of his shorts, arranged it on his head and secured it with its loop of black cord. Connie put her hat back on.

'What's he like to work with?' asked Mike.

'Sinnet? He and Rip are like buddies in a Hemmingway novel, so in our cave the testosterone level is about as noxious as the batshit. And his sexist attitude bugs me. He obviously regards women as the weaker sex and a source of temptation. Like yesterday when he said, "On behalf of some of the brethren here, I must ask you to cover up some more."' Connie convincingly impersonated Sinnet's southern drawl.

'He said what?'

'Personally I thought he was being stupid, but I don't want to offend anybody so I've tried to meet him halfway. Do you think I look okay?'

Mike wanted to say that he would find her disturbingly attractive in a bag lady's cast-offs; instead he said, 'Yes, fine.'

'And this morning we had a big disagreement. You know those enormous rocks in a deep pit at the back of our cave? I offered to wriggle down between them and see if there was anything interesting at the bottom. I'm the only one in our cave who's both agile and slim enough to try it, but Sinnet wouldn't let me. I thought he didn't believe a woman could do it so I challenged him and things got heated. In the end he said he wouldn't let a man try it either, so I accepted his decision and we shook hands.'

'I'm impressed with your commitment to the dig,' said Mike. 'That would have been above and beyond the call of duty even for a genuine volunteer.'

Connie gazed at the distant mountains with a lost-to-the-world expression, then she said, 'Did you say there was a place we could swim? It would be great to cool off.'

They followed a narrow track down to the wadi known as Nahal David, where a waterfall clattered into a small shady pool. Bathers wallowed idly in the water.

'I've got a swimsuit at the Centre,' said Connie, removing her hat and kicking off her trainers. 'If you'd suggested this trip before I left yesterday I would've brought it.' She unbuttoned her shirt, pulled it free from her shorts and tied it together above her midriff.

Mike sat to untie his trainers.

'Don't worry. In this temperature there's a lot to be said for swimming with your clothes on. When you get out, the water slowly evaporates and keeps you cool for ages.'

'Oh yes? I bet you engineered this whole thing because you like to see a woman in a wet shirt.'

She stepped onto a prominent rock and leaped into the nearest patch of clear water. Mike dropped his *keffiyeh* on the ground and followed her.

Some minutes later they emerged from the pool, collected their things and followed the outflow downstream. Pushing through a curtain of reeds that towered high above their heads, they found a secluded spot where a flowering tamarisk spread its dappled shade over a huge slab of rock. Connie sat down on the rock then lay back and stretched languorously.

'Mmm, you were right, Mike; this feels great.'

Mike sat beside her and she turned towards him, raising herself on her right elbow.

'So tell me, what does En-Gedi mean? All these biblical names seem to mean something.'

'Well, do you know the story in the Bible where King Saul comes here with his troops and suddenly needs the loo? He used a cave, not realising that David, whom he was trying to kill, was hiding at the back.'

'I vaguely remember it, but I don't see how it explains the name.'

'Well, I have a theory that before Saul went in the cave he scratched "Engaged!" on a rock outside, so he wouldn't be disturbed. Later the inscription got weathered until the third and fourth letters disappeared and the exclamation mark at the end was easily mistaken for a…'

Connie pushed him off the rock with a playful thrust of her foot.

'Mike, that was just awful! Even worse than your door handle joke!'

'Sorry. The real explanation…'

'You mean I'm supposed to believe this one?'

'…is that it means "the Spring of the Young Goat" – probably the ibex. You can still see them here if you're lucky.'

'Okay, I'll buy that.'

Mike lay down on the rock and faced her, his head resting on his left hand.

'Talking of names, how did you come to be called Sydney? It's an unusual name for a woman.'

'Not on my side of the pond. But there was a special reason in my case. My pop used to do business trips to Australia – he died when I was a kid – and he was there when I was born. He phoned every day to see if I'd arrived, and on the day I finally popped out he phoned from Sydney. It was a lucky escape.'

'How come?'

'A couple more days and he might've phoned from Wagga Wagga.'

Mike laughed. But the laughter gave way to silence. He was on edge now. As it was Friday the Reserve would close early for the start of *Shabbat*. The opportunity he'd carefully created had almost slipped away and he felt helpless to retrieve it, paralysed by a fear that Dave had misread the signs.

The silence dragged on, tense, awkward and pleading to be broken. And the only words he could bring himself to say were, 'I suppose we'd better go.'

But Connie's thoughts had taken a more creative turn. As Mike opened his mouth to speak she said, 'En-Gedi's in the Song of Solomon, isn't it?'

'Yes,' said Mike. The word squeaked out of him as though he'd inhaled a lungful of helium. He cleared his throat and tried again. 'Yes, in the first chapter.'

'"My beloved is to me like a sachet of myrrh that nestles between my breasts",' quoted Connie, moving closer to him and dropping her voice. '"My beloved is to me like a spray of henna blossoms in the vineyards of En-Gedi."'

After a pause Mike responded with the next verse.

'"How beautiful you are, my love! Indeed you are beautiful, with eyes like doves!"'

'"How handsome you are, my beloved, how perfect!"'

This time Mike's response came without hesitation. As the spring cascading from the cliffs above found a well-worn bed to flow in, so his feelings were finding their channel in familiar words.

'"Like a lily among thorns, so is my love among all other maidens!"'

'"Like an apple tree among the trees of the wood is my beloved among young men. I delight to sit in his shade, and his fruit is sweet to my taste."' Connie moved closer again, bringing their bodies almost into contact, and continued in a slow whisper. '"I am faint with love! O that his left hand were under my head, that his right arm embraced me!"'

All doubts banished, Mike complied and their lips met. It was a while before he resumed.

'"Your lips yield nectar, my bride; honey and milk are under your tongue!"'

'I can't follow that,' said Connie. 'Have you skipped a chapter?'

'Two, actually. Am I going too fast?'

'Uh-uh.'

'"How lovely are your sandalled feet, O royal maiden! The curves of your thighs are works of perfection"' – his hand moved appreciatively along her legs and over her left thigh, then on to her waist – '"your navel is like a goblet that never lacks wine, your stomach like wheat encircled with lilies, your breasts are twin fawns of a gazelle"' – between each word he placed a kiss on the exposed parts of her breasts, then, reluctantly following the dictate of the words, moving up to her neck – '"your neck is a tower of ivory, your eyes are like the pools of Heshbon…"'

'Don't stop, but could you skip the bit about my nose resembling a mountain of Lebanon? I'm still not quite at home with that comparison.'

Mike laughed and they kissed again. When they parted Connie said, 'I don't remember any more, so I guess I'll just say it up front: I love you, Mike.'

'And I love you, Connie.'

'Just hold me for a minute. Don't say or do anything, just hold me.'

He held her and became aware that she was sobbing softly.

'Connie, are you okay? What is it?'

'Relief, I guess. I was beginning to think this would never happen. You didn't seem to want me to get close. And then the bomb and the ambush… I was scared you'd die before… Oh God, I can't bear to think about it!'

He held her more tightly and stroked her hair. 'I didn't think it would happen either. It's been torture, falling steadily more in love with you and remembering what you said in Washington – that our relationship could only be professional. What happened to that, by the way? Did the CIA change the rule book?'

She eased out of his embrace, wiped the moisture from her cheeks and looked into his eyes.

'It's time I put you right on that. I'm not here for the CIA.'

'You're not? But I thought… I mean I assumed…'

'I came off the Swyver case after I screwed up in Washington. I'm on vacation. I joined the dig to see if there was any hope for us.'

'You joined... but this is incredible!'

'I lied a little on the application form – gave myself a respectable, conservative background. And I made a big deal out of the fact that I'd heard your lecture in Washington. I bet that's what did it.'

'I didn't mean that. I meant... are you saying that in Washington you already...'

'Before Washington. I started falling for you on the plane from Newark International.'

'But that's even more incredible! I talked incessantly about the Dead Sea Scrolls!'

'So? In *Brief Encounter* Celia Johnson falls for Trevor Howard when he's listing diseases of the lung.'

They laughed, embraced and lay down again on the rock. On the far side of the stream the bathers from the pool could be heard making their way towards the Reserve exit.

'Such a pity we have to go,' said Connie, gazing up into the tamarisk's delicate pink canopy. 'This is paradise.'

'I know. But if we stay much longer we'll be thrown out.'

'Like Adam and Eve.'

'With one big difference: we can come back next week.'

Chapter Seventeen

1

'You look like the cat that got the cream!' said Dave, shaking Mike's hand. 'You took my advice?'

Mike pulled a chair closer to the hospital bed and sat down.

'Yes. We went to En-Gedi like you suggested.'

'Great! So you proposed and she accepted? Congratulations!'

'Well, it wasn't like that exactly,' said Mike.

'Oh? So what was it like exactly?'

'I didn't actually ask her to marry me.'

'But that was the whole idea! What the hell's stopping you? Is it because Connie doesn't hold your *hashkafa*?'

'Hold my what?'

'Religious outlook. If you want my opinion…'

'No, nothing to do with that. I just think we ought to know each other a lot longer before…'

'But you said you'd known her since last November!'

'Yes, but… look, that's enough about me,' said Mike, avoiding an awkward explanation. 'How are you doing?'

'Oh, just fine. Thanks to you. From what I hear, you saved my life.'

'Hardly,' said Mike, with a self-deprecating wave. 'I'd say we both owe our lives to the guidance system in your Jeep. Why didn't you tell me it had one of those things?'

'Subject never came up. It's only meant to work at the Rapture.'

'I know; I saw the ad. How long are they keeping you here?'

'Only a few more days if I continue to make good progress.'

'That's wonderful!'

'The bad news is that I won't be able to rejoin the dig. It'll be a while before I can climb a rope ladder or wield a patishe.'

'Will you go back to Beer Sheva?'

'Well, I was wondering... I need to be around Jerusalem a while longer. Do you think they'd let me stay on at the Centre? I could do some computer stuff.'

'Haven't the security people finished questioning you?'

'Yeah, that's no problem. By the way, they think those guys who spoiled our drive were using Galils.' Dave could see that Mike didn't know what he was talking about. 'A Galil is an assault weapon developed by the Israeli military after the 1967 war. Takes a fifty-round magazine. Converts into a sub-machine gun.'

'Does that help identify the terrorists?'

'Not really. When I lived in the States you could buy a Galil for about two thousand dollars from your local Guns-R-Us. But I have my own theory.'

'Which is?'

Dave beckoned Mike closer and lowered his voice.

'You remember I told you some Ultra-Orthodox want to stop all excavation of ancient Jewish burials? Well, there are cases where an archaeologist has been the target of a *pulsa danura*, a religious decree which turns a murder into a good deed.'

'What?'

'It fits, Mike. We found a multiple burial and we didn't play it by the book. I know the later handling of the remains wasn't your decision, but you're the cave supervisor and I'm your assistant, and in the eyes of those *nudniks* that probably incriminates us. What I can't work out is who leaked the news. Did you mention the burials to anyone outside the team?'

'Only Baruch Zederbaum, and he's no friend of extremists. Have you said all this to the police?'

'Are you kidding? I can't risk getting the dig into trouble! Like I said the other day, if the authorities came down heavy we'd have to stop everything. Anyway, you'd better be careful, Mike. It's likely those assholes had you as their prime target; the security guys say most of the bullets hit my Jeep on the passenger side.'

2

The library was empty apart from Connie. She was sitting at a table, poring over several books and covering a notepad with shorthand. Mike crossed the room and sat next to her.

'Hi! How's Dave?' Connie took off her glasses and kissed him on the cheek.

'Still doing well. He sends you his love. Have a good field trip?'

'Great! Herodium was fascinating. And so's this.' She tapped an open book with her glasses. 'I've been getting acquainted with the Rev. Z Smith, trying to work out how to run a computer test on his so-called cipher, and I've made an interesting discovery. The Copper Scroll has sixty-four entries, right?'

'Right.'

'And you told me Smith found a reference to the caves of Nahal Shuhan in the forty-seventh?'

'Right.'

'Could you just take me through the main points of his argument?'

'But you've got it there in front of you.'

'Let's pretend I haven't,' said Connie, closing the book and putting it to one side.

Mike marshalled his thoughts.

'Okay. It goes something like this. The forty-seventh entry mentions "the Great Wadi", which Smith thinks is Nahal Shuhan. This is because the previous entry mentions Mesad, which he thinks is Masada, and the one before that mentions a place called Bet Tamar, "House of the Palm Tree", which he says is En-Gedi, famous for its palms. In other words he locates the forty-seventh cache in Nahal Shuhan because it's a big wadi near Masada and En-Gedi. He then turns to the details. The Scroll says the hiding place in the Great Wadi is an underground cistern by an aqueduct; but there's never been an aqueduct in Nahal Shuhan so he resorts to his cipher theory. After getting the gematria treatment, the hiding place becomes a cave in the wadi's southern cliffs. For an encore Smith turns back to the forty-fifth entry where he finds the term *herem*, "devoted to the Temple"; he assumes it means Temple vessels and that it relates to a whole group of caches. As a result – hey presto! – we have Temple vessels in one of the caves of Nahal Shuhan!'

'Not according to this,' said Connie, opening the book again.

'Here's the paragraph where he deals with sections forty-five through forty-seven. It contains no references to Nahal Shuhan, En-Gedi or Masada, and no mention of a cipher.'

Mike took the book in silence and read the whole paragraph from the beginning. It said:

> The pass of Bet Tamar should be sought at the eastern end of the Wadi Kelt near Jericho. Bet Tamar means 'House of the Palm Tree' and Jericho was called 'the city of palms' as we know from the Bible (Deuteronomy 34:3, etc.). Cache 45, described as 'devoted to the Temple', is therefore buried in a cave at the entrance to a defile in that region. As for cache 46, the fortress or stronghold (which is the meaning of *mesad*) is most likely the Herodian fortress of Kypros on the south side of the wadi. The treasure (9 talents of silver) lies buried nearby in a small opening in the rock. This brings us to cache 47. The 'great wadi' can only be the Wadi Kelt itself. The aqueduct mentioned there must be the ancient channel which still carries water today. The cistern, said to contain 12 talents, must lie near the mouth of the wadi, close to other localities in this section.

'It's utterly different!' said Mike. 'The book must have gone through more than one edition!'

'Three to be precise, and they're all here,' said Connie, picking another volume from the desk. 'You've just been reading the first edition and this is the second.'

Mike opened it at the title page.

'That's odd; it says nothing about revisions.'

'I know. Without reading every edition you can only tell them apart by comparing publication dates.'

Connie had inserted a piece of paper to mark the page dealing with caches 45–47. Mike turned to the place and read:

> Bet Tamar is without doubt En-Gedi, also called Hazazon-Tamar in the Bible (2 Chronicles 20:2). Cache 45, consisting of sacred vessels from the Temple, was therefore hidden in a cave in a nearby defile, almost certainly that known as 'the Ascent of Ziz' in Old Testament times (2 Chronicles 20:16). The fortress mentioned as the landmark for cache 46 was probably the Roman-period citadel at Tel Goren, some 500 yards to the south. The

treasure, described as 9 talents of silver, lies concealed in a small opening in the rock somewhere nearby. The 'great wadi' or 'great stream' of cache 47 can now be identified as Nahal Arugot, the perennial stream which passes 200 yards south of Tel Goren. The treasure, buried in a cistern near the watercourse, is said to be '12 talents'.

'Amazing, isn't it?' said Connie. 'He gets a completely different set of locations just by playing around with a few names. And still no sign of a cipher yet. He doesn't come up with that idea until the third edition. That's when the caves of Nahal Shuhan make their first appearance.'

She handed Mike the third edition and he browsed through it.

'This is the version I got from Swyver in January,' he said.

Connie put her glasses on and looked at her notes.

'The interesting thing is, most of the revisions are minor. These three caches are the only ones that change their locations drastically with every edition.'

'Strange.'

'It's like someone's looking for this buried treasure without finding it, and Smith has to go back to the drawing board each time to come up with alternative locations. By the third edition he's run out of obvious possibilities and comes up with the cipher theory to create some more. You said Smith isn't an archaeologist, so someone else must be doing the digging. I was wondering…'

'Sinnet!' said Mike.

'Exactly! Is there some way we could find out for sure?'

'I expect so.' Mike took the paper Connie had used as a bookmark, borrowed her pencil and scribbled down a few place names and dates. Then he got up from the desk.

'Father Joseph would know if there'd been a dig near the monastery, and I'll contact Baruch…'

Connie stood up and placed a finger on his lips. 'Okay, but don't do it right away.'

'No?'

'No.' Connie removed her glasses again and put them down on the desk. 'It's not often we get time away from other people in this place, so when we do I think we should take advantage of it, don't you? Put the paper down, Mike. You'll need both hands to

213

do this properly.'

3

'I wish I knew what those two were up to,' said Sinnet, watching Mike and Connie on a security video.

Parbunkel crossed Sinnet's office to take a closer look at the screen.

'I think that's French kissing.'

'I know that, Leo. I meant I'd like to know what they were doing a few moments earlier. Could you run this tape through a computer and enhance the image?'

'Chuck?'

'I don't mean so I can watch those two fools groping each other! I want to know what they were reading. See those books on the table? Could you isolate that part of the screen and give me a close-up without losing definition?'

'I can try.'

'Then do it now, Leo. And miss dinner if you have to.'

4

[Sixth (and final) extract from the journal of Effin L Clinger]

Day 19 (Sun. 21 May)

A wonderful service at the Garden Tomb, with no less a person than Dr. Kermit Bender preaching! He emphasized the importance of believing in the premillennial return of Christ, and I realized I'd neglected this aspect of the saving truth in my conversations with Totley. Must make every effort to correct the oversight.

Totley is in unusually high spirits and I can guess why: he's probably found a buyer for the stolen jar and is richer by several million dollars! It riles me to think of him getting away with it, but Dr. Sinnet seems determined to take no further action.

Spent the afternoon in the garden at the Center with Mrs. Hope-Parsons, discussing the benefits of regular flossing.

Day 20 (Mon. 22 May)

Back to the canyon. Haven't found the other sandal yet but Totley is happy for me to just keep on digging in my own corner. In other parts of the cave he and Alice Wesson have been finding all kinds of stuff – pieces of matting, willow baskets and such like.

During lunch I asked Totley outright whether he was a premillennialist, a postmillennialist or an amillennialist, and I warned him that all but the first position ran contrary to Scripture. He said, 'Actually, Effin, I'm a *pan*millennialist.' I said I didn't know there was such a position and could he please explain it. He smiled and said, 'I believe everything will pan out in the end.' Only an unredeemed cynic could make light of such a serious matter.

Day 21 (Tue. 23 May)

The Domestic Dental Repair Kit came in useful again today. The insoles of my boots kept working loose and bunching up at the toes, so at breakfast I glued them in place with 'Supergummit' dental cement. The boots are still comfortable as I write this at close of day.

At lunchtime I insisted that Totley explain *exactly* what he believed about the Millennium.

He said, 'Okay, let's look at context and genre.'

I sighed loudly. Mrs. Hope-Parsons and Travis Roston III moved a bit closer to listen.

Totley said, 'The Millennium is mentioned only in the book of Revelation which, like all apocalyptic literature, uses a complex metaphor-system.'

I sighed again but he ignored me and carried on. According to Totley the Millennium has to be 'an extended metaphor' because the sequence of events is too bizarre to be taken literally – the evil forces that get wiped out at Christ's return are resurrected after the thousand years and allowed to oppose God all over again.

'As I see it,' he said, 'by resurrecting those who were implacably opposed to the return of Christ, God gives them a chance to choose differently. He offers reconciliation to his worst enemies. The Millennium is a powerful metaphor for the incredible mercy of God.'

Travis Roston III said, 'I like that,' and Mrs. Hope-Parsons said, 'Thank you, Mike. I've always been troubled by those repeated descriptions of God's judgement, which seem so terribly severe, but you've given us a new way of looking at it.'

Beats me how intelligent people can fall for this liberal hogwash.

Day 23 (Thur. 25 May)

Mending my boots with 'Supergummit' was a big mistake. When I tried to take them off on Tuesday night I found they were glued to my feet. By that time everyone else was asleep so I couldn't ask for help. After struggling for about half an hour to prize them off I finally gave up and tried to sleep with them on, but it didn't work.

I was still awake when I heard someone getting up at first light. I crept out of the tent without waking Travis Roston III and found Mike Totley sitting on a rock, staring at the sky while shaving.

He whispered, 'Morning, Effin. Dawn in the desert is an awesome thing, isn't it?'

I said I had something else on my mind, and when I explained my problem he said 'Shit!' – for which I rebuked him. He suggested I stood in the shower for a while but I told him water wouldn't help, so he took a can of gasoline from one of the Land Rovers and poured it all over my feet.

'And if you complain, Effin,' he said, 'I'll strike a match.'

This was a needless threat as he was the one doing all the complaining. But I don't mind admitting he scared me. After all, this man had masterminded the theft of the Temple jar so he's clearly capable of desperate acts.

The gasoline had no effect on the powerful adhesive so Totley said he knew a good hospital in Jerusalem and would drive me there. When the others had got up he explained the situation and we set off. Harry Hah took pointless video footage of my feet as I climbed into the Land Rover. Totley delivered me to the hospital but didn't wait to see how I got on in surgery.

After my boots had been cut away and the insoles detached from my skin I was taken to a ward to wait for the local anesthetic to wear off. To my surprise Dave Hirschfeld was in the very next bed. He'd moved there from intensive care a few days earlier.

I took this God-given opportunity to explain that his recent misfortune pointed to some sin in his life but he wouldn't listen and said, 'You're off the planet, Clinger! Have you never read the book of Job?'

I think they moved him too soon, because when a young

nurse came by he pleaded to be taken back to intensive care. She just laughed. Dave and this nurse seemed to be on very familiar terms.

Left hospital in the afternoon and got a cab back to the Center where I spent Wednesday night. Couldn't write my journal because I'd left it in the tent. Slept like a log and woke late. Tried on my sandals and decided I could walk, so after Mrs Spittler had given me some toast and coffee I got a cab to a shopping mall and bought new boots. Then I asked the cab driver to take me out to the canyon, but he drove me to Qumran instead. I guess he couldn't believe I wanted to visit a canyon in the middle of nowhere. I tried to explain my real destination by describing the caves and the excavations but he kept saying, 'Plenty of caves here, and archaeology! This is the place!' But I finally made him understand that I wanted to go farther south and we set off again.

At about 1 PM he dropped me where the track to the canyon leaves the road. From there I walked the two miles to the camp only to find the tents all gone and nobody around. There was nothing for it but to walk back to the road and try hitching a lift to Jerusalem. After a long time I got one with an Arab in an old pick-up. He said he was a Christian but when I asked if he was a premillennialist he didn't seem to know the meaning of the word. I guess some important doctrines still haven't reached these parts yet.

At the Center I found everyone had arrived back from the canyon while I'd been gone – must have passed me when I was off the road at Qumran. They came back because of a major discovery which occurred during my absence: a whole archive of letters from the Bar-Kokhba revolt turned up in Miss Schluter's cave! There's so much material to work on, they decided to return a day early.

My feet were painful after all the walking, so I went to bed. This evening Mrs. Hope-Parsons brought supper to my room. She asked if I would take a look at her filling and check that it was still okay. I told her it was fine and would last until she died – or until Christ returned, which was almost sure to happen sooner.

'And then,' I said, 'we'll see who's right about the Millennium!'

She leaned close, patted my hand and said quietly, 'Effin, you worry about the oddest things. And please call me Cecilia.'

At that moment I experienced a strange tingly sensation, probably some after-effect of the Novocaine.

It's been a frustrating couple of days. Can't wait for tomorrow and a new start.

5

Chuck Sinnet sat in front of his computer monitor, massive chin thrust forward, his fingers drumming an impatient tattoo on the desk. When the booting-up was completed he found that nine email messages had arrived since Monday morning. Only one of them interested him. He read it, whooped loudly, then read it again. Moments later he was summoning Leo Parbunkel on the internal phone.

'A reply from Brush!' he said as Parbunkel entered the room.

Pulling nervously at his beard, Parbunkel sat down at Sinnet's desk and silently mouthed his way through the words on the screen.

Chuck,
Received your latest news. Very disturbing. As the expedition has accomplished its main aim, you must now terminate as soon as possible. Everything is ready this end. Be bold, and do whatever is necessary to protect Project Peter. Remember, in these final days THE END SANCTIFIES THE MEANS! God bless you!
Oral
P.S. I hope the protective suit arrived safely.

'So that's it?' said Parbunkel.

'Yes. Action at last, Leo!'

'We'll have to think of a plan.'

'I already have. We'll finish everything tomorrow.'

'Tomorrow!' The blood drained from Parbunkel's face. 'As soon as that?'

'Sure! No point delaying. Time's running out. The clock's ticking fast. We're almost out of rope. The countdown...'

'Okay, I get the picture. Just tell me the plan.'

Chapter Eighteen

1

Mike had mixed feelings about the early return to Talpiot. On the one hand, Friday would now be a full working day at the Centre so he and Connie had lost an opportunity to go back to En-Gedi. On the other hand he could now extend his evening with Baruch and Rivka Zederbaum. He'd originally planned to leave their apartment no later than nine o'clock, spend Thursday night at the Centre and drive back to the canyon very early next morning. The change of schedule meant he could sleep late on Friday and therefore spend longer with the Zederbaums.

This was just as well because Thursday night's meal was a leisurely Middle-Eastern affair and the conversation didn't turn to the matter of the stone jar until after the main course. Rivka Zederbaum, an elegant woman of about forty with strikingly sculpted features, was full of questions about the Nahal Shuhan burials and the Bar-Kokhba documents. It wasn't until she left the room to fetch dessert that Baruch said, 'You will be interested to know, Michael, that I have obtained the information you asked for on Saturday.'

'I hope it wasn't too much trouble,' said Mike.

'Not at all. I can confirm that an American excavated with a team of Israelis in Wadi Kelt in the late eighties. He continued alone after the Israelis had left but was soon forced to stop because he did not have his own excavation permit. More recently, this time with a permit of his own, the same man conducted a survey of the Ascent of Ziz. He became convinced that a particular slab of rock concealed a cave entrance and tried to use explosives to remove it. He was not allowed to proceed.'

'That all fits,' said Mike. 'And the man's name?'

'Charles Sinnet. From your face I can see this is no surprise. Is this the same man who claims to have found the stone jar?'

'Yes. He seems to have been looking for it for years, driven by an obsession with the Copper Scroll. And now I hope you're going to tell me what you know about it.'

Rivka Zederbaum brought Sephardic cakes and cream to the table. When she was seated Baruch continued.

'I'm afraid we have to venture into some rather arcane subjects before we come to the Kelal,' he said, 'beginning with the Jewish concept of corpse impurity.'

'Of course – the topic of after-dinner conversations in all the best circles.'

'God,' said Zederbaum, ignoring Mike's whimsy, 'is in one sense present everywhere, but we Jews believe he was present to a special degree, so to say, in the Temple. There, in the Holy of Holies, the glory of God dwelt among his people. For this reason the Temple was of extreme sanctity, more holy than any other place in the physical universe. And because God is the creator and source of all life anything connected with death is ritually unclean. So no one who had been in contact with a dead body could enter the Temple without first being purified. To enter it without purification was a sin punishable by death.'

Mike nodded.

'This is familiar ground so far. To be cleansed from defilement, people had to be sprinkled with the Water of Purification.'

'And do you remember how that was obtained?'

'The rite of the red heifer,' said Mike, 'as described in the book of Numbers, chapter nineteen. The cow was slaughtered and burnt, then its ashes were mixed with spring water to produce the Water of Purification.'

As Rivka Zederbaum got up to fetch the coffee she placed a hand on her husband's shoulder.

'You see, Baruch, Mike knows the Bible just as well as you, so you don't need to lecture him.'

'The Bible sets out the basic procedure, of course,' said Zederbaum, 'but as time went on the rabbis made the whole thing more complicated. For example: the Bible says the cow had to be red in colour and without blemish; the ancient rabbis had much debate about what that meant. The majority decided that to be acceptable, the cow could have no more than five hairs that were not red, and they had to be plucked out before it was sacrificed. And it could not have even two hairs that weren't red if they both grew from the same follicle. Indeed, Rabbi Joshua Ben Bathyra said that two hairs of the wrong colour were enough to disqualify the animal even if one was in its tail and one on its head!'

'Splitting hairs, you might say.'

Rivka Zederbaum reappeared with a tray carrying a cafetière of coffee, a jug of milk and three cups. 'You heard that, my dear?' asked Baruch.

'I'm afraid I did. Your jokes are as bad as ever, Mike.'

They moved to easy chairs grouped around a low table on which two Roman oil lamps burned with tall, wavering flames. Zederbaum resumed his narrative while pouring the coffee.

'Once a suitable cow had been found, the priest who was to perform the ceremony had to live for a week in the Temple enclosure, undergoing his own rites of purification. When the big day came, the priest and his assistants led the cow from the Temple courts across a bridge spanning the Kidron Valley to the Mount of Olives. This bridge was probably a temporary wooden structure, erected only when the ritual became necessary.'

'It must have been a huge undertaking,' said Rivka.

'No doubt. But it wasn't done very often. The ashes from each red cow lasted a long time. Tradition says that only six were burnt between the time of Ezra and the destruction of the Temple – roughly one every hundred years. Anyway, having reached a special place on the Mount of Olives the priest's assistants bound the cow and placed it on a big pile of wood. Facing west so that he could see the Temple, the priest took a knife and killed the cow, catching some of its blood in his left hand. Then he dipped the forefinger of his right hand in the blood and sprinkled it in the direction of the Temple. He did this seven times. Then he set fire to the wood.'

As he spoke, Zederbaum's hands enacted the slitting of the animal's throat and the sprinkling of the blood. These gestures, his solemn, ponderous delivery and the flicker of the oil lamps lent an eerie drama to the narrative. He paused and closed his eyes as though imagining the crackle of flames and the smell of burning flesh. Rivka recalled him to the present with an offer of more coffee and he continued.

'While the fire blazed, the priest took some cedarwood and hyssop, tied them together with scarlet wool and cast them into the fire to be burnt with the cow. The meaning of this ritual is quite lost, of course, and even the ancient rabbis could not explain its significance. Anyway, when the fire was burnt out the ashes were collected and ground to a fine powder. Then they were stored in a stone vessel.'

Zederbaum looked at Mike, awaiting a response.

'I said, Michael, the ashes were kept in a *stone vessel*.'

'Oh, I see!' said Mike as the penny dropped. 'We've finally arrived at the Kelal!'

'Precisely! You were correct the other day when you said that *kelal* simply means a jar, but to people versed in these subjects it signifies one jar in particular – the stone vessel containing the ashes of the red cow. It was kept in the courts of the Temple, as befitted its sanctity. Small amounts of ash were taken from it on the end of a stick and added to spring water, producing the Water of Purification. A priest used to dip a sprig of hyssop into the water and sprinkle it over the defiled person.'

'And do we know what happened to the jar when the Romans destroyed the Temple?'

'We have only tradition to guide us, which says it was preserved from destruction and the ashes used for purification for several more decades.'

'Seems a bit unlikely,' said Mike. 'If ritual purity was only necessary for Temple worship, why would they continue it when the Temple no longer existed?'

'The rabbis wanted people to conduct themselves as though the Temple services were still going on. They hoped to keep priests and people in a state of readiness for when the Temple could be rebuilt. As you know, a new Temple was one of the goals of Bar-Kokhba's rebellion. Rome's defeat of the rebels dashed that hope and that was perhaps when use of the ashes finally ceased. We will never know for sure. Tradition merely says the ashes were lost.'

'The rabbis lost the ashes? I didn't even know they played cricket! Sorry, Baruch,' added Mike as Zederbaum gave him a severe look. 'But I'm itching to know what you think about the jar Sinnet claims to have found. Could it be the genuine Kelal?'

Baruch Zederbaum finished his coffee and sat back in his chair.

'There are two ways of approaching that question. One is from the angle of historical probability. Let us suppose for a moment that at least one bit of the tradition is true – that the Kelal survived the destruction of the Temple. We can also suppose that sixty years later, at the time of Bar-Kokhba's revolt, there were still some ashes left. That is reasonable because the last red cow was burnt only ten years before the Temple fell. If the rebels had possession of the Kelal they might well have decided to hide it when the tide turned against them. And you have found plenty of evidence that Bar-Kokhba's rebels used the Nahal Shuhan caves.'

'So you think Sinnet had the real McCoy?'

'I said there were two ways of looking at the question. When you came to see me at Tell el-Mikhta you gave some cogent reasons for thinking the jar was a fake; my second line of reasoning leads to that same conclusion, and I happen to favour it. But we must start with more arcana. Did you know that some Zionist extremists still believe the Temple should be rebuilt?'

'I've heard the usual rumours,' said Mike.

'I'm afraid these groups are more than rumours. Do you remember an incident at the Temple Mount in 1990, when the Israeli police opened fire with automatic weapons into a crowd of Palestinians? Twenty-one people were killed, one hundred and twenty-five wounded. Those protestors had gathered because a group called the Temple Mount Faithful wanted to lay the cornerstone of a new Temple during the Feast of Succoth.'

'But the Dome of the Rock...' Mike began.

'They were proposing to dismantle it and transport it stone by stone to Mecca.'

Mike whistled.

'There are several such groups,' said Rivka. 'The Temple Institute, the Hand of Solomon... but they share a common purpose: to bring the terrestrial world into harmony with the dynamics of heaven. They believe there can be no true wholeness in Israel, no *shalom*, until the Temple has been restored. And this belief in the Temple's cosmic importance excludes concern for anyone else's interests or sensitivities.'

'All these groups are politically dangerous,' added Baruch, 'but the most extreme is one calling itself the Temple Foundation. Its leaders follow the teachings of a rabbi whom they call the Sagan – an ancient title meaning a deputy High Priest, so to say. They have long believed that the Temple will be rebuilt during the Sagan's lifetime, and because he is now old and sick they are becoming desperate.'

Baruch Zederbaum paused and looked at his wife, who took up the explanation.

'The Foundation is suspected of having an underground terrorist branch, but nothing has ever been proved. It maintains the public face of an academic institution; it has a library, publishes books and conducts research into the ancient Temple rituals. Like other groups of Temple activists, it claims to have traced the descent of priestly families to identify men who could serve in a new Temple, and it trains suitable candidates to perform the ancient rites, including animal sacrifices. They've even implanted genetically engineered embryos into cattle to produce flawless red cows.'

'Which brings us to the big catch-22 situation,' said Baruch. 'Are you all right, Michael?'

Mike's mouth had dropped open.

'Er, yes. Just finding this a bit hard to take in, that's all. The idea of reinstating animal sacrifice – the mind boggles!'

'As it should,' said Baruch. 'The Temple was more like a slaughterhouse than a synagogue, a mosque or a cathedral. It must have smelt like a McDonald's combined with an abattoir!'

'These Temple activists are a small minority of extremists,' said Rivka. 'Most of us think they're a bunch of nuts and we would find all that slaughter and burning of animals a big embarrassment. We believe the Temple is to be built in the heart, as it says in the Prophets: "To obey is better than sacrifice, and to listen to God is better than the fat of rams." But these groups believe they have a duty to rebuild the Temple in stone.'

Baruch nodded slowly in agreement. He suddenly looked sad

and tired. His wife touched him gently on the arm and said quietly:

'Baruch, you were going to explain the catch-22 situation?'

'Of course. To return to corpse impurity for a moment: this kind of ritual defilement is acquired in many ways – by visiting a cemetery, or just being in the same building as a dead body – and it never wears off. Only the Water of Purification can remove it, and since that has not been available for nineteen centuries all Jews are now held to be impure. Even men of priestly descent would be disqualified from officiating in a rebuilt Temple. To purify a priest, a new red cow would have to be burnt; but only a purified priest can perform the ritual!'

'Naturally,' Rivka interjected, 'many solutions have been proposed. For example, finding a woman of priestly lineage who is pregnant with a male foetus and having the child delivered and raised by robots in ritually pure conditions; at the age of thirteen he could become a priest and slaughter a red cow.'

'That's grotesque!' exclaimed Mike. 'Like the plot of a science fiction novel!'

'But it was suggested in a serious religious journal.'

Baruch Zederbaum leaned forward in his chair to take charge of the conversation again.

'Of course, such expensive, risky and controversial schemes would be unnecessary, *if*—'

Mike caught his drift. '...*if* someone could find the ashes of the last red heifer!'

'Exactly, Michael! The importance of the Kelal lies in its contents – the ashes!'

There was a pause while Mike tried to put all this together.

'So you think Sinnet was planning a hoax, and some of these Temple wackos took the jar before he could announce its discovery to the world? How ironic!'

'No, Michael.'

'No?'

'Think carefully. Did Sinnet believe he could fool every archaeologist in Israel? Extremely unlikely! If it hadn't disappeared, the jar and its contents would have been subjected to every conceivable scientific test. He must have known the jar would disappear before that could happen.'

'What? You mean the theft was pre-arranged? Sinnet is in cahoots with this Temple Foundation? But why the hell…'

'Because he wants to help the Foundation's cause. Aren't there Christians who believe the Temple must be rebuilt before Christ returns?'

'Of course, but this still doesn't track, Baruch. There are two major problems for your theory. Firstly, I doubt whether a fanatical Jewish organisation would accept help from a fundamentalist Christian.'

'But why not?' asked Rivka. 'Sure, the Talmud says no Gentile can help build the physical structure of the Temple, but it permits Gentile contributions of other kinds. Sinnet's provision of the Kelal would therefore be acceptable.'

'Your other problem?' asked Baruch.

'Well, wouldn't the Temple Foundation submit the jar to just as much scrutiny as professional archaeologists? If they've got research facilities…'

'You are assuming they would be objective. When people are desperate to believe, facts and reason get left behind. A few years ago an amateur archaeologist said he'd found some incense mixture from the Temple in a cave near Qumran. Scientific analysis didn't support his claim, but I know a rabbi who still believes it. So it's my guess the Temple Foundation will not question Sinnet's claim too closely, especially if he can back it with documentary evidence. And didn't you mention a connection with the Copper Scroll?'

As Mike's last objection dissolved he sank back in his chair. The Zederbaums exchanged glances and Baruch nodded. Then Rivka said, 'It's most important that you are careful about your own safety, Mike. Remember, the Temple Foundation is thought to have terrorist connections. In view of what happened to you at Tell el-Mikhta and on the Jericho road we think your interest in the Kelal has come to their attention.'

Mike resisted this vigorously.

'But surely the bomb at Tell el-Mikhta was directed against Baruch's dig! And Dave Hirschfeld thinks we were the targets of a *pulsa danura* by the Ultra-Orthodox, on account of the burials we found.'

'Unlikely,' said Zederbaum. 'A shooting out of the blue is not their style. If the Ultra-Orthodox were angered by the dig at Nahal Shuhan they would have been out there in force, or at the Centre, trying to close it down completely. But the involvement of the Temple Foundation would explain both the strange affair of the Kelal and the danger you've been in.'

Mike paled visibly. For a long time he said nothing. Rivka leaned forward and touched his hand.

'We've thought about this a lot, Mike. I'm sure Baruch is right. Take great care. Don't underestimate these people. I'm afraid some of our fanatics have advanced far in the doctrine that sins committed for a great cause become good deeds. Look at the massacre in the Hebron mosque, or Rabin's assassination... That's why we're asking you to be extremely careful.'

Mike continued to sit in stunned silence. The logic of their interpretation of events could no longer be denied yet he baulked at it, unwilling to believe he could be the target of anyone's hatred. Eventually he said, 'Thanks. Thanks for your concern, both of you. You've given me a lot to think about. And I promise I will be extra careful from now on.' He looked at his watch. 'I guess I'd better be going; it's very late.'

All three got up. Rivka and Baruch both embraced Mike fondly. He had a lump in his throat as they exchanged goodbyes. As he turned to the door a final query struck him.

'These Temple fanatics – they wouldn't be looking for the Ark of the Covenant as well, would they?'

Baruch Zederbaum shook his head.

'Why should they? The Ark was lost when the First Temple fell. The Second Temple functioned for almost six hundred years without it. Why do you ask?'

'Just wondering,' said Mike.

It was after midnight when he left the Zederbaums' apartment. As he drove back to the Centre his mind was awhirl with conflicting ideas. He parked the Land Rover in the compound and quietly let himself in by the rear door. As he stood in the unlit corridor with one hand still on the door handle a terrible thought froze him to the spot. If the Zederbaums were right, his would-be murderers had known that he was investigating the stone jar. But apart from Baruch Zederbaum, he'd told only one person…

'Oh, no! Please God, no!' he said aloud in the darkness.

2

Effin Clinger did not make any more journal entries after Thursday. Had he done so, honesty would have compelled him to report that his bowel movements had finally abandoned their usual regularity. While Mike was walking slowly towards his room thinking the bottom had fallen out of his world, Clinger was feeling as though the world had fallen out of his bottom.

The trouble had begun around eleven thirty with a vague sense of nausea, followed by terrible griping pains in his stomach. The diarrhoea had started about thirty minutes later. Since then he'd been ensconced in a toilet cubicle in the nearest bathroom. And he was clearly not alone in his sufferings. The sound of other men groaning and retching came to him from neighbouring cubicles, and volunteers who could no longer wait in line could be heard rushing along the corridor in search of an alternative bathroom.

Mike wandered to his room, oblivious to the moans of the sick and the occasional glimpse of a sprinting volunteer. Removing only his shoes, he fell onto the bed and lay in an agony of doubt and anxiety. His thoughts raced around a bewildering maze of facts and possibilities, desperately trying to construct a more palatable overview than the one suggested by the Zederbaums. He was still trying to do this when exhaustion, and the effects of a large meal, overtook him and he sank into a dream-troubled sleep.

Effin Clinger finally returned to his room and sagged onto a corner of his bed. The other bed in the room, normally occupied by Travis Roston, was empty because its owner was undergoing his own sufferings in a distant part of the building. Cautiously, Clinger lay down.

At first all seemed well but after a few minutes he sensed the onset of further colonic upheavals. He rose resignedly and plodded back to the bathroom, only to find every cubicle display- ing its *engaged* sign. Quickening his pace he made for the bathroom of the adjacent corridor, but that had no vacancies either. By now he was desperate. He did the only thing he could think of. He rushed back to his room, pushed his pyjamas down and launched himself backwards onto the small *en suite* washbasin. Just as he was congratulating himself on a piece of swift lateral thinking there was a loud crack and his makeshift lavatory broke away from the wall, pitching him face down onto the floor. As he pulled together his shattered composure he became aware of two things: his buttocks were being sprayed with cold water from a fractured pipe, and one of his front teeth was missing.

3

Mike watched Chuck Sinnet empty the contents of an ashtray into the Kelal and present it solemnly to a white-robed priest. Then the priest was carrying the Kelal slowly down broad white steps with the Temple portico towering behind him. His white robe became uncannily bright and he was no longer a priest but an angel with a golden sash across his chest, and behind him six more angels emerged from the portico, each carrying his own Kelal. But now they were not Kelals, they were seven golden bowls, and dense smoke billowed from the Temple and a loud voice commanded the angels:

'Go and pour out on the earth the seven bowls of the wrath of God!'

So the first angel poured out his bowl on the earth, and there was the sound of loud moaning, as of many people with severe food poisoning. Then things became confused as Mike's subconscious strove in vain to incorporate other background noises into the dream: the slamming of doors, people shouting, the revving of vehicles, the sound of tyres on gravel.

At last there was silence.

Chapter Nineteen

1

Mike was woken by Leo Parbunkel tapping on his door and whispering loudly. At first he thought he must have overslept but his bedside clock showed that it was only 6.30, a whole hour before breakfast. He rose groggily from the bed – still in the previous evening's clothes – put his shoes on and opened the door.

'It's the Ark!' blurted Parbunkel, still whispering. He had the look of a man who'd been awake all night – pale, haggard and red-eyed. 'The protective suit arrived this week and I've just been inside the treatment chamber! Some marks have started to show up on the box and I'm sure they're where the four golden rings were fixed for carrying it – exactly as described in Exodus, chapter thirty-seven! I think we might be ready for a press release, Mike, but I'd value your opinion.' With that he hurried off towards the lab.

Mike forced his fingers through his hair, as much to tidy his thoughts as his appearance, and followed reluctantly. When they arrived at the room with the heavy door Leo opened the combination lock and rushed to the console. The chamber beyond the window was already illuminated. The door to the right of the window swung open, revealing a small cubicle. Parbunkel led Mike inside and closed the door behind them. The cubicle contained a tall frame on which hung a bulky white suit in two parts, another white garment with thick tubes sewn into it, a transparent helmet and some breathing apparatus. A metal door connected the cubicle to the treatment chamber.

'Ex-NASA,' said Parbunkel, lifting the tube-infested garment from its hooks.

'You mean it's a spacesuit?'

'Modified by the boys at Swycorp. We didn't need the waste-disposal system, for example, and we've dispensed with the big outer helmet; the inner bubble-helmet is enough for our purposes, along with the flight cap containing earphones and a mike. We've kept the breathing apparatus, of course, but it's been scaled down. An astronaut carries a seven-hour supply of air, but that's been cut to about two and a half to reduce the size of the pack. Not that we'll ever need that much at one time; it only took me ten minutes or so to give the box a thorough inspection. We've also kept the water-cooled undersuit – which is this thing here. I'll explain how it goes on.'

It took Mike over twenty minutes to get fully kitted out. He had never seen Leo so agitated; his hands shook and he fumbled hopelessly as he helped Mike into the suit's various parts.

'Okay? Everything working?' Parbunkel's voice came over the earphones in the flight cap.

'Yes, I think so.'

Parbunkel moved to the console in the outer room.

'I'm releasing the electronic lock on the door into the treatment chamber,' he said, his voice a nervous croak inside Mike's helmet. Mike turned the handle, opened the door and stepped forwards into the cloud of hot, poisonous vapour.

'Close the door behind you, Mike. The temperature must be kept constant.'

Mike did as requested. Then he turned to the wooden box. At the time he attached no significance to the loud click of the electronic lock.

2

In spite of losing two hours' sleep during the night, Connie woke promptly to her alarm. After a visit to the showers she quickly dressed and brushed her hair. When she left her room again to go and have breakfast she was surprised to find Chuck Sinnet standing in the corridor, almost as though he'd been waiting for her.

'Morning, Connie. I was about to call on you. Thanks for helping last night. How are you feeling?'

'A little tired but okay. Any news of Cecilia and the others?'

'Food poisoning. Salmonella. They've all got it pretty bad. I'm afraid they'll be in hospital for at least another day.'

'Have you seen anything of Mike?'

'Oh, sure; he's fine. Got up early to work on the manuscripts. We'd better not disturb him – it's a delicate job. Listen Connie, with everyone sick except five of us we'll have to put some things on hold for a few days, and in the meantime there's something I'd like to try. D'you recall offering to climb down between those big boulders at the back of our cave?'

'Sure. You thought it was too dangerous.'

'I know, but I've been thinking it over. I was being over-cautious, and perhaps a little irrational. I guess you were right when you said I was unwilling to take the idea from a woman. So, if you can forgive an old man his foolishness, and if the offer still stands, I thought perhaps this morning…'

'Well, yes I guess. But I was supposed to be restoring pottery…'

'That'll keep. I thought we'd drive out to the canyon right away, before it gets hot. Leo's packed some breakfast so we can eat on the way.'

3

Mike examined the box, looking for clues to its method of manufacture. It was impossible to be sure, but in some indentations he thought he could make out the heads of relatively modern nails. Then he looked for the marks that Parbunkel had said were visible on the two ends of the box. There were indeed marks, but not where he expected to find them.

'I'm afraid I don't see how the golden rings could have been attached here, Leo. These marks are too near the middle. To take carrying-poles, the rings must have stuck out at the sides. Assuming they were riveted to the ends in some way, the holes for those must have been next to the corner. Do you follow me?'

Parbunkel didn't reply.

'Can you hear me, Leo?'

Still no reply. Perhaps there was something wrong with the intercom. Mike moved over to the window to try signalling, but there was no sign of Parbunkel in the outer room. He then tried to open the door but the handle wouldn't turn. He remembered the click of the electronic lock and unpleasant suspicions began to form in a far corner of his mind. At first he tried to dismiss them, clinging to the unlikely alternative that Leo had simply rushed out for a pee and would be back any minute. But as time passed this became less and less plausible. In spite of his water-cooled underwear Mike felt a bead of sweat trickle slowly down his back.

4

Connie sat on a rear seat of the Defender with Leo Parbunkel, who looked tense and drawn and said nothing. Chuck Sinnet and Rip Warholler were in the front seats, Sinnet driving like a lunatic as usual. The morning mist had almost dispersed as they descended from the central hills into the Jordan Valley. Slopes which three weeks ago had been dusted with green were now fading to the bleached brown of summer.

Sinnet suggested they ate. Connie was sorry to see that Parbunkel had packed a meagre amount of food and drink. She was never at her best until she'd eaten a good breakfast.

'I'm really grateful, Connie,' said Sinnet, driving with one hand on the wheel; in the other he held some Arab bread daubed with peanut butter. 'With most of the team sick, and Mike busy with the manuscripts, you're probably the only person who can do this. Leo isn't exactly a man of action, Rip is too well built to fit between the rocks, and with this old knee of mine I just don't have the flexibility. But you can do it, I'm sure. No problem.'

5

Mike soon gave up hope of opening the door. It was solidly constructed and didn't yield in the slightest when he threw his weight against it. The window offered no escape either, being very thick and firmly secured in its metal frame. Then he searched the walls for detachable panels, hoping to find controls that would stop the ejection of polyethylene glycol and lower the temperature – but there were none.

If his chances of escape were nil his hope of being rescued seemed no better. None of the volunteers knew of the underground lab's existence, and only Parbunkel and Sinnet knew the combination for the outer door.

Mike turned back to the window, shouting and pounding on it with his fists. It was a futile gesture, nothing more than a venting of frustration. Then, resting with his hands spread on the window and his helmet touching the glass, he noticed a clock on the opposite wall of the lab. It showed the time as eight o'clock. Mike reckoned he must have entered the chamber about fifty minutes earlier. Parbunkel had said the suit had enough air for two and a half hours and that he'd worn it for ten minutes or so himself. If that could be relied on, there were less than ninety minutes left.

6

'Ready, Connie?' called Sinnet from inside the Land Rover. Outside, Connie had donned a jumpsuit and was now fastening a climbing harness around her waist.

'Ready when you are,' she replied.

Rip Warholler ogled her surreptitiously while he placed a coil of rope over his head and settled it on his left shoulder. Then he went to the back of the Land Rover where Sinnet was busy selecting helmets.

'Are you sure she's going to fit down that hole?' he whispered. 'What about her... y'know... things?' He cupped his hands in front of his chest.

'What's the matter, Rip?' rasped Sinnet irritably. 'Are you getting cold feet about this?'

'No, sir!'

'Then quit worrying. She'll fit all right. You okay, Leo? Remember, as soon as you see us all disappear inside the cave, you drive to the top. We'll see you there. Oh, and by the way – the food poisoning was a great idea. I underestimated you.' He slapped Parbunkel on the back and jumped down from the Land Rover. 'Come on, Rip, Connie. Let's climb!'

7

Mike hated listening to the sound of his own breathing. As the ticking of a clock underscores the relentless march of seconds, so the hiss of every exhalation marked the steady diminution of his air supply.

Sometimes he tried holding his breath (which he found he could do comfortably for one and a half minutes), not to extend his life by some pitifully small amount but simply to stop the noise for a while. It was during one of these silences that the voice spoke. It was a pleasant, female voice with an American accent and it came from the earphones inside the flight-cap.

Its first words were simply, 'Hello, there!'

Mike was sitting on the floor at the time, leaning back against the wall. On hearing the voice he sat bolt upright.

'Hello!' he yelled. 'Connie, is that you? Tally?'

'Greetings from Swycorp Research,' said the voice.

'Who is that?' Mike demanded. 'Can you hear me?'

'We at Swycorp have done all we can to make this equipment safe, efficient and comfortable to wear.'

'Can you hear me?' shouted Mike, getting to his feet.

'We hope you've enjoyed using it. We would like to inform you that your air supply will run out in approximately thirty minutes. For your own safety, please make sure you can return to a normal environment and remove your helmet within that time. Thank you for listening to this recorded message, and have a nice day.'

8

Sinnet clipped the rope to Connie's harness with a karabiner.

'You sure you're ready for this, Connie?' The question echoed around the high vaulted cavern like a challenge.

'Sure,' she said, peering down into the chaotic jumble of boulders. The prospect of crawling through the narrow interstices, not knowing how far it was to the bottom and with only a helmet lamp to see by, was not one she relished; but she was determined to go through with it. During the last three weeks the patronising attitude of these two men towards women had irritated her more times than she could count, and she was not going to miss this chance to prove her physical courage and stamina.

'Okay, so let's do it!' said Sinnet. 'Remember, when you get to the bottom – assuming that's possible – look out for anything at all that might be a sign of human activity. If we're right in thinking the roof collapsed in the earthquake of 31 BC, there could be anything down there from flint tools to a bunch of scrolls.'

The first part of the descent was an easy, vertical funnel between the rocks, so Connie clambered down feet first. Then came the first serious constriction and some moments of acute discomfort. After that progress was easier again, though it involved a good deal of twisting and squirming. For about a minute Connie moved steadily down while Sinnet let out the rope. After another tight squeeze she found herself standing on a flat expanse of rock.

'Is that the bottom?' Sinnet shouted. He could no longer see her but the rope had stopped moving.

'No. It's the top of a giant boulder. It slopes away on one side and there's a gap just big enough to get through. I'm going on down.' Connie lay flat on her stomach and began to crawl forward.

Sinnet turned to Warholler and whispered, 'Okay, Rip; do it now!'

Rip Warholler hunkered down and grasped a large rock firmly with both hands. With a loud grunt he stood up, holding the rock waist-high. He guessed it weighed about two hundred pounds.

9

Mike found it impossible to prepare for death. For one thing, his mind was busy with unresolved questions: Had Connie really betrayed him? And if so, why? Was this part of the same game she'd started in Washington? Was the CIA supporting the Temple Foundation? Or had the Zederbaums been wrong after all? Round and round ad infinitum. Then there was the unreality of his current situation. Dying this way was almost too bizarre to be taken seriously. He expected to wake at any moment and catch the smell of hash browns wafting across the garden from the kitchen. In an effort to ground himself he touched the metal wall with his gloved hands, looked up at the lights shining through the dense chemical vapour, down at the spacesuit covering his body...

His thoughts were deflected again. The spacesuit reminded him of something. He wasn't sure what, because the memory wouldn't take on a definite shape, but it felt important, somehow connected with all his unanswered questions. Before he could pin it down it was gone, and he was thinking again about Connie and the Zederbaums and dying unprepared and wondering how on earth he could have been so stupid.

10

Crawling down the side of the giant boulder, Connie heard a loud thud and felt a tremor run through the surrounding rocks. With her heart pounding she quickly wriggled backwards to the flat top of the boulder and looked up. A shower of dust covered her face.

'Hey, what was that?' she shouted, blinking the dust from her eyes. 'What happened?' There was no reply. 'Are you guys okay?'

Still no reply. She pulled on the rope. At first it went taut but when she put her weight on it it came free, trickling down between the rocks until it lay loosely around her feet. Connie's first thought was that a minor earthquake had caused a rockfall, injuring – or worse – Sinnet and Warholler. She took some deep breaths to calm herself and began the return climb.

It took longer than the descent and in the tight spots she missed the help of the rope. Her full predicament became clear as she neared the top. She climbed on grimly until she could push against the rock that blocked her exit, and soon realised there was nothing she could do to shift it. She tried shouting again. Listening anxiously for a reply she caught the sound of voices, faint and distant.

Warholler had dragged the rope ladder up into the cave, detached it from its moorings and was now rolling it into a huge bundle.

'Okay, I'm ready,' he said. 'I'll climb to the top, then haul this end of the ladder up after me and anchor it so you can follow.'

'Thanks,' said Sinnet. 'Then all we have to do is wait for Leo. Steady as you go, Rip. See you in a few minutes.'

Connie could not make out the words of this conversation but it didn't sound as though Sinnet and Warholler were in any difficulty. Then she heard the steel gate at the cave entrance clang shut and the truth broke over her in a devastating wave.

She felt weak, her legs ready to buckle and drop her between the jagged rocks. With her failing reserves she scrambled back down, trembling violently and sometimes missing a hold, until she reached the top of the giant boulder again. It was a sanctuary of sorts, a place where she could rest without danger of falling while she tried to bring her panic under control.

She began by telling herself there might be an alternative route through the boulders, but a few minutes' exploration soon showed this to be a vain hope. All the gaps she tried were too small or led nowhere. She resumed her seat on the boulder.

Suddenly, blind panic could no longer be postponed. It rose like a tide, engulfed her, and she was sick. She hugged her knees against her chest, trying to control the trembling which shook her whole body.

Slowly the panic subsided and her fear took on a different quality, blended with anger against the men who had trapped her. She could not fully comprehend their motives but she assumed they had something to do with her involvement with Mike and his suspicions about Sinnet. In which case Mike was also in danger. Fear for his safety and frustration at her own powerlessness swept all other emotions aside and she cried out, 'O God, if you're there, help him! If the bastards haven't murdered him already, please save him!'

Her plea bounced back in broken echoes and faded into silence.

11

Mike's attempts to weave an acceptable tapestry from his tangled thoughts were getting him nowhere. It was theoretically possible, without involving Connie, to explain how the Temple Foundation had learned of his interest in the Kelal. Perhaps one of the dealers he'd questioned about the jar had in fact procured it for Sinnet, and this dealer might have told Sinnet about his enquiries; Sinnet in turn could have warned the Foundation that he was a potential nuisance and the Foundation could then have acted to nip things in the bud... An attractive idea, but was it true? He would never know – unless death brought that kind of knowledge, in which case he would know all too soon.

'Hello again!' said the voice from the microchip. 'You now have enough air for only five more minutes. Please return to a normal environment and remove your helmet. Thank you, and have a nice day.'

'Into your hands, O Lord...' said Mike, and waited.

12

Connie's mouth and throat were painfully dry. For ease of movement she was not wearing a water bottle; Sinnet had been carrying water for all three of them.

In the slender hope that water from the winter rains might have gathered at the bottom of the cave she resumed her attempt to get below the giant boulder. Crawling down its sloping surface she emerged into another, smaller open space. This time she had reached the true floor of the cave. The cavity was roughly triangular, bounded by the cave floor, the underside of the boulder and another large rock against which it rested. There was no sign of water but in one direction the floor sloped away into darkness.

Connie wriggled forwards on her elbows, directing the beam of her helmet lamp into the farthest recess. Suddenly she froze. Where the boulder met the floor, partially crushed beneath it, lay a human skeleton. The skull lay on its side facing her, grinning a welcome out of the darkness. Overcoming her revulsion, Connie moved closer on her stomach. The skeleton was draped in the remnants of a white garment, a rope girdle where its waist had been. There was no water anywhere.

13

The last few minutes of Mike's life seemed to be dragging on indefinitely. He slowly got to his feet to check the clock but as he turned to the window the recorded voice answered his question.

'Hello again! You now have enough air for only one minute. I repeat: one minute. Please return immediately to a normal environment and remove your helmet. Failure to do so will result in your biological non-viability. Thank you, and have a nice day.'

Mike was about to sit down again when he caught sight of the wooden box reflected in the window. He stopped and stared. It was as though the glass, reversing the image of the box, had also reversed his perception of it. Until now he'd only viewed it negatively, as a box that was decidedly *not* the Ark of the Covenant. Now he knew what it was.

His breathing quickened as he turned from the reflection to confront the real thing. He took a step forwards, stretched his arms wide and placed his gloved hands on opposite ends of the box. Then he remembered the computer images documenting its discovery, saw again the rock hewn passage stretching downwards into the hidden heart of the Temple Mount, and in another moment of shining clarity he knew why Sinnet and Parbunkel had really gone there. The explanation was as transparent as it was terrifying.

But right now the box itself demanded his attention. He tightened his grip on it and pushed. At first he underestimated its weight and it barely shifted. He braced himself and pushed again. The box moved noisily over the wire mesh, creaking under the strain, until it was tilting on the edge of the table. Mike let go and it fell, hit the floor with a loud bang and shattered into several pieces.

He bent down and rummaged among the debris on the floor. In the wreckage he found a lump-hammer, two hefty crowbars, a badly-corroded object that might once have been a jack, several handspikes, a block and tackle, a partially decayed tape measure and a stiffened coil of rope.

He suppressed his excitement, trying to keep each breath as slow and shallow as possible. Selecting the hammer he struck the window several blows. But the glass was armoured and refused to break, even when spiderwebbed with cracks. Mike took a slow, deep breath and held it. That gave him one and a half minutes to try something else.

Using the hammer and a handspike he set to work on the window frame. After bending back the metal at the bottom and on both sides he forced the crowbars into the rubber seal, one at each of the lower corners. Grasping a crowbar in each hand he then pulled with all his strength until the whole window burst from its frame and fell into the room.

Mike climbed through the hole, stepped away from the chamber and unfastened his helmet. With a prayer of gratitude, he took deep breaths of the lab's air-conditioned atmosphere. But his problems were not over yet. A mist of polyethylene glycol was pouring into the lab from the treatment chamber and he didn't know how to open the outer door.

Holding his breath again, he went to the console and was relieved to find that its keys bore self-explanatory symbols. He pressed one marked with dotted lines radiating from a nozzle; one of the console's winking lights went out and the susurration of escaping vapour died away. He pressed a key displaying a thermometer and another light went out. Then he noticed a symbol that might represent the blades of a fan. He pressed the key; a new light started winking and a whirring sound came from inside the chamber.

The mist began to diminish.

14

After shuffling backwards away from the grim remains, Connie removed her helmet and switched off the lamp. The darkness was total, deeper than the darkness of night or of closed eyes. She lay still, resting her face on her hands, and wept quietly with frustration and despair. Her only solace was that the end would probably come gently; first the lassitude of dehydration, then sleep, and finally an unconscious passage from sleep to death.

Chapter Twenty

1

It took Mike over an hour to get past the outer door of the lab. The combination lock had to be totally destroyed before it would yield, and by the time he'd finished, Mike had hammered all the corroded handspikes into strange shapes and bent one of the crowbars. Eventually the heavy door stood open. Grasping the serviceable crowbar he hurried out of the lab and along the passage.

On reaching the ground floor he moved cautiously, brandishing the crowbar to deter attackers, but encountered no one. Determined to confront Connie he made his way to the pottery room, remembering that she had been scheduled to spend the morning on restoration. The room was empty. On the benches stood rows of partially reconstructed pots, like huge prehistoric eggs recently hatched. But the instruments for measuring and drawing sherds were still in their trays; no one had been at work since last night.

Mike went through the rest of the southern building, using the crowbar to break into any rooms that were locked. In Parbunkel's office the computer screens were dead but there were files, printouts and a half-drunk mug of coffee on the desk; books – open face down to keep the page – lay scattered like shot birds.

Mike was about to move on when a printout, partially covered by one of the books, caught his eye. A closer look confirmed that it was a photograph of Connie. She appeared to be reading a book which was lying open on a desk and in her right hand she held a pencil poised over a notepad. By her left elbow lay another book, closed and with its spine facing the onlooker. The photo had been enlarged until individual pixels distorted some of the finer details, but the white classification number on the spine of the second book was clear enough to read.

Mike then examined the book which had been left on top of the printout. It was Smith's volume on the Copper Scroll and it had the same number.

The fact that Connie had been under surveillance put everything in a new light. Mike hurried to the accommodation block. In the corridor where Connie's room was located all the doors were unlocked and the rooms empty. The same was true of every other corridor he passed. He set about exploring the rest of the complex room by room and in every block the situation was the same. In normal circumstances the Centre was never left empty but now it had an eerie atmosphere of sudden dereliction.

As rooms were eliminated one by one Mike grew increasingly anxious for Connie's safety. Almost unconsciously he began repeating a verse from the Song of Solomon as he paced the corridors: 'O my dove, in the clefts of the rock, in the holes of the cliff, let me see your face, let me hear your voice...' Then he stopped in his tracks and wondered.

2

The two-seater Land Rover was far from ideal in view of its ageing gearbox, but it was the only vehicle left in the compound. Mike hurriedly loaded it with everything that might be remotely useful and set off through the suburbs of Jerusalem. Although he'd discarded the bulky outer spacesuit and the flight cap he was still wearing the white undergarment ribbed with coolant tubes and felt strangely conspicuous waiting at traffic lights.

After about one and a half hours he reached the turn-off for Nahal Shuhan. At the fork in the track he stopped to examine the cliffs below Cave D through a pair of binoculars. The rope ladder was gone. This not only confirmed his suspicions but left him with no hope of reaching the cave from below. He turned right, heading for the northern cliffs.

Second gear proved elusive so Mike had to take most of the mountain road in first. After a terrible journey around the head of the wadi, during which the old Land Rover frequently stalled and seemed on the verge of breaking down altogether, he pulled up on a familiar plateau above the southern cliffs.

It was very hot, perhaps over thirty degrees. Mike rummaged in the back of the Land Rover, found Sinnet's solar-powered baseball cap and put it on. At the edge of the precipice he lay flat on his stomach and cautiously peered over to check that no one was around. The only signs of human activity were the patterns of vehicle tracks on the distant canyon floor.

He couldn't see the entrance to Cave D from the top so he estimated its position. Then he went back to the Land Rover and reparked it in what he thought was a more suitable spot facing the ravine. After double-checking the handbrake he took out all the climbing gear and a heavy backpack. From now on success – not to mention his life – would depend on how well he remembered the rudiments of abseiling.

He put on the backpack and a climbing harness, clipped a descender to the latter and fed the rope through it. Following Sinnet's example he then tied the rope to the Land Rover's bull bars, wishing he knew as much about knots as his intestines apparently did. Carefully walking backwards to the edge of the cliff he dropped the rest of the rope over the precipice, feeling the pull of its weight as it uncoiled below him. He felt slightly sick. He took several deep breaths, prayed, and stepped back over the edge.

To begin with everything went well. Descending one careful step at a time he made slow but effective progress for about forty metres. Then the wall of rock began to curve away from him. It continued to curve away until his feet no longer touched it and he was simply dangling over empty space. Mike hadn't expected this. Too late, he remembered that Sinnet had used a different route, bringing them down slightly west of the cave. Then, as he was wondering what to do next, everything started to spin. He soon realised that this was no vertigo-induced illusion; the rope was in fact twisting, turning him round and round at steadily increasing speed.

Mike shut his eyes against a rising sense of nausea and tried to think. In theory there was no need for contact with the rock face; he could lower himself by simply slipping the rope through the descender. Opening his eyes he tried to gauge the distance to the cave. He was less than halfway down. Far below him an eagle soared, each careening arc taking it farther east towards the Dead Sea. The vast silence of the wilderness extended all around, heightened by an occasional creak from the twisting rope and the faint whirr of the fan in the peak of his cap.

Mike concentrated on his white-knuckled hands, willing them to relax their fearful grip on the rope. Eventually reason triumphed over instinct and his right hand allowed the rope to slide through the descender; he was moving again. The awesome landscape continued to revolve around him. Eventually he drew level with the mouth of the cave and realised exactly how ill-judged his starting point had been.

The ledge outside the cave didn't jut out far enough for him to reach it; it was a good three metres away. This was his worst nightmare. He looked up at the overhang from which he'd come and considered his chances of climbing back up the rope. He decided they were non-existent unless he jettisoned the heavy backpack, which contained his only means of getting inside the cave. He was left with only one option.

Kicking the air, he set himself swinging towards and away from the cave entrance. When his speed and direction were right he would release the rope and drop onto the ledge. It was a risky manoeuvre, made all the more difficult by the fact that he was still spinning, but eventually a moment came when he was facing the cave and swinging towards it with sufficient momentum. He let go of the rope and made a grab for the metal hooks which had once held the ladder.

3

Rip Warholler was baffled. The body he was supposed to remove from the Centre was nowhere to be found. Someone else appeared to have broken in and removed it already. Or perhaps they had managed to rescue Totley while he was still alive. But who could have known he was there? Whoever it was they had come well equipped, leaving behind a scene of utter devastation.

Pulling a phone from his pocket he tried the personal numbers of Sinnet and Parbunkel but got no reply from either. If all had gone well that was only to be expected; by now they should be on a flight to the USA. But clearly all had not gone well. He thought of contacting Swyver in person but that was a drastic move to be reserved for the most extreme circumstances. For now he would try to handle this himself.

After going through the rest of the Centre he ended up at the rear exit. He scanned the compound and realised the old Land Rover was missing. Afraid the problem might be spreading to Cave D he decided to drive back and check.

4

Mike lay still on the ledge, recovering from his surprise at being alive. When the dizziness had passed and his limbs had stopped shaking he pulled himself gingerly into a sitting position and checked his body for injuries. There were rope burns on his hands and bruises on his shins but nothing more serious. He removed his backpack and started to unfasten it.

A few minutes later the canyon's silence was shattered by the shrill scream of the rock slicer biting into the lock on the cave door.

5

The noise rang through the echoing darkness. Connie opened her eyes and wondered why she couldn't see anything. Completely disorientated she panicked and sat up, banging her head. The noise stopped. She began to think she'd dreamt it. Then came another noise, faint and metallic, that might have been the cave door opening. She sat very still, not even daring to breathe in case she missed something.

'Connie! Are you there? It's me – Mike.'

Connie tried to reply but her voice came as a hoarse whisper. Afraid Mike would go away again, she felt around for the caving helmet and banged it repeatedly on the floor.

'I hear you!' shouted Mike. 'I'll be down as soon as I've moved this rock.'

Connie wept with relief. She touched her tears with her fingertips and licked the salty moisture.

Knowing it would be impossible to abseil down a cliff with all the components of the rock slicer, Mike had brought only the disc cutter and the power pack. Without the dust extractor he preferred not to use it to break up the boulder; even if he wore a face mask the massive volume of dust might choke him before the job was finished. It would be his last resort. First he would try the simplest mechanical device of all. He reached for his backpack and pulled out the crowbar.

It took many minutes and all Mike's strength but eventually the hole stood exposed. From the backpack he pulled a bar of halva and a canvas pouch containing a canister of water. He squeezed the halva into the pouch with the canister, fastened it to his climbing harness and began to squirm his way down.

The route between the rocks was even more difficult for Mike than for Connie. For one nasty moment near the bottom he seemed completely stuck, unable to move backwards or forwards. Eventually he struggled free and dropped onto the giant boulder.

Realising he was close, Connie tried to call out. This time her voice was husky but audible.

'Mike, don't try to come any further… won't make it… lower the rope.'

Mike did as Connie suggested and a few minutes later her left hand reached up from the darkness. He pulled gently and soon the rest of her emerged. They cried, laughed and clung to each other for a long time.

'I thought you were dead,' said Connie. 'I figured that if they wanted to kill me they'd want to kill you too.'

'They did their best,' said Mike. 'I'll tell you about it later. Have some water.' He put the canister to Connie's lips. She began to gulp it and was convulsed by a fit of coughing. 'Steady. Not too fast. Just sip it to start with. I've brought some halva as well. It's good energy food.'

When Connie felt ready, they climbed back to the upper level of the cave. They sat down to rest just inside the cave entrance where Mike unpacked more food and drink and explained how he'd found her.

'I don't want to sound ungrateful,' said Connie, chewing a slice of dried grapefruit, 'but you should've gotten help instead of risking your life like that. What would have happened if…'

'Do you think anyone would have taken me seriously? It's a pretty bizarre story and I had no proof you were here. I could hardly expect the Israeli army to launch a mountain rescue mission because of a verse in the Song of Solomon. And secondly—'

'Is there any more halva? Thanks. You're wonderful. Carry on.'

'Secondly, Sinnet and Parbunkel are in cahoots with a secret organisation of ruthless fanatics. If I'm right about what they're up to, it's a conspiracy that could extend to the highest levels.'

'You mean we're in a trust-no-one situation?'

'I'm afraid so.'

'So what are these guys into? Smuggling antiquities?'

'Much worse, I'm afraid.'

'Narcotics?'

Mike shook his head.

'An illegal arms deal?'

'It's a long story. I'll tell you when we're on the road.'

'The road to where?'

'Well, we can't go north. The way I see it, Sinnet and Parbunkel, or some of their cronies, will have to go back to the Centre to dispose of my body – or at least to make my death seem like an accident. When they find I'm gone they'll try to track me down. I suggest we drive south, not stopping until we get to Elat. That way we should stay ahead of them. There's an airport at Elat and I'm hoping you'll be able to pull some strings and get us out.'

'So that's why you went to so much trouble to find me – I'm your passport to safety!'

Mike said, 'Connie, I love you,' and kissed her on the lips.

'I can hardly believe you did that,' she said, pushing locks of matted hair back from her face. 'I must be a revolting mess.'

'It would take more to put me off you than a coating of stale sweat, dried vomit and bat guano.'

'Love it when you talk dirty,' said Connie and returned his kiss. 'Now, what's the plan for getting out of here?'

Mike got to his feet and picked up the rope that trailed across the floor from outside. 'First I'm going to work my way along the ledge to get out from under the overhang, then I'll climb back to the top and...'

'Are you crazy?'

'Don't worry. Look, I'll fasten the rope to my harness with this figure-of-eight thing.'

'Mike, that figure-of-eight thing is called a descender. You know why? Because you use it when you're going down. It won't help you get back up!'

'But at least I won't lose the rope. And with the rope to pull on I won't be dependent on finding handholds all the way. In any case, we have no choice. Even if we could abseil to the lower ledges and climb to the bottom, the Land Rover's at the top and it's our only way out of here.'

'I'm afraid there's another problem; I could normally manage a climb of three hundred feet – I've climbed at Yosemite and I think I'm pretty good at it – but right now I don't have the strength or stamina. I'm sorry, Mike, but I just don't see how...'

'I've thought of that. When I get to the top I'll give you a shout and you tie this end of the rope to your harness. The other end is tied to the front of the Land Rover, so I'll just drive it backwards and pull you to the top.'

After considering the plan in grim silence Connie said, 'It sounds crazy to me, but I can't think of anything better so I guess we have to give it a try. We can't just sit here and starve.'

Mike bent down and kissed her on the forehead.

'Don't worry. I'll see you at the top.'

He paused at the cave door to put on the baseball cap.

'Has anyone told you,' said Connie, wiping a tear from her cheek, 'how completely ridiculous you look in that outfit?'

6

There is a point on the mountain road, just before it begins its detour around Nahal Jamin, from which Cave D can be seen clearly in the distance. Rip Warholler stopped his Land Rover at that point and scanned the cliffs through binoculars. Immediately he saw a white-clad figure moving uncertainly among the crags. The climber was so strangely dressed that Warholler wasn't completely sure it was Mike. Nor was it easy to tell whether he was on his way up or down, his movements were so erratic. But whoever he was and whatever he was doing he had to be stopped. Warholler cruelly slammed the Land Rover into gear and urged it forward.

7

Notwithstanding the confident tone in which he'd outlined his plan to Connie, Mike had no illusions about his competence as a mountaineer. He fully expected the climb to be hell every step of the way and it was. His progress was constantly impeded by flawed judgements, retraced steps and moments spent glued to the spot by fear. Fortunately, what he lacked in experience he made up for in stamina and sheer resolve. Eventually, breathless and bathed in sweat, he reached the top.

As soon as he'd recovered sufficiently he called down to Connie to tie the rope to her climbing harness. In response to a shout that she was ready, he got into the Land Rover, started the engine and began to edge it slowly backwards. All went according to plan until he was about sixty metres from the cliff; then the whine of the engine changed subtly and Mike realised something was wrong.

The rope was no longer moving. He put the Land Rover in neutral, letting it roll forward slightly to release the tension. The rope lay slack on the ground. Applying the handbrake he jumped down and ran to the edge of the cliff. The rope had slipped into a narrow crack and become firmly wedged. Connie, still more than twenty metres from the top, was looking anxiously up at him. He was about to reassure her that he would think of something – though he had no idea what – when a familiar and unpleasant noise started up behind him. Above the whine of a rock slicer Rip Warholler shouted:

'Having problems, Totley?'

Mike froze. Then it occurred to him that freezing while crouched on the edge of a cliff with Warholler approaching from behind with a rock slicer was not a good idea. He willed himself to stand and turn around.

'Well, well,' he said, feigning insouciance, 'this is a surprise.' He took a few steps away from the cliff edge. Brandishing the disc cutter effortlessly in one hand, Warholler took a step towards him. Mike looked around to see if anyone else had turned up. Apparently not. He could see Rip's Land Rover parked some distance away and it looked empty. The noise of his own vehicle's engine had obviously drowned out its arrival. He chided himself for not being more alert.

'If you really believe in God,' shouted Warholler, 'I suggest you say a quick prayer and get ready to meet him.' He took another step forward.

'And if you believe in God,' said Mike, 'I suggest you remember his sixth commandment: "You shall not commit murder."' He took a step sideways, away from Warholler and the cliff edge.

'This won't be murder,' said Warholler, moving to block Mike's escape. 'This is an execution.'

'In that case might I know the charge?'

'Opposing God's will.'

Mike could see only one outcome to this confrontation; his strength was no match for Warholler's and in his present exhausted state he couldn't count on his agility either. In any case, making a run for it was out of the question; he couldn't contemplate leaving Connie. But he was determined to postpone the end for as long as possible.

'But how can you be so sure you know what God's will is, Rip? What if you've got it all wrong?'

'Shut up, Totley! I gave up doubting a long time ago.'

'That's a pity, because doubt can be very constructive; *reculer pour mieux sauter*.'

'I said shut up! That's devil's talk!'

'Actually it's French. It roughly translates as drawing back in order to leap further.'

'I meant it's devil's talk to approve of doubt! That's why Dr Swyver is God's man for our times; he knows the will of God for sure!'

'So you would even commit murder on his instructions?'

'I told you, in my book this isn't murder! Now, are you going to jump, or does this have to get nasty?'

'You think jumping off a cliff isn't nasty?'

Warholler closed in.

'Dr Sinnet says that in Jesus's time they used to execute blasphemers by throwing them over cliffs, so this'll be kind of appropriate.'

'I think you'll find,' said Mike in a desperate bid to prolong the argument, 'that the *Mishnah* stipulates a cliff about four metres high for that purpose. Which means this one's a trifle too big.'

Unimpressed, Warholler continued his advance. Mike braced himself. He wasn't going to die without a struggle, however futile. Then, as Warholler approached the rope, it suddenly sprang taut from the ground. He tripped over it and lunged forward, grabbing at Mike's arm with his free hand. But Mike's firmer stance now gave him the advantage. With all the strength desperation could supply he wrenched his arm free, propelling Warholler towards the precipice. Mike fell to the ground at the edge of the cliff. Warholler plunged over into the void, his scream merging with the rock slicer's whine as both faded to silence.

In a state somewhere between relief and incredulity Mike stared at the vibrating rope. To his further amazement he saw, where it disappeared over the cliff edge, Connie's right hand grasping it. Then her left hand appeared, feeling for a purchase on the rock.

'Mike, help me!' she gasped. 'I'm pooped.'

8

'You okay?' asked Connie, watching Mike with concern. 'Shall I drive for a while?'

Mike shook his head, keeping his eyes fixed on the road. They had left behind the high plateau of Masada and the salt pans of the Dead Sea, heading south on the road to Elat and Aqaba. Mike hadn't spoken for half an hour.

'Are you still thinking about Rip?'

Mike nodded. 'I've never killed anyone before.'

'Mike, there are two facts you've got to hold on to. Number one: you aren't solely responsible for his death; we both are. Number two: it was self-defence; him or us.'

'I know. I just wish there'd been some other way.'

After another brooding silence Connie said, 'Look, this isn't just a problem for you, you know. It's bugging me, too. If you can't talk about it right now I respect that, but couldn't we talk about something else to take our minds off it?'

'Such as?'

'Well, you still haven't told me what Sinnet and Parbunkel are involved in. And you didn't finish telling me how you got out of that awful room.'

Mike thought for a moment, then said, 'Okay, I'll start with how I escaped. It leads on to Swyver's plan anyway.'

'*Swyver's* plan?'

'You know, the man who put the fun back into fundamentalism? He's clearly at the bottom of it. So you were right — back in Washington when you tried to tell me he was up to no good. I owe you an apology.'

'Accepted. Now can I please hear the rest of the story?'

'Okay. The treatment room. Like I said on the plateau, I couldn't open the door or the window and my air supply was almost gone. Then I realised what the box was.'

'The box Parbunkel said was the Ark of the Covenant?'

'Yes. I was sure it wasn't, but I hadn't really considered the alternatives. I'd half suspected it was a fake concocted by Parbunkel and Sinnet, but it suddenly struck me that it couldn't be. The marks on the ends were too obviously in the wrong place; an intelligent hoaxer would have got it right. The alternative was that Parbunkel's story was true; they'd stumbled across the box by chance and got carried away with the idea that it might be the Ark. When they first retrieved it the marks on the end didn't show up, so there was no evidence to contradict the theory.'

'So what was it?'

'A munitions box — or something similar — from the Victorian era; the kind of thing the army used to carry equipment in. The marks on the ends were rivet holes where leather straps had been fastened.'

'But what the hell was it doing in a cistern under the Temple Mount?'

'In the nineteenth century the caverns below the Haram esh-

Sharif were explored by several military men, like Charles Wilson and Charles Warren, both officers in the Royal Engineers. Another British army officer called Parker went down there in 1911. One of them must have left the thing behind. In fact it has to have been Parker because the others produced plans of all the chambers they entered, and they don't include the one where the box was found. And Parker left in a hurry, for reasons I'll come to in a minute. Anyway, it occurred to me that if I was right, the box might still contain some of Parker's equipment, including tools I could use to break out.'

'And it did? That's incredible!'

'And when I realised what the box really was I also understood why Sinnet and Parbunkel had been ferreting about under the Haram. It was Parker's expedition that gave me the missing clue. I don't suppose you know the story of Captain Montague Parker and his ill-fated quest for Solomon's gold?'

'I'm afraid not.'

'Not many people do. He was a kind of English Indiana Jones. His Jerusalem venture was inspired by an old manuscript, said to describe the hiding place of King Solomon's treasury. The manuscript mysteriously disappeared – the way these things do – but a report of its contents persuaded Parker that the treasure lay in a secret chamber below the Temple Mount. So he got together a bunch of like-minded aristocratic adventurers and in 1909 they arrived in Jerusalem with enough money to hire a workforce and buy equipment. On the surface they were an ordinary archaeological mission; apart from a couple of bribed Ottoman officials, no one outside Parker's own circle knew what he was looking for.

'They started by clearing a system of blocked tunnels, discovered years earlier by Warren. Archaeologically it was quite useful work, but by the spring of 1911 there was still no sign of any treasure. Parker became impatient and bribed more officials who let him excavate on the Haram itself, secretly and by night. After another week of futile explorations his tactics became even more outrageous.

'Beneath the Dome of the Rock there's a cave that's used as a place of prayer, and set in its floor is a round marble slab about a metre across. Moslem tradition says this covers an entrance to the realm of the dead but Parker thought it might conceal a secret passage. One night he and his men entered the cave and started hacking away at the floor. The racket was heard by a Moslem attendant whom Parker had omitted to bribe and he blew the whistle on them. Soon Jerusalem was full of wild rumours – that Parker had found and stolen the crown of Solomon, or that he'd brought in barrels of gunpowder to blow up the Haram esh-Sharif. The Moslem population was outraged and riots broke out. Parker and his team managed to escape but rioting spread until the whole city was in turmoil. It took several days to restore order. It was probably the most disastrous archaeological expedition ever – until ours, that is.'

'And you think Sinnet was carrying on the search where Parker left off? I guess it figures, in view of his obsession with…'

'No. More sinister than that, I'm afraid.'

Connie looked at Mike. Her lips parted but it was several seconds before she spoke.

'You're not suggesting… You are, aren't you? Oh, my God!'

'It all ties in – the Kelal, the attempts on my life…'

'The assholes! The stupid assholes! Mike, we've got to stop them!'

'I know. I was hoping you'd come up with a plan.'

They drove on in silence. Across the broad expanse of the Arabah the mountains of ancient Edom rose in folds of deep red and brown. Shadows were lengthening from the west.

Part Three
The Seventh Seal

There will be a battle, and terrible carnage before the God of Israel,
for this will be the day determined by him since ancient times
for a war of annihilation against the sons of darkness...
On the day of disaster, the sons of light and the forces of darkness shall battle together...

1QM (The War Scroll) 1:9–12

Chapter Twenty-One

1

[The White House, Washington DC, 11.30 a.m.]

President Patrick Thorn sat at his mahogany desk in the Oval Office perusing the latest printout from the situation room. He glanced up as Harry Hassenbacker, White House chief of staff, put the phone down and turned to face him.

'That was the last one, sir. They're all on their way.'

'Good. Thanks, Harry. You've done a great job.'

'Would you like to be left alone for a few minutes, sir, until they arrive?'

Thorn, a flat-featured slab of a man, responded with a barely perceptible nod. This was going to be the most important meeting of his presidency. He looked back down the path which had brought him to the White House in time for this turning point in world history and felt overawed by the privilege.

His career in politics had begun in the sixties, writing speeches for Nixon; his profile had been raised in the eighties when Reagan appointed him to liaise with the religious Right, then newly emerged as a political force; in the nineties he'd campaigned tirelessly against welfare, gun control, immigration, environmentalism and feminism, his paranoid rhetoric contributing hugely to the Republican swing in the 1994 mid-term elections. After that the presidency had been just a matter of time.

By 11.45 the men Thorn had summoned were all present. He surveyed their expectant faces.

'Okay, gentlemen, let's begin. I apologise for the urgent call but we've received intelligence that demands immediate attention. The fact is, there's been a dramatic development in the Middle East.'

His audience looked at each other uneasily as Thorn paused

and took a deep breath.

'Something of immense significance will shortly be happening in Israel. I've asked Joel to explain the situation to you just as he explained it to me an hour or so ago.'

All eyes turned to Joel Shepherd, national security advisor, a man whose round schoolboy face belied his experience and shrewdness. He straightened himself in his chair and began. He spoke without notes, but in the dull monotone of someone reading a script for the first time, precisely and without feeling.

'At shortly after 10 a.m. our time, Eugene Hayden, the CIA's deputy director of National Covert Operations, received a call from an Israeli air force base just outside Elat.'

Harry Hassenbacker interrupted to ask if he might enquire why the call had not been made to *International* Covert Operations. Shepherd replied brusquely that it was a long story with no relevance and carried on.

'One of our agents out there has uncovered a plot to blow up the Dome of the Rock in Jerusalem.' He looked at the predominantly blank faces of his audience and continued in a slightly patronising tone. 'For those who are unfamiliar with it, let me explain that the Dome of the Rock is a Moslem mosque which stands on the Temple Mount, the place occupied in biblical times by the Jewish Temple. There are certain groups in Israel, and indeed here in the United States, who dearly wish to see the Temple rebuilt. But the existence of a Moslem holy place on the site has always prevented the realisation of that goal. Blowing up the mosque would make it possible for their dream to become a reality. It is evident that a coalition of such groups is responsible for this plot, though their precise identity is unknown at this present moment in time.'

'If I may interject, Mr President,' said Harvey Weissman, Thorn's attorney general and by a wide margin the most learned man in the room, 'the Dome of the Rock is not strictly a mosque, it's a shrine. To be precise it was the first major Islamic shrine to be built, around thirteen centuries ago, and is the only shrine from that period to survive substantially intact to the present day.'

'So its destruction would be an act of vandalism,' said Hassenbacker, who was taking copious notes and wanted to get things straight.

'Its destruction,' said Weissman, his aquiline features reddening, 'would be a catastrophe of gigantic proportions! We're not just talking about some quaint building of historic interest here; we're talking about one of the holiest places in the entire Moslem world! If these ultra-Zionists destroy it there'll be an unprecedented international crisis; Islamic nations will accuse Israel of a crime against God; there'll be reprisals, an escalation of violence that no one can stop, ending in all-out war in the Middle East and probably beyond! So I'm waiting to hear Mr Shepherd tell us what's being done to stop this happening!'

Joel Shepherd was still stinging from the attorney general's correction. He hated being lectured at.

'I'm afraid it seems to be too late to prevent the building's destruction,' he said matter-of-factly, relishing the consternation on Weissman's face. 'A bomb has been concealed beneath the Temple Mount and there is unfortunately no access to it.'

There was general alarm at this news. Murray Chambers, secretary of state, was incredulous.

'What do you mean, no access? How the hell did it get there if there's no access?'

'Well, there was access, of course,' replied Shepherd with infuriating calm, 'but there isn't now. The only tunnel leading to the bomb is blocked by tons of masonry and concrete. We can therefore assume that the bomb will be set off either by a timing device or a radio signal. If the latter, any attempt to reach it to prevent the explosion will be futile. The group responsible for planting the bomb would detonate it instantly rather than see their elaborate plans come to nothing.'

The secretary of defence, Morton Walsh, leaned forward to speak, his Queen Anne chair creaking ominously under his considerable weight. Speaking slowly and deliberately he said, 'So you're telling us there's nothing we can do to prevent this disaster? The most powerful nation on earth has to stand by and watch while a few lunatics plunge the Middle East, perhaps the entire world, into war?'

At this juncture the president intervened. Apart from Shepherd he was the only man in the room who did not look deeply perturbed.

'Gentlemen, I think we need to put this in perspective. As Joel mentioned, there are groups here as well as in Israel who want to see the Temple rebuilt. They include Christians who are very good friends of mine. And you know why those Christians want to see Jerusalem graced once again with a Jewish Temple?'

Thorn picked up a Bible from his desk and read from a well-thumbed page:

'"And the heathen shall know that I the Lord do sanctify Israel, when my sanctuary shall be in the midst of them for evermore." Ezekiel, chapter thirty-seven, verse twenty-eight. That sanctuary, gentlemen, is the new Temple. The building of a new Temple is foretold in Scripture; therefore it is inevitable that it will take place. Furthermore, this is one of the last great prophecies to be fulfilled before the return of Christ. In short, the rebuilding of the Temple makes Christ's return imminent. So it may not be mere chance that it lies beyond our power to prevent the destruction of this mosque or shrine or whatever. We should seriously consider the possibility that we are witnessing the unfolding of God's purposes.'

There was a stunned silence, broken only by the antique chair groaning under Morton Walsh's bulk. Thorn hadn't talked like this since the Reagan era, when he'd espoused the view that Armageddon would be a nuclear holocaust, and it was widely believed that he'd renounced his infatuation with apocalyptic texts in favour of a more pragmatic approach to long-term policy.

General Tom Sandstrom, chairman of the Joint Chiefs of Staff, brought the meeting back to practicalities.

'Mr President, I assume the Israelis know what's going on and have had time to optionalise possibilities. May we know what action they're taking?'

Thorn turned to Shepherd and with a slight nod instructed him to continue.

'The IDF and Shin Bet have taken charge of the situation. As of now they are attempting to seal off the area around the Temple Mount to prevent loss of life. But when it comes to preventing the explosion they are essentially impotent. They have considered trying to reopen the tunnel which leads to the bomb but, as I said earlier, that is a high risk strategy which may provoke the bomb's immediate detonation. Shin Bet are therefore putting their best resources into locating the headquarters of the group responsible. The problem is, the clampdown on extremist groups in Israel in 1995 drove their remnants underground. Since then they have operated in almost total secrecy. The chances of identifying the people involved in this plot are very slender indeed and we should not pin any hopes on that approach.'

'The bottom line,' said Thorn, 'is that we must assume this bomb will go off, and make plans accordingly. To put it bluntly, gentlemen, we must plan for a war which the Bible calls Armageddon.'

Morton Walsh's chair finally disintegrated and the room shook as he hit the floor.

2

[The Pentagon, 8 p.m.]

Walsh chain-smoked his way through the latest intelligence reports, passing each page across his desk to General Sandstrom as he finished it. As he handed over the last sheet he stood up and began pacing the room, massaging his lower back. Sandstrom looked up.

'Are you all right, sir?'

'Pain's a bit easier, thank you, General.'

Sandstrom dropped the last page of the report onto Walsh's desk and shook his head.

'No fresh light there, sir.'

'No, General. I'm afraid you're right.'

There was a knock on the door and Gerald Sullivan of Central Intelligence entered.

Walsh motioned him to sit down and said, 'Well, Gerry, what news?'

Sullivan settled into a squeaking, overstuffed chair, wiped his brow with a sweat-stained handkerchief and began. He was clearly nervous and embarrassed.

'It's been difficult to get to the bottom of this, sir, but you were certainly right about one thing: there is more to this than Joel Shepherd disclosed in his briefing.'

'What do you mean, difficult to get to the bottom of it?' Walsh didn't like the sound of this. If Central Intelligence couldn't get to the bottom of something, then who could?

'There are two people involved, sir. According to Eugene Hayden one is a young female who works in Analysis and was merely in Israel on vacation; the other is not one of our agents at all, but an English male academic whom the woman was asked to recruit as a contract agent last November. But this is obviously a smokescreen; fabrication from start to finish.'

'You think so?'

'It's as plain as a cockroach in a bathtub, sir. Look at what they've achieved! I've no doubt these are two high-level covert operatives whose activities are so highly classified, their true backgrounds and training are not on record. I pressed Hayden for the facts, of course, but he stuck to his story. I've contacted MI6 in case the man is one of theirs but they adopted a deny everything policy. In fact, nobody admits to authorising this particular mission or knowing anything about it.'

'My God!' exclaimed Walsh.

'Yes, sir,' said Sullivan. 'I'll look into this more thoroughly when I get the opportunity, but I assume that's not a priority right now?'

'I suppose not. So, what was Shepherd holding back?' Walsh finished one cigarette, lit another and resumed his pacing of the room.

'The telephoned report of these agents claims an American connection with the extremists responsible for this bomb under the mosque, sir.'

'What?' Walsh began coughing convulsively. By the time the fit was under control he had tears pouring down his face. He borrowed Sullivan's handkerchief and wiped them away. 'What the fuck do you mean, an American connection?'

Sullivan's chair emitted a chorus of loud squeaks as he shifted uneasily.

'In brief, sir, they say the Reverend Oral B Swyver is the mastermind behind the whole thing. And we do have evidence that Swyver's been channelling funds...'

'Swyver!' gasped Walsh, stubbing out the cigarette he'd only just lit. He was remembering Thorn's words: '... there are groups here... including Christians who are very good friends of mine...' He asked, 'The same Swyver POTUS is friendly with?' He somehow felt more comfortable using the acronym. To have pronounced the president's name, even his title, would have given too firm a shape to his embryonic fear.

'Yes, sir.'

'So POTUS may have known—' He left the suggestion unfinished.

'It begins to seem likely, sir.'

Walsh sat down heavily at his desk, swearing as pain returned to his lower back. There was a minute's silence while his mind grappled with the developing scenario. Sullivan and Sandstrom looked at each other anxiously.

Eventually Walsh turned to Sullivan and said, 'Where the hell is Swyver now?'

'At his Bible Institute in Tennessee, sir.'

'I want him.'

'I anticipated that, sir. I already have agents in Tennessee.'

'And how soon can we expect results?'

Sullivan's chair discharged another volley of squeaks.

'Well, sir, a situation has developed...'

Walsh leaned forward, jowls pulsing.

'What kind of a situation?'

'It seems Swyver's being guarded by some weird militia types...'

'My God! Are you telling me this could become a siege?'

'Don't worry, sir. I sent our best agents...'

'Not the best, Gerry; the best are in Elat. I want those two covert operatives brought here fast. Have the Israeli air force fly them by military jet if you have to. Get on to it right away, and make sure no hint of this operation leaks out to the president or to Shepherd.'

3

[The White House, 12.30 a.m.]

Thorn and Shepherd strode briskly across the situation room, located in the basement of the White House. Shepherd moved ahead of the president and opened the door to the conference room. When they were both inside he closed it crisply, shutting out the chatter of bleeping computers and purring printers. Thorn checked his watch and turned to face a large video screen. He pressed a button on a remote control unit and the screen lit up with a life-sized picture of Sandstrom, who looked directly at the president. Five miles away, at the national military command centre in the Pentagon, Sandstrom was looking at a life-sized picture of Thorn and Shepherd.

'Well, Tom,' said the president, 'I hope you've got something for me. I'm sorry to say that Shin Bet have made no progress whatsoever.'

Sandstrom thought the president sounded more exhilarated than sorry.

'Well, sir,' he said, 'since the chance of averting the energetic disassembly of the Dome of the Rock is suboptimal, we've used our computers to generate projections of the level and course of volatility in the Middle East over the next several months.'

Thorn raised a quizzical eyebrow at Shepherd, who obliged with an interpretation.

'Nobody has a cat in hell's chance of preventing the explosion, so here's our guess at what's going to happen after the bomb goes off.'

General Sandstrom then sketched the total collapse of the Middle East peace initiative and the shifting pattern of alliances likely to form against Israel; he predicted the takeover of both Egypt and Syria by hardline Islamic fundamentalists, and the invasion of a divided and destabilised Iraq by Iran. All this would culminate, he speculated, in the successful invasion of Israel by a constellation of Islamic powers in about five months' time, concluding:

'In engagements of the scale expected, there is certain to be a high level of contingent ordnance, collateral damage and arbitrary degrees of health alteration. However, our projections suggest that containment in a subholocaust scenario might be possible.'

'A hell of a lot of people are going to die,' explained Shepherd, 'but there may not be a nuclear engagement big enough to wipe out all life in the region.'

'Is that all?' asked the president, addressing Sandstrom's image. 'What about the Russians?'

'This is a purely Middle East scenario, Mr President. There is no reason to believe Russia has the strength or the will to get involved. We have no intelligence to that effect.'

Pat Thorn shook his head.

'Yes we do, Tom. We have biblical prophecies, and they provide top-level intelligence. It's there in Ezekiel, chapters thirty-eight and thirty-nine. If you don't have a Bible get hold of one and read it right away. And take a look at Revelation, chapter sixteen, verse twelve. It predicts the drying up of the River Euphrates, allowing the advance of armies from the east. So you're wrong about Iran and Iraq, too. Expect an invasion of Israel by Baghdad. You'd better patch Ezekiel, Zechariah and Revelation into the computer. In fact—' He was about to say 'patch in the whole Bible' when it occurred to him that verses about loving enemies, being peacemakers and beating swords into ploughshares might confuse the issue. 'On second thoughts, that should do it. Then come back with an operations plan for our own involvement, approved by the chiefs. In the meantime, have the Sixth Fleet on standby alert.'

'Our own involvement, sir?' said the general. The idea was so at odds with Thorn's isolationist policies that Sandstrom thought he'd misheard.

'I think,' Shepherd explained patronisingly, 'the president believes we should prepare to enforce hemispheric hygiene.'

'Invade Europe?' gasped Sandstrom, visibly flabbergasted.

'Sure,' said Thorn. 'The neo-communists and Zhirinovsky's ultranationalists have both been making belligerent noises lately. We've got to be ready to move before they do. We've spent—'

Sandstrom was so amazed he did something he normally considered taboo; he interrupted the president.

'But, sir, you're surely not suggesting we pay any attention to rhetoric designed for internal consumption!'

Thorn waved a hand to dismiss the objection.

'As I was saying, we've spent four years rebuilding our strength and now it's time to live out our destiny. You know what the Bible calls us, Tom? "The young lions of Tarshish"! Well, the young lions are about to roar.' He pressed another button on the remote control and the screen went blank.

In the Pentagon, General Sandstrom turned to Secretary of Defence Walsh and said, 'I think the president is operating in a different information space, sir.'

Walsh nodded.

'He's a nut all right.'

A phone bleeped in his pocket.

He answered it, swore fiercely, then said to Sandstrom, 'More bad news. The Israelis aren't prepared to send those agents home yet. Something to do with further interrogation and medical care. I just hope they're not too late.'

Chapter Twenty-Two

1

Below in the middle distance a constellation of lights criss-crossed the darkness in regular lines.

'Is that it?' Connie shouted over the throb of the Chinook's engines. A soldier on her left nodded. As far as she could make out the BIOSES campus was the size of a small town.

'I still don't see why they want us here,' said Mike, speaking close to Connie's right ear to make himself heard. 'If a team of highly skilled agents have been trying to negotiate with Swyver for three days without success, what do they expect us to do?'

They had left Elat feeling more or less recovered from their ordeal but now, after traversing time zones for sixteen hours in various modes of transport, most of them too noisy to permit sleep, the strain was beginning to tell.

'I'll be out of my depth,' he continued, 'probably in the way.'

'I know, I feel the same,' said Connie, squeezing his hand, 'but let's wait and see, shall we?'

Details of the campus became visible as they descended. The tall fountains in the main lake were floodlit and the Power Tower had lights shining from every window; its roof was crowned by a spire-like antenna which glowed with neon strips, sending out spokes of light through a circle of smaller masts.

The helicopter landed inside the main gates, not far from a huge articulated truck. Other bulky shapes loomed nearby, difficult to make out in semi-darkness but ominously like armoured vehicles. Beyond them the burnt out shell of a gatehouse was dimly visible.

As two armed soldiers escorted Mike and Connie from the helicopter to the rear of the truck, a door opened to admit them. Suddenly they were enveloped by bright light and cigarette smoke. They both blinked with discomfort, becoming aware of monitors and banks of lights along both sides of a long room. Without saying anything the soldiers withdrew, closed the door and ran back to the Chinook.

Inside the truck the helicopter's insistent throb faded, giving way to a soft hum and the faint chatter of tinny voices leaking from headsets. A swarthy, middle-aged man with greying hair and a harassed expression stepped forward and held out a welcoming hand.

'Agent Patterson and Agent Totley, it's good to have you on board at last. I'm Agent Margelli. These are Agents Nash and Cooper.' He jerked his thumb in the direction of two younger men sitting at a long desk. Each wore a headset and was watching a monitor. Their workstations were cluttered with empty plastic cups and cigarette packets. Both looked up fleetingly and gave a token nod of acknowledgement.

'I believe you've been briefed somewhat on the way but I'll bring you up to speed,' said Margelli. 'There are a few hundred heavily armed militia men on the campus, including a handful in the Power Tower – exact numbers unknown. There are also perhaps two hundred BIOSES students on the thirtieth floor of the Tower – that's right at the top – whether of their own free will or not we don't know, but their presence is effectively a human shield. We've got soldiers posted at various points around the perimeter but we've got to be careful; Swyver claims the whole building is wired to explode if we fire on any part of it, killing everyone in there including himself. He may be bluffing but I wouldn't like to put it to the test.'

Connie was standing behind Nash and Cooper, looking over their shoulders.

'Are these both views of the Power Tower?' she asked, pointing at the monitors on the desk.

'That's right. This camera shows the whole building, and this one is zoomed in on the entrance so we won't miss any comings and goings. And we've got infrared and thermal imaging capabilities in case the lights go out.'

Mike was more interested in the wide-angle shot. In the foreground, only thirty or forty metres away, was a lake and its waters seemed violently agitated. Mike peered more closely at the screen and soon saw the reason.

'This may be a stupid question,' he said, 'but what are all those sea lions doing in the lake?'

'Agent Nash,' said Margelli, 'what's the latest on the sea lions?'

'They're playing around the fountains and eating the goldfish,' said Nash.

'But why are they there?' asked Mike. 'Are they standard on American campuses?'

'No. We put them there, Agent Totley. Had them brought in yesterday by truck from various sea life parks. We released them by the gate and they headed for the lake and dived in.'

'But – forgive me if I'm being dim – why order sea lions at all?'

'Well...' Margelli paused, clearly embarrassed. 'We were in radio contact with Swyver, trying to talk him out of this thing with the bomb, but all he'd say was that he was waiting for the seventh seal of the book of Revelation. Well, Agent Cooper here remembers his Bible somewhat and he recalled that Revelation is full of weird animals, so we figured that the seventh seal must be one of them. We thought we might get Swyver to talk if he thought the seventh seal had arrived. Of course, to be on the safe side we had to get seven, because if we'd only gotten one he might have thought it was the first, not the seventh. Now sea lions turned out to be the easiest kind of seal to get hold of at short notice so we hoped Swyver wouldn't be too particular about species or...'

'I don't believe I'm hearing this!' said Mike, pushing his fingers through his hair. 'The book of Revelation isn't talking about that kind of seal at all! It means the seals on a scroll!'

'Well, of course, we began to suspect an error when Swyver failed to respond. But at least it hasn't done any harm.'

'The goldfish might disagree,' said Connie.

Margelli became conspiratorial.

'Agent Totley, we'd be greatly obliged if you didn't mention this episode to our superiors.'

Mike didn't answer. He was staring over Margelli's shoulder at a neglected monitor on the opposite side of the room.

'Fascinating!' he said, walking over for a closer look.

'Oh, that,' said Margelli, dismissively. 'It started coming

through a couple of hours ago. We can't make any sense of it.'

'Where's it coming from?'

'The Internet. Visit any of Swyver's web sites and this is all you get. We think he's trying to confuse us.'

'Not terribly difficult, I imagine,' said Mike.

'What is it?' asked Connie.

'A photographic reproduction of a Dead Sea Scroll. And did you notice the picture just changed? I'll bet the whole thing is being displayed one column at a time.'

'A Dead Sea Scroll?' said Margelli, none the wiser.

'11Q19 to be precise, otherwise known as the Temple Scroll.'

'Temple...' mused Connie. 'Could it be some kind of signal?'

Mike looked at Connie, then back at the screen.

'Of course! Why didn't I see it straight away?'

'You can't have all the good ideas.'

'But this is crucial! If only we'd got here sooner...'

'So how does it work?'

Margelli beckoned Cooper and Nash to join them. They stubbed out their cigarettes and got up from the desk.

'This,' said Mike, tapping the screen, 'is one column of text from the longest of the Dead Sea Scrolls. Altogether there are sixty-six columns and they're apparently being screened in order, each being displayed for a few minutes before the programme moves on to the next. Unless I'm mistaken, what we're looking at now is column twenty-five, which is fairly typical of the whole thing. The top seven or eight lines are fragmentary, but the rest is quite easy to read – if you know Hebrew, that is, and you're familiar with this style of script. For example, this bit says: "You shall offer as a burnt offering for the Lord one bullock, one ram, seven yearling lambs and a male goat for the sin-offering" – describing the sacrifices made in the Temple on the Day of Atonement...'

'Just bring it home, Mike!' said Connie impatiently. 'What's the bottom line?'

'Sorry. The bottom line – of my explanation, I mean, not of this particular column of the scroll – is this: among a lot of idealised descriptions of Temple buildings, sacrifices, festivals and so on, there's one passage which mentions a new Temple to be built in the future, at the start of a new age. It says...' Mike paused.

'Yes?' said Connie, 'It says what?'

'It says... I'm quoting from memory, you understand, and there are a few doubts about the correct translation.'

'Mike, please! A loose paraphrase will do! Just tell us what it says!'

'Right. It says something like: "On the Day of Creation I will create my Sanctuary anew, establishing it for myself according my covenant with Jacob."'

Margelli, Cooper and Nash looked at each other dubiously. They'd been expecting something more explicit. Margelli said, 'Is that all?'

'Isn't that enough?' said Connie. 'It says a new Temple will be built, and that's what Swyver and these other nuts are wanting to happen.'

'So when the column containing that line appears on the screen,' Mike continued, 'that will be the signal – to someone in Israel, I assume – to blow up the Dome of the Rock.'

There was dead silence for several seconds while the three agents considered his theory. Cooper, a slight, pale man with a beard, glasses and untidy hair, was the first to speak.

'It doesn't track, Agent Totley. It would be far simpler for all the conspirators to just agree on a pre-arranged time. Why do it this way?'

'I think I see why,' said Connie. 'Doesn't the Bible say something about no one knowing in advance when the end of the age would come?'

'"Of that day or hour no one knows, not even the angels in heaven, not even the Son; no one but the Father",' quoted Mike.

'So even if Swyver thought he could calculate the year, he wouldn't dare claim to have calculated the day and hour. But Swyver also believes he's God's inspired agent, so it's my guess he's been waiting for a flash of inspiration in which God would tell him the precise time the bomb should go off. Until he received that revelation he couldn't possibly tell anyone else.'

'Brilliant! And that's what he meant by waiting for the seventh seal – the last seal to be broken, opening the scroll that reveals the end!'

'And a couple of hours ago,' Connie concluded, 'he became convinced it had happened so he activated this signal. Of course, the means of communicating with the faction in Israel must have been agreed in advance.'

Cooper nodded thoughtfully.

'And these people in Israel, how are they supposed to set off the bomb?'

'I can offer a guess,' said Nash, coming closer to the screen. He was a well-built black man with three days' growth of stubble. 'A VLF induction radio – sorry, that stands for Very Low Frequency – can transmit through several hundred feet of sold rock, so they could send a triggering signal that way. But they'd have to be pretty close, right in Jerusalem in fact, because induction radios can't cover long distances without phenomenal amounts of power. For example, you'd need the output of five big power stations to communicate over just twenty miles – totally impractical. To me, Agent Totley's idea makes a lot of sense. Swyver can't trigger the bomb himself because a VLF induction system can't be used for global communication, and because normal radio waves are absorbed by solid rock.'

'I'll buy that,' said Connie. 'Mike, can you tell us how much time we've got?'

'No problem. The crucial line occurs in the twenty-ninth column. If I'm right about this being column twenty-five, and if it's taken two hours to get to this point in the scroll, then each column must be on screen for about... let's say about five minutes. There – that confirms it!' The picture on the monitor had changed again. 'Definitely column twenty-six – the bit about the scapegoat. So at five minutes per column of text we've got just fifteen minutes before the crucial passage comes up.'

'Cooper,' said Margelli, 'contact Shin Bet with this information immediately, and put headquarters in the picture. Nash, how can we stop that signal?'

Cooper returned to his workstation.

Nash stared at the screen and shook his head. 'I'm afraid

there's no way of doing that. The signal goes straight to an Orbstat satellite and from there it can travel freely around the globe, making use of the world's telecommunication systems. Block one route and it'll kind of feel its way around cyberspace until it finds another.'

'Ironic, isn't it,' said Mike, 'when you consider that the Internet grew from something originally devised by the US defence department.'

'Couldn't we stop it at source?' asked Margelli, who had little interest in irony.

Nash shook his head again. 'Swyver has his own generators so there's no way we can deprive him of power. The only way to stop the signal is to take out the top of the building with an airstrike, destroying the transmitters. But even if Swyver's threat to destroy the whole building is a bluff we couldn't do that without killing all those people on the top floor.'

'So the president would never sanction it,' said Margelli, sinking hopelessly into a chair. 'My God, what a heap of shit! Any news from Shin Bet, Agent Cooper?'

Cooper swivelled his seat. He too looked profoundly despondent.

'They've taken the risk of reopening the tunnel that leads to the bomb. A team has entered the Temple Mount and started removing the rubble but they say there's no hope of reaching the bomb within fifteen minutes.'

'My God, my God,' intoned Margelli dismally, burying his face in his hands. A gloomy silence descended on everyone.

Mike watched column twenty-six give way to column twenty-seven, then he said, 'Is there any way you can put me in touch with Swyver?' Four pairs of eyes suddenly fixed on him, pleading with him to say something on which they could pin some hope. 'I know you had no success when you tried talking to him, but I think I've got a lever you didn't have. I'm afraid there isn't time to explain what I've got in mind. Every second counts. If you can connect me, please do it straight away.'

Nash, Cooper and Margelli exchanged glances.

'If anything goes wrong,' said Margelli, 'we'll all be left with our dicks in the wind.'

'Speak for yourself,' said Connie. 'Anyway, what have you three achieved apart from wiping out a lakeful of ornamental fish?'

After another second's hesitation, Margelli nodded to Nash, who sat down at his workstation and began punching his keyboard.

'Okay, Agent Totley, do what you can.'

Mike started towards the desk, waving a hand in front of his face to disperse the pall of smoke. Suddenly he hesitated. Connie went to his side.

'What is it, Mike?'

'This idea... it involves a gross piece of deception, a lie so enormous...'

'Well, if you can't do it, I will! Just tell me what to say!'

Mike looked into her eyes for a moment, then he put his hands on her shoulders and attempted an encouraging smile.

'It's all right, I'll do it.' He sat down at the desk.

Nash handed him a spare headset and wished him luck.

As Mike positioned the earphones he could hear Swyver speaking in unnervingly calm and casual tones.

'Hello, again, gentlemen. What is it this time? I'll be making an announcement in due course but I'm extremely busy right now.'

Mike adjusted the flexible wire that held a pea-sized microphone in front of his mouth. 'Hello, Dr Swyver. This is Mike Totley here.' There was no reply but Mike thought he could hear a background murmur of muted consultation. 'I said this is Mike Totley. Ms Patterson is here, too. We're both alive and well and we're right here on your campus.' There was still no response, so Mike continued. 'I'd like to draw your attention to the book of Revelation, chapter eleven, verse eleven. It concerns two witnesses, murdered because of their inconvenient testimony. Remember? "After three and a half days a breath of life from God entered the two witnesses, and they stood up on their feet, and great fear fell on those who saw them." Do you know how long it is since you had us murdered, Swyver? I'm sure you're aware that Israel's time zone is ten hours ahead of this part of the United States.'

After a pause Swyver's voice returned, but this time sounded dry and hoarse. 'Totley? Is that really you?'

'Yes, it is. I've several things to say to you, Swyver, starting with this: you must take the Temple Scroll off the Internet. You've seriously mistaken the will of God and you must stop the signal immediately. Do you hear me?'

There was another pause, briefer this time, then Swyver said, 'I'll stop it when I see you face to face, Totley. I'll radio my men to let you approach the building.'

Mike stood up, removed the headset and sighed, 'I was afraid he'd say that.'

Connie clutched his arm. 'What's happening, Mike?'

'I have to go in there to talk to him. Agent Margelli, there's one more thing I'd like you to do. Can you send a bulletin to all news agencies immediately, saying that Jerusalem suffered a major earthquake today? Say that a tenth of the city was destroyed and seven thousand people killed.'

'What?'

'It could make all the difference.'

Margelli hesitated.

'Trust him,' said Connie. 'Please trust him!'

'Okay,' said Margelli. 'Consider it done, Agent Totley.' He strode to the door and opened it.

Trying to keep a note of finality out of his voice, Mike said, 'God bless you, Connie.' Then he stepped outside and was gone.

2

The sea lions watched with interest as Mike walked briskly past the edge of the lake. In their experience the close approach of a human being meant that food was in the offing. The last goldfish had been chased and swallowed long ago and Mike looked like someone who might lead them to fresh supplies. They launched themselves out of the water and lolloped after him.

As Mike reached the glass doors in the pedestal of the Power Tower a voice from a concealed speaker croaked, 'Are you armed?' It sounded like Leo Parbunkel under stress. Mike spotted a camera over the doorway and addressed it.

'Is that you, Leo?'

'Yes. You'll be scanned electronically when you're inside and you won't get near Dr Swyver if you're armed.'

'Well, I'm not. Let me in, Leo.'

'Have you been followed?'

Mike looked around. 'Only by the seven sea lions of the apocalypse. Hurry up, Leo. Time's running out.'

'Okay, take the elevator down to the lowest level. You'll be met by a guard and brought to us.'

The doors hissed open. Mike stepped forwards and the sea lions crowded through after him.

3

Cooper turned from the desk.

'I've got Deputy Director Sullivan on the line, Agent Margelli.'

Gerald Sullivan had been pursuing his search for the truth behind Eugene Hayden's rigmarole and had finally realised that the rigmarole itself was the truth. Margelli picked up the spare headset and began to say, 'Agent Margelli here, sir—' but Sullivan cut him short.

'Those two people you've got there, Totley and Patterson. There's been a mistake. They're not high-level covert operatives. In fact Totley isn't any kind of agent at all. The CH-53 is on its way back to you and I want them choppered out of there as soon as it lands. Have them ready to go in precisely two minutes. Is that clear, Agent Margelli?'

'Yes, sir. But—'

'But me no buts, Agent.'

'Er... no, sir. But—'

'But what, man?'

'I'm afraid it isn't possible, sir. At least, not in Totley's case. He's not here.'

'Then where the fuck is he?'

Margelli glanced at the screen which showed the entrance to the Power Tower and saw the doors close behind the last of the sea lions.

'He's just gone inside the tower, sir.'

'Oh, my God!'

'He has a plan, sir.'

'What kind of a plan?'

'Er… I'm afraid I don't know, sir. He didn't have time to explain. But he thinks he can trick Swyver into shutting down a signal designed to trigger the bomb. Something to do with a verse in the Bible that says…'

'So you're allowing an untrained civilian to play some chickenshit psychological game with the lives of millions of people? Are you completely insane?'

'Well, sir…'

'Has he gone in there alone?'

'No, sir. He had some sea lions with him.'

'My God, you *are* completely insane! What else is going on there? Or am I going to wish I'd never asked?'

By now Margelli could guess Sullivan's reaction to Mike's request, but he took a deep breath and went ahead anyway.

'Totley wants a bulletin sent to all news agencies, sir, reporting an earthquake in Jerusalem and the loss of seven thousand lives. I was about to request authorisation…'

'Well, you can't have it!' snapped Sullivan. 'Let me make this absolutely clear, Margelli: from now on you don't try anything creative. Just stick to feeding me onsite intel. Understand?'

Chapter Twenty-Three

1

The man sent to escort Mike into Swyver's presence was called Gabe Detweiler. He was short-haired, short-necked and his battle fatigues barely concealed the fact that his well-developed musculature was turning to fat. Since 1993 Gabe had been a key member of a survivalist militia living in the wilds of Colorado. Several hundred such groups had sprung up in the aftermath of the Waco tragedy, inspired by renewed suspicion of the federal government. That none of them shared the Waco sect's peculiar beliefs was neither here nor there. In fact the new survivalists had plenty of peculiar beliefs of their own.

Gabe believed that a secret cabal of Freemasons, international bankers, occult illuminati and the Vatican was plotting to set up a global government and that a takeover of the USA by the United Nations would be the first step. In the past this cabal had engineered the French Revolution and the rise of Communism, so its power was not to be underestimated. Faced with such a threat it was the duty of every good American to pray for the return of Christ and stockpile an assortment of deadly weapons. Gabe himself was something of an expert on the latter, having studied survivalist classics such as *Bazooka: How to Build Your Own* and *Improvised Home-Built Recoilless Launchers*. But his all-time favourite was *The Do-It-Yourself Sub-machine Gun*, as evidenced by the nine-millimetre weapon that hung from his shoulder. In short, Gabe Detweiler was in serious need of psychiatric care.

The prospect of meeting Mike unsettled Detweiler. He preferred things to be black and white – especially white; he liked to know whether to embrace a man as a like-minded patriot or blow his head off, and he'd heard enough of Swyver's deliberations to realise that Mike's status was a disturbingly grey area. When Mike stepped out of the lift Detweiler still hadn't decided whether to be aggressive or deferential. He tried a compromise, speaking politely while pointing his sub-machine gun at Mike's head.

'That way please, sir,' he said, indicating the direction with a nod.

Mike turned and walked briskly down a low-vaulted passage. The floor was concrete, the walls and roof an arch of corrugated metal. Bizarrely, a public address system was dispensing country and western muzak, belted out by a high-pitched female voice which Mike had last heard on TV in Washington:

> I'll be safe in Heaven's walls
> when the final trumpet peals,
> as the fiery judgement falls
> and he opens all the seals…

They passed through a pair of steel doors that slid open automatically at their approach and closed again behind them. Beyond this point other doors were set in the walls.

'In here,' said Detweiler, stopping and gesturing with his gun. 'Please.' He opened the door and drew back, inviting Mike to go first.

Mike stepped over the threshold into a room that was part office, part control centre. Straight ahead, with a map of the world as a backdrop, Swyver sat behind a desk facing the door. The wall to his right consisted entirely of rows of monitors and facing it, seated before a large console, was Leo Parbunkel. The wall to Swyver's left was lined with shelves of books and file boxes. Between Swyver's desk and the bookshelves Chuck Sinnet reclined insouciantly in an easy chair. Sinnet and Parbunkel were dressed casually but Swyver was wearing a suit and tie, ready to address the nation.

'Is he clean?' asked Swyver.

'As a whistle, Brush,' said Parbunkel.

Mike wondered fleetingly what a whistlebrush was. Swyver beckoned him forwards. Mike advanced and stood a few feet in front of the desk. Detweiler closed the door and stood guard with his back to it.

'Take a close look,' said Swyver, watching Mike but addressing Sinnet and Parbunkel. 'I only met Totley once, last November;

you've been with him every day for three weeks. Is this him?'

Sinnet and Parbunkel approached Mike and scrutinised him.

'Well, it sure looks like him,' said Sinnet warily.

'I'd swear to it,' said Parbunkel in an awed whisper. 'See those scratches on his right hand? I noticed those when I helped him put the protective suit on!'

Mike had the odd impression that he was being talked about in his absence.

'Of course it's me,' he said impatiently. 'And I can prove it. On the morning Leo sent me into the treatment chamber to die, he was wearing dark blue trousers and a green shirt that clashed, and the shirt had stains down the front – probably some chemical he'd been using, because he never wears a lab coat. And as he led the way to the basement he waffled about a press release on the Ark of the Covenant – which, in case you're interested, was really a nineteenth-century munitions box. That's right, isn't it, Leo?'

All three stared at him in silence. Parbunkel had turned deathly white.

'Look, I can repeat the whole of that morning's conversation if you like, but only after you've stopped that signal. There can't be many seconds left before you all make the biggest mistake of your lives!'

After a pause, which tested Mike's nerve to the limit, Swyver said quietly, 'Put phase one of Project Peter on hold until further notice.'

Parbunkel scurried back to the console, pressed a series of keys and waited anxiously for the result. 'Phase one on hold,' he reported. 'The sequence is frozen eight seconds before the detonation signal.'

Mike gave a sigh of relief and said a silent prayer of thanks.

'Okay, Totley,' said Swyver. 'So, you are who you say you are; but whether you're *what* you say you are is another matter. So start talking, and if you don't convince me Leo will reactivate the signal.'

2

The sea lions were delighted to find that the lobby of the Power

Tower contained a wide variety of fish: twin-spot wrasses, striped headstanders, regal tangs, orange chromides, African monos, maroon clownfish, sabretooth blennies, rosy barbs, pearl gouramis, tuxedoed platies, red tigers, scats, moors, harlequins and sucking catfish. Unfortunately they were all swimming around in glass columns more than twice the height of a human being and there was no obvious way to get at them.

One of the sea lions approached the nearest column and peered into it. A little group of moors gathered to stare back with bulbous eyes. The sea lion yelped and lunged forward, slamming the upper half of its body against the glass. This had no obvious effect except that the moors, and several scats and rosy barbs which shared the same pillar, performed panic-stricken gyrations. The sea lions honked with excitement and frustration.

Six of them were Californian sea lions, the kind that commonly make a spectacle of themselves in zoos and circuses, but the seventh belonged to a rarer and much larger species. It was a male Steller's sea lion, four metres in length and weighing 1,300 pounds. The sea lion which had launched itself against the pillar backed away with respect as this enormous creature lumbered forward to repeat the experiment. This time the glass pillar rocked visibly. For a moment it looked as though it might settle back on its base again but the movement of its 175 gallons of water rendered it irretrievably unstable. Its top described an ever-widening circle in the air until it fell to the marble floor with a startling noise.

Being made of reinforced glass the pillar survived the impact, but its contents spewed from the open end like grapeshot from the mouth of a cannon. A mixed shoal of moors, scats and rosy barbs was dispersed across the lobby by a spreading wave.

3

'The other fatal flaw in your interpretation,' said Mike, 'is that it completely ignores the New Testament angle. Jesus predicted the destruction of the Temple but said nothing about it being *rebuilt*! In fact the only time he mentions a replacement Temple, he's said to be talking metaphorically about himself. And Revelation reworks the prophecy of Ezekiel so that a future Temple is replaced by "the throne of God and of the Lamb". You see what all this means? You claim to offer the definitive Christian interpretation of prophecy but you miss out the specifically Christian ingredient – Christ, who supersedes the Temple!'

Mike's passion was utterly sincere. He might have deceived Swyver to gain an audience but now he was venting his true convictions in righteous anger at Swyver's overweening presumption. Swyver stared back at him throughout, pale but poker-faced, saying nothing. Chuck Sinnet seemed to be contemplating his own hands, folded on his lap. Only Leo Parbunkel betrayed any emotion. His eyes roved the room, his fingers played alternately with his beard and the headset on his lap, and his twitching face was beaded with sweat.

Mike stepped closer to Swyver, leaned forward and rested his fists on the desk.

'And when you do find room for Christ, what kind of a Christ is he? Not the Christ who showed his power by giving up his life, not a Christ of redemption and forgiveness. Your Christ is an ideological bully, smashing opposition with short-haired military efficiency, using brute force to dole out punishment and demand loyalty. In short, your Christ is a perversion, more akin to the Beast of the Apocalypse!'

He thought he saw a flicker of fear in Swyver's eyes and pressed home the advantage.

'You've turned the values of the kingdom of God upside down, Swyver! "Blessed are the peacemakers, for they shall be called children of God" – but you've portrayed the quest for peace in the Middle East as a work of the devil, simply because it runs counter to your interpretation of prophecy! Did it never occur to you to measure that interpretation against the straightforward words of Jesus? Couldn't you see that your crass literalism was leading to a total distortion of his message?'

At this point, Swyver's face underwent a subtle change. Very slowly he sat back from the desk and folded his arms across his chest. Without breaking his eye contact with Mike he said, 'Leo, would you mind sampling the international news agencies for reports of an earthquake in Jerusalem?'

4

The water drained away down the lift shafts, leaving the last few fish twitching and helpless on the marble floor. But the moors, scats and rosy barbs provided little nourishment, and as soon as the sea lions had devoured them they turned their attention to another glass column. This one contained harlequins, blennies and sucking catfish, and the latter at least looked a respectable size.

But once again the meal was disappointing. The fish turned out to be much smaller when floundering on the ground than they had seemed while swimming behind thick glass. The sea lions, however, were relentlessly optimistic. A third column crashed to the ground, followed shortly by a fourth.

5

Parbunkel turned to the console. Teletext from various sources filled screen after screen.

'Don't see anything yet,' he said.

Mike's pulse began to race.

'No mention at all,' said Sinnet, a few moments later. 'He was lying, Brush!'

A cold smile pulled at the corners of Swyver's mouth.

'Look,' said Mike, 'it's irrelevant whether I lied to get in here; what I've been saying stands or falls on its own merits! And a moment ago you began to recognise the truth of it, I know you did!'

'Rotweiler,' said Swyver, continuing to stare straight at Mike.

'Detweiler, sir.'

'Detweiler, get rid of him. We've been wasting precious time.'

Mike fought down his fear and carried on.

'Why won't you speak to me, Swyver? You're afraid, aren't you, because you know I'm right!'

'Take him away and let's get back on track. It's time to unleash the vengeance of God!'

'You haven't a clue what you're talking about! The vengeance of God is about justice, but your home-made apocalypse can only increase the world's toll of death and misery!'

'Execute him outside the main entrance,' said Swyver, as Gabe Detweiler led Mike to the door. 'I want his friends to see it happen. Let them know that we take evil seriously here. Leo, reactivate the signal.'

Mike still refused to give up. 'Have you forgotten Zechariah chapter four, verse seven? "Not by force, nor by power, but by my spirit, says the Lord"!'

'So what about First Chronicles chapter twenty-two, verse sixteen?'

'Matthew twelve, verse six!'

'Haggai one, verse eight! Detweiler, get him out of here!'

'That's completely irrelevant and you know it!'

'Shut up, you piece of shit!' snarled Detweiler, pushing Mike through the door. 'Follow the passage, and remember – I'm right behind you!' He was glad to have everything cut and dried at last. Now he knew that Mike was an agent of Satan he could despise and abuse him appropriately.

Mike walked down the tunnel in a daze, stunned by this latest turn of events. What had happened to the news bulletin Margelli had promised to arrange? Was the CIA totally incompetent? Now he was about to die for nothing and the world would fall into chaos.

> ... we'll have a ringside seat
> as the sinners feel the heat,
> on that great and glorious day that's coming soon,

rejoiced Barbi-Jo Butterfield.

They arrived at the lifts. 'Get in, demon-spawn!' barked Detweiler as the doors opened, 'and stand over on the left.' He followed Mike inside and backed over to the right. Keeping his eyes fixed on Mike he ran the fingers of his left hand down the control panel and pressed the button for the lobby. When the doors opened again the floor looked wet and there was a powerful smell of fish. Detweiler sniffed the air.

'What's been going on here?'

'I've no idea,' said Mike, though he suspected the involvement of sea lions.

'I'll have to check this out. Move to the back of the elevator and stand in the middle where I can see you. If you make the smallest move you'll die right there!' Keeping his home-made sub-machine gun trained on Mike, Detweiler backed warily into the lobby. His eyes flicked from side to side, taking in more and more of the devastation as he moved farther away from the lift.

Mike made a decision. He would walk straight out of the lift, forcing Detweiler to carry out his threat. That way Connie wouldn't have to watch him die. He put one foot forward.

'Hold it right there!' Detweiler snapped. 'I waaaaaaaaah!'

He'd been about to say 'I warned you!' but his right boot had slipped on a sea lion's excrement and shot from under him.

As Detweiler hit the ground Mike leaped for the control panel, punching the button for the top floor.

6

'Okay, Brush,' said Leo Parbunkel. 'The programme's up and running again, but it can't pick up exactly where it stopped, so we're back at the start of the column twenty-eight countdown.'

'So how much time is left?' asked Swyver.

'As of now, four minutes and twenty-six seconds.' Parbunkel wiped the sweat from his face and stood up. 'After all that excitement I need the john. I'll be back in a couple of minutes.'

He hurried down the tunnel, past the nearest toilet, through the automatic doors, and summoned a lift. Guilt had been eating away at him for days and it hadn't been assuaged by seeing Mike alive; in fact hearing Mike refer to 'the morning Leo sent me into the treatment chamber to die' had intensified it. He now hoped that if he could undo the wrong by saving Mike's life the dreadful gnawing sensation might go away.

When he reached the lobby the scene before him was totally unexpected. Detweiler lay spreadeagled on his back, apparently unconscious, and Mike was nowhere to be seen. As far as Parbunkel could tell without walking all around the cloister, the twelve glass pillars had all been felled; the floor was wet and strewn with waterweed and the lobby stank like a fishmonger's shop. And yet, surprisingly, there were no fish to be seen. He called Mike's name several times but there was no response.

Baffled, he turned back to the lift. He was about to step inside when he noticed that the floor indicator above the other lift was flashing double figures: seventeen, eighteen, nineteen... He guessed where Mike was going and decided to follow.

7

'Twenty seconds left,' said Sinnet. 'Looks like Leo's going to miss the big moment.'

'I'm afraid he's not cut out for all this,' said Swyver, putting on a headset. 'He may be great at the technical stuff but he can't handle pressure. It's a shame I had to send Willard on ahead.'

'Ten seconds.'

'Can't wait to see what the other big news channels do with *this* story!'

'Five, four, three, two...'

Then the lights went out and the screens faded to black, plunging Swyver's bunker into total darkness.

8

The power failure occurred just as Leo Parbunkel stepped out of the lift on the thirtieth floor. For about half a minute he stood still in the blackness, not sure what to do next. Then the dim emergency lighting came on and there in front of him, leaning against a wall with his arms folded, was Mike.

'So it *is* you, Leo. I thought I recognised your distinctive wheeze.'

'Mike! Are you okay?'

'Fine, thanks. My life's in danger, of course, but I've got used to that since joining your dig. And how about you? Keeping well?'

'I meant... I mean...'

Mike came closer.

'What exactly are you doing here, Leo? And why did the lights go out when you arrived?'

'I think there's been a power cut, but it was nothing to do with me. I came to see if I could help you.'

'Oh? Are you trying to tell me you've changed sides?'

Parbunkel's eyes wandered uncertainly.

'Sorry Mike, but I can't just... I still think Oral's got it right.'

'Does that mean you've reactivated the signal?'

'Yes.' He looked at his watch. 'The bomb will have gone off by now.' Mike turned and smote the wall with his fist. 'I'm sorry, Mike. And I'm sorry about... you know... what happened at the Centre. That's why I'm here – to make amends. I want to make sure you get out of here alive.'

Mike suddenly grabbed Parbunkel by the collar.

'Leo, is it true there are two hundred hostages somewhere on this floor?'

'Almost that many. They're in the rotating restaurant. Except it won't be rotating now the power's down. And they're under armed guard.'

'Then you'd better do some quick thinking, because I'm not leaving without them.'

9

'Good, we've gotten emergency power,' said Swyver.

Chuck Sinnet scanned the rows of flickering monitors.

'I'm afraid the security cameras are still down. How about the Scroll signal?'

Swyver shook his head.

'If you mean can we restore the link with the satellite, no way; emergency power is insufficient. We need power from the generators and we seem to be getting zilch.'

'Here's our problem!' said Sinnet, pointing to a winking light on the console. 'There's a fault in the circuit from the main transformer!'

'Then all we have to do is switch to the back-up,' said Swyver, his resolve returning. 'But it has to be done manually. Right at the bottom of the stairs there's a room with lots of switches and fuses...'

'Leave it to me,' said Sinnet, getting up from the seat by the console. 'Will the steel doors open on emergency power?'

'No problem, Chuck; I can operate them from here. Wear Leo's headset and I'll talk you through the procedure.'

Sinnet picked up the headset and hurried from the bunker.

10

'So, any suggestions, Leo?'

'Erm…' said Parbunkel, whose brain seemed to have seized up.

'Look, these armed guards you mentioned…'

'Militiamen, like Detweiler. Half a dozen of them, with M-16s.'

'Do they know you? Would they respect your authority?'

'I guess so.'

'And I assume there are some stairs in this place?'

'Sure.'

'Then it's simple!' said Mike. 'You go in there and tell them there's been a change of plan: the students are to be taken down to the ground floor and allowed to go.'

'But they'll wonder why I came all the way up here to tell them. They're wearing headsets.'

'Say the headsets can no longer be used because you think the CIA can pick up your frequency. That should stop them trying to contact Swyver as well.'

'But what if the reverse happens? What if Oral talks to them before they get to the bottom? It's too risky, Mike!'

'No, it isn't. You also tell them the CIA are trying to send fake messages by impersonating Swyver's voice, so they're to ignore everything except your personal orders.'

After an irritating pause, during which he pushed part of his beard up to his mouth and sucked it, Parbunkel said, 'But Mike, I still don't see how that gets you out of here.'

'Just show me where the stairs are and leave that to me. I'll hide behind a door or something and when all the students are on their way down I'll pop out and mingle with them. What about it, Leo?'

Parbunkel seemed on the verge of agreeing when another snag struck him. 'But what about me? If Oral finds out that I—'

'You can say I forced you to do it. And I should warn you: it's very close to becoming the truth! Come on Leo, *please*!'

'Well, I...'
'Yes?'
'Could you just run all that past me again?'

11

Sinnet's destination was a room located directly below the lift shafts. Conduits carrying power cables rose through its ceiling into both shafts, from where they continued up through the core of the Power Tower. By following these conduits some 2,000 gallons of water had drained into the room from the lobby. When Sinnet opened the door, the 2,000 gallons of water burst out, throwing him with deadly force against the opposite wall.

12

When Gabe Detweiler returned to consciousness, he was surprised to discover darkness all around him. Like a small child who wakes in the night and reaches for a much-loved teddy bear, Detweiler felt for his sub-machine gun and was relieved to find it lying at his side. Instinctively he rolled onto his stomach and adopted a firing position. In the darkness, however, he could not see anyone to fire at.

Then the emergency lighting came on. He slowly rotated his body through 180 degrees to scan his surroundings. On discovering that he was alone in the lobby, he stood up and rubbed the back of his head where it had struck the marble floor. He adjusted his headset, which had been dislodged by the fall, and realised that he ought to report Mike's disappearance.

On the other hand Mike had to be somewhere in the building because the doors wouldn't open without the correct security procedures; if he could find Mike and finish the job, no one need ever know there'd been a hitch. He noticed that both lifts had stopped on the top floor and decided that that was the place to look.

In the rear of the central column that housed the lift shafts there were two doors, each giving access to its own stairwell. Detweiler sprinted around to the nearest of these and found his way barred. A creature which he mistook for a dead whale lay across the threshold. Undeterred, he pressed on to the second door. This was not blocked, but in order to reach it he had to weave his way between the sleeping forms of the other six sea lions.

Detweiler was surprised by the presence of all these marine mammals in the lobby. Apart from Mike, the only person in the Power Tower who'd seen them enter the building was Leo Parbunkel, and Leo had been so shaken by Mike's arrival that he'd failed to mention them. A less single-minded person than Detweiler would have stopped to wonder what they were doing there, but he merely grunted and carried on.

Once through the door, he took the stairs two at a time. At the sixth floor, however, he adjusted his stride to one at a time, and at the tenth he slowed to a plodding walk. By the fifteenth floor he was climbing very slowly indeed and at the twentieth he resorted to progressing on all fours. Suddenly, above the roar of his breathing and the pounding in his ears he heard Swyver's voice coming through his headset.

'Detweiler?'

'Sir!' he gasped.

'Have you dealt with Totley?'

'He's gone, sir.'

'Good,' said Swyver, hearing only what he expected to hear. 'Now here's another job for you. It's extremely urgent. I want you to go to right down to the bottom of the stairs and look for Dr Sinnet. If you don't find him let me know and I'll tell you what to do next.'

His legs shaking, Detweiler turned and began the descent. On reaching the ground floor he realised that this particular stairwell didn't go any further. To reach the lower levels he needed access to the other one. Unable to face a climb of even one storey to reach it, he decided to see if he could get past the dead whale.

He was tiptoeing gingerly between the dozing sea lions when one of them lifted its head and let out a disagreeable yap. One by one they all woke up and thrust their noses at him, honking inquisitively. Through the corner of his eye Detweiler saw that the creature by the stairwell – which was clearly neither dead nor a whale – had also raised half of its huge bulk off the ground and was lumbering in his direction. No survival manual he'd ever read had envisaged this situation, but in the end it all boiled down to the same thing: you took out everyone and everything that looked remotely hostile. He prepared to open fire.

'Detweiler!' blared Swyver's voice in his earpiece. 'Are you there yet? What's keeping you?' He sounded anxious and irritated.

'Seals!' shouted Detweiler. 'I'm surrounded by them! I'm going to—' He was cut short by the Steller's sea lion nudging him hard in the back and knocking him to the ground. Before he could recover his sub-machine gun the big sea lion flopped forward to lick him and his right arm was immobilised beneath its enormous weight.

'Can't move!' he gasped, 'I'm being – Oh God! – licked... all over!'

13

Alone in his bunker, Swyver turned to a microphone on the console and switched it on.

'Can you hear me, Margelli? So, you thought you'd surprise me by sending in a team of navy SEALs, did you? Thought I wouldn't expect them three hundred miles inland? Well, now it's your turn to be surprised! I told you I could destroy this whole building but you obviously didn't believe me. Now watch this!'

The top five storeys of the Power Tower exploded, sending flames and debris out into the darkness.

'Oh, God!' said Margelli, watching the catastrophe in infrared. 'This'll make Waco look like a day at the beach!'

The domed roof and its forest of masts collapsed into the thirtieth floor. With almost impossible slowness the tall spire fell, end over end, and crashed to the ground. Then the next five storeys exploded, and the next. The whole upper half of the tower was blazing like a giant torch. The explosions continued, ripping the building apart section by section.

Connie turned away in despair.

'Wait! Look!' shouted Cooper. 'There are people scattering from the base of the Tower! Someone's trying to lead them this way!'

A final massive explosion sent a wave of flame rippling out from the roots of the building. The last thing they saw were running figures diving into the lake. Then a shock wave rocked the truck and the screens went blank.

Chapter Twenty-Four

1

Mike opened his eyes. There was a pain in his right foot. Sunlight, sliced by a blind, fell in strips across the hospital bed. A clock on the wall said it was 11.30. Aware that he was not alone he turned and saw Connie sitting at his bedside, smiling.

'Welcome back!' she said softly.

'Connie!'

'How're you feeling?'

'Horribly groggy. What happened?'

'You've been sedated. You were in agony when they pulled you out of the lake. Seems you ruptured your ankle ligaments when you jumped. They wouldn't let anyone see you last night, so I've been waiting for you to come round. I'll tell the nurse you're awake.'

Mike took her hand and tried to sit up.

'Not yet. What happened to the others, the hostages...?'

'Don't worry, they all got out.'

Mike sank back onto the pillows, his face grave, almost bitter.

'What's wrong, Mike? I said they're all safe.'

'If only I could have stopped Swyver sending that signal! I can't put all the blame on Margelli. If I'd handled it better...'

'Didn't you know? You *did* stop him!'

'But Leo said...'

'Well everything's fine! The bomb's been made safe.'

For a few seconds Mike was unable to speak, his eyes filling with tears of relief. Then he pulled Connie close and hugged her.

'Oh, Connie, thank God for that!'

'Yes, thank God!'

'But I'm afraid we may not be out of the wood yet.'

Connie sat up.

'Meaning what?'

'When Swyver told Leo to pause the signal, his exact words were, "Put phase one of Project Peter on hold." If blowing up the Dome of the Rock was only phase one, what the hell's phase two?'

'Does it matter? Swyver's out of the game, his network's in ruins...'

'But he might have set something in motion...'

'Relax, Mike! Even if he did it's not your problem. As soon as you're ready someone from the CIA will come and talk to you; you can tell them what Swyver said and leave the rest to them, okay?'

Mike sighed and nodded.

'I'd better go,' said Connie. 'The nurse will want to see you.'

As soon as she'd gone a nurse and doctor entered the room. After a brief examination, Mike was given a light meal and allowed to shave. His next visit was from two CIA investigators, a tall balding man who asked a lot of questions and a junior colleague with a laptop, who took everything down. The interview left Mike exhausted and when the men had gone he slept again.

He woke up shortly after three o'clock and found Connie once more at his bedside.

'Hi! You're looking a lot better.'

'I feel better. In spite of a lengthy interrogation by one of your friends.'

'One of my superiors, you mean.' Connie presented him with a bag of grapes. 'If you think you can stand it, I've a question of my own.'

'Thanks. Fire away,' said Mike, sitting up in bed and taking a grape.

'I just want to know how you did it.'

'But you know how – the old witnesses raised from the dead ploy. Works every time.'

'What I mean is, normally you'd rather chew your own feet off than tell a lie, but you fed Swyver that baloney about the two witnesses like a regular bunco artist! How did you square it with your conscience, or God or whatever?'

Mike bit thoughtfully into another grape. 'I didn't rationalise it at the time but I suppose I see it this way: Jesus said the most important commandments are to love God with all your heart, soul, mind and strength, and to love your neighbour as yourself; "There is no other commandment greater than these." So if these commandments ever come into conflict with another, it's an unequal contest.'

'In other words you considered the greater good?'

'Touché!' said Mike, recalling his outburst in Washington. They both laughed, then Mike was suddenly thoughtful again.

'What is it?'

'Not sure. When my thoughts went back to Washington it seemed as though a particular memory was trying to surface. It's not the first time it's happened. I've a feeling it has some connection with this phase two mystery. I told the CIA people about it, but my mind won't let it go.'

'You need a distraction. I'll fetch you a book to read. Any special requests?'

'Actually,' said Mike, taking hold of Connie's hand, 'a long, sumptuous kiss would do me more good than a whole pile of books.' But her kiss was uncharacteristically restrained and afterwards she stared almost guiltily into the bag of grapes. She tried to move her hand away but Mike tightened his grip. 'I thought something was wrong when you didn't kiss me earlier.' She made no response. 'Well, are you going to tell me what it is?'

Connie looked trapped. Her explanation still needed working on. She closed her eyes for several seconds and took a deep breath.

'Has nobody told you what's happening out there? You're being fêted as the man who saved the world! Your picture's in all the papers, your face introduces every news bulletin, and soon it'll be on the front of every magazine; you'll be offered fantastic sums of money for your story, there'll be radio and TV interviews, all kinds of people will want to be seen with you; you could probably run for president and win it at a walk!'

'Wouldn't I have to become an American first?'

'What I'm trying to say is that your life is about to change dramatically! You could do anything, *be* anything you wanted!'

'And you've got a rule against kissing men who get their names in the papers?'

'Mike, be serious!'

'Very well. And this is as serious as I've ever been: I love you, Connie.'

Connie paused, finding it difficult to continue.

'I love you too. But you've got to understand… however you thought your future would turn out, it's going to be very different now. Lots of new opportunities… I don't want to be a dead weight. We've not made each other any long-term promises so if, when you're making decisions… I mean, if I don't seem to belong in the new picture you mustn't feel obligated…' Her voice breaking with emotion, she pulled her hand free and rushed to the door.

'Stop!' shouted Mike. Connie froze, her fingers on the handle. 'I've already made one decision and what you've just told me doesn't change it. Will you marry me, Connie? And can we please make it as soon as possible?'

2

From: waterman@rangac.co.uk
To: m.totley@semeia.net
Date: 2 June 2000
Subject: Book

Dear Mike,

After much hassle I manged to get your temporary email address from a bolshy secretary in Whitfield. Said she wasn't sure you'd want me to have it! I read about your escapades in the papers. Never thought of you as the Indian Jones type.

Anyway, am writing to tell you I'm staring a new monograph series, and your book on end-time beliefs would be ideal way to lunch it. So, if you're finding tim to finish it in midst of your explots, I hope you'll sned it in my direction. Let me know if want furter information on royalties etc.

Yours ever
Giles

★

From: m.totley@semeia.net
To: waterman@rangac.co.uk
Date: 2 June 2000
Subject: Book

Dear Giles,

Do you never check your emails before sending them? This time you managed eight typos in only nine lines. Please don't give my address to anyone else; you were never meant to get your hands on it in the first place.

I don't believe a word of this stuff about a new monograph series. You are simply angling for my book (in which you've previously shown no glimmer of interest) because you think my new-found fame will push it into the bestseller lists and make you a fat profit.
Thanks, but no thanks.

Yours
Mike

★

From: blanchard@sun.bbc.co.uk
To: m.totley@semeia.net
Date: 3 June 2000
Subject: interview

Dear Dr Totley,

You are a hard man to track down! I eventually got your email address from a mutual friend, Giles Waterman.

We are including a feature on the Swyver Affair in tomorrow's Sunday programme on Radio 4, and as part of that we would like to do a live, down-the-line interview with you. You will be followed by a Christian impressionist who will try to encapsulate the Book of Revelation in a series of hand and mouth noises. I'm sure you'll agree it will make a terrific combination! I look forward to your speedy reply.

Yours,
Andromeda Blanchard (PA to the Producer)

★

The Bible Institute of the South-Eastern States
Memphis
Tennessee

2 June 2000

Professor Mike Totley
Crowne Plaza Hotel
250 North Main Street
Memphis TN 38103

Dear Professor Totley,

Please forgive this breach of your privacy and allow me to introduce myself. Following the recent tragic events at the Bible Institute of the South-Eastern States, a special committee has been set up to oversee the Institute's future. I am writing on behalf of that committee.

After some difficult deliberations we have taken the decision to keep BIOSES in existence as a center for Christian learning, but with a much altered theological basis and orientation. As part of the process of reconstruction we hope to appoint a Dean of Studies, part of whose task would be to ensure sound theological content across the curriculum. We were unanimous in wanting you, Professor Totley, to be that person. A full job description is enclosed.

I would also point out that, should you accept the position, you would have the freedom to design and teach your own courses in the biblical area and to lead excavations in Israel to train archaeology students. In that connection you may be interested to know that our Center for Biblical Archaeology in Jerusalem has reopened. We have appointed Ms. Talia Schluter as its new director.

We trust you will give our offer your prayerful consideration, and we look forward to hearing from you.

*Yours sincerely
Oscar Short*

★

From: m.totley@semeia.net
To: schlutert@cenarc.conserve
Date: 3 June 2000
Subject: Dig etc.

Dear Tally,

I've just heard about your promotion – congratulations! I can think of no better person to get things back on track and I wish you every success.

I don't know what plans there are for wrapping up the Nahal Shuhan dig, but if you can get enough staff together I recommend exploring the lower section of Cave D. In circumstances which I don't need to spell out, Connie discovered a human skeleton and the remains of a white garment. As you know, Josephus says the Essenes wore white. There may well be scrolls in that cave, and if Chuck Sinnet hadn't been so tunnel-visioned he would probably have found them.

Speaking of Connie, she and I are getting married in two days' time. If you have an address for Dave I'd like to let him know. Look forward to hearing from you.

Best wishes
Mike

⋆

From: schlutert@cenarc.conserve
To: m.totley@semeia.net
Date: 4 June 2000
Subject: Center news

Dear Mike,

Thanks for your kind and generous letter. I hardly know what to say, remembering how I failed to stand up to Chuck and Leo when you needed support.

Great news about you and Connie! Not a complete surprise, though – Dave's been predicting it. Thanks for the advice about Cave D. At the moment I have no permanent staff here except Mrs. Spittler. The volunteers have all gone home apart from Drew and Dave. They're helping me get the records of the dig in shape so I can publish a preliminary report. Dave goes back to Beer Sheva in a few days – reluctantly – seems he's formed a relationship with a nurse at the hospital – but Drew is staying on. He's a tower of strength.

Please come back and see us as soon as you can – with Connie, of course.

Best wishes
Tally

⋆

From: m.totley@semeia.net
To: hirschfeld@cenarc.conserve
Date: 6 June 2000
Subject: Various

Dear Dave,

I was wondering how to get in touch with you when I had an email from Tally. I hope you're still making a good recovery from the Wadi Kelt incident.

In view of the advice you repeatedly gave me, you'll be pleased to hear that Connie and I were married yesterday! We weren't able to have a normal wedding or you would have been invited. If we'd made conventional plans, issued invitations and so on, the paparazzi would have turned up in force and ruined it. So instead, we did it quickly and quietly. Connie's mother and her sister, Canberra, were there, and a man called Nash from the CIA combined the jobs of best man and security chief. A woman priest led the service in a relaxed, sensitive way which we both appreciated.

At the end of the week we'll be leaving Memphis for a delayed honeymoon but at the moment we're kept here by an enquiry into the events at BIOSES; forensic scientists are still poking around in the ruins of the Power Tower and they want me on hand in case I can answer any fresh questions that come up. We're staying in a posh hotel at the CIA's expense, so can't complain.

The media attention is a bit overwhelming at times and I have to keep reminding myself that my role in the so-called siege of BIOSES was really not that great. My attempt to persuade Swyver to abandon his lunatic plan was actually a failure; it simply delayed things while more effective agents played their part. I refer, of course, to the troupe of sea lions which unfortunately perished in the explosion. As far as the forensic people can tell, water which the sea lions spilt from a dozen huge fish tanks found its way into a room full of electrical gubbins, where it caused the failure of Swyver's main power circuit. The rescue of the hostages is also something I can't take sole credit for. I couldn't have done it without Leo, whom the media continue to malign in spite of my protests. Along with Swyver,

Leo is still missing, presumed dead, and so cannot defend himself.

The fate of both men is actually a mystery. As I expect you've heard, a body identified as that of Chuck Sinnet was recovered from the mangled bowels of the building, but no trace has been found of either Leo or Swyver. Stories that Leo escaped from the Tower with the rest of us and fled unseen into the darkness are mere speculation. It's more likely that his misguided loyalty drove him back to Swyver's bunker. Although the bunker itself was destroyed by the final blast, a network of tunnels has been discovered connecting it with other buildings on the campus. Connie's theory is that Leo and Swyver escaped via one of these and are now holed up with some of their end-time militia friends. In Leo's case I'd like to think she's right, but the world would be a safer place without Swyver.

If you have time to reply before Saturday we'd love to hear from you.

God bless you,
Mike

3

Connie nestled in Mike's embrace and gave a little sigh of pleasure.

'Was that okay?' asked Mike.

'No. It wasn't okay, it was beautiful.'

'After nearly ten years of celibacy it might take me a while to get into my stride.'

'I've got no complaints so far. But if it improves your confidence, honey, you can practise on me as much as you want.'

'Thanks.' He gave her an affectionate squeeze. 'What shall we do today?'

'Well, Magevney House isn't far. That's the oldest surviving house in Memphis, built in 1836.'

'My love, I don't mean to denigrate your heritage, but in England there are whole streets older than that! I'll show you some when we go to Whitfield.'

'Well, Mud Island's real close as well,' suggested Connie.

'Let me guess; that's a hands-on museum of Mississippi alluvium, with over two hundred and fifty different varieties of mud for visitors to smell and handle.'

'It's nothing of the kind! If you've seen *The Firm*, it's where the bad guys almost catch up with Tom Cruise but he gives them the slip.'

'Then let's go there; if the paparazzi track us down we'll know what to do.'

'Would you make some coffee while I have a shower?'

They both got out of bed and Mike put on his dressing gown. Then he boiled a kettle, filled a cafetière and walked over to the window, gratified to find that his injured foot gave only mild discomfort.

From their suite high in the Crowne Plaza Hotel he could see right across the Mississippi. The scale of everything was so vast that all motion appeared sluggish. The progress of ships was barely discernible. On the far side, a freight train of incredible length snaked slowly southwards.

He poured himself some coffee, turned to a desk with a computer on it and sat down. On his move to the hotel the management had provided complimentary Netscape facilities. He switched the computer on and the monitor went through its usual warm-up routine. Eventually it informed him that there were no new email messages on the server.

Connie emerged from the shower wrapped in a towel.

'Anyone been in touch?' she asked, rubbing a second towel over her hair.

'No. I was hoping Dave might've replied, but there's nothing yet.'

'You ought to go easy with that thing. Research shows it can undermine authentic relationships.'

'But email has revived the art of letter writing, given it a sense of immediacy. It's probably the most fun anyone can have sitting down.' He was about to get up and pour Connie's coffee when she placed a hand on his shoulder, pressing him back onto his chair.

'Sorry, honey, but I can't let that go unchallenged.' She sat astride his legs, facing him. Loosening the towel around her body she let it fall to the floor. Then she slipped the other towel behind Mike's neck and gently drew his face towards her breasts. He nuzzled them appreciatively.

'How fair and entrancing you are... O daughter of delights! You are as stately as a palm tree... your breasts like its clusters of fruit... I will ascend the palm tree... take hold of its fruit...' He stroked her nipples with his tongue while running his fingers down the well-defined valley in the centre of her back.

Connie let go of the towel and reached down, parting the folds of Mike's dressing gown. 'Let us hurry to the vineyard... there I will give you my love... all choice delicacies are ready... both new and old I have in store for you, my lover...'

As Connie adjusted her position Mike glimpsed the animated Netscape logo on the monitor behind her. Inside the rectangular design a shower of glowing meteors streamed passed a giant N towards the curve of the earth's surface. He sat back as though stung. His hands slipped from Connie's buttocks and fell to his sides. The colour drained from his face.

'Oh, honey, your Power Tower's collapsed! Did I do something wrong? Is it too soon after the last time?'

Mike opened his mouth but had difficulty speaking.

At last he said, 'I know what phase two is!'

Chapter Twenty-Five

1

Connie handed Mike a fresh cup of strong coffee and sat down on the edge of the desk. She was wearing a bathrobe and brushed her hair as she talked.

'So is that the secret of good control? You think about one of life's great mysteries until the very last moment? Perhaps I should try it. Next time I don't want to come yet, I'll try to work out who murders the chauffeur in *The Big Sleep*.'

'Connie, my conscious thoughts were completely taken up with you! But subconsciously I must have been fretting away at the problem for days, and then suddenly I saw it...'

Connie put her hairbrush down, got up from the desk and sat on Mike's lap with one arm around him.

'I'm sorry, I shouldn't be going on at you. You'd better give me the whole thing from the beginning. But to be honest, honey, it sounds to me like you've been watching too many of those trashy doomsday movies – *Asteroid, Deep Impact, Armageddon...*'

'A Bible would be useful.'

'I think I saw a Gideon Bible in the cupboard by the bed.' Connie got up, found the Bible and returned to Mike's lap.

'Thanks. Do you remember what Swyver said when we saw him on TV in Washington, quoting verses about an earthquake and giant hailstones? Well, put all that together with this from Revelation chapter eight: "The first angel sounded his trumpet, and there followed hail and fire... and the second angel sounded his trumpet, and as it were a great mountain burning with fire was cast into the sea... and the third angel sounded his trumpet, and there fell a great star from heaven, burning like a torch..." It goes on to describe pollution, darkness and plague, resulting in death for a third of the world's population. The second phase of Swyver's apocalyptic scenario *has* to be an asteroid strike. That explains why he called the whole scheme Project Peter; Peter is Greek for a rock, so the name applies equally well to the Dome of the Rock and to the rock – the asteroid – that will hit the earth!'

'It's an ingenious idea,' said Connie, perusing the Bible as it lay open in Mike's hand, 'but with a fatal flaw. An asteroid would have to turn up at just the right moment, which seems improbable to put it mildly. There's no way Swyver could stage-manage a cataclysm on that scale – you said so yourself in Washington.'

'And I'm beginning to think I was wrong. But we'll have to go back to Washington to confirm it. How soon could we fly there?'

'You want to go to Washington? Today?'

'As soon as possible. These faint memories that keep surfacing – that's where they all come from. And I think they're the key.'

After a long moment's thought Connie leaned towards the desk and picked up the phone.

'You know, if you hadn't been right about the bomb in Jerusalem, I'd say you were nuts.'

2

A rock the size of a mountain hurtled towards the earth. As it seared through the atmosphere it began to glow like a rogue sun. Blazing chunks broke off and scattered. Then came a blinding flash and an overwhelming noise. Lakes vaporised and whole forests turned instantly into clouds of ash, swirled skyward by a sea of roiling flames. Shock waves spread around the world rupturing the boundaries of tectonic plates, causing massive earthquakes and volcanic eruptions. Tsunamis invaded coastlands with destructive force. A choking pall of smoke and ash began to spread like a stain across the globe...

'In 1989, a large earth-crossing asteroid passed the exact spot where the earth had been only six hours earlier. Prompted by this close call, a group of scientists lobbied the government's Space Subcommittee to formulate plans for coping with a potential catastrophe.'

Once again the IMAX auditorium was empty apart from Connie and Mike. But this second private showing had been harder to arrange. The film had been out of circulation for five months and had had to be brought from storage.

Mike leaned closer to Connie.

'This next bit's one I remember well. I was feeling really sick.'

'Using technology created for the Strategic Defence Initiative, we are now developing space weaponry capable of deflecting an asteroid from a collision course with the earth.'

An irregular lump of rock, resembling a giant potato, rotated end over end while a space probe with extended solar panels approached it like a small bright fly. Then the fly struck one end of the potato and there was a bright flash. The potato altered its spin and moved slowly off the screen.

'And this was where we went out. So it's possible, at least in theory.'

'Sure – in theory. But Swyver owned communication satellites, not space weaponry!'

'Our knowledge of asteroids will soon be greatly increased by a project called Neoren – Near Earth Object Rendezvous. Launched by NASA at a cost of one hundred and thirty million dollars, the unmanned spaceprobe Neoren 1 will rendezvous with asteroid Moros and transmit data…'

Connie clutched Mike's sleeve.

3

Gerald Sullivan paused outside Morton Walsh's office and checked his watch. He was early, but he knocked and entered anyway.

'You're early!' said Walsh.

'Sorry sir, but this is a very grave matter.'

'My God! You look terrible!'

Sullivan's face was ashen, his hair dishevelled. Without waiting to be asked he eased himself into the same overstuffed chair that he'd occupied before. This time, however, he would make sure Walsh did some of the squeaking. He opened his briefcase and pulled out a document of several stapled pages.

'Take a look at this.'

'Cigarette?' offered Walsh. Sullivan declined but Walsh took one for himself. He skim-read most of the first page, then stopped. 'What is this, Gerry? I thought you sent this kind of bullshit straight to the shredder!'

'We do – usually. But this came from Connie Patterson, sir. If you read on you'll find there's plenty of supporting evidence.'

'You expect me to understand all this in a couple of minutes?' said Walsh, leafing through the rest of the document. 'It's got equations, calculations…'

'In summary, it concerns the Neoren Project. As I'm sure you know, the spaceprobe Neoren 1 will engage with an asteroid called Moros in less than forty-eight hours. Its alleged mission is simply to orbit Moros and collect data, but Patterson believes it's equipped with a nuclear weapon for defence against earth-crossing asteroids.'

'You mean she's claiming Moros is an earth-crossing asteroid?'

'No, sir. Moros never comes closer than ten million miles. She believes the aim is to test the technology in a no-threat situation, altering the trajectory of Moros by a small but verifiable amount.'

'Then why the hell hasn't everybody heard about it?' demanded Walsh dismissively.

'With respect, sir, that's as obvious as a cockroach on a white rug. Apart from the political objections to putting a nuclear weapon into space, if people knew about this mission there'd be rumours that Moros was dangerous and we'd be faced with global panic.'

Morton Walsh lit another cigarette and got up to pace the room.

'I assume you've asked NASA for confirmation?'

'Yes, sir; but you know the old line about NASA meaning Never A Straight Answer.'

Walsh looked relieved.

'So then I approached General Sandstrom.'

'And he denied it too, I expect?' Beads of sweat were forming on Walsh's fleshy face and jowls.

'To begin with. Until I told him I'd already been briefed about the project by you, sir.'

'You sonofabitch, Sullivan!'

'As I've said many times before, sir, it would be wiser for the Pentagon to tell us things at the beginning. We always find out sooner or later.'

Walsh slowly returned to his chair.

After drawing heavily on his cigarette for several seconds he said, 'All right, so Neoren 1 is carrying a one hundred kiloton nuclear bomb and it's mission is a hot strike rendezvous with Moros. Dammit, that girl must be smart!'

'Very smart.'

'But I still don't see how this supports the cockamamie claim on the first page.'

Enjoying the upper hand Sullivan leaned forward, his fingertips together, elbows resting on Walsh's desk.

'The software contract for Neoren 1 went to Swycorp, the research and development arm of Swyver's empire.'

'So, this is a free country!'

'We both know that's not exactly true, sir. In this case there's evidence that Swycorp got the contract because of illicit, personal intervention by the president.'

Walsh stubbed out his cigarette, his eyes fixed on Connie's paper.

'The evidence is in there?'

'Page four. The truth is as plain as a cockroach in a plate of grits.' While Walsh gagged on the thought of this culinary combination Sullivan summarised Connie's argument. 'Patterson's theory is that Swycorp modified the software for Neoren 1; as a result the nuclear device will deflect Moros onto a collision course with the earth.'

Walsh loosened his collar. 'And?'

'These equations, supplied by the Planetary Science Institute in Tucson, are an attempt to predict the consequences. Moros is a couple of kilometres across…'

'Not big, then,' said Walsh hopefully.

'The exact scale of damage will depend on things like composition, density, speed, angle of entry, all of which are unknown, but it's likely that on impact it will explode with a force of at least one million megatons, devastating an area of four million square kilometres.' Walsh stared blankly. 'If you're having problems envisaging that, sir, it's about half the area of the United States. But the damage caused by ejecta and subsequent fallout would be global. We could expect up to a third of the human race to die, in keeping with Revelation, chapters eight and nine, where its says…'

Morton Walsh was having one of his coughing fits, tears mingling with the beads of sweat on his face. This time Sullivan had brought a spare handkerchief. Walsh accepted it and, as the fit subsided, began mopping up operations.

'But... but didn't NASA run some kind of test on the software before they launched this goddam thing?'

'Yes, sir. But the technician who did the job has since moved on and can't be traced, and records of the tests have disappeared with him – which more or less confirms Patterson's theory.'

'My God!' said Walsh, pulling out another cigarette. 'I'll order the immediate destruction of Neoren 1. We'll say an on-board malfunction caused...'

'I'm afraid that won't be possible; NASA can't get the probe to respond to any signals. We're about five months away from the biggest catastrophe in human history.'

4

Mike paused and looked back. Connie was still swimming, her long hair spread like a fan on the cobalt water. He waited while she emerged naked onto the pebbled beach and followed him up stone steps warmed by the sun.

'That was great,' she said, as they reached the shaded terrace together. They looked down between dark spires of cypress trees to where sloping olive groves met the Ionian shore. 'In fact this whole place is just perfect!'

'And the cream on the cake,' said Mike, 'is that no one knows we're here.' They embraced and kissed. 'I still think you should have told them, you know.'

'Told the CIA where we're spending our honeymoon? You've got to be kidding!'

'No – told them that Swyver's doomsday device has been a useless piece of space junk since 1 January.'

'I disagree. It'll do them good to sweat. They almost got you killed, remember.'

Mike held Connie without replying. A soft breeze soughed in the cypresses.

'What're you thinking, honey?'

'Just relishing the irony,' said Mike. 'A Millennium nut thwarted by the millennium bug.'

'Very good! But now I want you to put all that out of your head. I don't want a repeat of last time.'

'Last time?'

Connie put her arms around his neck and whispered, '"Be like a young stag, my beloved, on the cleft mountain..."'

Mike fell eagerly into step. '"I will go... to the mountain... of myrrh, to the hill... of incense..."' he said, between increasingly zealous kisses.

'"All choice delicacies... are ready... both new and old... I have in store for you... my lover..."'

'"Many waters... cannot quench love... no flood... can sweep it away..."'

5

Nathan Willard picked up the phone and pressed Swyver's personal code.

'"Lift ye up a banner on the high mountain!"' responded Swyver.

'The guests have arrived, sir,' said Willard.

Swyver resumed the quotation: '"The noise of a multitude in the mountains, like as of a great people!"'

'There are only about a two dozen, sir.'

'Numbers don't matter, Nathan. The armies of heaven are with us.'

'Yes, sir.' He put the phone down and made his way to the circular meeting hall, one of several blast-proof concrete domes which sat like blisters on a high plateau in the Absaroka mountains. Swyver entered a few seconds later, walked over to a lectern and surveyed the remnant of his following.

'My friends, the Lord has put us through a severe test of faith in recent times but by his grace we have shown ourselves worthy!' Several voices muttered Amens. 'And God has shown his approval by revealing to me the error in my calculations. To cut a long story short, I had failed to realise that one of the half-weeks of Daniel chapter nine, verse twenty-seven – symbolic of three and a half years – should have been added to the other totals. This means we have time to rebuild our resources, re-establish contacts and remove our enemies. Gentlemen, our God-given goal is as clear as ever! The manifold blessings of the Millennium still await those who remain faithful to the end…'

Postscript

From the final chapter of *Misunderstanding the Millennium: Apocalyptic Thinking from 200 BC to AD 2000*, by M J Totley.

In earlier chapters we saw how the Essene branch of Judaism took certain Old Testament themes and developed them to produce the concept of cosmic degeneration and its apocalyptic outcome. Alongside these ideas, perhaps because of them, the Essenes' sectarian tendencies eventually gave rise to the fanatical separatists of Qumran. For reasons still to be explored, the darker Essene traits were hardly preserved at all within Judaism, but thrived at the margins of its unruly offspring, Christianity. We were able to follow a twisting but continuous line of descent from the Qumran Essenes, through the 'Apostolic Brethren' and other doomsday cults of the Middle Ages, to Waco, Heaven's Gate and the Swyver phenomenon.

In the light of our survey the roots of Swyver's apocalyptic discourse will need no explication. The date-fixing urge of the Millerites, the dispensationalism of Darby and Scofield, the strident, right-wing rhetoric of Lindsey are all obvious contributors to the heady concoction.

Swyver's psychology, on the other hand, is harder to probe. Much has already been written of the parental expectations which may have driven him to increasingly overweening spiritual ambition; of the carapace of unbounded self-belief that protected him from ridicule and insulated him from reason; of his need to see his beliefs vindicated on the world stage, which may have prompted his absurd act of hubris. Looking at the wider context, some have applied Fenn's thesis that fascist tendencies are exacerbated by a sense of time running out.

I leave it to others to plumb these murky waters, confining myself to the one, trivial-sounding observation that Swyver *lacked a sense of humour*. It has been said that only terrorist systems possess no comedy, and Swyver's outlook had become almost indistinguishable from that of the terrorist. Hence parallels have rightly been drawn between the Swyver phenomenon and the Japanese cult of Aum Shinrikyo which, in 1995, staged its own dress rehearsal for the apocalypse by releasing sarin nerve gas into Tokyo's subways. I find it significant that Kuschel speaks of 'the humourless apostles of catastrophe who love to conclude... that all creation is fallen and ripe for apocalyptic destruction'.[1] Laughter, he observes, fosters self-critical detachment and has the power to de-fanaticise. I believe it is no coincidence that the Essenes of Qumran imposed penalties on members who giggled.[2]

---

[1] Kuschel, Karl-Joseph, *Laughter: A Theological Reflection*, SCM, 1994, p.96.
[2] 1QS (The Community Rule) 7:16.

Bibliography

For readers interested in sources of fact and inspiration.

Boccaccini, Gabriele, *Beyond the Essene Hypothesis*, Grand Rapids, Eerdmans, 1998

Boyer, Paul S, *When Time Shall be No More; Prophecy Belief in Modern American Culture*, Cambridge, Mass., Harvard University Press, 1992

Colson, Charles, *Kingdoms in Conflict*, New York, Zondervan, 1987

Gibson, Shimon and Jacobsen, David M, *Below the Temple Mount in Jerusalem*, Oxford, Tempus Reparatum, 1996

Lindsey, Hal, *The Late Great Planet Earth*, New York, Zondervan, 1970

Shahak, Israel, 'The Third Temple and a Red Heifer', *Middle East International*, 22 March 1984

Tabor, James D, 'Apocalypse at Waco', *Bible Review*, October 1993, pp.24–33

VanderKam, James C, *The Dead Sea Scrolls Today*, Grand Rapids, Eerdmans, 1994

Wolters, Al, *The Copper Scroll*, Sheffield, Sheffield Academic Press, 1996

Yadin, Yigael, *Bar-Kokhba*, London, Weidenfeld and Nicolson, 1971